ALSO BY LORELEI JAMES

The Blacktop Cowboys® Novels

Corralled
Saddled and Spurred
Wrangled and Tangled
One Night Rodeo
Turn and Burn
Hillbilly Rockstar
Wrapped and Strapped
Hang Tough

The Mastered Series

Bound
Unwound
Unraveled
Caged
Schooled (*novella*)

The Need You Series

What You Need
Just What I Needed

HILLBILLY ROCKSTAR

A BLACKTOP COWBOYS® NOVEL

LORELEI JAMES

JOVE
New York

A JOVE BOOK
Published by Berkley
An imprint of Penguin Random House LLC
375 Hudson Street, New York, New York 10014

Copyright © 2014 by LJLA, LLC
Excerpt from *What You Need* © 2017 by LJLA, LLC
Penguin Random House supports copyright. Copyright fuels creativity, encourages
diverse voices, promotes free speech, and creates a vibrant culture. Thank you for buying
an authorized edition of this book and for complying with copyright laws by not
reproducing, scanning, or distributing any part of it in any form without permission.
You are supporting writers and allowing Penguin Random House to continue to
publish books for every reader.

A JOVE BOOK and BERKLEY are registered trademarks and the B colophon
is a trademark of Penguin Random House LLC.

ISBN: 9781101990285

Signet Eclipse trade edition / August 2014
Jove mass-market edition / February 2017

Printed in the United States of America
1 3 5 7 9 10 8 6 4 2

Cover art by Aleta Rafton / Bernstein & Andriulli
Portrait of the author by Russell Lloyd Jensen © Sage Studios

Chapter One

$\mathcal{A}$fter country music star Devin McClain finished a performance, he needed three things: a shower, a woman and a beer.

Not necessarily in that order.

He'd just handed the naked blonde a towel when someone started pounding on his hotel room door.

Devin snagged a complimentary robe and lifted an eyebrow at the curvy woman who hadn't bothered to cover herself. "Please tell me that ain't a jealous boyfriend lookin' for you."

"No," she said in a breathy whisper.

He wandered to the door and peered through the peephole. What was his road manager, Crash Cavanaugh, doing here? Devin opened the door. "What's goin' on?"

Crash's face was pasty white even beneath his beard. "Jesus, Devin." The burly man barreled in and pulled Devin into a bone-crushing hug. "I'm so glad it wasn't you. Sucks for JT, but damn, man . . ."

"What happened?"

"It's . . ." His gaze flicked over to the woman peeking around the bathroom doorframe. "Hey, darlin'. You wanna shut the door so I can have a private word with my boss?"

"Sure."

The door closed.

Now Devin was well past alarmed. "Crash, start talkin'."

Crash stilled. Then his eyes met Devin's. "Who knew you'd be in a hotel room tonight instead of on your tour bus?"

"You. I probably told Jase and Gage. I pretty much grabbed my duffel and . . ." What was the blonde's name? "Gretchen and I skipped the party to head straight here."

"Did you tell JT that he could crash on your bus tonight?"

"No. Why?"

"Looks like he decided to take a nap in your bed. Someone got onto the bus and beat the shit outta him with a baseball bat."

Devin's entire body seized up. "Are you fucking kiddin' me?"

"No."

"How is he?"

"Unconscious and in the ICU. He'd probably be dead if Check hadn't dropped off your guitar after the show. He noticed the bus door was open—which it ain't ever supposed to be. He went inside and saw your hat on the dresser, your boots on the floor and someone in the bed underneath the covers, blood everywhere. He thought . . ."

"It was me."

Crash nodded. "He freaked out, called 911 and tracked me down. Big mess when the ambulance arrived because people were still hanging around after Dixon Davis's concert ended. Only when the stretcher came out of the bus did we see that it was JT." He ran his hand down his beard and sighed. "Scariest fifteen minutes of my life, man. Don't know if there were any reporters around. But there were plenty of fans with cell phones. Rumors are gonna run rampant. You don't need that."

"I could give a damn about any of that when JT's in the hospital." Devin dropped onto the sofa. "Give me a minute to get my head on straight and then we'll go to the hospital."

"I don't gotta tell you that this bullshit has escalated. Which means we're making some changes effective immediately."

"Now's not the time—"

"It goddamn *is* the time," Crash said hotly. "The threats are real, Devin. Whoever has been doin' this the last eighteen months kicked it up a notch tonight."

He said nothing because the guilt was choking him.

"You oughta know I called Scott Rosenthal."

Devin's head snapped up. "Why would you call my agent? He doesn't need to worry about—"

"His high-profile client's well-being and safety?" Crash interjected. "I ain't about to argue the parameters of your agent's job besides that it's his right to know." He threw his shoulders back. "Fire me if you want, but I'm done helping you hide this crap from everyone. Rosenthal is meeting us in Denver the day after tomorrow. And lemme tell you, it took some fast talking on my part to convince him not to pull you out of tomorrow night's sold-out show in Denver."

"Jesus. He doesn't get to decide that."

"According to him, yes, he does."

Fuck.

"In the meantime, the cops want to talk to you." He jerked his chin toward the bathroom. "Probably wanna talk to her too."

Devin's eyes narrowed. "Why?"

"To make sure this wasn't some sort of publicity stunt."

"That's bullshit."

"Then why did they ask me if you were violent and might've gone on a rampage after finding JT in your room?"

"Come on. You can't be serious."

"You're in the public eye. Neither of those scenarios is out of the realm of possibility to people who don't know you."

"I don't know which is worse. That they'd think I'd beat the shit out of my bus driver to get my name mentioned in the news, or that I beat the shit out of my bus driver for daring to sleep in my bed. Christ. Do I need a damn alibi?"

"Don't snap at the messenger," Crash cautioned. "I'm just passing on what I heard. This is standard procedure."

"Where are the cops?"

"Waiting for you downstairs."

"Awesome." Devin snagged clean clothes out of his suitcase.

Crash angled his chin toward the bathroom. "You want me to handle her?"

Too many times Devin had used Crash to deal with groupies who'd overstayed their welcome. "I'll explain the situation."

"Where'd you meet her?"

"In the media room. She's the features reporter for the Kansas City newspaper."

"Never a dull moment with you. I'll tell the cops you're on your way down." He left the room.

Devin snapped the last button on his shirt before he rapped on the bathroom door. "Gretchen?"

The door flew open and the tiny blonde stormed past him. Clutching the towel above her ample cleavage, she spun around and glared at him. "Don't bother to *handle* me; I heard everything." She snatched up her clothes and mumbled angrily to herself as she jerked them on.

"This is not how I planned to end the evening."

"Me either." She shimmied her skirt up her thighs. "God. I know better than this." After she pulled the sleeveless black shirt over her head, she glared at him. "I've worked very hard to maintain a professional reputation. And now I have to tell the police that I've been up here with you for the last hour?"

He kept his tone even. "It was your choice to come with me."

She wobbled on one foot as she pulled her boot on. "I'm aware it's my own fault for being blinded by your celebrity, by your devastating good looks, by your Western charm and by your voice . . ." She inhaled a deep breath. "That deep voice of yours is liquid sex . . . It sucked me in like a siren's call."

There wasn't anything he could say at this point.

"I don't suppose you'd tell them that we were up here finishing the interview from earlier?" she asked hopefully.

Devin shook his head. "I don't lie. Especially not to cops. Especially not in a situation like this one, where someone has gotten hurt."

Her eyes turned shrewd, and he realized she'd slipped into reporter mode. "There's a story there. Do you have a stalker or something?"

He automatically hedged. "I've had a string of weird things happen."

"Think it's a pissed-off boyfriend or husband of some woman you had a fuck-and-run encounter with?" She smoothed her hair in the mirror above the dresser. "Because you do have quite the reputation."

"Didn't seem to stop you from dropping to your knees in front of me, did it?"

Devin probably deserved her fiery glare, but hey, she'd been a willing participant.

∞

The interrogation with the cops didn't take long—everything Devin had told them about his whereabouts was verified with the hotel manager and Gretchen. Every minute of his time after he walked offstage had been accounted for.

As soon as they were alone, Crash said, "Rosenthal and Carl Carlson are expecting us to meet with them and the security firm in Denver. There is no way in hell you're getting out of it this time. Don't get so pissy. Rosenthal is trying to protect your ass."

"More like protecting his asset," Devin muttered.

"If you've got a better idea, I'm sure he'd love to hear it."

If Devin had to be saddled with security, he'd damn well choose it himself. No way would he allow a security detail to clog up his bus and hamper his creative process. He'd allow one person to travel with him. *One.* He'd agree to more security in the arenas and to and from events, but not in his personal space.

Although his bus could easily house the five members of his band, he insisted they have their own bus—a contract stipulation he'd had since he'd hit the big time and that wasn't about to change now.

Few people understood that with all the time he spent on the road, his bus was his haven. The one place he didn't have to be on—he didn't have to be Devin McClain, country music star. He could just be Devin Hollister, a Wyoming ranch kid who'd made good.

"Uh-oh. I know that look," Crash said as they turned the corner into the hospital's parking lot.

"What look?"

"The one that says you've got something up your sleeve that ain't no one gonna like."

Devin scrolled through his contacts list. "Hang on. I gotta make a call before we go in."

"Dev, it's midnight."

"She's up. And it's eleven in her time zone. She wouldn't know what to do if I called her at a normal time." He listened as the line rang five times.

"So didja finally get yourself thrown in jail and you need me to wire you bail money?" she drawled in that sexy twang.

He laughed. "Tex-Ass darlin', I love that you're so optimistic when it comes to me."

"Hillbilly rockstar, I've been a party to your wild partyin' ways, so it's not such a huge leap to imagine you've gotten yourself ass deep in alligators. Hang on a sec," Tanna said. "Stop bein' so fucking smug, Doc. Yes, I know you won."

He heard Fletch's deep laughter in the background.

"What's goin' on, T?"

Tanna sighed. "I bet Fletch it was his cell phone ringing and not mine, since he's on call this week. So thanks, buddy. You cost me an hour's worth of sexual favors, which I've just learned will require him using lube *and* vibrators on me."

"You ain't complaining."

"True. Fletch says hey and thanks. So why *are* you callin' me?"

"I need a favor. I just found out that I'm getting a security detail on this next leg of the tour. I'm not happy about it, so I'd prefer to choose my own babysitters. Is your brother, Garrett, still in the private security business in Denver?"

"Yes. But I have to say up front, his business has really taken off."

"That's good because I want the best. Trust me; the promotion company will definitely make it worth his while. I thought I'd call him in the morning, but I couldn't remember the name of the company. Can you text me that and his phone number?"

"Sure. And, Devin, darlin', you know I'm gonna ask if everything is all right."

"Everything is fine. Just takin' precautions. Better safe than sorry."

"Good. I'll send Garrett's contact info. Take care, wild man."

"Always do. I'm jealous as hell that you've got Fletch to take care of you." He meant that. Part of him had always hoped he and Tanna could make a go of it, but after seeing her with his childhood friend Fletch, he knew they were perfect for each other.

Crash gestured to the phone after Devin had hung up. "Was that the hot, feisty barrel racer you used to pal around with?"

"Yeah. Her brother runs . . . Well, you heard the conversation."

"I heard the lie. Look, I know you oversee every aspect

of your career, but you've gotta realize that Rosenthal and Big Sky Promotions won't waver in this edict. And if the security company ain't up to snuff . . ."

"It will be." God, he hoped so. "Come on. Let's go in and check on JT."

Chapter Two

⟅⟆

*L*iberty Masterson had just finished her daily requirement of PT—thirty minutes of cardio, followed by
thirty minutes of kickboxing and fifteen minutes of takedown drills. Right after she hit the showers, she'd check
in at the onsite gun range.

This was the best job ever.

The only way it could be any better was if she got to
blow shit up.

*You used to do that in the army and it wasn't all that
fun, remember?*

Yeah, but people were shooting back at her. This was
different. She was paid very well as a member of GSC
Security—no more living hand to mouth in the world's
sandboxes. She absentmindedly rubbed the jagged scar
below her collarbone, the literal parting shot that had
ended her military career.

She blotted the sweat from her face and scanned the
empty training area. Most of the guys she worked with

were on assignment. She missed the camaraderie of her coworkers and she hadn't sparred with anyone in a week, so she was antsy.

Joe, the boss's second lieutenant, poked his head in the door. "Liberty, got a minute? Garrett needs you to do something for him."

"Do I have time to shower?"

"A quick one. Then meet me out front."

"Be right there." After rinsing off her body, she scraped her wet hair into a bun. Then she slipped on her uniform— black dress pants, gray blouse, black blazer and black boots. Lastly, she strapped on her gun.

Ready to rock and roll.

She took the stairs at a run and cut through the parking garage to the front of the building

A luxury motor coach idled at the curb, Devin McClain's face and his name plastered down the entire length of the bus. She'd never been a big country music fan, but she recognized the cowboy singer. His rugged good looks and heart-stopping smile were even more impressive billboard sized.

Joe trotted over with a clipboard.

"What's going on? You bring in live entertainment for the annual employee barbecue?"

"You wish. This is a potential client. He's inside with Garrett right now, but the boss wants you to catalog all the possible security breaches for this bus. Then head up to the second-floor conference room and we'll go from there." He passed over the clipboard.

"Will do. Is the bus locked?"

Joe scowled. "No. The door wasn't even completely latched when I got down here."

"Anyone on board?"

"Nope. It's all yours."

She nodded and got to work.

∞

Fifteen minutes later, Liberty entered the conference room. Joe pulled out a chair next to him, but the four guys on the opposite side of the table didn't miss a beat in their conversation.

Devin McClain was stretched out in his chair, arms folded over his chest with obvious belligerence. He wore a ball cap pulled low so half his face was obscured.

The man in the three-piece suit next to Devin ended with, "What we're asking for is a minimum of two, and we want them 24/7."

"No," Devin said with an emphatic shake of his head. "That ain't happening."

Three-piece-suit man sighed. "That is not your decision to make anymore."

"The hell it isn't. This affects me the most, so it should be solely my decision."

Garrett scrawled across his notebook. "How long is this 'Heroes and Heartbreakers' tour?"

"Four months," the bearded man sitting on the other side of Devin said. "The shows take place at a mix of smaller venues, like county fairs and casinos, and at bigger event centers, like stadiums. This leg of the tour bounces all around the Southwest for three months. Then there's a ten-day break before finishing the final three weeks of the tour on the West Coast."

"We'll need a copy of the full schedule," Joe said. "So we can see the security setups at the performance sites."

"We don't normally contract out for that long with one person, let alone two," Garrett pointed out.

Devin scowled. "I don't need two full-time security

guards. I'm still not convinced I need even one. I'm leaning toward callin' this whole thing a gigantic waste of everyone's time—especially mine."

Liberty kept her face schooled, but she was thinking, *Wow. Diva much?*

Garrett must've been thinking along the same lines because his gaze hooked hers. "Why don't you tell Mr. McClain and his . . . advisers what you found on your security check of the tour bus?"

Liberty addressed the bearded guy, who appeared to be in charge. Holding up the clipboard, she pointed to all the red check marks. "These are considered security weak spots. I found more than a dozen. The first one? Door to the bus wasn't shut, let alone locked. And upon examination, the lock is nonfunctioning."

"Maybe the person who beat the shit out of JT busted it when he broke in," Devin said tightly. "We haven't had time to get it fixed, and it worked fine before that."

She had no idea who the JT person was. "Or maybe the fact it was broken beforehand and no one had checked it made access easier?" she said coolly.

"What are you insinuating?"

"Nothing. I'm stating facts." She waggled the clipboard at him. "Your current security measures are downright laughable, Mr. McClain, since you don't seem to have any."

Silence.

Liberty shot Garrett a look. He wasn't wearing a frown that indicated she'd stepped out of line.

"Who exactly are you?" Devin said to Liberty with a slight sneer in his tone.

Garrett leaned forward, locking his gaze to Devin's. "Liberty works for me as a security specialist. And before you further insult her, I'll point out that she spent years in the army, working for various security task forces. She knows what she's talkin' about. Questioning her qualifications is not only an insult to her but to me, so tread lightly."

Devin held up his hands in mock surrender. "I apologize to both of you." He directed his next question to Liberty. "Please summarize what you see as the biggest security risks."

"First, it sounds like you have zero personal protection right now."

"I wouldn't say zero. I have security escorts at the larger event centers."

"That's your biggest mistake right there, especially if you've been dealing with any kind of personal threats. You need daily personal protection. Did you have security guards in Kansas City?"

"Yes."

"Where?"

"Inside the arena."

"Did they escort you from the bus inside the building?"

He shook his head.

"Whose decision was that?"

"Mine. I usually walk with the band."

"That would be the first thing I'd change. More than safety in numbers, you need professional security. I doubt your drummer would know what to do if you were attacked."

The bearded guy laughed and covered the noise with a cough.

"What else?"

"Take your face and your name off the side of the bus. That's just inviting trouble. If having your face billboard sized is a vanity thing, get over it. A nondescript vehicle cuts your security risks in half since no one knows you're on board."

Devin's mouth tightened, but he didn't respond.

So she continued. "There are four bunk spaces, but it looks to me as though they're being used to store random sh—stuff. It's an easy place for someone to hide or to hide something. The band doesn't travel on your bus?"

"The band travels in a separate bus, as do the roadies who handle the equipment."

"How many buses are in the Devin McClain traveling show?"

"There are three tour buses and two semis."

"We're getting sidetracked here," three-piece-suit guy interjected. "I need to know if GSC can handle Devin's security needs."

Garrett tapped his pen on the table. "I'm getting mixed signals. Who makes the final decision on this?"

"I do," Devin said, keeping his focus on Garrett. "So let's cut to the chase. Here are my revised security requirements. One security specialist who will blend in with my crew. While security is your main concern, privacy is mine. I require time alone to work. I understand this person will need to be close by at all times, but you all need to understand that if I have to choose between my safety and my ability to make music, the music will win every time."

For the first time, Liberty understood Devin's underlying frustration with the situation.

"Give me time to confer with my team. Any last questions before we duck out for a few?"

Liberty's stomach pitched when Devin aimed those intense blue eyes at her. "Anything else you want to add?"

The cool tone wasn't only a challenge, but his clear displeasure that she'd voiced an opinion. Because she was a woman? Or because she'd dissed his operation? She let her gaze flit across the men on his side of the table, three-piece-suit guy, bearded guy and a guy wearing a cowboy hat who hadn't said a word. "Brutal honesty, Mr. McClain? You've reached a high level of success in the music world. You deserve a nicer bus than that piece of shit parked out front, especially if your safety truly is their number-one concern."

The man didn't even crack a smile.

Just as they were walking out the door, the guy in the cowboy hat said, "Hold up." He meandered over and handed Garrett a sheaf of paper. "Here are the rates we're prepared to offer for this contract. So you know we're serious." Then he murmured something to Garrett.

Interesting. Liberty wondered if Devin McClain knew what his safety was worth.

After the cowboy hat guy trotted off, Garrett and Joe conferred in low tones. She wanted to eavesdrop, but something in their stiff postures worried her, so she hustled into Garrett's office.

A few minutes later, Joe plopped next to her in the chair opposite Garrett's desk.

Garrett refilled his cup of coffee before he took his seat. He unfolded the paper and raised both his eyebrows before passing it to Joe.

"That good, huh?" Liberty prompted.

"Holy fucking shit would be appropriate here." Joe squinted at the paper. "This is one of the highest pay rates I've ever seen."

Liberty snorted. "It'd have to be since Mr. McClain is a dickhead and no sane person would ever take on the assignment."

"Liberty."

Although she'd been chastised, she pushed her point.

"Why are you even considering taking this job? It's not like GSC needs the work."

Garrett sighed. "It's a personal favor. My sister, Tanna, went through a rough patch, and Devin was always there for her in ways I couldn't be. So I owe him. And he's more messed up about this latest incident than he's letting on." He summarized the past trouble in Devin's world. She was shocked someone in Devin's position just kept going about business as usual—as if none of the threats mattered or had affected him at all.

"Liberty?"

Her gaze snapped to Garrett's. "Sorry. What did you say?"

"I asked if you've ever met Devin before."

"No. Why?"

"You know the connection between your sister and mine is what brought you to my attention in the first place. Tanna and Harper are both married to men who grew up in the Muddy Gap/Rawlins area. That's where Devin is originally from."

"I've heard Harper and Bran talk about him, and I guess he goes back there sometimes, but I've never met him."

"I'm hopin' that'll work in our favor," Garrett drawled.

"I don't follow."

Garrett and Joe exchanged an oddly wary look.

"Should I shoot myself in the foot now?"

Joe laughed. "And everyone says you don't have a sense of humor."

She scowled at him and then said to Garrett, "Go on."

"The best—hell, the only solution—is to send you out on tour with Devin McClain. And hear me out before you pull your gun on me. You've been begging us to send you on assignment. You are an excellent trainer, but this is a better training opportunity for *you*. Not only because of the money for us."

Liberty fought the urge to laugh. It was always about the money. "With the big swinging dick that Devin McClain wields, there's no way he'll agree to having a woman as his personal security. No way in hell."

"It'll be his only choice if he wants to hire us." Garrett fiddled with his pen. "The rest of the guys won't agree to be away from their families for that long. Not only that. You've asked for a job like this for the past four months. Here's your chance to jump to the next level and prove you're qualified for fieldwork."

"Slathering on compliments?"

Garrett smiled. "And you're deflecting them. I don't say it unless it's true—you know that about me."

"Yes, but I'm still on probation." Garrett required a year of probation for all his new hires. While it sucked that the slightest infraction could get her shit-canned, it ensured the ones who hit the twelve-month mark were worthy of carrying out the sometimes dangerous work the job demanded.

"In four and a half months you'll be within a week of permanent status. You take on this job, I'll give you that last week."

"Sorry, but no. I'll pass."

Joe and Garrett exchanged another look.

"What now?"

"This information doesn't leave this room. The promoter has sweetened the pot. There's a hundred-thousand-dollar bonus if the bodyguard lasts the entire tour. So if you agree to take this assignment, in addition to getting paid your regular rate, we'll let you keep the bonus."

She perked up at that prospect. "Seriously? Every penny?"

"Every penny, and I'll kick in enough to cover the taxes on it."

That money would provide a hefty down payment on a house. Roughly four months out of her life would make her dream of home ownership a reality, and she'd get experience in the field that would increase her base pay rate. Win-win.

"Deal."

Joe slapped a twenty-dollar bill on the desk. "You suck."

Garrett swept the money into his desk drawer. "I warned you not to bet against me, Joe."

"What the hell kinda bet did you two make about me?" Liberty demanded.

"That you'd be more interested in the money than living in close quarters with one of *People* magazine's hottest men in music."

Liberty rolled her eyes. "Seriously, Joe? You haven't learned anything about me in the past eight months? I oughta make you pony up twenty to me for the damn insult."

Joe grinned. "I almost wish I was going along to see you bust this guy's balls on a daily basis." He leaned forward and pleaded with Garrett. "Please let me be the one to tell our client that Liberty is his new bodyguard."

"Fine, but you'd also better warn him that Liberty is . . ." Garrett laughed. "Never mind. He can figure it out for himself."

On the way out, Garrett stopped her. "The head of the promotion company was very clear in this offer. McClain isn't to know anything about the performance bonus. If you tell him about it, it voids that part of the contract."

"My lips are sealed. I promise."

"I know I can trust you."

"But I don't know if I can trust them."

Garrett waited for her explanation.

"We both know they'll pay you at regular intervals while I'm on assignment. So I want their guarantee that I'll have that bonus no later than three days *after* the end of the tour. I don't want to wait ninety days while they dick around about payment."

He smiled. "Excellent point. Are you sure I can't talk you into takin' an admin position when your probationary period is up?"

"Do I still get to Taser people from behind a desk?"

"No."

"Then no way."

Chapter Three

❧

*W*hat the hell was taking them so long?

Devin fought the urge to get up and pace; instead he focused his frustration on his agent. "All of JT's expenses are bein' taken care of, right? Including transportation back home so he can recuperate?"

"The legal team wants to run it past accounting—"

"I didn't ask about the legal team. They weren't in that hospital room. They didn't see the damn bloodstains on my bed. The man took hits that were meant for me—"

"Don't say that," his agent warned. "Neither you nor the tour promotion company is claiming any culpability for the attack. I know you're upset, but this situation is a lawsuit waiting to happen. We don't need any more ammo fired at us."

Carl Carlson, the head honcho from Big Sky Promotions, nodded. "You just go right on telling folks that the beefed-up security is a requirement of headlining as one of the hottest solo tickets in country music. Remember, we're allowing this meeting at your request. Be warned, son. I will overrule you if they don't propose a security plan that I approve of one hundred percent."

"That woman already gave us all the answers to our questions about security problems."

"No. She gave us the tape to fix the leaks, but we still need someone keeping watch so no more unexpected leaks show up. Console yourself with the fact we're not demanding two bodyguards."

"Fine. But I'd better have a different goddamn tour bus in four days, when we leave for Salt Lake City." It'd been humiliating enough having his name and his face plastered on his bus—he'd always hated that—but it really chapped his ass that anyone would believe he actually *wanted* that blatant promotion.

The door opened and the GSC trio walked in.

Devin tried to keep his focus on Tanna's brother, but his gaze kept landing on Liberty, the ballbuster, which annoyed him; the chick was nothing special to look at. She wore shapeless monochromatic clothing, her angular face was free of makeup and her eyes were a nearly colorless gray. He wasn't even certain of her hair color since she'd plastered it to her head and secured it in a bun.

Garrett's associate Joe, a bruiser the size of a small truck, took the reins. "As you're aware, we don't normally contract for such an extended amount of time, but we've figured out a way to make it work."

Devin knew the only reason GSC had taken this appointment was because of his friendship with Tanna. "And I appreciate that."

"Luckily for you, our security specialist has agreed to take the job."

"Who?"

"Me."

Oh no. Oh, *fuck* no. Devin looked at the woman and found her staring back at him . . . with zero emotion. His mouth opened before his brain engaged. "You seriously think I'll let a woman protect me? That goes against the way I was raised and everything I believe in. Men protect women, not the other way around."

"You wanted discreet security," Garrett pointed out. "And Liberty is the best possible solution."

"You do have a lot of women hanging around, Dev. No one would think twice about her bein' there," Crash added.

"Does she *look* like the women who hang around my shows?" Devin snapped. "No one in their right mind would ever believe I'd be with a woman like her."

That brought a flush to Liberty's cheeks, and Devin felt like a dick for saying it—even when it was true.

"Devin, can you not jump to conclusions?" his agent asked. "This sounds to me like the ideal solution."

"Tryin' to pass her off as my girlfriend?"

"We were thinking more along the lines of a personal assistant," Garrett said.

"That theory will be blown when she's conferring with the event security, wearing an earpiece and holstering a firearm under her business suit. Or if she perceives a threat and pulls a gun, because she—and no offense, sweetheart— looks awful trigger-happy."

She set her forearms on the table. "You have no idea how true that statement is. But right now the person I'd be gunning for most is you, *sweetheart*." Then she smiled.

Holy shit. The smile completely transformed her face— but Devin wasn't sure if it was a good thing or a bad thing because the grin straddled the line between sexy and evil.

"I know it's hard for you to keep your morbid sense of humor in check, Liberty, but please try," Garrett drawled.

That wasn't exactly a reprimand from her boss. Christ. The woman had threatened to shoot him. Had no one caught that?

Devin bristled. "I'm not joking when I say that you're not even close to my type."

"I assure you, Mr. McClain, you're no more my type than I am yours."

"Does your type have breasts and a vagina too?" It slipped out of his mouth before he could stop it.

Rather than bristle, she looked at each of the men beside her. They seemed . . . amused. Or maybe slightly scared of what she might do or say next.

"I'm not a lesbian—not that it would matter if I were. I'm very good at my job, but I see you've got too much ego to find that out for yourself. I doubt it's your naturally protective male instincts telling you that it's a crime against nature to hire me, but more your testosterone-laden fear that someone—your fans, your friends, your family in Wyoming, your way-hotter-than-me female groupies—will think less of you for having to hire security at all."

It pissed him off that she already had his number. If she could read him that well, how quickly could she assess a potentially dangerous situation? "Go on."

"People want a piece of you. People think they know you through your music. While ninety-nine percent of your fans are just normal, everyday people who love music, it's my job to be concerned about that other one percent who boarded the crazy train. And, honestly, if it's only about appearances for you, wouldn't you rather people know it takes only one butch woman to protect you instead of two former linebackers? That makes you look badass, not weak."

Damn. This woman was really, really good.

So he shocked the shit out of her by saying, "So much for my theory that you're the *fade into the background with your mouth shut* type."

"Only when it's warranted, sir."

Devin directed his question to Garrett just to see if she'd become outwardly indignant. "Has she ever saved someone's life?"

"Absolutely. She's a bona fide hero," Joe inserted with pride. "Two years ago, while serving in Afghanistan, she took three bullets as part of a security detail. The intended target was . . . ?"

"An ambassador to the UN," she supplied.

"Did you know him?" Devin asked.

"No. But that didn't matter because I did my job— which was protecting him."

"Liberty received an honorable discharge." Garrett paused. "If you have any further questions, please address Liberty directly."

"Fine." Devin locked his gaze to Liberty's and said, "Everyone out. I want to talk with G.I. Jane one-on-one."

After the door closed and they were alone, Devin said, "No offense. I really don't want to hire you. Not because you're a woman, but because I don't want to hire anyone."

"I'm aware of that."

"You should also know that I'm not sexist, but—"

"In my experience, men who say that usually are sexist."

He fought a sigh. "You don't give an inch, do you?"

She maintained eye contact. "After spending more than

a dozen years in the military, I'm good at doing what I'm told. But I was also in a position of command, so when I issue an order, I expect it to be followed. I suspect you're not the type to follow orders—from men or women."

G.I. Jane had definitely hit the nail on the head. Devin scrubbed his hands over his face. "Look. I'm not an asshole."

"In my experience, men who say that—"

"Usually are assholes. Yeah, yeah, I get it." He paused, needing to take a different, less antagonistic tack with her. "How'd you know I'm from Wyoming? Did you read my bio?"

"No. My sister lives outside of Muddy Gap."

"Who's your sister?"

"Harper Turner."

His jaw dropped. "Are you fuckin' serious? Hot, sexy beauty queen Harper is your sister?"

"Hard to believe, isn't it?" she said with a hint of humor. "Harper got the looks in our family and our little sister Bailey got the brains."

"What did you get?"

"Resolve."

Not the answer he expected.

As they stared at each other across the table, ready to battle, Devin realized her eyes weren't a boring hue, but almost a shimmery silver.

What the fuck? Since when do you give a shit about her eye color? Focus. "What now?"

"How about you listen to my stipulations before I hear yours? We can go from there."

He motioned for her to bring it.

"If you hire me, I will be by your side 24/7. I have one job: your bodyguard. I don't fetch coffee. I don't cook. I don't clean your tour bus. I don't chauffeur you around. I don't wash your clothes. I don't run errands. I don't mix drinks. I don't answer your fan mail. I don't procure groupies for you to fuck. I don't get on my knees and suck you off. I'm not paid to kiss your ass; I'm paid to protect it."

No confusion on her job expectations.

"Now, what were your concerns?" she said frostily.

"You're a little prickly, aren't you?"

"If you'd dealt with as many pricks as I have over the years, you'd know some of that attitude was bound to rub off on me."

He laughed. "Well, my set of conditions is a bit different. You protect me, but you don't get to judge me. I like women, I like sex and I have a lot of both. I'm up late, which means I sleep late, but that don't mean I'm lazy. I work out at least every other day, so you need to keep up. That said, I need time alone to write, and the only time that happens is when I'm on my tour bus. I'll be one hundred percent safe while we're traveling down the road, so during that time, you'll need to entertain yourself."

"Not a problem."

"My biggest stipulation is that you can't tell anyone you're my bodyguard, especially your sister. I don't need this spread among my friends in Muddy Gap."

"GSC is discreet and professional. I have nondisclosure agreements with them, and I'm fully prepared to sign them with you. I don't talk about my work with anyone."

"I appreciate that. Now, here's my final concern. Crash will tell everyone associated with the tour that you're my new personal assistant. However, when you store your stuff in my tour bus, no one is gonna believe it. They'll assume we're fucking. Will that be a problem for you?"

She shook her head. "I don't care about anything except doing my job."

Devin raised an eyebrow. "Even if it means I'll parade groupies past you?" he countered. "You prepared for the questions from my bandmates? You don't care if they think you're a star fucker? You can honestly act like you don't give a shit who I fuck as long as I'm givin' it to you on a regular basis? Because in my past experiences, no woman ever deals well with that."

That gave her pause. Then she offered him that evil smile. "Maybe since I'm a more . . . masculine-acting woman—your words, not mine, Mr. McClain—that means I proudly embrace the same I-don't-give-a-damn attitude that men do when it comes to casual sex."

"You gonna toss my knee-jerk comment about your physical attributes in my face every chance you get?"

Liberty cocked her head. "Yep. You wouldn't have said it if you didn't mean it, which means you have to accept that I won't forget it. You're used to saying whatever pops into your head, and I doubt anyone ever calls you out on it. Be warned: I will."

"So noted."

"And I don't shy away from asking what I need to know."

"Such as?"

"When was your last relationship that lasted longer than a box of condoms?"

He refused to let her get a rise out of him. "Four years ago."

"Then no one is expecting you to suddenly become monogamous."

"True." He took a sip of his cold coffee. "But I'll expect you to look like the type of woman I'd hire. Or have in my bed."

She scowled. "What does Devin McClain's type look like?"

"Not that." He gestured to her outfit. "Wearing a getup like that will be a dead giveaway that you're not who you claim to be. And I'm not all right with that. You shouldn't be either. Darlin', you gotta blend."

Instead of bristling, she nodded. "Understood. But I won't wear constricting clothing. I can't run in high heels. My gun needs to be accessible at all times."

"Will you always be carrying?"

"It'll depend on the situation. But, yes, I'll either have a handgun or a stun gun on my person, which is standard in the personal-protection business regardless of your gender or mine."

Devin didn't want this—he truly felt he didn't need it. But in the case of picking the lesser of two evils, he'd choose her. He managed a smile. "You're hired. I play Denver tonight and Cheyenne tomorrow night. The tour leaves in three days. See that you're ready."

"I will be. And thank you." She pushed back from the table. "I'll bring the others back in so you all can iron out the final details." She slipped out the door.

He closed his eyes. Given how much they'd butted heads in the past hour, he'd better stock up on headache medicine.

After a minute, the chair next to him squeaked, but he kept his eyes closed. His agent said, "Everything all right?"

"I guess."

"Choosing her is the smart move, Devin."

Like they'd given him a choice. "Why? Because I'm not attracted to her in the least?"

His agent cursed softly, then leaned closer. "No. Because it's what the tour promoters want. After agreeing not to play the song that's brought everyone a buttload of trouble, and following their security demands, you'll be seen as a team player. They'll reward you. Mark my words."

"Great."

"It will be."

Devin opened his eyes. Liberty had retaken her seat but wouldn't meet his eyes.

Carl and Garrett were passing papers back and forth. Everyone else was silent.

Wasn't long before Liberty said, "Garrett, you need anything else from me right now?"

"No. If you have something else to do, feel free."

She stood and left the room.

Talk about a hasty exit. His gaze connected with Joe's, and the level of animosity surprised him. Then Joe murmured something to Garrett and took off after Liberty.

What had happened? Was his new bodyguard involved with one of her bosses?

Before he could ask about the Joe/Liberty dynamic, he was hit with a barrage of questions. Now that he'd been muscled into agreeing to full-time security, the remaining negotiations didn't interest him. He tuned out, focusing on the tune in his head that'd been giving him fits over the past week.

He heard a soft sigh and glanced over at Crash. His road manager was bored out of his skull too.

"We're done here," his agent said. "You and Crash are meeting Carl and me at our hotel to finalize tour plans."

"How am I supposed to get there? I came on my bus. And since ridin' around in it is like painting a bull's-eye on me . . ."

"Garrett will escort you. Get anything you'll need off that bus. The transport company providing the new bus will transfer the rest of your belongings."

Devin grinned. "Hot damn. Do I get to choose my bus this time?"

Carl shook his head. "But I guarantee it'll be top-of-the-line, with all of the safety recommendations. Only the best for our best and brightest."

Carl's slimy smile dimmed Devin's happiness. No good deed was offered without strings. But he knew how the game was played. If he acted grateful, maybe those strings wouldn't choke him.

"We'll see you at the hotel." Hands were shaken. Then his agent and Carl left him and Crash alone with Garrett.

Crash stood. "I'll get your guitar. I know that's all you really give a shit about."

"My day travel duffel is in the first bunk." He kept an emergency bag packed at all times. That came in handy when he was called to fill in for last-minute gigs and had to hop on a plane at a moment's notice.

"Got it. See ya down there."

Garrett stood. "I'll give you the nickel tour on our way down to the parking garage."

He followed Garrett into the hallway. "I appreciate you makin' this work, Garrett."

"I guarantee you'll find Liberty a better fit into your lifestyle than the guys from LaGruder Security." He punched the elevator button. "As it is, you'll get a taste of that type of protection the next couple of days."

Devin frowned. "What do you mean?"

Garrett crossed his arms over his chest. "You really are the last to know. Carl already hired two bodyguards from LaGruder. They'll be with you until Liberty takes over."

"So I've got two fuckin' babysitters?"

"I wouldn't use that term around security specialists," Garrett said dryly, "as it tends to piss them off. But, yeah, LaGruder is the big dog in this town in the personal-protection business. That's why Carl picked them sight unseen."

Devin changed the subject when they stepped into the elevator. "How's Tanna? I haven't had a chance to talk to her much."

Garrett's eyes warmed slightly. "Happy. Busy. She's still runnin' the circuit, but she's struggling to stay in the top fifteen. I know she has her heart set on back-to-back world titles. But she and Fletch are tryin' to start a family, and she wants that even more." He paused. "And don't worry that I'll tell Tanna anything. I don't fuck around when I promise my clients confidentiality. I have the same policy for those who work for me. No one in Wyoming knows that Liberty is on my payroll."

"How's that possible?"

"Tanna mentioned to me that her friend Harper's sister was lookin' for work after bein' discharged from the military. I contacted Liberty and interviewed her."

"I get it. I'm sold on her." Mostly. If he had to be saddled with a babysitter, he'd prefer someone with a personality—even an abrasive one—to humorless goons.

They stopped outside a large window that looked into a workout room with weight machines, heavy bags, speed bags, and training dummies. Two people in full gear were sparring on the mat. Even through the glass, Devin could hear the sound of the gloves striking against flesh and the safety gear. Neither one held back.

"Do they always train this hard?"

"Yes, if they want to be employed here."

"How long will they go at it?" Devin asked.

"Until one falls."

"Why'd they pair up like that? Seems the bigger guy has a huge advantage over the smaller guy."

"Because threats come in all shapes and sizes. My employees train against each other, but I also bring in other specialists in different martial arts disciplines so they don't get complacent with their skills."

"With a setup like this, and your employees being mostly ex-military, I'd suspect you were running a private black ops group and not just a personal security company."

For the first time ever, Garrett Barker smiled. It wasn't a friendly smile. And the man neither confirmed nor denied Devin's comment.

Scary shit.

Devin refocused on the fighters, watching as the smaller guy landed a punch to his opponent's gut and then swept his legs out from under him.

"And we have a winner," Garrett murmured.

The victor offered a hand to the loser to help him up. Then they removed their gloves and helmets.

The smaller "guy" wasn't a guy after all, but Liberty. And her opponent was big Joe. The man was actually limping as they walked off the mat.

Devin knew why Garrett had suggested a tour—to show him Liberty in action.

"Never underestimate her," Garrett said softly.

He didn't respond. He watched Liberty and Joe peel off their protective gear as they continued their conversation—an intense and intimate one, if the familiar way Joe touched her cheek was any indication. When she smiled at Joe, her face full of joy and her eyes shining, it didn't matter that she was soaked in sweat or what she wore; Liberty Masterson was the most compelling woman he'd ever seen.

Not attracted to her at all? Bullshit. Maybe that's your problem. You are attracted to her and she's not your usual type.

The next four months in close quarters with this woman just got a whole lot more complicated.

Chapter Four

❧

$\mathcal{S}$parring with Joe hadn't taken the edge off. Liberty still wanted to beat the shit out of someone, namely one smarmy-ass country singer.

Because I am not attracted to her in the least.

Motherfucking son of a bitch, that stung.

It wasn't the first time she'd heard that. Usually she blew it off, but this time it weighed on her and she didn't know why it stung so much.

Maybe because he's one of the sexiest men you've ever met.

No lie there. The man had it going on. Lanky—but a holy-shit well-built lanky. Broad chest, equally broad shoulders, muscular arms beneath his tight long-sleeved T-shirt. His face hit the perfect mark between rugged and pretty. His hair had to be ten different shades from pale blond to a rich, dark brown. Neither the color nor the riot of curls that made all those hues stand out had come from a bottle, and damn if those sexy, loose curls didn't just beg for a woman's fingers to get tangled up in them. That million-dollar smile of his was way more potent in person than on the pages of a magazine—not that the man had bestowed that infamous grin on her. But even when he had smiled at Garrett, it hadn't reached his piercing turquoise blue eyes. The constant wariness in them didn't bother her; in fact, it would make her job easier. Better to have a cautious client than a cocky one.

Liberty climbed into her car and dropped her head back, closing her eyes. Even the new-car scent of her pride and joy—a baby blue Mustang—didn't settle her like it normally did. She ran her hands over the steering wheel as her mind raced.

How was she supposed to completely make herself over into a simpering, insipid, scantily clad groupie in three days? It'd take two weeks to get an appointment with a brain surgeon to suck half her brain out. She snorted. Few besides herself appreciated her sense of humor.

She didn't know where to start in assembling a new wardrobe. There'd been an adjustment period after she retired from the army, transitioning from wearing the required uniform to choosing civilian clothes. Comfort, not fashion, was her priority. So, yeah, she could admit her clothing was boring. She had two styles: not work clothes and work clothes. Her not work clothes consisted of ratty sweats and baggy T-shirts, worn jeans, long john tops and camo shorts. Her work style wasn't any better. She owned one sundress, which she'd bought on a whim. Her official work wardrobe was black, black and gray. Black pants, black jackets, sturdy black shoes. But she'd mixed it up and bought suits in navy blue and dark brown. The good thing was, it didn't take her long to get ready in the morning.

Times like this she wished her sister Harper lived closer. Although Muddy Gap was a lot closer to Denver than Fort Bragg, where Liberty had been stationed for years. She glanced at the clock. Noon. Probably Harper was doing ten thousand things at once, but she called her anyway.

As always, Harper's breathy sex-phone-operator voice was ruined by little boys' shrieks in the background. "Hey, sista. I was just thinking about you."

"I assume you're at home?"

Harper laughed. "How could you tell? Jake, get down. No, Tate. He doesn't need your help."

Liberty grinned. Those two little boys were a handful. But they were sweet as well as wild, and she loved them with a fierceness that surprised even her. "How are my darling nephews?"

"Needing a nap. Or maybe just Mama is. I'm fixing lunch before I pass them off to Bran for the afternoon. I'm heading in to the store. What's going on in your life?"

"I need your help," Liberty blurted. "Like really need it to the point I'm about to have a damn panic attack."

"Hang on a sec. Bran just walked in."

Liberty heard, "Hey, hot mama," and imagined Bran kissing Harper's neck, like he did whenever they'd been apart for more than five minutes. They were so crazy in love it'd be sickening if not for the fact they shared that love with everyone around them. From the instant Bran had married Harper, the gruff rancher had considered Liberty as much his sister as Harper's. He'd been such a pillar of strength for both her and Harper in the months during Liberty's recovery and after leaving the military.

So she couldn't be jealous of her sister's good fortune; Harper deserved the happiness she'd found with Bran.

Still, Liberty secretly believed that type of forever, soul-mate love was a fluke.

"Heya, sis. Come visit us soon. The boys miss you," Bran said into the phone. Then the sounds of background noise faded.

"Okay, now tell me why I'm getting a panicked call from you," Harper said with concern. "You're never panicked."

Liberty exhaled slowly. "After eight months of training, I've scored a long-term assignment where I'll be traveling. At the meeting today, the client insisted that I"—it pained her to admit this to her beautiful, fashionable sister—"look less dowdy and more hip to fit in."

"Your jerk of a client said that to you? Good Lord, Lib. How much is the guy limping? Or did you just shoot him?"

She loved how quickly Harper got indignant on her behalf. "Neither, because he's right. I have no sense of style. I've always told you I don't care, and that was true when I was on active duty, but now? Now I'm embarrassed to admit that I'm thirty-five years old and I'm so over-whelmed by all of it—girl hair, makeup, clothing—that I don't even know where to start."

"Well, sweetie, you came to the right place. Take a deep breath. We'll get you through this."

"Thank you."

"Oh, you'll be cursing me when I tell you that I've been waiting for this day to come, and I've prepared for it accordingly."

Liberty frowned. "How did you prepare for it?"

"Please. Did you forget I own a clothing store? I see thousands of pieces of merchandise every year. And ever since you got this job, when I saw something that would look great on you, I've set it aside."

"Christ. Like some kind of Liberty-becomes-a-fashionista hope chest?"

Harper laughed. "Exactly. I know you like baggy, comfortable clothes and I kept that in mind when I picked pieces that are . . . absolutely nothing like that at all."

Liberty groaned but admitted, "God, you annoy me, but I love you anyway."

"I know. I've set aside two dozen pieces. Some will work well together, some need another piece to complete the outfit, but they're all stylish and yet fit with your personality, job and lifestyle. When do you need them by?"

"We leave Denver on Monday."

"Okay. Not a problem. I'll overnight them to you today . . . under one condition."

"What's that?"

"That we finish every ensemble tomorrow afternoon—including shoes. Which means you will take me along as your personal shopper and we'll be on FaceTime for as long as it takes."

Don't groan. "That sounds"—like torture—"good."

"You're such a liar. I'll include ideas of what I think will finish off the outfits and where you can find individual pieces. We'll start at department stores." Harper paused.

"What?"

"Is money an issue?"

"Depends on if you're sending me shopping at Saks or Kmart."

"Places like Nordstrom, Dillard's, Forever 21, Charlotte Russe and Anthropologie will work just fine."

"Then I'm good." Now that the hundred-thousand-dollar paycheck loomed, she could afford to spend a little of her nest egg.

"What about hair and makeup?"

"I was hoping you'd have all the answers for that too."

"That's something you need to handle on your own. But let me ask Bernice if she knows anyone in Denver who specializes in makeovers."

Bernice. That crazy woman who told her she had the perfect face for a crew cut. Liberty had enough problems looking feminine without that. "I'm not sure—"

"Bernice won't steer me wrong. I promise. As far as makeup, I'll text you a list of basics you need in your tool-box. Then I want you to go on YouTube and watch 'how-to' segments. I'd suggest a department store makeup counter, but I know you, sis; you're hands-on. The best way to learn is to do it yourself. And this time you have to learn. Your job depends on it."

Some of the tension melted out of her. "You don't have any idea how much I appreciate this."

"Yes, sweetie, I do. I'm really tickled you came to me first."

"As the former Miss Sweetgrass, you're the expert. I never even considered calling anyone else."

"I wish we could do this in person." She paused. "How long will you be on assignment?"

"Four months. But I get a ten-day break after three months so I promise I'll drive up and hang out with you and your boys."

"We'd like that. And maybe before you leave you could FaceTime with Tate and Jake? They love the stick horses you sent."

She grinned. Spoiling her only nephews was her right. "Sounds good."

"I'll text you Bernice's salon recommendation and I'll

talk with you tomorrow. Love you, Lib. Thanks for need-ing my help."

"You might be sorry you said that," she warned. "Love you too. Kiss the fam for me."

Four hours later, Liberty was sitting in a beauty chair, facing a mirror. The stylist had spent fifteen minutes offer-ing suggestions about color changes and style.

Now the decision rested solely in her hands. She looked at her baby-fine, reddish brown hair, which brushed the tops of her breasts. Over the years she'd worn her hair either long or short, no in between. She'd never changed the color. She'd never really cared before now.

Be daring. And face it—even a shitty haircut eventually grows out.

"So? What'll it be?"

Liberty smiled—although it looked more like a gri-mace. "Do it all. Cut it. Color it. I don't want to recognize myself when you're done."

∞

Two days later . . .

Devin studied the outside of his new tour bus. No gigantic image of his grinning face, no signage at all about who was on board. But there was no doubt this still looked like a rockstar's bus. The inside was even better. He had a big master bedroom and decent-sized master bathroom. The promotion company had even found a bus with only two bunks instead of the standard four. This one had a second bathroom as well as a small alcove where the bunks would've been. The main living area had a half-wall on both sides that allowed for separation from the kitchen.

The driver's area was enclosed like the cab of a semitruck. The only access was through a sliding glass window.

His roadies had unloaded his bags in his bedroom and stashed his favorite guitars in the closet. He didn't give a damn if his clothes got wrinkled; he cared that his guitars were protected and accessible.

Crash wandered over with an update. "We're loaded. The equipment trucks are gone. The roadies' bus is following. We're waiting on Tay, but the rest of the band is ready to roll." He peered over the top of his sunglasses. "Where's your new personal assistant?"

"Who knows? I haven't heard from her. If she ain't here in ten minutes . . . we're still leaving."

"Nope. Sorry. I got my orders, Dev. We're waiting on her."

"Goddammit. This is so fucking stupid. I don't need—"

As he spoke, two arms circled his waist and he jerked away violently.

Yeah, maybe he was a little on edge.

He whirled around and saw the shocked face of his string player and songwriting partner, Odette.

"Geez, Devin, jumpy much?"

"Sorry, darlin'." He hugged her. "You all set?"

"Yes. Thanks for scoring us a new bus too. It's sweet. Steve and I will be breaking in that king-sized bed very soon."

"TMI, little O. And if you tell me that my drummer's got the right rhythm, I will put you two lovebirds in a single bunk and rotate Tay, Gage, Leon, and Jase into the bedroom."

She whapped him on the chest. "That's just plain mean. Sounds like someone needs to get laid."

"You have no idea." Although he had groupies lined

up for him before and after shows, in the past eighteen months, after all this shit started going down, he hadn't fucked any of the women he'd invited into his ready room. He'd kept sexual contact to blow jobs and hand jobs. If those women lied and bragged he'd banged them, well, he didn't give a damn. He couldn't go back and change the manwhore reputation he'd built over the years—most of which had been exaggerated anyway.

A jacked-up Ford truck screeched into the parking lot and the driver slammed on the brakes. A scrawny, bearded guy leaped out of the cab and climbed onto the back bumper, lifting suitcases out of the truck bed and tossing them to the ground.

Just then Tay came around the back end of the truck, yelling obscenities at the man.

"You have got to be fucking kiddin' me," Devin said. "Is Tay an asshole magnet?"

"Yep. This dude followed her to Denver from Kansas City. They were going at it like rabbits. We were in the room next to theirs," Odette said.

Then Tay took a swing at him with her laptop bag.

The guy ducked, jumped back into the truck and sped off, tires spitting gravel.

"Looks like another breakup to me," Crash muttered. "Can't wait for her and Jase to start fucking and fighting again . . . *Not*."

Jase, the laid-back lead guitar player, and Tay, his keyboard player and backup singer, had an on-again off-again relationship. Their fights—and subsequent makeups— were loud, obnoxious and the main reason after Odette . . . Devin never got involved with a woman he worked with.

"Is Jase here?" he asked, watching Tay head toward the band's bus, Odette hot on her heels.

"He left with the equipment truck," Gage said behind him.

"Wise choice."

"A hundred bucks says they're back together by Friday," Leon, his steel guitar player, said.

"Whose turn is it to run the pool?" Steve asked.

"Gage did it last time," Crash said. "I reckon it's Devin's turn."

"Get your bets and money to me by showtime."

"Who're we waiting for?" Gage asked.

Just then a gorgeous baby blue Mustang pulled up. The driver's-side door opened, and a pair of boots hit the concrete. He saw only a flip of the woman's hair and her jeans-clad backside—and sweet baby Jesus, what a sweet backside it was—before she was hidden, rooting around in the open trunk.

Even as his suspicions surfaced, his head was telling him *no*, that couldn't possibly be her.

The trunk shut, and she started toward him. Wind tousling her shoulder-length auburn hair, her hips swaying in jeans that hugged her every curve. With a duffel bag slung over her shoulder and another one clutched in her other hand, she flexed her well-defined arm muscles. Her cherry red lips curved into a smirk as she fastened her gaze on him.

Holy mother of God. It was a miracle that he managed to keep from drooling. Or from cursing at the sky because the fucking universe had a sick sense of humor.

Or maybe this is karma beating you with the stupid stick for boldly proclaiming that you didn't find Liberty Masterson attractive. And for challenging her to look the part of your groupie entourage.

What a cruel joke—his groupies never looked that goddamn good.

Devin had about ten seconds to prepare himself before she reached him. Good thing he had his sunglasses on—maybe they'd keep his eyes from popping out of his head.

That's when his gaze landed on not one but two bruisers behind her. One guy carried two suitcases; the other guy hefted an enormous cooler. Given the sheer size of the first guy, he could've been a Broncos linebacker or a WWE wrestler. The second guy was a mirror image of the first.

Liberty offered a quick smile. "Sorry I'm late. I had to grab a few last-minute things." She set down her duffel bags. "Which bus is ours?"

Devin pointed to the forward bus.

"Sweet upgrade. Guys . . . do you mind?"

Immediately, Hulk #1 and Hulk #2 carted the suitcases and cooler aboard the bus. Then they were back, awaiting Liberty's instructions.

She stood on tiptoe to get in Hulk #1's face. "You'll make sure she's protected? No matter what?"

"Baby girl, don't worry. I promise I'll take as good care of her as you do, okay?"

"Okay." She smiled and pressed something into his hand.

Then the guy picked her up off the ground and spun her around, giving everyone his massive back so no one could see if he was laying a big steamy kiss good-bye on her or copping a feel or what. Then he tossed her to Hulk #2, where she received the same treatment, except Hulk #2 slapped her ass and whispered in her ear before he set her down and lumbered back to the car.

It was surprising the King Kong twins fit into the front seats.

She didn't turn around until the car was out of view. "Sorry. I have separation anxiety."

"At bein' away from them?" Devin asked sharply.

Liberty gave him a *you're-an-idiot* look. "No. From my car."

"That's *your* car?"

Another *you're stupid, Captain Obvious* look from G.I. Jane.

Crash said, "Happy to have you with us, Liberty."

Odette rejoined them. "And who *are* you exactly?"

"Liberty Masterson. I'm Devin's personal assistant."

A beat passed, and then she laughed in Liberty's face. "Right. So how long have you been *personally* assisting him? Since you met him in the bar last night?"

Liberty didn't respond. She merely stared at Odette until she backed down.

Devin stepped forward, taking his life in his hands when he draped an arm over Liberty's shoulder. Not only did she look good; she smelled good. "Liberty is handling the venue logistics, my promotional appearances, and all that stuff I hate doin' and Crash is too busy to deal with since I'm headlining this time. So to keep everything streamlined, she's traveling on my bus."

Looks were exchanged, eyebrows were lifted and Odette nudged Tay and muttered, "Personal assistant, my ass."

Then Devin introduced Liberty to his band.

"Nice to meet all of you. But if you'll excuse me, I have to get the rest of my shit on the bus so we have an on-time departure—since keeping Devin on schedule is part of my job."

Her bright smile was totally fake; Devin choked back a snort.

She reached for the straps on her bags and Devin

moved to help her. The damn woman was so stubborn that they played tug-of-war until he shouldered her aside. "Now, sweetheart," he said through gritted teeth, "what kind of a man would I be if I stood by and watched you struggle with your luggage by yourself?"

She smiled—the devious one that made his stomach drop. "You'd be like every other man on the planet." She picked up the smaller bag and hoofed it to the bus.

Devin was so focused on the mesmerizing way her butt jiggled that he didn't budge until Crash elbowed him.

"Quit standing there and move it. I'm right behind you."

He snagged the handles and let out a grunt. Had she packed cannonballs in here? He trailed behind her, trying like hell—and failing miserably—to keep his eyes off her ass. So he nearly plowed into her when they entered the bus.

"Holy friggin' hell." Liberty had stopped in the living area and was gawking.

"Keep movin'. I've gotta get these bricks unloaded," he grumbled.

"Funny. Which bunk is mine?"

"Both. Since you're the only other passenger."

"Sweet. I wondered where I'd put everything."

Devin dragged the duffel bag the last few feet. "I figured you'd be the type to pack light, not drag four bags along."

"Guns and ammo take up a lot of room."

She had to be joking.

But the look on her face said she wasn't.

Devin pointed to the area below the first bunk. "There are locking drawers for all your firepower."

"Thanks." Liberty didn't ask for help hoisting her bags.

"All right. See you guys in Salt Lake because I don't plan on stopping."

Liberty looked at Crash. "You're on the other bus?"

"I'm driving the other bus." He grinned. "How do you think I got my name?"

"I'm thanking the universe I'm not riding with you."

After Crash departed, Devin stood there like a dumbass, staring at her.

Of course she caught him staring. "What?"

"You look . . . different."

Her gaze sharpened. "You *told* me to look different, remember?"

"Yes, but I didn't think you'd look like this." His admiring, borderline lustful gaze swept her body from head to toe and back up.

"Seriously? I get the slack-jawed response that Sandra Bullock got in *Miss Congeniality* after her makeover and there's no one around to see it?"

"And that's where the comparison ends, because there ain't nothin' congenial about you."

She blushed but kept her stubborn chin lifted.

Feeling ornery, he didn't let it go. "I find the section of blue hair . . . interesting. Why'd you do it?"

"I swear a blue streak and thought my new, improved look should reflect that."

Devin laughed. "It worked. You look"—fucking fantastic—"incredible."

Her silvery eyes turned a dark, stormy gray. "It's a damn good thing you're not attracted to me in the least, don't you agree?"

Now he looked away. That'd been an asshole thing to say. And the fact she'd overheard it? Now he knew why she'd given him the cold shoulder at the GSC offices.

"Takes two to two-step, darlin'. You swore I'm not your type either."

Her startled expression indicated she'd forgotten that.

"Now, we done with this who's hot and who's not sniping so I can show you the rest of the bus?"

"We're done."

"Come on."

Liberty was properly awed by their luxury traveling coach. "I spent so many years riding in the back of transport trucks and in Humvees, I doubt I'll get used to this. This place is way nicer than my apartment. It's a little surreal."

"For me too," he confessed. "Even after a dozen years in this business, I keep expecting I'll wake up and find it's all been a dream." Why had he told her something so personal? Now she probably thought he was even more of a pussy.

Yeah, you hauling her luggage proved you're one badass dude.

Three knocks sounded outside the door. "Just wanted to let you know we're taking off."

Liberty moved and offered her hand. "I'm Liberty, Devin's personal assistant."

"I'm Reg." The rotund guy in his midfifties shook her hand with much enthusiasm. "Happy to meet you, ma'am. If either of you needs something, hit the intercom switch. It'll turn on the light on my dashboard. Since I wear headphones, it's best that you approach me that way and not through the beer window. Better not to scare the dickens out of me and I end up wrecking the bus."

"Good point."

Devin watched as Liberty put away her groceries— every bit of it labeled. "You don't have to do that," he said when she added a big *L* to the side of the milk. "I ain't gonna steal your food."

"Sorry. Habit left over from military life."

"Why'd you bring your own food anyway?"

"Because when we're out, I have to eat where and when you do. But because we're in public, I'll be so busy watching the perimeter, I forget to eat. I make sure to have decent food available for when I have uninterrupted time." Then she pulled out her own one-cup-at-a-time coffeemaker.

Devin didn't know why that annoyed him.

Yes, you do. That means she won't be making coffee for you.

"Once you get settled, we need to go over a few things," she said.

"I'm settled now. What's on your mind?"

"This job is unlike a normal job where I work twelve hours and then I'm off shift for twelve hours. I won't have a partner to relieve me. And it'd be unhealthy and unwise for me not to have any downtime. I certainly hope you don't expect me to work twenty-four hours a day for the first three-month leg of the tour without a break."

"Of course not," he scoffed. "Don't forget I'm used to bein' alone on my bus, doin' what I want, when I want, with no distractions and no one to answer to."

"You're most protected when we're traveling, so I'll take my downtime when we're on the road. That'll give you the quiet time you need to work. I'll just hang out in my bunk or I'll stay in the part of the bus that gives you the most privacy."

Devin nodded. "That'll actually work really well for me."

Relief crossed her face. "Good. But as soon as the bus stops, I'm with you at all times. No exceptions unless I'm handing you off to an event security team."

"Then what will you be doin'?"

"Limiting access to you."

He snagged a Red Bull from the refrigerator and kept his temper in check. "Limiting access meaning . . . keeping groupies away from me? Because we already discussed my conditions on that."

Liberty studied him. "And I said I didn't give a fuck who you fucked as long as they pass my safety parameters. Which are: None of the ladies can bring purses, handbags or backpacks into your ready room. No more than two women at a time in your ready room. I will be stationed outside the door the entire time you're . . . entertaining your fans."

Was she fucking serious? She'd be listening outside the goddamn door?

She shook her finger at him. "I'm not a pervert; nor will I get off hearing you getting off with your groupies. But this is a nonnegotiable point, Devin."

"Fine. Whatever. Let's practice havin' separate downtime starting now. I'll be in my room. See you in Salt Lake."

Chapter Five

❦

See you in Salt Lake.

Talk about dismissed.

She couldn't help but feel relieved Devin had squirreled himself away in his master suite. The sooner they got used to each other and a routine, the better.

Yet after Liberty had gotten settled, she still felt . . . unsettled. She paced the length of the bus, worried for the first time that she wouldn't last three days in this situation, let alone four months.

Think about the money.

Taking a deep breath, she crawled into her bunk and pulled the curtain closed. She surfed the Internet, answered e-mail, checked out the new real estate listings in the Denver metro area. She killed two hours.

She exited her bunk and realized the soundproofing in the bus must be fantastic because she hadn't heard any music.

Her stomach rumbled, so she fixed herself a sandwich. Since she hadn't figured out how to operate the TV system, she brought her laptop into the eating area and watched two episodes of *Dexter*. She'd just washed and dried her lunch dishes when Devin appeared.

"Hey." He glanced at the dish towel. "You already ate?"

"Yeah."

"Shoot. I was lookin' forward to you fixin' my lunch."

Liberty's eyes narrowed.

Devin laughed. "Kidding." Then he opened the pantry door. "Always interesting to see what gets stocked for me."

Of course he wouldn't do his own food shopping. He had minions for that. She said, "Heads will roll if they bought the wrong kind of peanut butter," a little snottily.

He peered around the fridge door at her. "You think I'm some spoiled-ass male diva, don't you?"

"Are you?"

"With some things. Mostly on the performance side. Expecting a certain kind of venue and promotion from the record label. When I reached the level of success that I could request things like uninterrupted time before a show, a private ready room, and my own bus, I figured I'd earned it. I did my time on the road, playing in every small-town bar across the country, livin' out of an equipment van with three other guys, eating peanut butter sandwiches three times a day because that's all I could afford, sneaking into truck stops to shower because we couldn't scrape together enough money for a motel room."

She felt her cheeks heat at her preconceived ideas about him.

He rolled a can of diet soda between his hands. "I know what it's like to starve to make music. It sucks to play to a crowd of ten people who'd rather have country music piped in than listen to a live band. At my lowest point, I had to get a job at a horse farm and stop touring because I was flat broke and didn't have the cash to replace our shitty van that died." He cracked open the soda and drank. "I had a shady agent who promised me the world and basically put me in performance hell for a year. I damn near gave up when a scout for a big Nashville label deigned to attend one of my shows and told me I'd never make it in the music business. But I decided to prove him wrong." He grinned. "Yeah, I'll admit it's sweet revenge every time I see him now and pretend I don't know who the hell he is."

Liberty smiled.

"I've been on both sides. And, darlin', it's just plain human nature to prefer the side that offers more creature comforts and fewer creatures."

Devin rummaged in the refrigerator and dumped a prepackaged salad into a big bowl. Then he sprinkled chopped chicken on top and poured dressing over everything. After he slid into the bench seat opposite her, he looked up. "What?"

"Nothing."

"Surprised that I'm eating something green?"

"Maybe a little."

He speared a chunk of chicken and spinach. "I learned the hard way, after my first tour, not to exist on snack food and junk food. I put on twenty pounds, and it sucked havin' to get it off."

"It's obvious you take care of yourself now and keep in shape. You look great." Shit. Why had she said that?

Devin smiled before he shoveled in a bite.

Liberty let him eat without asking questions. She peeled an orange and ate half.

When he finished his meal, he washed and dried his dishes and put them away, which surprised her.

Maybe you shouldn't be making assumptions about Devin McClain. You didn't like him making them about you.

Then he took his seat again and looked at her. "Go on and ask the questions I see in your eyes."

"So you weren't an overnight success?"

"Guess that depends on who you talk to about the definition of overnight success. I started playing in local bands in Wyoming when I was seventeen. Moved to Nashville when I was eighteen, confident I'd hit the big time in a year, dumb-ass hick kid that I was." He shook his head. "I landed my first real recording contract at age twenty-four. The album did well right outta the gate, so everyone assumed I was an overnight success. When I heard the stories from really talented guys who had a much longer, harder road than I did, I guess six years could be considered overnight. It's been a decade since that first album was released."

"So when did the money, the fame and the groupies become a way of life?"

"That happened really damn fast. *Boom*. I had two number-one hits off that album and two that hit the top ten. I won the best new artist award. I opened for Brooks and Dunn; at the time they were the biggest act in country music. I spent a year on the road. When I got back to Nashville, I bought a house, a couple of cars. Lots of guitars." He reached for her orange and tore off a segment. "I burned through a helluva lot of money in a short amount of time. The label had been pressuring me to put out another record. Problem was, I didn't have enough material."

"What does that mean?"

Devin looked at her. "You sure I'm not boring you with the *This Is Your Life, Devin McClain,* story?"

"No. It's fascinating. Having fame, fortune and an

entourage is so different from my life, or the life of anyone I've ever known. As your personal assistant, I should have a better idea of who you are other than what your official media bio says."

His penetrating blue gaze roamed over her face—almost as if he were seeing her for the first time. "Ain't no one gonna believe that you're just my personal assistant, Liberty."

A wave of heat steamrolled her. Holy crap, the man simply oozed potent sexuality when he put his mind to it. Her heart raced and her palms sweated just from the smoldering way he looked at her. What would it be like to have him touching her as he murmured in her ear with his deep, raspy voice?

Sheer. Fucking. Heaven.

She managed to toss off a breezy "Guess we'll see, won't we?"

He grinned, well aware that he'd gotten to her. "First off, as my personal assistant, you should know that my legal name is Devin McClain Hollister. When I started out, there was an artist with the name Gavin Hollister, so we used my middle name."

"It'll be easiest if I stick to calling you McClain. Finish the story."

"I'd written all my own songs on my first album. I had finished maybe . . . four during that yearlong tour. So the label handpicked another half a dozen songs from other songwriters for me. I didn't like a single one of them. But I was new to the business and the label, which had successfully put out hundreds of records, had to know what they were doin', right? Rather than delay the release of a new record, I fell in line—against my gut instinct—and recorded those shitty, clichéd songs."

"What happened?"

"The album tanked. Big-time. Only one song cracked the top hundred—a song I'd written. I still went on tour to promote the album, but wasn't part of the primo gigs. I wasn't a failure, but I'd slipped a notch." He popped an orange segment in his mouth and chewed. "That slip gave me some clarity. I understood there'd be an ebb and flow to my career, no matter if I hit that upper level of megastar success that so few do. I needed to be prepared for when I started the descent back down because it would happen at some point—it happens to everyone."

That was way more insightful than she'd expected.

"I realized two things. First off, for me it was about putting out music I was proud of—no more slapping crap on a record just to make someone else's deadline. I needed to surround myself with other musicians who had the same vision, which is why my band has stayed together. The music we create in the studio and on the road is because we gel as a group. I retained control of the only part of the business to me that matters, and that's the music.

"Second, I had to make my time on the road productive. The best thing I ever did was learn to write music anywhere— on the bus, in a restaurant or in a hotel. I stopped limiting myself to havin' the perfect conditions, and the result was the music became . . . truer somehow. But at the end of the day, I'm an entertainer. I'm not curing cancer. I hope I'm providing songs that hit home for people, make them think or laugh or cry, or just provide them with a catchy chorus they can sing along to. I'm lucky I get to do what I love every damn night. And I'm gonna enjoy the hell outta this journey while I can."

Liberty let that sink in. It didn't sound like Devin was repeating a PR company's suggestion, but rather his true thoughts.

"You're awful quiet over there, G.I. Jane. Whatcha thinkin' about?"

She crossed her arms over her chest. "Honestly? I get the *life is a journey, not a destination* mind-set, but when did your fans start thinking you belonged to them? I read the case reports, and you've had some crazy things happen over the years that would've made me hire a full-time bodyguard a long damn time ago."

"Which incident?"

"Inez Vanderpol."

He sighed. "My first superfan."

"Didn't she stalk you too?"

"As much as a sixty-six-year-old woman can stalk someone, yeah. She ended up in a mental hospital in Ohio."

"What happened?"

"It's really fuckin' bizarre. After my third album, she joined my fan group. When she learned that I'd been born on the same day her first husband had died, she was convinced he'd been reincarnated in me."

Her mouth dropped open. "No way."

"Yep. And get this: Her husband had also been a musician. So she started following me on tour. I saw her at every concert. She left flowers, and, uh, inappropriate gifts for me at every stop. I was new to that sort of attention, so I thought it was harmless."

"Meaning that she was harmless."

"Exactly. Then, when I had my final fan meet and greet for the year in Nashville, she literally tackled a woman I was talkin' to—just for talkin' to me. She was hitting her, screaming at her to keep her hands off me—her husband. Big public mess. I had to get a restraining order. Then I didn't hear anything from her until my next album came out. She showed up at concerts again and wrote me really long, really sexually explicit letters."

"What format did she send them in?"

Devin looked uncomfortable. "She e-mailed some to the contact e-mail on my Web site. The ones she hand-wrote?" His gaze met hers. "She stuffed them under the door at my house."

"Jesus."

"Then the letters took an even more bizarre turn toward crazy town. She threatened to kidnap me so she could help me remember my previous life."

"As her husband."

He nodded. "I had a two-week break from touring, came home and found her in my house."

Liberty's stomach pitched. "Did she hurt you?"

"No. She tripped the alarm when she broke in and evidently she hid in my closet when the cops came. They didn't find her and locked up the house. When I got home later that night, she was waitin', naked, in my bed."

"Oh, Devin."

"It was so fuckin' sad. I felt bad for her, but at the same time, it pissed me off she'd gotten into my private space and was snooping through my stuff. It bugged me so much I sold that house and bought one with a gate around the entire property. I also purchased a cabin and some land up by Flathead Lake in Montana." He offered a sad smile. "I figured if I ever needed total privacy, no one would find me there."

"What happened to the woman?"

"The cops came and took her in. Her grown children were shocked by her delusions and got her psychiatric help. I didn't follow up on her. I haven't seen her since."

Liberty got up and grabbed a bottle of water.

"Is there something you're not tellin' me? Has she been released or something?"

"No. But Garrett did have GSC follow up on her. Just to see if there was a link to the attack on your bus driver. But she's been in an Alzheimer's care facility since two weeks after the incident at your house."

"So there's no connection."

"Nope."

"I think the attack on JT was random. Some meth-heads breaking into a fancy bus, lookin' for cash or drugs or something to pawn. Not some psycho fan wantin' to harm me," he stated flatly.

They were back to this again. *The promotion company is overly paranoid and I don't need you* argument.

Liberty stared at him suspiciously. "I might believe that if the reincarnation lady was the only example. But we've seen the files, Devin. There have been lots of other incidents. Even paternity cases."

"*One* paternity case three years ago. I knew the woman in question would be a problem because she showed up at rehearsal the day after I banged her, claiming I'd proposed to her. She even wore a big fake diamond. After security threw her out for trespassing, she swore she'd get even with me."

"Is she the one—"

"Who sent her two brothers to my next gig so they could beat the fuck outta me? Yeah."

She frowned. "I don't remember a report like that."

Devin drained his soda. "Because I didn't report it. Her puny brothers cornered me and had me on the ground when Crash and Sarge, the head of my road crew, intervened. I was so fuckin' embarrassed about it that I told them if they ever told a soul I'd fire them both."

"Save me from the fragile male ego," she muttered.

"After everything I've told you, you're actually surprised I have an ego?"

"No. You have to have some ego in your business." She leaned forward. "Hiding something like that is due solely to wounded male pride and doesn't help someone like me who's protecting you. How many other unreported incidents are there?"

He shrugged. "I haven't read your reports, so I don't know." A challenge lit his eyes. "Which incident were you referring to when you said, *Is she the one*?"

"The woman who said she cowrote one of your songs. Then, when you wouldn't meet with her, she would stand outside your bus and throw rocks at you?"

"Another delusional person. She ambushed me at five concerts before we caught her."

"Getting hit with a rock is better than a bullet."

Devin lifted a brow. "Ever been beaned in the back of the head with a rock?"

"Yes, and I've been shot, so I can say that taking a bullet hurts much worse than getting stoned."

"Shit. Sorry. I wasn't thinking."

"What about your relationship with China Marquette?"

He groaned. "Mistake. Big mistake. I'd never dated an actress and had no fuckin' idea the media shitstorm I was in for when I broke up with her. The woman is psychotic."

All guys thought their exes were psycho. "She's the wholesome girl-next-door star on the Disney Channel's most popular family show. How psychotic could she be?"

Devin leaned forward. "She blew up my car."

Liberty's jaw dropped.

"That incident didn't make the papers. Neither did the one where she unloaded two hundred live chickens in my garage and let them die while I was away on tour for a month. Can you imagine the smell? Of course, there was no way to prove it. There were a dozen other things she did that no one would believe. She only ended her smear campaign when I threatened to release a sex tape we'd made. The raunchy things that girl begged me to do to her would've destroyed her career. And no, I don't feel a damn bit guilty because she was out to destroy me."

"Nice world you live in," she mumbled. "Are the other incidents I read about easily explained away too?"

He bristled. "Probably. To be honest, there've been so damn many I've forgotten some. But I won't be a prisoner to fame, Liberty. I won't let the couple of nut jobs out there have power over me and how I live my life." He stood. "Anything else about me that you wanna pick apart?"

Pick apart? He'd freely offered up the information. "I'm just preparing myself for what I might run into over the next few months."

"There's no way you can prepare for it because when the weird shit happens to me, I'm never prepared. Even if it's similar to something I've faced before." He disappeared down the hallway without another word.

And he called her prickly? Sheesh.

Looking out the window didn't give her any idea where they were. She hit the intercom. "Reg? How far are we from Salt Lake City?"

"An hour and a half."

"Cool. Thanks."

She watched another episode of *Dexter.* Then she checked to make sure she could get online so she could log onto *Call of Duty* during her downtime. She so rarely got to play during the day. It'd be interesting to see the difference between daytime and nighttime gamers.

She ate a protein bar and double-checked her hair and makeup. Maintaining her new style hadn't been as time-consuming as she'd imagined. Plus, she did look more professional. Just wearing a little lip color softened her mouth, which she'd always thought was too harsh looking. Spike and Zeke—Joe's brothers who'd dropped her off—had even whistled upon seeing her feminine side. Of course, she'd immediately threatened to knock them on their asses if they believed girly clothes had changed her.

The look on Devin's face when he caught sight of her? Priceless.

The bedroom door opened, and he walked past the bathroom and down the hall.

After slipping her gun in her waistband holster, she went to the front of the bus.

Devin had draped a suit bag across the bench seat.

When she glanced over at him, he was blatantly checking her out. She could blush and ignore it or call him on it. "Do I pass inspection?"

"More than pass. Good enough that I'd make a pass at you, but I suspect you're armed." His dark gaze swept over her again. "You carrying right now?"

"Yes."

"Where?"

She lifted her blouse and showed him a modified holster that stayed snug against her body but gave her easy access to her weapon.

"I'll be damned. Sometime you'll have to show me how fast you can pull."

Her gaze never wavered when she said, "I sincerely hope that's something you'll never see."

Properly chastised, he said, "What kind of gun is that? It looks small."

"It's a Kahr Arms PM45. It's compact with the stopping power of a forty-five." Liberty changed the subject. "What do you usually do first when you get off the bus?"

"Track down Crash and Sarge and see if there were any problems with setup. Then the event staff shows up."

"Event staff. Who is that?"

"The head honcho responsible for bringing acts like mine into the venue. His or her assistants."

"And your security."

"They take me backstage. Show me the food service room and my ready room." At her blank look, he said, "A ready room is just my private room. I require one at every venue—regardless of the size of the venue. The room can be decked out like a five-star hotel room or a canvas tent, or anything in between." He pointed to the suit bag and the duffel. "Since I can't send my guitar guru, Check, to the bus anymore to get things I'll need in my room, that's my clothing for tonight and tomorrow night."

The bus slowed down. While Liberty was taking in the sights of Salt Lake City, Devin leaned back with his eyes closed. She couldn't imagine how much pressure he was under, playing to a sold-out crowd two nights in a row. She wanted to ask him if he ever got nervous before going onstage, but he radiated that "back off" vibe, so she stayed quiet.

Once they'd parked in the back of the lot between the other two tour buses, Devin stood and put on his cowboy hat. "You ready for this?"

"Not really. How about you?"

He bestowed that million-dollar grin on her. "Darlin', I was born ready. I live for this. Come on, let's hit it."

Chapter Six

~~~

*L*iberty acted cool, like being backstage at a Devin McClain show was no big deal. But secretly she was as excited as the first time she shot a grenade launcher.

The preshow activity had put her on edge. Luckily, Devin had two escorts as he entered the back door of the event center and two more inside. She didn't think the big events would be the problem anyway, but the smaller county fair venues. When Garrett had suggested canceling the preshow or the aftershow party, the promoter had refused. Devin agreed. Interactions with his fans were a big part of the tour. He wouldn't disappoint people who had paid extra for their tickets for a chance to meet him.

Devin had a no-contact rule prior to the performance. When she'd asked him about it, he said he needed time to get his head on straight and warm up before he walked onstage. So tonight he'd shooed her out of his ready room and she'd prowled the halls, watching the multitude of people it took to put on a show this size. From the catering staff to the media personnel, the roadies, the tech guys, the crew who traveled with the opening act.

She finally understood why he needed solitude. He had to be overwhelmed by everyone who wanted a piece of him. She wondered if it'd be a zoo tonight at the after-party that kicked off his headlining gig.

The crew removed the last of the opening act's equipment, and Devin's roadies had the switchover completed in ten minutes. The arena went dark. The crowd started chanting, "Devin, Devin, Devin."

Devin's band took the stage under the cover of darkness. Liberty peeked around the corner and saw the two security guards escorting him.

He'd changed into tight jeans with a metallic sheen and a black and silver button-up shirt open to his sternum, revealing a gray tank top. He'd rolled up his sleeves and donned a black cowboy hat. Those tempting curls ringed his face when he put on his hat. She smiled when she saw the same pair of scuffed-up boots he'd been wearing since this morning.

He adjusted his microphone, his earpiece and the strap on his guitar before he said, "Hello, Salt Lake City!" and moseyed to the center of the stage.

The roar of the crowd was deafening. Their reaction gave her goose bumps.

The lead guitar played a riff, the drums joined in and the show got under way.

And what a show it was.

No wonder his concerts sold out. The man was electric onstage. He had a great rapport with his band, making sure they got time in the spotlight. He danced a little. Male strippers had nothing on him—he knew exactly how to move that very fine body for maximum effect. He played a rock cover tune, all his biggest hits, and at one point he stripped it down to him and his guitar, with Tay on background vocals.

In that moment, she understood it wasn't the spectacle of his stage show that caused that *wow* factor, but the man himself and his music.

Ninety minutes and two encores later, he exited the stage for the final time. But his night wasn't over.

Amid the congratulations from the crew for the great show, he headed back to his ready room. Liberty followed behind the security escorts and caught the door before it slammed in her face.

Keeping his gaze on hers, he uncapped a bottle of water and drank deeply. His clothes clung to his body, completely damp with sweat. Then he began unbuttoning his shirt.

Liberty's mouth went dry at the sight of the sculpted muscles of his shoulders, arms, and chest. Using a bootjack, he removed his boots and his hands went to his belt buckle. "Are you really gonna stand there and watch me strip without sayin' a word?"

"Are you really gonna strip in front of me and expect me not to watch?" she retorted.

Devin laughed. "First night on tour and you're already bustin' my balls. So what's up?"

"Just wondering if you want me escorting you to the party, or if you'd prefer security. And how long before you're ready."

"I need to shower, so you go on. Tell the security guys to stick around."

She nodded. Just as she reached the door, it opened and a well-endowed blonde paused in the doorway. "Can I help you?"

"I'm supposed to meet Devin here."

Liberty wondered how often that statement worked for these groupies. Her gaze dropped to the lanyard with the backstage pass. "Sorry. He's—"

"Very happy to see you," Devin inserted behind her. "What's your name again?"

"Eve."

"Beautiful name, doll. Come on in." He took her hand and tugged her into the room.

When Liberty spun around to protest that this strange woman, whose name he hadn't even known, had gained access to him by flaunting her tits, she was momentarily sidetracked by his bare chest. How did the man maintain that physique when he spent most of his time on a tour bus playing guitar?

Devin murmured something to Eve and snaked his hand around her waist. He said, "I'll see you at the party," without meeting Liberty's gaze and shut the door on her.

She wanted to knock until he opened the door again and point out this woman could be dangerous and should be frisked for weapons—but then she realized how ridiculous that sounded. Eve's outfit defined skimpy.

The security guard to the right smirked at her. "Yes, she's clean. We checked her. And the five others waiting in line behind her."

She glanced at the ladies glaring at one another from various spots in the hallway. "Just make sure he makes it to the party after he's done."

Liberty cautioned herself against a morality judgment. He was a guy who used his celebrity for easy sex—no different from most of the men in the public eye.

What she didn't understand? Why some women were so eager to drop to their knees for a guy they didn't know.

Did they brag to their friends about giving a celebrity a blow job? Did they think they were so good at sucking cock that a guy like Devin would fall in love with them? She snorted. Men weren't picky about blow-job technique. Any woman who put a dude's dick in her mouth was good at giving head.

"Hey, Liberty, wait up."

She stopped and faced Odette.

Odette hadn't changed clothes; she still wore the iridescent skirt and sequin tank top from the performance. "I wanted to apologize for earlier this morning. I was rude to you. I'm sorry."

Liberty started walking. "Apology accepted."

"It's just . . . I've known Devin a long time."

The way she emphasized *known* meant one thing. "How long were you and Devin together?"

She blushed. "A year. Being in close quarters on tour and thinking we were in love is something that a lot of musicians go through with other musicians. I've been with Steve for five years now. So we're proof that on-the-road romances don't always end in disaster." Odette looked around. "Where is Devin?"

"Taking the edge off in his ready room."

She stopped again. "You're okay with him banging a groupie on the first night of the tour?"

Liberty shrugged. "I'm his personal assistant, remember?"

"But you've got to be more than that," Odette blurted. "Devin never lets anyone stay on his tour bus. And you've pretty much moved in."

"All the better to offer my personal assistance whenever Devin needs it." God. It burned her damn tongue to say that, but she let Odette assign meaning to it.

Odette looked . . . sorry for her. Then she dropped it.

"Let's see what delectable morsels the promotion company ordered for us tonight. The first and last nights of tour are usually when they go all-out on the food."

Liberty was pleased the security guards manning the outer door checked everyone's passes. The half of the room cordoned off for fans was packed, while on the other side, a couple dozen people milled about, holding drinks but not eating.

"Hang on," Odette said and vanished into the crowd.

This type of situation made her jumpy. Too many people. Too many ways to get to Devin. She checked out the other four security guys inside the room. Even though they were staying alert, she couldn't drop her guard. But since Devin wasn't here, she should probably eat.

She wandered over to the tables loaded with fancy food. Beautifully crafted rolls of sushi, skewers of roasted meat, mini pulled-pork sandwiches, bread with several different pesto and tomato toppings, artisan cheeses, creamy dips for the bowls of hand-cut potato chips. She didn't see any of the freeze-and-heat type of grocery store appetizers she was used to. Next to the bowls of brined olives was a mountain of fresh-cut vegetables and plates of exotic fruit. At the end of the table she spied trays of chocolate desserts with swirled rainbow-colored icing and gold flecks that she was afraid to touch.

A deep voice behind her said, "Seems a waste, don't it? All this pretty, expensive damn food and no one has touched it."

Liberty faced Crash. "I don't see a plate in your hand."

"So let's be the first ones to load up."

She piled her plate high. "What happens to all this food if no one eats it?"

"Depends. Devin has stipulations in his contract that

if we're near a kids' home or a women's shelter, they get first dibs. If we're close to a military base or a veterans' facility, it gets delivered to the mess hall. Boomer, our sound guy, is the resident do-gooder, so he makes sure it goes someplace besides in the damn garbage."

"I'm glad to hear that. I know soldiers would be thrilled to get grub this good."

They found a table that gave her a decent view of the room.

"I'm assuming there haven't been any problems tonight?" Crash asked.

"None."

"Were there women waiting for him at the ready room after the performance?"

Liberty shook her head. "That shit's been stopped."

Crash nearly choked on his sandwich. "No women at all?"

"Don't pity the poor man, Crash; he's with a woman now. The others are allowed to wait in the *hallway*, and they'll be checked out before they get near him. From what I can see, the biggest threat to his safety is him suffocating from all the ladies who want to dog pile him."

He laughed. "And a few men too. But it ain't as bad as all that. A lot of what you'll hear about him and his um . . . appetites are bald-faced lies to sell sleazy magazines." He crunched a chip. "His bandmates think you're his new girlfriend and the PA thing is just a front."

"I know."

"You don't have a problem with them thinking you're a pushover for letting him fuck whoever he wants while you're supposedly in his bed every night?"

Her gaze met his. "Makes it easier all around if they think I'm a pushover. And to be blunt, I don't give a flying fuck how they judge me. It's not like I'll become besties with any of them."

"Harsh."

"You, Devin and I know that I'm not here to make friends. So the first time Odette asks me to have lunch with her and Tay and I decline, they'll be fine. But the third or fourth time I say no, they'll think I'm so cock whipped that I can't leave Devin's side even for a lousy hour. I'm good with that too. Because I won't be having girl time or lunch with them. Ever."

Crash's eyes turned serious. "You're better at this job than I thought you'd be. Just think. We only have sixty-seven more performances to get through."

"Since Devin isn't very forthcoming about his band-mates, can you give me a rundown on each one? Hookups, history, length of time Devin's been working with them?"

"Most of them have been with him since his third album. Jase is the lead guitar player and he's on again, off again with Tay. Tay is the keyboard player and backup singer. Odette is our string virtuoso. She and Dev were involved for a while, but now she and Steve, our drummer, have been together for years. Gage is the bassist. Leon plays slide steel. They've both been with him since the beginning."

"Are they studio musicians when they're not on tour?"

He shook his head. "Someone at Devin's level could hire top-notch studio musicians and tour with them. The record label suggested that, but Devin is loyal. He trusts all of his band members and considers them his family. At one time he approached the label about rebranding themselves as the Devin McClain Band, but they shot him down."

"He's amazing in concert. I was pretty blown away, to tell you the truth."

Crash nodded. "I've managed his road crew for eight years and I've not lost the excitement of seeing him onstage."

The sea of people parted, clapping started, signaling the star had arrived.

Liberty had wondered if Devin would show up with a woman on his arm, but he came solo.

Coming solo was probably rare for him since he had women lined up, ensuring he didn't have to take himself in hand. She snickered. Not PC. But hey, at least she hadn't said it out loud.

Devin looked around, saw Crash and beckoned him over.

"Duty calls. Enjoy your break. I figure he'll be ready to head back to the bus in an hour."

Liberty watched him doing the meet and greet, and she could tell he genuinely enjoyed it. He must've had his picture taken a hundred times. He signed T-shirts, ball caps, posters and CD covers without missing a beat or losing his smile.

Finally, the crowd thinned. But he wasn't done. Looked like he had media interviews. During that time, he'd finished a bottle of water. She thought she caught him staring longingly at the food table, but he didn't stop what he was doing to eat.

She had the strangest compulsion to fill a plate with food and force him to sit.

Don't go there. It'd set a bad precedent. You're not his caretaker; you're his protection.

But the truth was, Devin McClain looked like he needed a caretaker.

∞

"Thank you so much. I appreciate y'all comin' to the show tonight."

Devin realized there wasn't anyone else waiting in line to talk to him. Before that changed, he headed for the food tables, only to find most of the food gone, except one mini sandwich and a handful of chips. Better than nothing. He devoured it in about five seconds and glanced up to see Liberty watching him.

She wore the blank expression of someone who's seen it all, done it all and was bored with it all.

That expression didn't change one iota as he wandered over to her. "Did you have a good time tonight?"

"Not as good as you've had."

Of course she'd point that out. "I meant the show. What did you think of it?" Why had he asked when he knew how brutally honest her answer would be?

"It was . . ."

"What?"

When Liberty leaned forward, her silver eyes shone with pleasure. "Fucking spectacular. I've never seen anything like it. And it's lucky you had other security keeping an eye on your safety because I couldn't look away from you . . . I mean from the show."

Devin grinned. "Thank you. I mean it."

She pushed a plate of food toward him. "I noticed by the time you got a break there wasn't much food left. I didn't touch this. Go ahead if you want it, although it is cold."

There was a glimpse of the real Liberty, the thoughtful woman behind the gun. "Thanks again."

"So what happens now?"

"Usually after the first show we have a meeting with the crew to talk about problems. In fact, they're all waitin' for me in the arena right now."

She eyed the security guys. "Their shift is about up."

"Let them go. I'll be surrounded by people the rest of the night. You're here to escort me back to the bus."

As Liberty spoke to the security team, Devin couldn't help but admire the way she dealt with them. Professionally, with a hint of don't-fuck-with-me charm that should've been off-putting but was effective.

Devin knew he shouldn't be having those thoughts, but even after just one day, he realized he'd never met a woman quite like Liberty. And he looked forward to getting to know her better.

She nudged him. "Come on, slowpoke. Crash has beckoned you over, like, two times."

"Sometimes I'm a little spacey after the performance high wears down."

"I imagine it's hard to shut off that adrenaline rush."

He looked at her. "How do you know that? You're a performer?"

Liberty shook her head. "I assume it's similar to being in a firefight. The intensity puts you on another plane, and when it's over . . . you don't crash right away. You want to do something that'll keep up that level of intensity."

Shocking that she did understand. Was this her way of telling him she thought having a woman to take the edge off after he got offstage was okay?

"But just because I get it doesn't mean the women you use and discard do."

And . . . there it was. Judgment. Before he could remind her who he fucked wasn't any of her fucking business, she spoke again.

"Get moving. They're waiting on you."

Devin grabbed a beer from the cooler and joined his crew. For the next half an hour they dissected the show from start to finish. By the end of his second beer, they'd changed the lighting on a few songs and decided on a short rehearsal tomorrow to get a better balance between the fiddle, the drums and the guitars.

Liberty waited in the wings and fell into step with him as they exited the arena.

"You up for a poker game tonight in your fancy-ass new 'I'm a rockstar' tour bus?" Jase asked.

"Nah, man. I'm whupped."

"And he's got press meetings in the morning," Liberty reminded him.

"Catch ya later." Jase took off.

Crash said, "You've got that hospital visit tomorrow before rehearsal."

He felt Liberty stiffen beside him. "I know."

They reached the bus. Liberty deactivated the alarm and unlocked the door.

"You'll have to show me how to do that," Devin said.

"Why? Chances are you'll never be unattended."

There was a cheery thought.

Reg peered through the beer window. "You're back later than I expected."

"Been a long day."

"I hear ya. All was quiet tonight, except for some girls yelling how much they loved you."

Devin blushed. "Thanks for sticking around."

As soon as Reg was gone, Liberty locked the doors and pulled the curtains. Then she got right in his face. "Why didn't you tell me you had another commitment tomorrow?"

He scowled. "It's personal."

"It's personal," she repeated. "Since the moment I signed on as your *personal* security, I'm in your *personal* business, Devin, all of it. What don't you get about that?"

Would it piss her off if he mentioned how hot it was when fire flashed in her eyes and she went toe-to-toe with him? Definitely. Might be worth getting shot at.

He shrugged. "It's not a big deal."

"Then what is it?"

In lieu of answering, he returned her icy stare.

"Fine. Since I didn't plan extra security for a personal hospital thing, you'll have to cancel."

Devin herded her until her back hit the wall. "No fuckin' way. I will be there. So think of this as your chance to prove that you—just you—can protect me."

She waited for an explanation, her bodyguard mask in place.

"Where I'm goin' is a hospital—a children's cancer hospital—so you can't wear your gun."

"Oh, this just gets better and better."

"Suck it up, G.I. Jane. And you'll put on a happy face for those kids, understand?"

"How much media will be there?"

Stung, he stepped back. "None. Jesus. You think I'm doin' this for some media attention? What kind of publicity-hungry asshole do you think I am?"

She threw up her hands. "I don't know! I don't know you, okay? And this caught me completely by surprise." She inhaled a deep breath. "How many people know you're going there tomorrow?"

"Crash. I didn't mention it to my agent, and I forbade the tour promotion company from turnin' it into a media spectacle. I don't do this for any reason other than it makes me happy to put smiles on those kids' faces. Even for just an hour."

Her eyes searched his. "No bullshit. This is really important to you, isn't it?"

"Yes."

"Why?"

He collapsed against the wall, shoving down his resentment that he had to share something so intensely personal with her. It was one of the few private things he had left. "These kids that have cancer . . . they deal with so much pain and so much uncertainty. Days, weeks, even months in the hospital. I remember how my little sister would talk about how much she loved it when 'special' people came and did things with them."

A moment of silence passed. "Your sister had cancer?"

"Yeah."

"What happened to her?"

A sharp stab of pain still lodged in his heart every time he thought of her. "She was diagnosed with leukemia when she was seven. The treatments didn't work on her, and she passed on two days after her ninth birthday."

"How old were you?"

"Sixteen. She was the sweetest girl in the world. And she suffered . . ." He swallowed hard. "It about killed all of us—me, my mom and dad and older sister, Renee—to watch her, knowing we couldn't do a goddamn thing about it. So when I'm on the road, I make time to hang out with kids like her."

Liberty's hand pressed against his chest, over his heart. "I'm sorry. God, Devin, I'm so fucking sorry. I can't imagine your loss. And I'm sorry that I questioned the reason why you were doing it. It was a dick move on my part."

Shocked by her apology, he opened his eyes, surprised to see a sheen of tears in hers. "I don't talk about my family. Very few people know about her. The grief . . . then and now, it's private, you know?"

"No, I don't know. Thank you for telling me."

Devin placed his hand over hers. "I know you don't want to be my confidante, but we will be livin' in very close quarters, so I hope we can be friends."

She blinked at him and opened her mouth. But she shut it and nodded. Then she slid her hand free.

"It's after midnight. You a night owl?" he asked.

"I'm more an *early to bed, early to rise* type. So I'll call it a night. I don't have to warn you not to leave the bus or let anyone in, do I?"

"No. I'm lookin' forward to some alone time." He smirked. "Just me and my big-screen TV."

"Have fun. You'll have to show me how to run it."

"The TV in my bedroom?"

Liberty rolled her eyes. "No. The one right there." She pointed to the forty-eight-inch screen that dropped down from the ceiling.

"I can do that."

Halfway down the hall, she stopped. "What was your sister's name?"

Why did she want to know that? He said, "Michelle," and she had no idea how hard it was for him to choke out.

"Pretty. Night, Devin."

Chapter Seven

～

The next afternoon Liberty accompanied Devin to the children's hospital.

She waited outside the room, letting him do his thing with the kids. They stayed for nearly two hours. As they walked out, in a moment of sympathy, she'd taken his hand. He'd squeezed her fingers and kept her close enough to his side that their arms brushed. The intimacy in their simple touch hinted at a deeper connection between them—which was as scary as it was thrilling.

But on the ride back to the event center, he pulled away into total silence.

Devin was waylaid outside the arena doors by a couple of enthusiastic female fans. He chatted with them for several minutes and called over one of his roadies to hand out backstage passes. Liberty heard him tell his admirers to come to his dressing room in an hour, when he finished rehearsal.

The girls squealed with excitement after Devin disappeared inside.

Un. Fucking. Real.

Her internal mantra of *no judgment* was drowned out by the loud woofing sound in her brain, reminding her that country music star Devin McClain was a dog.

During rehearsal, she stayed in the shadows of the stage, feeling naked without a weapon. She'd agreed to leave her guns locked up on the bus while they were at the hospital. She should've insisted they stop to get them after the hospital visit, just to be safe. But the only danger Devin appeared to be in right now was getting run over by his raging libido.

After the stage cleared, she hung back while Devin talked to Crash. Her curiosity threatened to get the better of her, but she forced herself to stay in place, out of earshot of their conversation.

When Devin cut down the hallway to his ready room, Liberty followed.

Crash fell into step with her.

"What's up?"

"Dev wants some time to chill. He'll stay in there until the concert starts. He said to tell you to go back to the bus."

"So the security we hired is already here?"

Crash shook his head.

"Guess that answers that."

"Liberty, he doesn't need—"

"Don't cover for him. I don't give a damn if he's dangling from a fucking trapeze with those two chickies who flashed their tits for backstage passes. He can fuck both of them until he's dehydrated from losing excessive body fluids. But I *will* be stationed outside the door the entire time. At least until arena security arrives. We clear on that?"

Crash sighed. "Yes."

"Do I need to make it clear to Devin again why I'm here?"

"Maybe. Hell, I don't know. He's in one of them moods where—"

"He needs naked fan adulation to help him through his rough day?"

"Goin' to those kids' hospitals does him in every fucking time. But he keeps doin' it, and afterward, he needs a distraction or two. Surely you can understand that."

"We all have different coping mechanisms. If he wants to wallow in pussy for a few hours? Great." Not really, but Devin's coping mechanism was none of her business. Her business was keeping him safe. "I just hope the walls provide a decent sound barrier."

The ladies who'd been given passes by the roadie showed up. Liberty eyed their clothing—too little of it to hide weapons. Then she blocked the door. "Purses, please."

The first woman, a busty brunette in her midtwenties, glared at her. "What?"

"Your purses need to remain outside with me."

"Why?"

"Because I said so." Liberty shrugged. "Take it or leave it, but those are the rules."

The big-haired, big-boobed blonde demanded, "Who are you?"

"The person keeping you from hanging out with Devin McClain if you don't hand over your handbags," she said tartly.

The door opened, and Devin lounged in the doorway. "Are you ladies gonna argue with my personal assistant or are you comin' in?"

"Of course we're coming in," the brunette cooed. "Just wondered why we can't have our stuff."

"Can't take the risk of cameras or cell phones. Don't worry. She'll keep an eye on it, won't you?"

"Absolutely, *sir*." Tempting to snap off a salute.

Devin raised a brow at her sarcastic response. Then he focused on his fawning fan girls. "Now that I know you two lovelies can follow the rules, let's see how many of them rules you're willin' to break for me."

Un. Real.

The door closed after the two women handed over their bags. She heard the lock slide into place. At least his big head was still somewhat present and he'd remembered to engage the lock.

Crash dragged a folding chair over for her. "Might as well be comfortable. Anything else I can get you?"

"A clipboard? So it looks like I'm doing something besides sitting out here listening to him doing his fans."

He laughed. "I can bring you the schedule for the next two weeks, and you can double-check the security recs."

"That'd be great."

The hallway remained deserted. But the quiet wasn't a blessing—she could hear every moan, groan and giggle drifting out from the room. Or possibly that was her imagination. Either way, she made a mental note to always carry earplugs.

Time dragged. She'd begun to make little hash marks every time she heard "Yes! Yes! Yes!" when someone said her name. Her head snapped up.

"You're Liberty, right?"

She squinted at the guy with longish brown hair, a soul patch and a sweet smile. His bulging biceps indicated he hauled heavy objects. "Yes, I am. Who are you?"

"Name's Check. I handle the band's instruments."

"Do they call you Check because you're the guy who says 'Check, check' into the microphones before the show?"

He groaned. "Original, huh? But no one would know who you were talking about if you said my given name—so Check is easier."

Liberty smiled. "Did you need something?"

"Saw you sitting here and came by to say hey. I wondered if you'd met the other equipment guys."

"Just Boomer and the dude with the cigar."

"That's large-and-in-charge Sarge. He's head of stage setup, front-of-house merchandise stalls and roadies."

Liberty's gaze landed on Check's tattoo—a marine insignia. "A jarhead, huh? How long?"

"Eight years." He cocked his head. "Which branch owned your soul?"

"Army. Twelve years. Been out a little over two."

That seemed to impress him. "A lot of us guys in this line of work did our time in uniform."

They started bullshitting about the life that only those who'd lived it could understand. Swapping good-natured insults. Trying to one up each other with stories.

Then Sarge showed up, bringing chairs for himself, as well as Mike—who oddly enough didn't handle the sound system—and Rick, who rotated between driving the equipment truck and the band's bus.

For the first time in days, Liberty was completely in her element.

She'd just finished a story with "I don't give a flying monkey's ass if you're a fuckin' general. Find me some goddamn coffee or I'll shoot you myself," and the guys were laughing uproariously when the door behind her opened.

The laughter died. Immediately, Check, Rick, Mike

and Sarge pushed to their feet. Check said, "See ya around. Come have a beer with us some night."

She looked up at Devin, who wasn't wearing the smug smile of a sexually satisfied man but an expression of annoyance.

The groupies sauntered out, each stopping to whisper in Devin's ear before snatching their purses. "Can't wait for the show tonight," the busty brunette tossed over her shoulder.

Neither she nor Devin said anything as the women sashayed down the hallway. It surprised her that the blonde didn't throw out her back from the exaggerated sway of her hips.

Liberty stood and stretched. Rather than say, "Finished already?" she opted for, "Ready to go back to the bus?"

"I've decided to stay and work on new material until the show starts."

She glanced at her watch. "Backup security should be here soon. I'll make sure they don't bother you." She grimaced when her ass connected with the hard metal seat again.

"You wanna sit in here?"

So she could choke on the scents of sex and cheap perfume? Uh, no, thanks. "I'm fine."

"Are you hoping your roadie admirers will come back and entertain you?" he said sharply. "You guys were incredibly fuckin' loud."

"Did it hurt your vocal cords to have to shout out your climax over our conversation in the hallway?" The instant she said that, she wished she could take it back. *Not professional, Masterson.* "Sorry. That was out of line."

Devin said nothing.

She kept her features schooled as she flipped through

the notes she'd taken, hoping he'd get the hint and return to his love nest.

No such luck. Devin crouched beside her. "My roadies ain't dumb. Didn't any of them question why a woman with a military career would be parading around as my personal assistant?"

Her gaze squared off with his. "First of all, *sir*, I worked as a personal assistant to my CO during my third tour, so taking this job isn't such a stretch. And you're right; those guys aren't dumb. They've been there. They know what it's like to flounder after leaving the military." She dropped her voice. "Second, my position with you is confidential. I'd never violate that for a cheap laugh or easy camaraderie. But I will be working with these guys for months. By being on good terms with them, I can better protect you."

"Bein' on good terms means you're gonna take them up on their offer to drink beer?"

Jesus, if she didn't know better, she'd think Devin was jealous. "No, *sir*."

"Would you have a beer with me?"

What the hell? "No, *sir*. I don't drink on the job."

Annoyance flashed in his eyes. "Stop with the *no, sir* bullshit. We both know that sarcastic *sir* is your verbal shorthand for asshole."

The man saw far more than she credited him for. How would she survive four months with him when they'd managed to piss each other off at least once a day for the last two days?

His warm fingers slid beneath her chin, forcing her to look at him. Why did he have to have such compelling eyes? Why did her damn heart skip a beat when he touched her?

"I don't want to always be at odds with you, Liberty."

"Me either."

"Good." His face softened. "I forgot to say thank you for comin' to the hospital with me today."

Don't be sweet. She had a better handle on things when he was being a douche. "You're welcome."

"I was serious about you havin' a beer with me once we're locked down in the bus tonight and on the road."

"We'll see."

"Woman, you don't give an inch, do you?" He sighed softly and stood. "You'll be at the show tonight?"

"Of course."

He smiled, a genuine smile, not the practiced media smile he used with everyone else. "I'll see you then. Right now, I'm feelin' inspired to write."

"I've heard good sex will do that." *Jesus, Liberty. Can't you just keep your fucking mouth shut for once?*

"Don't believe everything you hear." He walked into the room and shut the door behind him.

∾

The second night's performance was better than the first. Everyone was in high spirits. Devin had fulfilled his media and fan requirements the previous night. No groupies hung around backstage. Strangely enough, Devin sat in the arena and watched his stage set being torn down.

What was he doing? Making sure the roadies did tear-down to his specifications? Dissecting his performance?

Liberty kept an eye on the brooding singer, watching as he tapped his fingers on his thigh, lost in some rhythm inside his head. She'd never spent time around artistic types. She wondered how people like Devin dealt with the constant pressure of life in the fishbowl.

When he stood and scaled the arena stairs, she intercepted him at the top of the aisle.

"I should've known you'd be close by."

"I thought you'd be used to your lack of privacy by now."

Devin shook his head. "To be honest, I don't want to get used to it. That's why I find myself in the stands after a performance." He turned and looked at the stage. "Sometimes I look at all this and can't believe it's my life."

Not what she'd expected from him.

He faced her again. "I'm ready to go to the bus."

As they approached the motor coaches, Liberty noticed Reg sitting in a lawn chair beside the main door. Having a guard outside the bus indicated someone inside the bus was worth guarding. It wasn't a security measure she'd asked for. So who had implemented it?

Reg stood when he saw Devin. "We ready?"

"Yeah. Did Check bring my guitar?"

"It's inside." Reg punched in the code and turned the key to open the door. "I need to hit the john, and then we'll be on our way."

Devin grabbed his guitar and disappeared into the back.

Only then did Reg say, "A couple of guys were hanging around tonight. Both in their midtwenties. Don't know if they were together, but it concerned me enough I tried to take their pictures, but the damn things didn't turn out. Too dark."

"Did they say anything? Ask you whose bus it was?"

"Nope. They just paced about fifty feet away like they were waiting on someone."

"Thanks for keeping an eye out, Reg. But from here on out, I'd rather you were in the driver's seat or in the arena. You sitting out there during the performance is just inviting trouble."

He nodded. "Will do, Miss Liberty."

As soon as they were on the road, Liberty ditched her

personal assistant clothing. She slipped on a pair of baggy athletic shorts and dragged on an old army T-shirt. Then she washed the gunk off her face, slathered lotion on her skin and returned to the kitchen to make herself a sandwich.

Strange to think her life on the road tonight wasn't much different from her normal routine. She checked her phone for text messages and settled in to flip through her stack of Denver real estate magazines.

With the hundred-thousand-dollar bonus, she could jump up a price bracket in her house search. She'd focused on condos close to work rather than a place in suburbia, but the possibility of that money meant she could consider other options—like a funky loft in downtown Denver.

"House hunting?" Devin said behind her.

Liberty quickly slammed the magazine shut. "Give me a fucking heart attack. I didn't expect to see you tonight."

Devin pulled two bottles of beer from the fridge. "I thought we agreed to have a beer."

"I'm not sure if that's such a good idea. I'm still on duty."

"Technically, you're off the clock and on your own time since I'm safely ensconced on the bus."

She studied him, seeing he'd changed into loungewear. His feet were bare. He looked relaxed. Like a normal man. Not a superstar who'd just rocked an arena with ten thousand screaming fans. "Fine. One beer."

Devin grinned and passed over a Shock Top. He sat on the opposite end of the couch so their feet met in the middle of the cushion. "Why'd you say you were surprised to see me?"

"You snatched your guitar. I've already figured out that means you'll be working."

"I snapped a string on it tonight and I wanted to make

sure Check had fixed it because I plan to use it tomorrow during the day."

"How many guitars do you have?"

"On tour? Six acoustic. I use two a night. Jase, my lead guitarist, has more than a dozen with him."

Silence fell between them.

Liberty sipped her beer and looked anywhere but at him or his stupidly sexy feet. God. Who had sexy feet? Devin McClain did. The man had sexy everything. She should've stayed in her damn bunk. Besides, she didn't do casual *let's have a beer* chitchat very well.

"Why'd you tense up?" he asked.

"Because this is fucking weird."

"For me too," he murmured. "But it doesn't have to be. Let's get to know each other." He playfully stroked his bare toes across hers, which sent an electric zip of awareness up her legs. "I'll go first. Who were those two guys who dropped you off in Denver?"

"Zeke and Spike."

"How do you know them?"

"They're bodybuilders who weight-train with us at GSC. I've struck up a"—*fuck-buddies relationship*—"special friendship with them outside of work."

"Both of them?"

"Why not? They're hot, they don't talk much and they like to share. Double the pleasure, double the fun." She silently dared him to say something snarky about her sex life.

He studied her for a beat. "Any problems tellin' them apart?"

"Does it matter in the dark?"

Devin laughed. "Nope. Now you ask me something."

Liberty thought about it for a moment. "When did you

learn to play guitar? And not the slicked-up official bio version."

That question seemed to surprise him. "A guy I went to school with had one. He never played it, but every time I was at his house, I picked it up and dinked around. My folks were in such a state of grief after Michelle died that they would've said yes to anything, so bein' a typical selfish teen, I asked them to pay for lessons. The guy I initially learned from was an old bar cowboy. After him, I studied with a high school music teacher. He taught me how to write music. After I moved to Nashville, I hung around with studio musicians and realized I'd never be lead guitar material."

"So do you have to practice?"

"Nope. But I do play every day, especially if I'm working on songs." He swigged his beer. "Do you play anything?"

Liberty shook her head. "We moved around. There wasn't money for instruments or lessons. Singing along with the radio is the extent of my musical skill."

"What kind of music do you listen to?"

She smirked. "Will you yell at me if I admit I'm not a big fan of country music?"

"That's it. You're fired." Devin sighed. "What do you listen to? Opera? Jazz fusion?"

"Hilarious. No. I listen to metal and pop. But I downloaded two of your songs."

The beer stopped short of his lips. "You don't like country but you bought my music? Why?"

"I liked the songs."

"Which ones?"

"'Chains and Trains' and 'Better Days.'"

"Really? Those aren't my most pop-sounding songs."

"They're the only ones I recognized during your sets. But I'm sure I'll know the words to everything by the time this tour is over." *Way to sound like a simpering fan girl.* "Which is your favorite song to perform?"

"I get asked all the time which songs I've written are my favorites. I can't admit publicly that some of my best-selling songs are my least favorite ones to perform."

"Why?"

"Not because I'm sick of playin' them, but because I wasn't in a good place when I wrote them." Devin started to pick at the paper label on the beer bottle. "That doesn't seem to stop me from writing the darker stuff."

"What are you working on now?"

"Something light, pop-based and fluffy that I can sell for a shit ton of money. Dixon Davis has asked for some demos."

"Have you written for him before?"

"Nope. Every one of his songs has gone number one in the last five years. It'd be major if he recorded one of my songs."

Liberty held her bottle to his for a toast. "Here's hoping the muse works overtime for you."

Devin touched his bottle to hers. "Amen."

With the warmth of his body close to hers and the ease of them being together, she realized how easy it'd be to get sucked into his raw magnetism. Because the really disconcerting thing? He gave off pure male charisma without even trying.

Her stomach gave a little flip, imagining him aiming his I-wanna-fuck-you smoldering stare at her on purpose. She tried to tell herself she wouldn't become weak-kneed and slack-jawed like all the other women in his orbit, but she knew it was a lie.

Especially when she looked over at him and witnessed that breath-stealing smile dancing on his lips.

Her head screamed *retreat*.

She dropped her feet to the floor and forced a yawn. "Wow. Look at the time. Am I tired. I'll see you tomorrow."

Liberty didn't run to her bunk—but it was damn close.

⁀

Devin counted to ten. Then twenty. He drained his beer, which didn't curb his desire to chase her down.

Problem was, he didn't know what he'd do with her once he caught her.

He traced the mouth of his empty beer bottle. Ever since the moment she'd stepped out of that baby blue Mustang, he'd known he was in deep trouble. Maybe it made him a dick, but her transformation had floored him. He sure as hell hadn't expected her to look like that. The woman he'd met in the GSC offices was commanding, but very much a plain G.I. Jane. And, yeah, he'd issued the challenge because he figured she'd blow him off. That she'd show up wearing a lipstick smirk as the extent of his demand that she blend in with his crew. In fact, that was the woman he'd wanted, because it would've been a fuck ton easier to keep her at arm's length. To keep their relationship professional.

So here it was, two goddamned days into this tour, and he wondered how the fuck he'd keep his hands off her for the next four months.

His raunchy, I-wanna-fuck-everything-that-walks side jumped in. *Jesus, what is your deal? You had two hot groupies blowing you six hours ago. And tomorrow night, you could have two more. This is your life—and what a great fuckin' life it is. Gorgeous women throwing themselves at you, agreeing to your every sexual demand— including hot girl-on-girl action.*

Somehow he managed to shut that greedy voice down, because that wasn't him.

When had sex become a spectator sport for him? He'd jerked off more in the last six months than at any time since his teen years. The only difference now was the sexual scenarios happened live in front of him instead of on his computer.

He hadn't been balls deep inside a woman's pussy in ages. He'd become content letting his groupies blow him. Then he'd watch two—or sometimes three—naked chicks sucking and licking each other in an effort to turn him on. Which it did. But near the end of the live sex show, he ended up jacking off, or he'd gotten a hand job, before he sent the ladies on their way.

Today had been no exception.

After leaving the hospital, Liberty had taken his hand, almost without conscious thought. And he'd had the urge to pull her into his arms and hold her until the desolate feeling subsided. But on the drive back, he reverted to that mind-set where he needed mindless physical contact, not thoughtful consideration.

So he'd given in to the lure of quick sexual thrills, but all the while he'd heard Liberty's throaty laughter outside his ready room.

That'd fucked him up big-time—because he realized he'd rather be out there with her.

The woman was wreaking all sorts of havoc with his life as he knew it. Only time would tell if that was a good thing or a bad thing.

Chapter Eight

◆

*L*iberty wasn't sure how the first day of their long bus ride together would go. She knew Devin had given instructions for the bus not to stop until they needed gas. He hadn't indicated whether that meant he planned to load up on truck stop food, or if he'd leave his bedroom and fix himself something to eat at some point.

Since she was off duty when they were confined to the bus, she settled in her bunk. Next stop she'd get more pillows because two wasn't cutting it. Should she watch the backlog of movies she'd been saving on her laptop? Or catch up on the TV shows she'd been dying to watch?

Best get business out of the way first. She logged into her e-mail account. Garrett didn't require daily reports, but after years in the military, she preferred a daily log of her duties and any issues. That way, if there was a problem, she could usually narrow down the parameters on where the misstep had occurred.

Maybe it was overkill, giving intel on the groupies

who'd ended up with Devin. But Liberty suspected if she didn't jot down the details, at the end of four months, she wouldn't remember a single one.

How did Devin keep them straight? Or was he beyond the point that it mattered? When had he become the kind of guy who used and discarded women? After his rise to fame? Or had he always had women dropping to their knees in front of him?

Not your business.

True. She attached the report she'd finished and sent it off. She surfed the Internet and quickly got bored with page after page of useless information. Slipping on her headphones, she lounged against the wall and cued up the first season of *Sons of Anarchy.*

She'd made it through the first three episodes when she heard footsteps pass the heavy curtains.

Looked like the songwriter was out of his sanctuary.

Her stomach rumbled. Should she fix herself lunch? Or would Devin prefer to eat by himself? Would he ignore her? Engage her in conversation?

God. When had this professional situation morphed into junior high school lunch table drama?

When you admitted to yourself that you're attracted to Devin in a big way.

With that thought in mind, she ignored the stomach growls and watched the next two episodes. She finally ventured out and heard muffled music from behind Devin's closed door.

She'd just finished a "healthy" microwave meal when the bus slowed. Liberty peered out the window as they started up the exit ramp, seeing one of those super truck stops spread out on the right. She watched the other tour bus carrying the band pull into one of the gas bays. As soon as they stopped at the stall behind, she could see the interest two high-end tour buses generated.

Liberty headed toward the back of the bus and knocked on Devin's door.

"It's open."

She stepped into Devin's domain. His bed was made. He wore camo shorts with a white wifebeater. His feet were bare. He hadn't shaved. Didn't look like he'd combed his hair either. But he still looked damn good—too good. He'd propped himself against the padded headboard, amid half a dozen pillows. A notebook was spread open on his right side, and he held an acoustic guitar.

"Hey. What's up?"

"We've stopped for gas. I wasn't sure if you were getting off the bus or not."

"Hadn't thought about it." Strum, strum. "Why?"

"If you get off, I get off too."

When Devin aimed that famous grin at her and drawled, "Sounds fair to me, darlin'," she blushed crimson.

"You know what I meant."

"Any idea on how long we'll be here?"

"Are some stops longer than others?"

"Yes. If the bus needs an oil change or tires rotated, it can take up to a couple of hours. If that's the case, I hit the fitness facility and run on the treadmill."

"Since when do truck stops have fitness facilities?"

"Years, I guess." Devin reached up and pressed a button on the intercom system. "Reg?"

Half a minute passed before Reg's voice boomed through the speaker. "What can I help you with, Mr. McClain?"

"How long is this stop?"

"Probably take an hour before it's all said and done."

"Cool. Thanks." Devin set his guitar aside and scooted to the edge of the bed. From a bottom drawer, he pulled out a pair of running shoes. His gaze met hers after giving her a thorough toe-to-head inspection. "You workin' out with me?"

"Depends on the security of the facility." She retreated. "I'll get ready in case. Don't leave the bus."

"Wouldn't dream of it."

Five minutes later, Liberty was trying to figure out where to put her stun gun—damn yoga workout pants were skintight—when she felt Devin's breath on the back of her neck. A tingle traveled down her spine.

"You're seriously takin' a stun gun into a workout room at a truck stop in the middle of bumfuck Arizona?"

She snagged a nylon jacket and slipped a stun gun in the pocket before she spun around. "That's my job. I'll sit outside while you're working out."

"I see how it is. You just don't want to hop your cute buns on a treadmill."

Liberty snorted, ignoring the cute buns comment. "You wish. On the treadmill or on the track, I'd wipe the floor with you, guitar slinger."

"Bring it."

"As much as it pains me to decline . . . I'll have to." She punched in the code to unlock the door and exited the bus first. As she waited for Devin to alight, she noticed a small crowd had gathered.

Devin had slipped on a brown and gold University of Wyoming ball cap and a pair of sunglasses. A white wire for his earbuds was draped around his neck and he held an iPod. He stopped in front of Liberty and spoke loudly.

"I don't think he's getting off the bus. Said something about takin' a nap."

Clever man. Making the people think the real "star" wasn't showing his face. Liberty closed the door and armed the alarm. Then she put herself between him and the crowd as they walked to the closest door.

Crash waited inside for them. "Fitness room is yours for one hour," he said to Devin. Then he looked at Liberty. "No offense, but it'll look weird—not only to bystanders, but to the band—if you're manning the outside door. Better for me to hang out here and you to stay with him inside."

Devin grinned again. "Appears we can have us a treadmill race after all."

They turned the corner, and Crash led them to a wide, heavy door with a square glass window inset. Liberty peeked inside. The room had two treadmills, an elliptical machine, a rowing machine and a weight station. Unlike other fitness rooms, this one had no windows. No mirrors either.

Devin ditched his shades, but kept on his cap. She hung her jacket over the back of a chair after she removed the stun gun. She shoved it into the cup holder and climbed on the machine.

He whipped off his shirt.

The man definitely kept in shape. The thick slab of his chest was sculpted from his pectorals down to his rippled abs. His broad shoulders, biceps, triceps and forearms were well defined.

She managed to tear her gaze away and focused on poking buttons to warm up the ancient machine. But she felt him staring and glanced over at him again. "What?"

"Ain't you gonna take off your T-shirt?"

"No."

"It's hot in here."

"So?"

"So, I'll bet you're wearin' a sports bra under that shirt."

No, she was wearing a compression bra. Her large breasts were the bane of her existence. She downplayed them with the help of athletic clothing. "I'll pass."

"Well, sweetheart, when you're feelin' like passing out from heat exhaustion in this tiny airless room, don't say I didn't give you a chance to level the playing field."

"You're such a gentleman. But I'll remind you I spent years in the desert. I ran in full combat gear when it was one hundred and ten degrees out. So, *sweetheart*, I'm sure I'll be just fine." She laughed again at Devin's look of alarm. "What?"

"You're bluffing."

"Only one way to prove it."

"Fine. I'm in. How about . . . whoever gets the most miles in thirty minutes wins?"

"What's the prize?"

"Loser has to cook supper for the winner after the show tonight."

"Deal."

Devin slipped in his earbuds. "Ready, set, go."

Liberty watched the display as she started to run. Keeping her mind on her progress and not letting her gaze wander to Devin proved harder than she'd imagined. She adjusted her breathing at the five-minute mark and again at ten minutes. By the time she'd hit the halfway point, she'd found her rhythm.

She wished she'd grabbed a towel; sweat ran down

her face. She swiped it away with the back of her arm and saw five minutes left. Time to sprint. Liberty bit back a laugh when Devin's footsteps hit the rubber harder and faster.

By the time the machine shut off, she was very winded. And she wondered how smart it was to be exhausted; she was supposed to be protecting Devin, not competing with him.

He gasped, "How far did you get?"

"Four point five miles," she wheezed. "How about you?"

"Three point nine." He hopped off the machine and tossed her a towel.

"Throwing in the towel?" she taunted as she mopped her face.

"Yes." He bent forward, bracing his hands above his knees. "I might puke. That's my fastest fuckin' time ever and I still didn't beat you."

She chugged a cup of water from the dispenser. "How often do you do cardio?"

"Three times a week. Usually forty-five minutes at a whack."

Liberty said nothing. She just took another long drink.

"What's your cardio workout?" he asked.

"Thirty minutes. Six days a week. Sometimes seven. Plus an hour of other physical workouts that vary."

"How do you stand it? I fuckin' hate this shit."

She handed him a cup of water. "First, it's my job to be in top physical condition. Second, if you'd ever been injured to the point you worried you'd ever be able to do what you used to . . . staying fit becomes a priority."

Devin's gaze snapped to hers. "Shit. I'm sorry. I said that without thinking again."

She shrugged.

He glanced at the clock. "I'm ready for a shower."

Liberty peered through the window but didn't see Crash. She slipped on her jacket, pocketed her stun gun and said, "Come on."

But Devin reached the door first. He looked over his shoulder. "Can't a guy catch his breath? Not everyone is a supersoldier like you." He opened the door.

She started to follow him out. "Suck it up. I used to smoke a pack of cigarettes a day before I got fit."

"I was fucked before I hit that first mile, wasn't I?"

Her laughter died as a guy charged at Devin from out of nowhere.

Just as she moved to intercept, Devin pushed her back into the room. Then he was slammed against the door.

"I knew I recognized you, you son of a bitch," the guy yelled. "It's your fault that she left me!"

Seething about Devin shoving her out of the way, she pushed against the door, trying to move the psycho's fat ass.

Before Devin responded, Crash was there, pulling the guy free and knocking him to the ground. His eyes met Liberty's, and he shoved Devin the opposite way so she could get out.

"Get him to the bus." When Crash hesitated a half a second, she bit off, "Now!"

They disappeared, but she didn't look away from the assailant still on the floor. He could've been twenty or forty; hard to tell beneath his ginger-colored beard. "How long have you been following him?"

The guy looked confused. "Just from the parking lot. Saw them buses and knew someone who thought they were hot shit had to be on them. Then I heard the name Devin McClain and figured I could get a little payback."

"Payback for what?"

"He ruined my fuckin' life. My wife left me because of him."

"Let me get this straight. Your wife was sleeping with him?"

"Are you stupid? She left me after she heard that song he wrote 'Good for Nothing.' She said it was a wake-up call for her and I ain't seen her since."

"Looks like maybe she wised up." Liberty leaned closer. "You oughta wise up too. I'd better never see you anywhere around him again or he'll press assault charges. Understand?"

He nodded, and she noticed he had sunflower seeds stuck in his beard. Gross. After she pushed to her feet and backed away, she looked around. Thankfully, the incident hadn't drawn an audience.

Liberty took her time returning to the bus, attempting to keep her temper in check.

∽

Devin figured Liberty would barrel into the bus, loaded for bear, hissing and spitting and yelling. He half feared she'd zap him with her damn stun gun to show her displeasure with him for reacting . . . like a man. He'd acted instinctively. She couldn't fault him for that.

Yes, she could. Because he was entirely at fault.

Even Crash hadn't stuck around after chewing Devin's ass; he'd hightailed it to the other bus to leave Devin to deal with his bodyguard on his own.

So, reeking with sweat, he waited in the main living area to have this out with her.

The door opened. And closed. He heard the beep of the alarm being engaged. Then she appeared from the deep stairwell and stopped in front of him. She leveled that scary-ass stare for about thirty seconds before she closed her eyes.

Devin couldn't stand the silence. "Liberty—"

"Don't. Say. Anything."

That shut him up.

She locked those steely eyes to his. "Don't ever do that again. Let me remind you: I protect you. That's what I am paid to do. You shoving me aside impedes my ability to do my job. I am not the one who's had death threats leveled at me. I am not the one whose bus and home have been broken into. But because of those things, I am your personal security 24/7."

"I'm sorry."

Liberty released a slow breath. "I am too. You need to know that I have to report this incident to GSC, who will pass it on to the promotion company."

"Jesus. Why?"

"Because like it or not, they are paying me to protect you, and you didn't allow me to do my job today. This is my livelihood, not a fantasy where I'm spending months getting wild on the tour bus with a country rockstar. If I don't report it, won't it appear that I have something to hide? Who gets the blowback from it? You?" She shook her head. "Me. If you don't trust me to protect you, then I'll have to find a replacement you can trust."

Was she . . . threatening him?

Her face held frustration and determination but no malice. "I won't put you or myself in jeopardy. We've been on the road three days, Devin, and we've already had a major problem."

"It won't happen again. I swear."

The look on her face said she didn't believe him. "Excuse me. I need to talk to Reg before we take off."

He'd be pissed off by her dismissal if he didn't feel like such a fool. And things had been going so well between them.

You're surprised you fucked up something else in your life? Isn't that the way it goes? One step forward and two steps back?

Devin grabbed a beer from the fridge and headed to his room. In the shower, he let the hot water pound on his back while he chugged the icy cold beer. Reality hit him. What if that guy'd had a gun? Or a knife? Those fifteen seconds could've turned out completely different.

Fuck.

Fuck, fuck, fuck.

He fucking hated this. How the hell was he not supposed to react instinctively when a threat surfaced? It wouldn't have mattered if Crash or Gage or Odette had been behind him. He would've done the same damn thing. He also hated that a couple of unknown, unseen crazy mother-fuckers could upend his life. Force him to change how he lived and who he was.

Bitching, moaning, whining wouldn't change a damn thing. Being proactive only got him into trouble. So for the time being, he had to trust in someone besides himself. Not his choice and completely out of his control, but in order for this bullshit to end, he had to let Liberty do her job.

He toweled off, slipped on a pair of boxer briefs and dropped into a push-up position. Four sets of twenty-five got his blood pumping. He switched and did three hundred ab exercises. Then he finished with a series of plank poses.

As Devin dabbed the sweat from his face and neck, he figured he probably should've waited to shower, but push-ing his body had delivered the desired effect; he'd calmed down. He'd centered himself and was ready to offer

Liberty the apology she deserved. But first he needed to work on his music.

Because at the end of the day, no matter where he was, that driving need never abated. He could prop his feet up anywhere, strap on his guitar and slip into the skin of what—who—he was meant to be. A singer. A songwriter. A modern-day wandering minstrel plying his trade in hopes to earn a few coins and a little respect.

And it stung that in trying to earn Liberty's respect, he'd lost it.

Chapter Nine

❧

*T*hree weeks had passed since the truck-stop altercation.

After the incident, Liberty kept all interactions between them strictly professional. No sharing a meal or a beer or even a laugh on the bus. On the outside, it looked like nothing had changed. They worked out together. Liberty escorted him on his visits to children's hospitals. She remained stationed outside the door of his ready room even though he hadn't "entertained" any fans since Salt Lake City. Something had shifted, and he hadn't been in the mood for that type of female companionship. Instead he'd used the time to fulfill his media requirements so afterward he could concentrate on songwriting.

Whether it was Liberty's vigilance or just plain luck, there'd been limited security issues in the last three weeks. That's not to say a few situations hadn't arisen where his ability to give her the reins was tested, but he'd done it. Happily. Without even a single pat on the back from her.

Yet, in the last week, he'd sensed a thawing in her cold attitude. She'd actually initiated a couple of conversations that didn't revolve around his security. And he'd lapped up that little bit of attention like a starving dog.

Things were tense all around with his bandmates and his crew. Tay and Jase were back at it. Odette and Steve complained about having to trade off the bus's one bedroom with them. Sarge had issues between the roadies and ended up with a fist to the jaw when he broke up a fight.

Crash was tired of playing referee between all factions.

Since they had two days off and not a long distance to travel between gigs, Devin decided they needed to blow off some steam. Over the years, when this tension arose—because it always happened at some point during the tour—they'd organize a softball game. Or team up for laser tag. Or race go-carts. But this time, they needed a more extreme activity.

He was finishing a conversation with his agent when the buses turned off the highway and crossed to a county road. Naturally, that brought Liberty out of seclusion. Devin hadn't seen her today, and he took in her bare feet, faded jeans and the flowing floral blouse that fell to midthigh. While he understood her clothing had to conceal her gun, her long, baggy shirts also covered up her ass—which was a damn crying shame.

She peeked out the window above the kitchen sink. "Why aren't we on the highway?"

"Change in plans. We're gonna have a little fun today. And before you ask, yes, we weighed the risk factors, and Crash already contacted the promotion company. They rented the place out for the entire day. And night."

Her gaze sharpened. "What fun thing do you have planned?"

Devin grinned. "A paintball fight. There's also a camp-ground on the property, so we'll circle the buses, have a campfire, drink some beer, throw some horseshoes and give everyone, including the drivers, a night to just chill out."

"Paintball," she repeated. "You do realize paintball guns are actual *guns*?"

"There's where the fun part comes in."

"And you're telling me that you just decided to put yourself in danger—"

He held up his hand to stop her impending tirade. "The Big Sky HR department personally signed off on all of the crew. I'm not in any danger from any of the people on these buses. Big Sky also approved this outing and paid for it. I'm assuming they didn't announce that Devin McClain was reserving the place for his touring entourage."

"You didn't think to run this idea by me first?"

So that's what'd put the starch in her spine. "It's not a security issue—it's a personnel issue. And I'm tellin' you now, aren't I?"

Liberty glanced down at her feet. He saw her inhale deeply before she dragged her gaze back to his.

"Darlin', I don't like that smirk you're wearing. What gives?"

"Oh, I was just imagining if I wasn't tasked with guard-ing you how much I'd love to plug your ass with a dozen paintballs."

Devin leaned closer. "Bring it. Obviously, you and me have some issues to work out too."

Her humor fled. "Sorry. That was unprofessional."

"Liberty, I was kiddin'. As long as we're actually talkin' for a change, instead of avoiding each other on the bus and faking a happy relationship in public . . . I have to know if you're ever gonna forgive me for the mistake I made that day at the truck stop."

"I heard every word of all fifteen apologies you gave me."

But it wasn't enough. He knew she'd reported the incident. What she didn't know was Devin had called both Garrett at GSC and Carl at Big Sky. He swore to them the crazed-fan ambush had been a wake-up call and he wouldn't fight any of the security requirements for the rest of the tour—but only if he could retain Liberty. The men had conferred and agreed to let her stay, but warned him another incident like that would end her employment with him.

Devin didn't kid himself. Pulling Liberty from this duty wouldn't be to reprimand her—but to punish him. It wasn't a coincidence that Carl mentioned the LaGruder goons as replacements if he screwed up again. Just thinking about those *Robocop* clones caused him to shudder.

"Did you have something else to say?" she prompted.

"Actions speak louder than words. And I've followed your instructions over the last three weeks. When that woman accosted me at the meet and greet two weeks ago, I didn't try to handle it on my own. I immediately called for security."

Liberty just blinked at him.

"Last week when the PETA protestors rushed me in the parking lot because of my support for Wyoming furriers, I didn't engage them, even though I wanted to beat their hemp-wearin' asses for their urban ignorance of real life in the West."

"I sensed that," she said dryly. "Although adding the

PETA—People Eating Tasty Animals—bumper sticker to the back of the bus was a little over-the-top."

Devin held up his hands. "Totally Sarge's idea. I swear."

"Look. I realize it's been difficult to change your normal reactions of self-protection first, so I appreciate that you've been working with me, instead of against me."

"So you know I don't wanna backtrack and lose all the ground that I've gained. Which is why you should rise to the challenge of bein' on a paintball team." He displayed a sly smile. "Against me."

"No way, guitar slinger. You want to participate in a paintball fight? Fine. But I'm not letting you out of my sight, so it appears you and me are partners."

That wasn't what he'd been going for. "I already promised to be Crash's partner."

"Too bad you'll have to renege," she said sweetly.

"How will I explain why I'm partnered up with you when I won't let Tay and Jase, or Odette and Steve partner up?"

She shrugged. "Tell them you're a terrible shot and you need me to teach you how to be a straight shooter."

"FYI, sweetheart, I am a damn good shot. I've been huntin' since I was five." He issued a challenge. "Or maybe you want to partner with me because you have lingering combat issues and you expect me to keep you from goin' ballistic."

Liberty paled.

Shit. With as many times as she'd been in the thick of overseas conflicts, she probably did have some issues from that. He stepped forward and curled his hands around her biceps. "Dammit, Liberty. I'm sorry. I wasn't thinking. I'm a jerk."

She stared at him, clearly debating what to say.

"Come on. Chew my ass." His hand slid down her arm to her wrist. He then formed her fingers into a fist and brought it up to his jaw. "Or better yet. Punch me."

Then she did the oddest thing. She opened her fist and cupped his face. "I've witnessed the stubborn set to this jaw too many times to count in the last month. Even if I did pop you one, I'd probably hurt my hand."

He chuckled. "Probably."

Liberty lazily skimmed the razor stubble coating his cheeks, and he suppressed a shudder of pleasure. "Or I'd scuff up my knuckles on this sandpaper."

Devin let the caress linger, reveling in her simple show of affection. With every gentle sweep of her fingers, he felt that inexplicable pull toward her getting stronger. She fascinated him on so many levels; he'd never met a woman like her before.

"Damn, man. Are you out of razors?"

"You don't like the scruffy look?"

"Not on you."

"Shoot. I believed I was lookin' all hip, bein' emo and shit."

She murmured, "You're too much of a manly man to ever look like a hipster."

He cocked an eyebrow. "Was that a compliment?"

Her hand stilled and their gazes collided. "You don't need me to tell you that you're too handsome and charming for your own good, Devin McClain."

She immediately retreated.

Dammit. Looked like he'd blown it again.

The bus stopped.

Devin watched shamelessly as she bent over to slip on her shoes, hoping for a glimpse of her ass.

Then she whirled around and caught him looking.

"Unreal. Are you so hard up for female attention that even *I'm* starting to look good?"

"Darlin', that low opinion of yourself sure as hell ain't comin' from me."

"I'm too masculine-acting for you, remember? You'd have no problem keeping it professional between us because you're not attracted to me in the least, right?"

"Wrong." Devin caged Liberty against the wall, blocking her retreat.

"But you said—"

"I know what I said. I've also admitted that I was an ass and I've apologized for that too. I thought we were beyond that." His eyes searched hers. "Please tell me we can get beyond that."

"Don't."

"Don't what? Remind you that it doesn't have to be all or nothin'? You won't even talk to me about any of this. Not even after I've been following every one of your damn rules—to the letter."

"How generous of you to quit fucking groupies night and day."

"That was my choice, not because of some edict from you," he shot back.

"And why *did* you close yourself off from all that easy pussy?"

"Because none of them . . ." Jesus. He wasn't giving her the satisfaction of confessing that the women vying for a piece of him had lost appeal after he'd started to become friends with her. "I realized none of them are worth my time."

"And I am?"

"That's what I'm askin' you. Can we move past what was said and done in the last month and start things over?"

A hopeful light entered her eyes before she banked it. "You're right. We're both a little stubborn—"

"Ya think?"

She punched him in the stomach—just hard enough to get his attention.

Hard enough to get him fucking hard.

"I swear you are the most exasperating man I've ever met."

Devin grinned. "So that means I'm memorable? Sweet."

"Move."

He stepped back. Right before she closed the door to the bathroom, he clapped and said, "Good talk."

He heard her laugh.

That had to be a good sign, right?

Liberty appeared a couple minutes later, hair fluffed, gloss on her lips, cheeks rosier.

Devin doubted that Liberty the soldier had stopped to fix her hair and freshen her makeup before heading out of the barracks. And part of him would rather see her in dirt and camo than lip gloss and a tailored blouse.

Since when? You're the one who insisted she blend, remember?

She snagged her stun gun from behind her . . . pillow? When she glanced up, she said, "What?" a little brusquely.

"You sleep with a weapon under your pillow?"

"Yep. I'd keep sleepwalking to a minimum if I were you."

Two loud thumps sounded on the side of the bus.

Liberty brushed past him and unlocked the door. "Hey, Crash."

"I want you to know that I had no part in this unscheduled stop. I tried to talk him out of it."

Traitor.

The rest of their conversation was in low tones, which also annoyed him. Devin stopped at the top of the stairs. Both Liberty and Crash looked at him guiltily. "What?"

"Nothin'. I'm of the same mind-set as Bert. The two of you need to partner up."

Bert. He fucking hated the nickname his road crew had given her. Bert was a guy's name. In the last month, Liberty had shown him that she was far from the butch persona he'd initially believed her to be, so the name really grated on him.

Devin braced his hands on the rails and leaned over the stairs. "Crash, do me a favor and stop callin' her Bert."

"Why?" Liberty demanded. "You afraid people will think your latest squeeze is a man?"

Devin's gaze never left hers. "It's not about me. Bert is a crusty old guy's name. Liberty is a beautiful name, and it fits you and what you stand for so perfectly."

Her mouth dropped open.

Gotcha, darlin'. He grinned.

"I don't wanna know where the fuck that came from," Crash said. "Anyway, you and Liberty will take a rash of shit for bein' partners, so I hope you've got a good cover story."

They reached the front entrance and stood behind the crew as a young kid recited the rules.

During a pause, Sarge asked, "So we're not on teams?"

"No, sir. Everyone has a partner. Who you ended up with was luck of the draw."

"Except for Devin and Liberty," Crash pointed out.

More grumbles. Some loud enough he could hear.

Odette piped up first. "How come you two get to be partners and no one else who is a couple does?"

"Because I'm the boss and I knew you'd all be gunning for me. I needed an extra edge, which I got because Liberty is an expert paintballer."

Once the guy started speaking again, Liberty's warm lips connected with his ear. "I should be upset you're so good at stretching the truth, but I'm more annoyed that you put me in the line of fire with that 'expert' comment."

He bit back a groan. The whisper of her breath sent gooseflesh rippling across his body. He held in another groan when the scent of her skin hit him. Why did the woman always smell like chocolate and vanilla? He wanted to bury his face in her neck and run his lips across her heated flesh to find out if she tasted like pure decadence.

"Devin?" she murmured.

"I'm fine," he said loud enough that two roadies turned and looked at him.

"As long as there aren't any other questions, I'll meet you all in the equipment room in fifteen minutes."

Sarge whistled. "Sweatshirts for everyone in the truck."

"That's one way to make sure we all look alike," Tay grumbled.

Jase slapped her ass. "Wrong. You'll still be the sexiest one out there. What say we have a murder/suicide pact? Then, when these clowns are shooting at each other, we can sneak back to the bus and take extra time scrubbing each other clean."

"I hope their shower is bigger than mine," Liberty said. "There's hardly room for just me in there."

"You're welcome to use my shower whenever you want," Devin offered.

That took her aback. "Sure. Thanks. Maybe I will."

Devin steered her toward the equipment truck. Crash and Sarge were whipping gray sweatshirts into the air. "That's a good way to get rid of the shit that isn't selling."

He snatched the shirt Crash lobbed at him.

Liberty held hers out and squinted at the image. "Who decided that a—"

"Microphone in front of my open mouth was a good idea? It looks like I'm about to suck a big dick, huh?"

She laughed. "Yes."

"I normally donate leftover clothing to homeless shelters or to the reservations in Wyoming, but I'd be happier to burn these motherfuckers at the bonfire tonight."

"At least you can laugh about it."

"Better than cryin'. Come on. Let's get ready to kick some ass."

After they'd changed and were walking back, Devin said, "What's the plan?"

"Try not to get nailed with a paintball," she said dryly.

"Besides that. Don't you have a stealth-attack strategy?"

"Nope. Shoot first, shoot often."

They stood in line for paintball markers—aka paintball guns—and masks. Once everyone had been outfitted in the protective outer layer, the paintball master went over the rules. "What you're playing is a variation of woodsball—a capture-the-flag game. We have four acres of game area behind us in which we've placed ten flags. Your goal is not to capture just one of the flags, but as many flags as you can." He held up a helmet. "On the top are dowel holders for the flags. If you capture a flag, you must display it."

"So other players can kill you and steal your flag?"

The guy grinned. "Yep. Finding the flags isn't the problem. Keeping them without getting taken out is the issue. If your partner is taken out, you're not automatically out. You can still win. Immediate kill zone is anywhere near the heart or head. Three paintball strikes anywhere on your body puts you out. Any questions?"

Liberty raised her hand. "Why are there only five slots on the top of the helmet if there are ten flags? Shouldn't there be ten slots?"

"Sweetheart, no one has ever captured more than five flags."

Sweetheart? That was condescending. Although . . . sometimes Devin called Liberty *sweetheart*. Did she get that look of extreme annoyance on her face when he did it?

She gritted her teeth in what was supposed to pass as a smile. But he knew if the game master were playing this round? He'd be the first one in Liberty's crosshairs.

Good thing G.I. Jane was on his side.

∞

Two hours later they were down to three teams and a couple of renegades.

"Can you see who's behind that big oak tree thirty yards to your right?" Liberty asked.

"Sarge."

"Shit. We'll have to go around and try to flank him from the back."

"But he's alone. There's two of us and one of him."

"Which just means that Check, his partner, also a military guy, is someplace close, watching his six."

If it made him a pervert to get a boner when she slipped into military speak, so be it, because that was fucking hot.

"How do you know Check hasn't been taken out?"

"Sarge wouldn't be so visible. He's trying to draw us out so Check can take the shot."

"Where's the last flag?"

Liberty peered around the cement block, making the four flags on her helmet wave in the breeze. "I think that big roadie dude went after it." She snickered. "He's too broad a target for even *you* to miss, McClain."

"Fuck you very much, Miz Deadeye. Jesus. Were you ever a contender for *Top Shot*? They dig hot military women on that TV show, especially when they outshoot them macho guys."

She rolled her eyes. "They'd cream my butt on that show."

I'd like to cream on your butt.

He had to quit thinking about her ass and focus. "So, we goin' after him?"

"Yes, sir. On three, keep as low to the ground as you can and shoot on sight." Liberty shifted into a crouch.

"Shoot him in the back?"

"Always. There are no rules of engagement in paintball like there are in war." She checked her ammo supply and looked at him. "One. Two . . . Three."

Devin mimicked her stance, a funky kind of duck walk, until they cleared the last section of hedge.

Then Liberty had her gun up and she'd clicked off three shots in a row at close range.

Pow.

Pow.

Pow.

The big roadie turned around and Devin plugged him in the chest. "Aw, fuck me, man. How many shots do I got on my back?"

"Three. And that's more than enough for you to hand that flag over," Liberty said and motioned for Devin to retrieve it.

"No wonder you wanted her on your team," he complained to Devin.

With victory on his mind—mostly whether he could get away with laying a big kiss on her as they toasted their superior teamwork—Devin forgot to employ the stealth tactics Liberty had drilled into him. He pushed upright and walked forward to snag the flag when he heard a rustling noise beside him.

He froze as Check sidled out of the woods, his gun pointed at Devin's chest, a maniacal grin on his face.

Everything happened in slow motion as Liberty launched herself in front of Devin, taking all three paintballs meant for him, right in the chest.

As Liberty hit the ground, she shouted, "Devin! Shoot him!"

He raised the muzzle and squeezed off his last four shots. Then Sarge rushed him. Using Liberty's body as a shield, Devin bent down, retrieved her gun and pumped three paintballs across Sarge's torso. Then he set the gun aside and rolled Liberty to her back. "Baby, are you okay?"

She raised her eyebrows at his term of endearment but didn't comment. "I'm fine."

Devin dragged his finger through the red paint decorating her protective chest plate. "I can't believe you took a bullet for me. Three bullets." Although this had been fun and games, the reality was that Liberty would've dived into real gunfire to save him.

Risked her life for his.

What kind of crazy person signed on for shit like that?

"Devin."

Dazed, he looked at her. "What?"

"You can quit putting compression on my chest. I think the danger of me bleeding out is long past."

That's when he realized he had one hand in the middle of her chest and the other wrapped around her neck. And he was close enough he could give her mouth-to-mouth if she needed it.

Maybe you need it.

"Seriously, Devin. Let me up."

He bent closer. "You'll really put yourself in the line of fire for me."

"Yes."

Something changed in that instant. The dividing line between her professional responsibilities to him and his personal feelings for her should've widened. Instead, Devin felt them erode completely.

By the panicked look in her eyes, he knew she was fully aware of the shift.

"Devin—"

"Don't deny you feel it too. There's no goin' back for us, Liberty."

Before she could argue, he stood and offered her a hand up.

Pow, pow, pow rocked him on his feet, and he whirled around.

Boomer shot him one more time in the center of his chest. Then he stopped and pushed up his goggles. "I believe, as last man standing, all those flags belong to me and I win the game."

Devin laughed. He couldn't believe that mild-mannered Boomer had outlasted them all. "Yep, buddy, you sure do."

Liberty rolled to her feet. "What's next on Devin McClain's fun agenda?"

"Horseshoes." He draped his arm over her shoulder as they walked out of the wooded area, and she didn't try to shrug him off. "Wanna play?"

"Pass."

"Volleyball?"

"Pass."

"Mini golf?"

"Double pass."

He sighed. "You're shooting down all my fun ideas."

"Because my idea of fun is shooting stuff. We've done that today. I've had my quota of fun."

"So, you're just goin' back to the bus?"

"Yep."

"Will you at least come out of your hidey-hole and eat with us? Roast some marshmallows? Sit by the campfire?"

Liberty stopped and faced him. "Why is it important to you?"

"It's not for me; it's for you." Devin rested his hand on her shoulder and reached up to wipe away splatters of paint from her face. But he succeeded only in smearing it and making it look even more like blood. "Fresh air and a cold beer will do you some good."

"Probably. But this is time for you to hang out with your crew without me hovering. You should enjoy it. Given the rest of your tour schedule, it'll be pretty rare."

And it was really rare his bodyguard admitted that he was safe enough not to have her by his side.

The thing was, he *wanted* her by his side tonight.

"You're off the clock. You've earned some alone time in the bus." Devin hated to play this card, but he was shameless. "But in keeping with our cover, my crew will ask questions on why you're not around at all when you always are. So you need to put in an appearance for a few hours at some point."

"Then I'll forgo the weenie roast, but I'll be there for the bonfire."

It wasn't all he wanted, but it was something.

Chapter Ten

❧

*E*veryone seemed to be enjoying the campfire.

Even Liberty, who'd had her fill of the great outdoors during the years she'd spent living in military tent
encampments, could admit it was a beautiful night. Away
from urban sprawl, and with just a sliver of moon showing
in the inky sky, the stars shone brightly.

Bottles and cans of beer were nestled in tubs of ice.
Bags of chips and s'mores supplies were scattered across
the picnic table.

The mood of the band and the crew had mellowed. The
roadies were congregated on the left side, laughing and
bullshitting while the paired-off band members, Tay and
Jase, Odette and Steve, were snuggled together in front of
the campfire. Although she and Devin shared a log, he
was talking across the fire to Leon and Gage, so she felt
like the odd woman out.

Story of your life, Liberty.

Fighting the melancholy, she closed her eyes and

listened to the crickets and other bugs creating a nighttime symphony. Every once in a while she heard a coyote yowl.

Devin scooted closer before he spoke softly. "You all right?"

"I'm fine. Why?"

"You're awful quiet."

"I'm always quiet around other people."

"You yammer on when it's just you and me."

Liberty cracked her eyes open to glare at him, but he wore the charming smile that indicated he was yanking her chain. "Funny."

He set his hand on her thigh. "I know this ain't your thing, so thanks for hanging out tonight."

"No problem."

"Hey, Dev," one of the roadies yelled. "Why don't you get out your guitar and sing? Like them old-time cowboys used to do after a long day of working cattle."

"Don't you guys get enough of me bellowing at the top of my lungs every night?"

She smiled. At times the man was surprisingly humble.

A chorus of no's rang out, followed by the "Devin, Devin, Devin" chants that he heard before his shows started.

Devin drained his can of beer. "None of y'all better record this, 'cause after a few drinks, I can't guarantee it'll be my usual stellar performance." Before he could get up to retrieve a guitar, Check brought him one. "Thanks."

The road crew moved in closer. Liberty wondered why Devin seemed nervous when he regularly played in front of a crowd of thousands.

He strummed a few chords. He didn't look up as he started to turn the random warm-up notes into a recognizable song. The strange thing was—the song he picked wasn't one of his. Liberty didn't recognize the tune, but whatever it was, the raw emotion in it captured her heart and then wrung it out.

No applause followed when he finished singing, and she realized it was because no one wanted to break the spell.

Devin continued to mesmerize with the next four songs, each a different style: first a bluesy number, then a stripped-down rock ballad, followed by a Motown classic and finishing with a crossover pop megahit. He nailed every style, needing nothing but his voice and a few guitar chords to showcase his mastery over all types of music.

His crew clapped and whistled when Devin took a break. Crash handed him a bottle of water. Liberty watched as Devin's throat muscles worked, the liquid soothing those golden vocal cords.

He sighed gustily after he drained the water. "Thanks."

"You need another?"

"Nah. I'm good."

People milled around, getting more beer and loading up on snacks.

"Are you gonna take requests?" Boomer asked.

"Sure. Give me a minute, though."

"No problem."

"You take requests?" Liberty asked.

He glanced up and her stomach swooped. The look in his eyes was forceful, but he spoke to her very softly. "Yes. So here's your chance to get me to play something you might actually like."

Her cheeks heated—and not from the campfire. "I like your music, Devin. It's not the typical country dreck."

"I've moved out of the dreck category?" He aimed his panty-dropping grin at her. "Darlin', I'm gonna get a big head if you keep complimenting me today."

"Too late," she retorted sweetly.

Devin leaned closer. "Name a song."

"Seriously?"

"Seriously."

"Anything?"

"Anything."

"Why?"

"Because I want to play something just for you."

The man was throwing her all sorts of mixed signals today.

No, he's not. You're just not ignoring them—or him— for once.

"How about . . . 'Learn to Fly' by Foo Fighters."

He smiled. "Excellent choice. A favorite of mine too."

That surprised her. "Really? But I thought . . ."

"That I'd only listen to country dreck?" he teased.

"Yeah."

"Nope. I love all kinds of music. I have great taste. I listen to stuff that'd surprise even you."

"Such as?" she challenged.

"You're demanding proof that I have good taste in music?"

Liberty snorted. "Dude. Everyone thinks they have great taste in music and they want to prove to everyone else just how cool they are. That's why you see guys in their fifties driving around with their windows rolled down, cranking out AC/DC, Skynyrd, the Eagles or Springsteen. The ladies from the eighties are just as bad, zipping around in minivans blasting Bon Jovi, Journey, Def Leppard, Whitesnake and U2. And don't get me started on the rap booming from teenagers' windows, which is only marginally less annoying than some forty-year-old white guy trying to look hip by listening to Kanye West or Jay-Z at ten billion decibels."

Devin laughed so hard she worried he'd fall off the log. Finally, he stopped laughing, but he couldn't quit smiling. "God, woman, you crack my ass up. But you're exactly right." He strummed a couple of dissonant chords. "But you didn't weigh in on those folks who listen to country dreck."

"I'm sorry I called it that. I'll admit I have a new appreciation for country. And I find the fans way more diverse than in other styles of pop music. I mean, at your concerts I see grandparents, young kids, teenagers and twenty-something guys and their friends. Which tells me the music speaks to a larger segment of the general population."

"Country music doesn't try to be offensive or controversial." He frowned. "My recent brush with controversy was totally unintentional."

So far, Devin hadn't played the song in question in concert. Which was a shame because it was a great song.

"Sometimes that lack of passion makes it generic. That's what makes it so gratifying when something I write stands out. I don't mean a song that hits the top of the charts, but one that resonates with listeners. I'll never forget the first time I was onstage and the audience knew every word to my song and were singing along so loudly I couldn't hear anything in my earpiece. It was unlike anything I could've ever imagined."

She knew when he feared he'd revealed too much, and he was about to say something that'd make light of how he'd opened up to her. So she beat him to the punch. "After almost a month on the road with you, I know all the words to all your songs."

He pointed at her. "Now, I'm gonna look backstage during a performance to see if you're tellin' me the truth or just stroking my ego. And since you tossed down the challenge, how about if we swap iPods tomorrow before we work out?"

"Deal. But if a Christina Aguilera song comes on, I might accidentally crush your iPod beneath my foot on the treadmill."

He laughed. "Harsh. Have you ever really listened to the words of 'Beautiful'? There's a pretty powerful message in that song about true beauty beyond outward appearances. Listen to it with an open mind."

Again, she picked up on the underlying message in his words, and it caused her pulse to race.

During their exchange, Devin hadn't looked away from her. The man was stunning in the campfire's glow. Her fingers itched to trace every contour of his rugged face. See if she couldn't smooth away some of the shadows.

"Are you playing another song? Or the two of you gonna sit here makin' moon eyes at each other all damn night?" Sarge complained.

That broke the moment.

Liberty looked around. How long had everyone been watching them?

What does it matter? Everyone assumes you're in Devin's bed every night anyway.

Devin cleared his throat. "I've got a few more songs in me before the campfire smoke starts fuckin' with my voice."

Before Liberty could suggest they call it a night, he strummed the opening chords to "Learn to Fly." And he kept her transfixed until the very last note.

Then his head came up. Their eyes met, and once again it was as if everything around them faded into the background.

Applause and wolf whistles erupted. He mouthed,

"Thank you," and gave her a sweet smile she'd never seen before.

Before she did something fan girly like throw herself at him, Crash's booming voice cut through the noise.

"Dev. We gotta add that cover tune to the set list. Your fans will go nuts for an acoustic version of that."

Devin shook his head. "Not everything needs to be exploited."

"But—"

"I said no." He looked at Boomer. "You had a request earlier. What was it?"

"'Friends in Low Places.'"

"I resemble that one. At least tonight."

Boos rang out.

By the time he reached the chorus, it'd turned into a sing-along. The next tune was also a drinking song that everyone chimed in on. Liberty hated to call a halt to the fun, but she could tell the smoke was really bothering him.

As soon as she stood, she felt all eyes on her. "Go ahead and boo me, but I'm taking Devin to the bus."

No one booed, but several people protested.

Then Devin was on his feet. "Cut her some slack. She's only doin' her job."

A roadie said something that made everyone laugh.

Check wandered over and took the guitar. "Thanks for playing tonight."

"My pleasure." Then Devin said, "Good night," to everyone before he turned and they started the long walk toward the bus.

Liberty broke the easy silence between them. "Thanks for pestering me to sit by the campfire. Fresh air did do me some good."

"The last time I just chilled out beneath a starry sky

was last spring. A year ago, I was home for a week during branding. Hank and Abe Lawson put me to work. So did Kyle and Celia Gilchrist. I usually help Bran out, since they all brand right around the same time, but I had to get back to Nashville and missed it."

"I was there that year. First and last time." She shivered. "Not my idea of fun. I conveniently had to work this year."

"I actually enjoy it. Seems to be the only time I can really catch up with everyone."

"I mostly stayed in the house and took care of Jake."

"You're close to Harper."

"Very. Are you close to your older sister?"

A beat of tense silence passed. "Not really. It's not like we had a falling-out or anything."

"That's too bad, especially since you both lost Michelle. I'd think that loss would've brought you closer." When she realized how judgy that sounded, she quickly said, "Because I lived apart from Harper for so long, it's good to be within driving distance. It surprised me she's not the way I remembered her."

"Like what?"

"I always thought we were polar opposites. I was tough; she wasn't." She shook her head. "My beauty queen sister with the soft heart and the soft voice . . . I thought she'd have a soft will. But nope. She's made of strong stuff."

He bumped her with his shoulder. "Must run in the family."

"I am a marshmallow around her boys. I love how she is around them."

"How's that?"

"Happy. She's exactly where she's meant to be. For the longest time, neither of us thought we'd ever have that. A place of our own."

The ground crunched beneath his boots. "Do you have it?"

"I'm working on it." *And you're helping me achieve that goal, even though you don't know it.* "How'd we get on this subject?"

"Does it matter? I like talkin' to you. We were on track to getting to know each other before the truck stop—"

"I've moved on from that incident," she said in a rush.

Devin slowed their pace. "Personally? Or professionally?"

"Both." What was it about the dark that made it easier to talk? "I just didn't . . . don't know how to bring it up."

"How about . . . *Devin, I miss our witty banter on the long bus rides.* Or more accurately: *Devin, I miss insulting you at every opportunity.*"

She snorted. "You *need* someone to insult you to keep your head from swelling like a Macy's parade balloon."

He reached for her hand and squeezed. "See? I missed this. Give me another one."

"Believe it or not, I don't have an arsenal of insults."

"Damn. 'Cause some of them were really creative. I heard you muttering under your breath last week, callin' me an arrogant asshat."

Liberty laughed softly.

"Maybe you've built up a store of compliments for me?" he asked hopefully.

"Not any of those either."

"Double damn." He swung their joined hands. "So I'll give you one. Thanks for takin' bullets for me today."

"I hope paintballs are the only kind I'll ever have to take."

"Me too. But I am gonna drop a note in the suggestion

box about not using red paint. Because that fucked me up. Bad."

Her too, but she wouldn't admit that to him.

Once they were locked in the bus, she said, "I'm tired. Think I'll call it a night."

Devin looked as if he didn't believe her.

"What?"

"I dunno. Five minutes ago you seemed . . . restless."

She wouldn't admit to him, either, that being so close to him had her all kinds of revved up. But her usual ways of dealing—booze, sex, grappling—weren't feasible, so she'd go with option four: playing *Call of Duty* for a few hours. She faked a yawn. "Sorry. I'm fading fast. I'll see you in the morning." Halfway down the hall, she stopped. "Don't forget to—"

"Leave my door unlocked. Yeah, I know the drill by now."

Liberty grabbed her pajamas and changed in the bathroom. By the time she finished brushing her teeth, flossing and coating herself with lotion, Devin had turned off all the lights in the front of the bus. She listened at his door, expecting to hear the muted sounds of his TV or guitar, but it was quiet.

Her excitement level was still high when she crawled in her bunk and cracked open her laptop. While she was waiting for the connection, she fluffed her pillows and slipped on her noise-canceling headphones.

Cracking her knuckles might've been a little over-the-top, but she kept that superstition before she jumped into the fray.

Ready, set, go.

It was like coming home. Kicking ass and stomping over

the dead corpses on her way to empty a rebel safe house. She'd cleared the space of civilians and had tossed in a grenade to keep the rebel forces from returning to reclaim the structure when Devin ripped back the curtain.

She released a small scream and tore off her head-phones. "What the hell?"

He got right in her face. "Just gonna crash, huh?" He pointed at her laptop screen. "Is that after you pulverize an entire city with your stockpile of weapons?"

Liberty glared at him and hit pause. "You play?"

"Not very often." He squinted at the screen. "Holy shit. What level are you on?"

"Veteran."

Then, without warning or even asking, he bullied his way into her private space. "Scoot over."

"Hey!"

"What? I wanna watch the expert soldier do her thing."

"Fine." She moved closer to the wall. But they were still shoulder to shoulder. She hip-checked him. "Crowd-ing me much?"

"I'm a big guy. I take up a lot of room."

"Good thing you don't have to sleep in this bunk."

"Quit complaining. This is a helluva lot bigger than some of the bunks I've slept in over the years."

"It's definitely not made for two people."

She realized her mistake when he crowded her even more. "It can be pretty comfy for two; it's just someone's always gotta be on top."

Rather than get sucked into his smoldering eyes, she refocused on her laptop screen. "You'd know all about that, wouldn't you?"

Devin chuckled. "Without apology, darlin'. Want me to show you so you're in the know too?"

Yes. Please. "No. Now hush. You're breaking my concentration."

As the game progressed, Liberty realized Devin was hell on her ability to focus. The man was just so solid. And warm. He smelled good too, like sun-warmed pine and clean cotton. And sex.

Okay, maybe not sex, but she couldn't be this close to him and not have everything remind her of sex. With him.

He didn't ask a bunch of questions. He seemed content to watch her play. After about an hour, her neck hurt and her eyes started to droop. It'd be easy to rest the side of her face against his biceps and doze off.

"You okay?" he murmured into her hair.

"Getting sleepy."

"Me too. I think it's time to hit the hay."

She smiled against his arm. Except . . . When had she cuddled up to him? Why hadn't he moved her?

"What?"

"Nothing."

Devin's rough-skinned fingers slipped beneath her chin, lifting her gaze to his. "Tell me."

"I haven't heard the phrase 'hit the hay' for a long time."

"What can I say? I'm a bumpkin."

That's when those intent blue eyes sucked her in. "You're too polished to ever be a bumpkin, especially in public."

"But in private?"

"In private . . . you're just you."

"You say that like it's a good thing."

"It is. Like tonight at the campfire. Another artist would've played his own music, but you covered everyone's but your own. And when Crash suggested you add the cover tune in your show? You said no."

"You seem surprised that not everything I do is calculated to sell more records or concert tickets or charm the pants off the female fans."

Stung, Liberty jerked her chin out of his hold. "Forget I said anything." She logged off the game and powered down her laptop, ignoring him completely even when she could feel his breath stirring her hair.

"It seems whenever you say something nice to me, I don't believe it. Then I open my mouth and insert my foot. Bein' antagonistic with you isn't my intent."

She sighed. "I know. I'm at fault too. I just don't know what to do with this."

"That makes two of us." He scratched his head. "The logical part of my brain says it was better when we had no personal interaction. I don't wanna listen to logic this time, Liberty. And I don't think you want to either."

How hard would it be to redefine the parameters of this relationship? Scary to think it wouldn't be hard at all. That they'd been circling each other the last three weeks. Waiting for the right moment to make the change. "Look, it's late. We can have this discussion another time, okay?"

Devin scooted to the edge of the bed and ducked out of her bunk. "I'll let it go for now, but we can't keep ignoring it." He placed his right hand on the curve of her jaw and swept his thumb over her cheekbone. "Sweet dreams, sweetheart. Thanks for today. It's been one of the better days in recent memory."

Not fair the man could be so damn sweet that he made her ache. She shut the curtains and curled up in her bunk. But sleep was a long time coming.

Chapter Eleven

～

*D*evin was awakened by a loud scream. Immediately, he scrambled out of bed.

He'd left his bedroom door ajar and paused inside the doorframe instead of racing out—per his bodyguard's request.

Then he heard it again. A lower-pitched scream this time, followed by a loud "No, no, no! Please, no!"

Thumping sounds echoed back to him, and he realized Liberty was thrashing around in her bunk, not wrestling with an assailant.

Devin ripped open the privacy curtain, hoping like hell Liberty wouldn't shoot him on sight.

The illuminated strip running the length of the hallway allowed enough light for him to see she wasn't armed. But she was rolling around and kicking, bucking her body as if someone—or something—was holding her down.

She let loose a pain-filled cry that chilled him to the

bone. That's when he knew he had to wake her—regardless of whether she came out swinging.

He leaned in, placing one hand on her forehead while at the same time clasping her left hand in his other hand. "Liberty. It's me, Devin. You need to wake up."

She thrashed and violently moved her head back and forth, trying to shake off his hand, moaning, "No, no, no."

As his eyes moved over her, he noticed her face was damp—from sweat or tears? His gaze moved lower, and he saw her bottom lip was swollen and bloody from where her teeth had dug into the tender flesh.

Jesus. What images had her sleeping mind conjured to elicit this reaction? He squeezed her hand and tried again. "Liberty. Wake up. It's okay. You're safe."

Her body went scarily still. Then she turned her head and her eyes opened.

His stomach pitched at the look of horror in those silvery depths. "Hey." He smoothed her hair back from her clammy forehead.

Liberty blinked, and panic crossed her face. "Devin? What're you . . . ?" She struggled to sit up. "What happened?"

"Nothin' happened. Besides you havin' a nightmare. I heard you and came to see if you were all right." He tucked a hank of hair behind her ear. "No need to get up."

"Move." She dodged his touch and swung her legs—her shapely bare legs—over the edge of the bunk.

That's when Devin noticed she slept in a pair of very short running shorts and a baggy US Army Rangers T-shirt. Before he could lighten the mood, since she was clearly agitated, she snapped, "I'm fine."

"Liberty—"

"I said I was fine." She stared at her feet. "Go back to bed."

Devin stood and headed toward the kitchen. After snagging a bottle of water, he returned to her, twisted off the plastic cap and handed it to her. "Here."

"Don't treat me like a child. Just . . . leave me alone."

"Like hell." He wrapped his hand around her jaw and tipped her head back, but the damn stubborn woman kept her eyes closed. Frustrated, he grabbed her hand and curled her fingers around the bottle. "Drink it."

She shook so hard she spilled water all over her legs and her shirt. She took two sips—he had no idea how she managed to swallow anything through her clenched jaw.

Goddammit, the woman was hanging on by a thread. He grabbed the bottle from her shaking hand and screwed on the cap. Threading his fingers through hers, he pulled her to her feet. "Enough. You're comin' with me." He towed her down the hallway.

"Devin—"

"Don't argue."

"But—"

"Shut. Up." He stopped at the end of his bed and kicked the door shut. "Crawl in."

Liberty didn't move.

"Fine. Want to do it my way? Where I pick you up and throw you into my bed?"

She shook her head and crawled to the far side of the mattress.

Devin moved in behind her, dragging her body against his with his chest pressed to her back. Then he yanked the covers over them.

She gave a token protest until Devin said, "Suck it up. I'm not letting you go until you stop shaking." He nuzzled the back of her head. "Relax. I've got you now."

If anything, that caused her to tremble harder.

Devin just held on. He didn't say a word. Not even when he felt her silent tears trickling down her face and dripping onto the sheet. Not even when the trembling abated, but she wiggled, trying to get free.

After a while, she settled. He had no idea how long they remained like that, body to body, each wrapped in unspoken thoughts.

Liberty didn't pull away even after she expelled a long, loud sigh. "I'm sorry I lost my shit."

"No worries. You wanna talk about it?"

She stayed quiet so long he figured that meant no.

But then she sighed again. "I hate when this happens."

"Does it happen often?"

"Guess it depends on your definition of often. I haven't had one of these in months."

"These . . . meaning what?"

Another bout of tense silence. Then she said softly, "A flashback. It's not fair to call it a combat nightmare, because I didn't end up in the combat situations my fellow male soldiers did. I can't imagine what those guys are going through."

"What was the flashback?"

"We were in the second wave of soldiers that were sent over there. I was young and cocky. Hell, we were all cocky. Gonna kick some Middle Eastern ass. We were trained, but goddamn were we unprepared." Her breath became labored, and she fought to even it out again. "Within three months of our yearlong stint, we'd lost four key people out of our company. One was Maria. My roommate. We were inside the fence. She headed to the mess hall about two minutes before I did. A sniper took her out. One second she was ready to eat another shitty meal and the next, she was dead. Afterward I kept asking myself what was so damn important that I hadn't been walking with her. Maybe I could've . . . saved her."

Devin kept his mouth shut, not pointing out that if she'd been with her friend maybe she'd be dead too.

"So I get to relive that moment over and over. Sometimes exactly as it happened and sometimes the parameters change, but it always ends up the same—with me covered in Maria's blood."

"I can't imagine." It seemed far too natural to offer her comfort. He rubbed his cheek against the back of her head, her soft hair teasing his lips. "What happened after?"

"I pretty much closed down. Did my job but went out of my way not to make more friends. It was a lonely, miserable time, and I swore I wouldn't reenlist. I'd get out and work at fucking McDonald's if I had to. But by the time I returned to the States and reunited with my home unit, I'd changed my mind."

"How many times were you sent over there?"

"Four."

Jesus.

"A one-year deployment each time. Plus six months of specialized training with UN peacekeeping units."

"Was the last stint when you were shot?"

"Yeah." She paused. "But I don't have nightmares about that. Too many other things haunt me that there's no room for more."

Devin didn't know what to say.

Liberty wiggled—a hint for him to let her go. "Uh, thanks, for, ah, you know, but I'm better now. I'll just go back to my bunk so you can get to sleep."

But he kept her locked in his embrace, letting her know she didn't have to run away from him. Letting her know he had no agenda besides holding her, offering her a little security and comfort in the middle of the night. He braced himself, expecting her to fight, but her breathing slowed and she crashed.

He forced himself not to think of her smooth, bare legs entwined with his. Or her toned abdomen where his palms rested. Or the warmed chocolate scent of her skin. He simply held her.

As he finally drifted off, he realized he couldn't remember the last time he'd fallen asleep with a woman in his arms.

∞

The door to Devin's bedroom flew open, and instantly, Liberty pushed him flat on his back and rose on her knees in front of him.

Odette skidded to a halt. Her gaze winged between them and she grinned. "I knew I'd catch you two in bed! Personal assistant, my ass."

Devin looked at Liberty, wondering if she'd make a smart retort about it being the first and last time they'd be caught in bed together.

But she just shot him a sexy smirk over her shoulder and said, "Busted," before she faced Odette and Crash. "Was there a reason you interrupted us?"

"We're about to take off and little O insisted you two had plans to write together today." Crash paused and looked at Devin. "Is that true?"

"Yeah. What time is it?"

"After nine," Odette said. "We won't reach the Pine Hills County Fairgrounds until four. That leaves us six hours to work on new material while we're rolling down the blacktop."

"Fine. Let us get dressed and we'll be right up." He looked at Crash. "Tell Reg we're ready to roll."

Odette offered a little wave and disappeared.

Crash watched her until she was out of earshot. "Sorry about that, but you know how she gets. She was through the door and down the hallway just as soon as I entered the alarm code."

"She's damn lucky Liberty wasn't armed." He sighed and jammed his hand through his hair. "Next time call first. This is not the way we needed to be woken up this morning."

"Understood. I'll have Odette make coffee." Then he shut the door.

Liberty hopped off the bed. She paused with her fingers on the door handle, but she didn't turn around. "Thanks for last night, Devin. Sorry to be such a pain in the ass. It won't happen again."

"Are you worried about what Odette thinks of you?"

She shook her head. "I'm more worried about what you think of me."

That shocked him, but not as much as what she said next.

"Some bodyguard I am, huh? Shaking and goddamn crying in the middle of the night to the point that you had to fucking coddle me—"

"Stop." Devin was on her, clamping his hands on her shoulders. He didn't turn her around—allowing her the privacy of keeping her face hidden, but he refused to hear her excuse for showing him that she wasn't infallible. "To be honest, I'm glad you showed me your human side— even if it wasn't intentional. I was beginning to think they'd turned you into some kind of robotic supersoldier during your stay in the military hospital, because, darlin', you're always so coolheaded. You don't miss anything. While I'm thrilled that you excel at your job, since it's protecting my ass, I'm glad that I could be there for you when you needed someone."

She exhaled.

Devin spun her around. "Have you tried to talk to a counselor about what you're dealin' with?"

Her whole body went rigid again. "No."

"Why not?"

"None of your business. Drop it or I'll drop you."

She acted tough. But something didn't fit. Why wouldn't the queen of the killer stare-down meet his eyes when she leveled a threat at him? "Liberty."

"Move."

"Look at me."

"No. Just . . . move, okay?" she said, barely above a whisper.

Devin took a chance, hoping she wouldn't bite him or rack him when he placed his fingers beneath her chin and lifted her face. "What happened? Weren't we getting along for a change?"

She nodded.

"Then what's wrong?"

Her icy pale eyes finally connected with his. "Go back to being a dickhead. It's easier to deal with than when you're acting nice to me."

"Jesus. Seriously?"

Liberty jerked her chin out of his hold. "Seriously. Now, get out of my way."

That's when Devin noticed the labored state of her breathing. The pulse point in her neck was throbbing. The irises of her eyes were huge, not wary but darkened with a look he hadn't seen on her before. Desire.

"That's why you got so pissy?" He wanted to say,

Because you're not hiding the fact you're attracted to me? But he decided that would send her scuttling back into her shell. So he settled on, "Because you've realized I'm not such a bad guy?"

"Yes. This isn't real. We're forced together because of professional circumstances, not because we choose to be together."

"Bullshit. I chose you as my personal security. And I know Garrett gave you the option of saying no to me. But you didn't. So some part of you wanted to be here with me. Maybe it was strictly professional at first, but things change. We've been on this path since the moment you stepped on this bus with me. You aren't denying that, are you?"

After a long pause, she shook her head.

"So, baby, talk to me. Please."

Liberty turned and faced the door again. "I . . . can't."

"You can. I opened up to you about Michelle, and, sweetheart, that's damn rare. There's no judgment between us. You already told me some of what you're dealing with. Maybe it'll help if you tell it all. Just rip off the bandage instead of letting the wound fester."

She blew out a long breath. "Maybe you're right."

He waited. He'd wait all damn day if that's what it took to help her through this.

Her body tensed, and then she started to speak. "During my third deployment, I was involved with an officer. That's taboo, especially since he was my commanding officer. Somehow we managed to keep our relationship a secret. Two months before our deployment was up, the vehicle he was riding in hit an IED. I was in the transport truck directly behind them and saw it happen. I jumped out and ran to the wreckage because I thought I could save him."

Devin was sensing a theme here.

She shuddered. "But once again I was too late. Everyone thought I was some kind of hero for trying to save our beloved CO. I actually got a commendation. No one ever knew the truth of why I disobeyed a direct command. I had to pretend I was only doing my job when I had the horror of watching my lover die in my arms. That's the nightmare I relive."

"Christ." He rested his forehead to the back of her head. "I'm so sorry. How long ago did it happen?"

"Five years. After that, I didn't care whether I lived or died. I didn't snap out of it until my body took the bullets meant for someone else and I saved the ambassador's life. I couldn't save my friend. Couldn't save my lover. So the *third time's a charm* rule worked for the ambassador."

"Liberty."

"No one knows this shit about me. I don't know why I'm telling you."

"I don't know why either, but you can trust that I won't break your confidence. Trust that this doesn't change anything between us."

Such a liar you are, McClain. It changes everything.

"Thank you." Without another word, she pushed him aside and walked out.

Devin sagged against the door. No wonder she'd gotten into the personal-protection business. No wonder she had a hard time letting anyone get close—they had all died on her.

Sound familiar?

Turns out they weren't so different after all.

∞

Stupid, stupid, stupid. Why had she told him about Sean? She stopped violently scrubbing her hair and stood under the showerhead to rinse away the explosion of bubbles.

Because Devin was right; you needed to tell someone.

But why him? Tit for tat since he'd told her about his sister?

No.

She'd told him because even when she'd tried to push him away, he wouldn't let her. She'd taken a chance and trusted him. If her trust was misplaced . . . well, she'd deal with whatever resulted.

Since Odette was around, Liberty had to do a full hair and makeup job. During the day, when Devin locked himself in his room and worked on music, she didn't bother getting dolled up until they were forced to leave the bus.

She slipped on a pair of wide-legged olive-colored cropped pants, a sleeveless black blouse ruched down the center and patterned with swirls of gold, olive and plum. When she slipped on her gun before the show, she'd don the boxy black jacket that covered it. Concealment undergarments allowed her to keep her weapon by her hip, at the small of her back, or under her armpit. She regularly switched out the spandex-like garments. Wouldn't do to get complacent, always wearing her gun in the same place.

Hair fluffed, personal assistant face on, she exited the bathroom as the bus swerved slightly. She smacked right into Devin's hard chest.

"Whoa there. Careful." His long, strong fingers circled her biceps as he steadied her. "Wouldn't think you'd feel the twists and turns in a vehicle this size, would ya?"

"You sure Crash isn't driving this bus?"

Devin grinned. "If Crash was drivin', we would've tipped up on two wheels for sure."

"Scary thought." Liberty noticed that he maintained a grip on her arms, and his smile faded. "What?"

Then he did the oddest thing; he angled his head, lightly trailing his nose up the side of her neck. "Sweet Jesus, woman. Why do you always smell like chocolate and vanilla?"

Her skin broke out in gooseflesh from the heat of his breath and the warmth of his mouth against her skin.

"Every time you leave the bathroom in the morning after you shower, I swear I get a whiff of brownies. Then I come to find out that sweet-smelling temptation is all you."

"It's, ah, my cocoa butter lotion and my vanilla bean shampoo," she admitted in a breathless rush.

"Whatever it is, it blows my train of thought completely."

Was she supposed to apologize?

Devin raised his head and stared into her eyes. "You doin' all right?"

"I'm fine."

Then he dropped his gaze to her mouth. "You really did a number on your bottom lip."

"I imagine it was a misguided attempt to keep myself from crying out."

"Does it hurt?"

"Some."

"Maybe this will help." Devin dipped his head, placing a butterfly-soft kiss across the spot. He eased back and stared into her eyes. When she didn't utter a peep of protest, he kissed her again. Just as softly. But he didn't stop at one kiss. He brushed his mouth across hers over and over. Teasing her. Making her want more. But leaving it entirely in her control to take it.

So she did. Liberty wrapped her hand around the back of his neck and turned the soft glide of lips into an open-mouthed kiss, packed with passion and laced with lust.

Devin didn't push her against the wall or clamp his hands on her ass and grind their lower bodies together. He put every bit of his energy into the kiss, drugging her with the fast-slow-fast movements of his tongue. Tasting her thoroughly and letting himself be tasted in turn. He traced her upper lip with his tongue and then the lower lip. They paused, their lips barely brushing, and breathed each other in.

It was glorious.

"Omigod! Are you two at it again? It's been, like, fifteen minutes since you rolled out of bed," Odette said, and then she was trying to insert herself between them.

But Liberty wouldn't let go of his neck, and he had a lock on her eyes.

"You kissed her so hard she's bleeding? Dammit, Devin, you don't have to act like such an animal all the time."

That's when Devin's gaze moved to Liberty's mouth. "Looks like we opened up that cut on your lip."

"I don't care."

The heat in his eyes when he looked at her again made her belly cartwheel.

"I care," Odette inserted. "Go put Vaseline on it or something." She poked Devin in the chest. "Get your guitar and get up front. You've been a lousy songwriting partner the last three weeks, and we're behind on new material."

Devin made a whip-cracking sound.

Liberty snickered.

Odette muttered and stormed off in her four-inch heels.

"Duty calls. You gonna be all right?"

No. She would be thinking about that kiss all damn day. "Yeah."

He grinned. "Me either. But we'll talk about this later." He headed to his room for his guitar, and Liberty crawled into her bunk.

Chapter Twelve

◆

*W*hile the tour bus was luxurious, it also gave Liberty claustrophobia when she had to hole up in her bunk for more than just sleeping time.

Devin hadn't told her to keep out of the main living area when he and Odette were working, but it'd feel weird to sit around and watch as they created music.

During the day when they were on the road, Devin pretty much kept to himself. Occasionally, she heard the strains of his guitar, but when he was in the back of the bus, she mostly stayed up front.

But for some reason, today she hadn't pulled the divider between the front and back spaces. So the music and their voices drifted to her in her cozy alcove across from her bunk.

"No, that bridge is too close to the one on 'Alibis and Ammo,'" Odette said.

"It'll sound different when we add bass and drums."

"Not different enough. Jase, Gage and Steve will take

the easy way and play what's familiar to them, so this has to sound unique."

"How about no instruments? Just my voice?"

Silence. Then, "That would work. Let's hear it from the top."

Devin sang about love being broken beyond repair.

The haunting vocals coupled with the words caused goose bumps to break out across Liberty's skin. She fought the urge to cry. What had happened in his romantic life that caused so much bone-deep sorrow?

After that she couldn't concentrate on her work. She listened as they fine-tuned rollicking drinking songs, followed by a sappy ballad. Somehow she held back her laughter as they discarded the words *scour, dour, shower* and *plower*, which were meant to rhyme with *flower*.

Odette said, "How much of what we've been working on is for your next album?"

"Some. Most. Hell, I don't know. My audience knows what they're getting with me. Some of what I've written isn't my style. Doesn't mean I don't think it's good. It'd just be better suited to someone else."

"For instance?" Odette prompted. "Because everything I've heard today is suited to you."

He strummed a few chords. "I've been workin' on something. It's a little rough."

Liberty closed her eyes when he started to sing, letting his velvety smooth voice wrap around her like a silken promise. The song spoke of a great divide. By the second verse, she understood what the words meant. Standing on the precipice of something great but being unable to take that first step. This time when Devin finished, Liberty was crying. Not an escaped teardrop or two but a flood of tears.

Odette cleared her throat. "Uh, hate to tell you, but

that song is all you. Keep it stripped down like that, in that almost confessional whisper tone, and I guarantee it'll be a hit. Guarantee it, Dev."

"When did you become the psychic type who can see into the future?"

"I don't gotta have any special mind skills when my ears work just fine. That song is amazing."

Devin said something that made Odette laugh.

Then, before Liberty prepared herself, Devin's footsteps echoed toward her. He stopped when he saw her in the sitting area. "Oh. Hey. I hope we weren't disturbing you."

"Not at all."

His eyes narrowed. "What's wrong?"

Shit. "Nothing."

"Then why is your face wet like you've been cryin'?"

"Probably got dust in my eye when the air-conditioning kicked on."

"Try again."

"Allergies. I think I'm allergic to Oklahoma."

Devin crouched down. "Sweetheart, I know something caused the tears that made your makeup run."

She tried to discreetly wipe under her eyes, and her fingers came away black. God. Sometimes she sucked so bad at being a girl.

Devin sighed, stood and walked to the bathroom, returning with a handful of tissues. "Here."

"Thanks."

He was being so sweet, which was probably what spurred her to blurt out, "How do you do it?"

"Do what?"

"Write songs like that? Heartbreaking and beautiful with so much raw emotion."

"It's gotta be good if it makes the toughest woman I know cry."

Liberty didn't look at him. She just twisted the soggy tissue and said, "Don't make fun of me." Then she felt his warm fingers beneath her chin as he tipped her head up, forcing her to look at him.

"I'm not. I'm not bein' flip when I say I don't know. Some songs just come easy. Some I work on for months and can't seem to get right. That song? It . . ." His eyes were dark and so conflicted she couldn't help but reach for his hand.

"Devin. Sorry I pried. You don't have to tell me."

"I would if I could, but even I don't know where that song came from. I started it when I was havin' one of them days. Where the gap between where I was and what I wanted just kept getting wider. But even back then the song wasn't ringing true, so I set it aside. Just in the last couple days I was able to get it where it needed to be."

"I don't know anything about music, but Odette does and she's right. It's an amazing song."

"Thank you." He swept his thumb across her knuckles. "You don't have to hide back here. You're welcome to sit with us while we're workin'."

"It wouldn't bother you if I watched you?"

"I play in front of crowds more than five thousand strong damn near every night."

Devin moved closer.

He continued to stare at her, as if she were a challenge. Or maybe a puzzle. "This . . . attraction between us is makin' you nervous, isn't it?"

"Very."

"Why?"

"Because it's probably not a good idea."

"Why not?"

"I work for you." After she'd said it, she knew it didn't sound very convincing.

"Technically, you work for Big Sky Promotions, not me." His lips grazed the section of skin below her temple. "Is that the only reason?"

"No."

He nuzzled her ear. "Give me another reason, Liberty."

"That voice of yours in my ear is scrambling my brain."

"Mmm-hmm. Still not a valid reason, so if you don't want me to kiss you, say no."

"I can't."

"Can't what?" he said as he nibbled on her jaw.

Tingles shot across her skin. "Can't say no because I really want you to kiss me again."

He smiled against her cheek.

"And that pisses me off."

Devin brushed his mouth across hers in a barely there kiss. "Is that a challenge for me to kiss the mad outta you?"

"No. But—"

"Liberty."

"What?"

"Shut. Up." He slanted his lips over hers and dove in.

The heat was instantaneous.

And so was the interruption.

"Omigod! Seriously? I'm on a bus with the equivalent of horny teens." Odette marched over and tugged the back of Devin's shirt until he stood up. "Work. Now. No more breaks."

"One minute."

"No. Now," Odette insisted.

"I said I need another minute," he snapped. "Go back

up front or I'll get Reg to stop the goddamn bus and I'll throw you off myself."

Yikes. This sexually aroused side of him was hot.

"Whatever." Odette stomped away.

Then all six foot three, two hundred ripped pounds of sexually aroused male loomed over her. "We'll talk tonight after the show. Set some boundaries and all that since you love rules so damn much."

She smiled and shocked him by pulling him down for another steamy kiss. "It's a date. Now go sing me a pretty song."

∞

The show had been off tonight. Most people in the audience didn't notice, but he knew, and that's all that mattered.

After their encore, Tay approached him. "Dev, I need to talk to you."

"About what?"

"It's personal."

He moved to the edge of the stage to hand Check his instrument.

"Crying to Devin, are you?" Jase taunted behind them. "Typical of you, Tay. You've never been able to fight your own battles or even make your own decisions."

Tay whirled around and shouted, "Shut up! This doesn't concern you."

Jase all but threw his favorite guitar at Check. "The fuck it doesn't. And, bitch, if you're gonna be badmouthing me to Devin, I got a right to defend myself. And I have a goddamn say in this decision. This affects me too."

"Bitch?" Tay yelled. *"Bitch?"* Each time she yelled louder. "I haven't begun to show you my bitchy side, asshole. God. I fucking hate you. What did I ever see in you?"

"Back atcha, babe. But the truth is, you were too busy

trying to stuff my cock in you at every opportunity to ever really look at me."

Jesus. Not again with these two. Always going for the low blow.

"And look where that got us!" Tay picked up a microphone stand and swung it with all her might at Jase's head.

Jase ducked, but the corner of the base caught the edge of the riser and bounced back. It would've clipped Devin in the face if not for Liberty's quick action—snagging it midair and knocking it to the ground.

Odette, Steve, Gage and Leon looked at her like she'd morphed into a superhero, but that reaction was short-lived when Crash stepped between Tay and Jase, bellowing, "Enough! Everyone's got shit to do. Get it fuckin' done. Now."

Tay burst into tears, which brought Odette to her side.

None of the rest of the band moved, but the crew scattered.

"She has a legitimate reason for being upset." Odette put her arm around Tay and glared at Jase. Then at Steve for good measure.

Crash threw up his hands. "I warned you two." He pointed to Tay and Jase. "Get it figured out—how to work together after you've stopped fucking—because I sure as fuck am *not* putting up with this bullshit the rest of the goddamn tour. You work for him." He jerked his thumb at Devin. "But as tour manager, I have total hiring and firing discretion, and I will happily can both of your asses if you don't start acting like professionals instead of love-lorn teenagers. Got me?"

Jase walked away, and the rest of the guys followed.

Crash said, "Dev, I need you to check out a couple of things during teardown before the buses take off."

"Fine."

Tay gave Devin a tear-filled look as Crash lumbered off.

Fuck. He hated being in the middle of this. He spun around, right into Liberty.

She set her hand on his chest and raised both eyebrows.

"Don't ask. Ain't the first time they've dragged everyone into their shit, and it won't be the last."

"Will Crash really fire them?"

"I'd say no, but between the extra security concerns and working with ten different opening acts for this leg of the tour, he's hanging on by a thread."

"I thought bands' fighting was made up to sell more records."

"Not hardly." He placed his hand over hers on his chest. "Thanks for keeping me from getting a blow to the head."

"That's my job."

He wished it weren't. He wished he could pull her into his arms, drag her back to the bus and lose himself in her for a few hours. "I can't wait to be alone with you tonight."

"Same here. But we are going to talk first, right?"

"Devin? I still need to talk to you," Tay said behind him.

"About what?"

"I'm not being a drama queen when I say I can't stay on the bus with Jase tonight. I can't."

Devin turned around. "Tay—"

"I'm serious this time. I'll quit the tour before Crash can fire me if he tries to make me ride on the band bus."

"What do you want me to do?"

Tay wiped her tears. "Let me stay with you on your bus. Just for one night. Please. I'll sleep on the couch. Or on the floor. But I can't . . . handle being around Jase."

"What about tomorrow night? And the night after that?" he demanded. "This problem ain't goin' away."

"I know. But he's pressuring me. We're together all the time, so I don't have a moment's peace just to think."

Devin loomed over her. "If you're asking this because you want Jase to believe you're in my bed—"

"Puh-leez," Odette inserted with a snort. "That'd be a little crowded since we all know Liberty is in your bed."

He counted to ten. "I'll be sorry that I asked, but I need to know what's goin' on between you and Jase this time."

Tay looked at Odette and then burst into tears again. "I'm pregnant."

His jaw dropped.

"Yes, Jase is the father." She inhaled a shuddering breath. "You saw how he was tonight. Can you blame me for being unsure about whether I want to keep it?"

Devin put his hands up. "I am not takin' sides on this. You've got one night, Tay. *One.* Tomorrow night you're either back on the band bus or off the tour. Got it?"

She nodded. Then she threw herself at him, sobbing. "Thank you."

Devin looked at Liberty over Tay's head and mouthed, "I'm sorry."

Liberty's expression didn't change. But as soon as Tay released him, she stepped between them. "Hang on one second and we'll head to the bus and get you settled."

Odette said, "I'll grab your stuff."

"No. There will be no *stuff* grabbing besides a toothbrush and bedding," Devin warned. "One night doesn't mean tonight and all day tomorrow. We'll be in Oklahoma City by ten a.m. That's when my hospitality ends, Tay. Understand?"

"Yes."

Liberty took him aside. "Once I'm in the bus, I'll have to stay since I don't trust Tay not to create a chance for a security breach in her distracted state." She inhaled. Exhaled. "Which means the security guys will have to stay with you until teardown is done."

"Got it." Devin ran his finger across her jaw. "Will you be in my bed when I get there?"

"No. And I need you to lock your bedroom door tonight."

"Jesus, Liberty. Tay isn't gonna try to sleep fuck me or something."

"That's not what I'm worried about. She's emotional, and people in a mind-set where emotions overrule normal thought processes are capable of doing things you'd never expect. To guard against that, I'm telling you to lock your door."

She had the don't-question-me look on her face, which meant arguing was moot, and if he tried, well, she'd make her alternate suggestion even more extreme. "Fine. But I want all your firearms locked up tonight. Every. One. The last thing I need to worry about is you shooting a pregnant woman while I'm locked in my room."

"No problem."

They stared at each other.

"This isn't at all how I wanted our night to end."

"Me either."

Chapter Thirteen

❧

*E*arly the next afternoon, since Devin was under the watch of venue security, Liberty returned to the bus to take a shower after her workout.

With no one around, she stripped in front of her bunk. She jammed her workout clothes in the overflowing hamper and laid her outfit out on her bed. Hitting the light switch in her tiny bathroom, she realized the overhead light wasn't working. No windows meant she'd have to shower in the dark, and that wasn't happening.

No big deal; she'd use Devin's shower. Her mind bounced from thought to thought as she headed down the hallway. The door to Devin's room was ajar. She pushed it open, her eyes automatically sweeping the space. He always made his bed. The man was a serious neat freak.

Liberty entered the tidy bathroom and slid the pocket door closed. This space was so luxurious she couldn't believe it was on a tour bus. Skylights provided natural light in the slate-tiled shower and above the double vanity.

With the funky angles of the walls, the shower didn't need a door. She cranked on the water and stepped into the enclosure. Five showerheads blasted water at her; one from above and two from each side. She closed her eyes and sighed. The heat and steam and solitude were heavenly. No wonder Devin spent so much time in his master suite.

She reached for her shampoo and remembered she hadn't brought her toiletries with her. There was something that felt really intimate about using Devin's shampoo and body wash, but she didn't have a choice. She drew the line at using his razor.

Some oddly happy impulse spurred her to hum while she scrubbed her hair. Her humming morphed into belting out the 70s power ballads currently stuck in her brain, starting with Carly Simon's "You're So Vain." She'd just segued into the chorus of Linda Ronstadt's "You're No Good" when the bathroom door slammed open and Devin's angry voice filled the space.

"Jesus, Tay, I've told you a million fuckin' times to stay out of my shower . . ." Devin froze inside the doorway.

Liberty froze too.

However, Devin's eyes weren't frozen in place for long.

His gaze moved from her face, down to her breasts, then followed the center of her torso to the juncture of her thighs. His gaze returned to her breasts for several long moments. Then his eyes roamed over the curve of her hips and her thighs, briefly dipping to her feet before zooming back up to focus entirely on her breasts.

He said, "You're not Tay."

No shit.

"Sweet mother of God, Liberty Masterson. You've got the most rockin' body I have ever seen."

Oh wow. Now, there was a compliment. She was pretty

sure she blushed from head to toe, but she couldn't look away from the molten heat in Devin's eyes. Her skin erupted in gooseflesh, causing her nipples to harden.

Devin growled. He reached in and shut the shower off. Ignoring that he was clothed, he stepped into the enclosure with her, crowding her until her back hit the wall. Although he'd braced his hands by her head, he'd left enough space between them so he could still stare at her chest.

Liberty's heart raced. Despite the water dripping down her body, her mouth had gone desert dry.

"Two things I wanna know," he said to her breasts. "First. Why hide these? Jesus. They're spectacular." Then his gaze—his hungry gaze—returned to hers. "I've lived with you on this bus for a month. I've worked out with you. Hell, I've even had my arms around you in my bed. And, darlin', I'm unapologetically a breast man. I notice them. So there's no way I should've missed these beauties. No way. Unless you were purposely hiding them. Were you?"

She swallowed hard. "Yes. I wear a compression sports bra."

"Why would you do that?"

"Because these jiggling things are a pain in my ass. I started binding them when I joined the military."

"But—"

"You say they're spectacular? All they've ever done is get in my way. I wanted the guys in my unit to see me as a soldier, not a woman. It's a habit now because I'm still mainly working with men. I'm taken more seriously in my profession when I don't display distracting mounds of flesh. And I shoot better."

His eyes softened. "Doesn't it hurt you, though? To bind them all the time?"

"I'm used to it."

"You don't have to hide them from me anymore. Because, darlin', no offense, but now that I know about your gorgeous rack? I'm gonna be lookin' at your chest way more than is probably healthy."

"Or wise."

Devin laughed. "Maybe." His gaze zeroed in on her breasts again. "But even though I know you're always armed, I'd still be willing to take my chances to get my hands and my mouth all over you."

"Devin, you're making me uncomfortable."

"Now you know how I've felt since the moment you stepped combat boots on my bus." His gaze traveled up to her lips. "We never talked about setting some parameters in this relationship."

"I am not discussing it when I'm naked!"

"Would it be easier to talk about if I was nekkid too?" he said in that deep, silky tone of his.

Yes! "No!" She closed her eyes. "Please. Back off and let me get dressed."

"No."

Her eyes flew open, and she saw he'd closed the gap between them, leaving her trapped against the wall and by his eyes. "What do you want from me?"

"Your promise that we'll have an honest conversation about what's goin' on between us. As soon as possible." His eyes narrowed. "And, darlin', lose that defiant look. Don't insult either of us by pretending we're still just protector and protectee after those kisses yesterday."

"But . . . we are that."

"We can be so much more than that, and you know it." He slanted his mouth over hers. The kiss started out sweet but quickly caught fire. Even as Devin kissed her, he didn't touch her anywhere else. He focused on putting every bit of passion into the kiss.

Just like before, she lost her need for control when he put that wicked mouth on hers.

When he finally broke their lip-lock, a full-body shudder worked though her and she expelled a loud "God."

"I wasn't imagining it." Devin pushed back. This time, his gaze didn't leave her eyes. "The day is a wash as far as us getting time alone to talk without interruption. But tonight? As soon as that bus door closes and we're on the road, you are mine, understand?"

She just blinked at him.

"Liberty? Say something."

"I'm not sorry I used your shower."

That dazzling smile appeared. "Me either." He handed her a towel. "But you've gotta move your sweet ass outta here. I need to shower too and I only have so much willpower."

After he closed the door, she realized he never asked her about the second thing he wanted to know.

∞

For this part of the tour, Devin had two new opening acts. The first night Big Sky required all three acts to convene in the ready room after the first rehearsal. Devin wasn't happy about the interruption to his preshow solitude. Liberty wasn't happy with the two dozen extra people running around.

The promotion company had gone all-out—the catering was outstanding. The bands and their crews fell on the food like starving teenagers. Liberty stationed herself in the corner, observing the crowd while nibbling on a mini pastrami sandwich. She'd mentally sorted band members from roadies when Devin beckoned her over.

She ditched her plate and wiped her hands.

Crash stood on Devin's left side, a redheaded bombshell on his right. Or more accurately, the redheaded bombshell was plastered against Devin. Resting her head on his biceps. Putting her hands on his chest. Pressing her hip into his groin when she stood on tiptoe to speak with him.

Jealousy seared Liberty's gut like a red-hot poker. She wasn't sure who annoyed her more. The hot little number who assumed it was all right to put her grabby hands all over Devin. Or Devin, who wasn't telling said hot little number to keep her mitts to herself.

As soon as she reached the group, Devin reached for Liberty's hand and sidestepped the redheaded leech. "Hey, darlin'. You ate?"

"Yes. Did you?"

"Workin' my way in that direction. But first I wanted to introduce you to our opening acts." He pointed to the pouting redhead, who up close looked to be about twelve. "This is Jesse-Belle Archer. She's a big talent coming out of Alabama. Keep an eye on her because she's goin' places."

Liberty choked back a laugh at Devin's warning. She offered her hand. "Nice to meet you."

"Who is she?" Jesse-Belle demanded of Devin, ignoring Liberty completely.

"My personal assistant," Devin said, keeping an arm around Liberty's shoulder.

"Personal assistant, my ass." Odette snorted. "Those two are inseparable. We can hardly get them off Devin's bus. Be warned, Jezebel. You wanna talk to Devin, you gotta go through her first."

Liberty withheld a laugh at Odette's use of *Jezebel*.

"It's Jesse-Belle," she corrected. "I'm sure there won't be an issue if I need to speak to Devin alone, artist to artist."

Like hell there wouldn't be.

Two scruffy-looking guys approached, hands in pockets, booted feet shuffling nervously. "Hey, Devin. Heard you wanted to talk to us?"

"Liberty, this is Lee Stoltz and Eric Hofer, from Double Trouble. We're with the same record label, and they'll be opening the show for the next ten stops."

"I'm with the same record label too," Jesse-Belle pointed out, cutting off Liberty's response.

Devin, Lee and Eric made small talk about guy stuff, ignoring Jesse-Belle. Liberty had a moment of sympathy for the girl, knowing firsthand how hard it was to be excluded from the boys' club.

But her sympathy vanished when Jesse-Belle interrupted with "Come find me later, Devin. I've got more important things to do than listen to these two blather about nothing interesting." She stomped off in a huff.

Eric drawled, "I reckon it's time for her afternoon nap."

"Yeah, maybe if she throws a hissy fit, her mama will let her stay up past her curfew tonight," Lee added.

Devin laughed. "You've worked with her before?"

"Worked with half a dozen young things just like her. They're interchangeable."

Not very flattering.

"What Eric means is the label is tryin' to broaden everyone's fan base by creating an interesting slate of musicians for every tour," Lee said. "We've been lucky to open for lots of different acts in the past year. And we're happy the bosses at the label put us with you. It's an honor. Me'n Eric have been big fans of your music since your first album."

"I appreciate you sayin' so. One thing you oughta know—the label didn't assign you to this tour. I requested Double Trouble."

Lee and Eric exchanged a grin. "Way cool, man. Thanks."

"If you'll excuse me, I need to eat before they tear down the buffet." Devin steered Liberty to the tables of food. After a minute or so of standing there, he hadn't grabbed a plate.

"What's wrong?"

"Nothin' looks good."

"It is all good, trust me."

"I do." He tugged her close and kissed her forehead.

She froze at his public display of affection. Granted, he hadn't started macking on her, but it was the first time he'd acted like she was more than his personal assistant.

He noticed she'd stiffened up. "You okay?"

"I don't know if I'm ready for this."

"Ready to be in my bed?"

"Ready to be all kissy-face and hand-holdy in public. Especially when I'm supposed to be alert to our surroundings."

His beautiful blue eyes cooled, and she knew he'd misunderstood.

"When I feel you looking at me, or when you touch me, I forget about everything—including doing my job. As much as I like the promise of this new intimacy between us, it throws me off when we're out here." She placed her hand on his chest. "And out here is where I need to be extra vigilant about your safety."

"I get it. And thanks for clarifying that for me. I'll cool it when we're in mixed company." Devin's fingers circled her wrist and he placed a soft kiss in the center of her palm. "But when it's you and me alone? Cool is the last thing I'll be. I'm so hot to be all over you I'll be lucky if I make it through the show tonight."

"But . . . aren't we talking? Setting up some parameters about this first?"

He shook his head. "You know how wired I am after I walk offstage. For the past three weeks, since I've just said no to groupies"—he bestowed that megawatt smile—"I've been punishing myself, takin' cold showers or doin' sit-ups and push-ups until I wanna puke. But tonight—and every night from here on out—no more punishment. I'm gonna get what I want."

"Which is what?"

"You. In every dirty, raunchy scenario I've fantasized about."

Her pussy clenched in sheer happiness.

"Out here? I've accepted that you're in charge of my safety. But the only parameter I'll have when we're alone is that you're no longer in charge." He rubbed his mouth over the back of her knuckles. "See you after the show."

∞

Devin managed to finish half his food. He changed into performance clothes—nothing spangly or weird, but his fans paid good money for tickets, and they deserved to see that he'd put effort into his appearance. Some singers were content arriving onstage in an old T-shirt, holey jeans, and a ratty ball cap. Once in a while he did that. But tonight seemed like a special occasion.

Then, to kill time before he went onstage, he propped his bare feet on the coffee table and picked up his guitar. He strummed the melody of the song he'd been working on for the last month. He had the words and music to the chorus. But the opening chords escaped him. He'd intended the theme of the piece to be getting that second chance only to blow it again. Nothing worked. After an hour of restless plucking, he set aside his guitar.

Two beefy security guys lounged outside his door and immediately snapped to attention when he walked out.

"You ready, Mr. McClain?"

"Yeah."

A guy flanked him on each side, and they traveled the maze until they reached the backstage stairs.

Devin automatically looked around for Liberty. She accompanied him only when the security was light. No sign of her.

You'll see plenty of her tonight.

He snagged a bottle of water out of the tub.

Check started handing out guitars. Devin didn't bother to strum to see if his was tuned, because Check was more anal about that than he was.

Steve bounced from foot to foot. Odette ran her bow across her strings. Tay chomped her gum and blew big pink bubbles at Jase. Gage and Leon leaned against the back wall, lost in discussion. Just another preshow night. And like always, Devin sent up a silent prayer of thanks to the universe that he got to do what he loved for a living.

"You ready?" Crash asked, like he always did.

"Yep."

"Let's get your gear on. The set changes ain't takin' long." Crash handed him the earpiece and the remote pack.

Then Crash shook his head at someone who'd come up behind them. Devin felt the air change as the bodyguards closed rank. He kept his gaze on Crash. "I don't wanna know who that was or what's goin' on, do I?"

"Don't worry. It's bein' handled."

"By who?"

"Me. Because Little Miss I-Think-I'm-Hot-Shit does *not* want Liberty comin' down on her about security breaches. She has no idea that Liberty would chew her up, spit her out and use her bones to pick her teeth."

Devin laughed. "My woman is something, all right."

Crash lifted both eyebrows. "Since when is she your woman?"

"I'm starting to think since the minute I set eyes on her."

"Jesus. I knew it."

"Knew what?"

"Knew you'd be bangin' her at every opportunity. No woman alive is immune to that Devin McClain superstar charm."

Devin bunched his hand in Crash's shirt. "Watch it. Not that it's any of your goddamn business, but Liberty and I haven't had sex."

"Are you kiddin' me?"

"No."

"That's worse. Way worse."

"Why?"

But before Crash answered, Devin was prompted by his earpiece.

The applause was thunderous as his band appeared, instrument by instrument, starting with drums, followed by guitars and, finally, Odette's fiddle. The crowd quickly changed the chants into "Devin, Devin, Devin," so when he crossed the stage, he could hardly hear himself think.

Goddamn, he loved this. There was nothing like it in the world.

"That's one helluva a fine welcome for this Wyoming cowboy. What say we crank it up loud tonight? Get this party started right?" Jase jammed on the opening chords for "Bring on the Party" and that wall of sound washed over the stage again.

Yep. He had the best job in the world.

Chapter Fourteen

❯

"**G**ood night, Oklahoma City! Y'all have been awesome!" Devin and his band took their final bows after their encore. As soon as the stage went black, he slipped off his guitar strap and was the first one to reach Check and the instrument-loading bay.

"In a hurry tonight, Dev?" Check asked.

"Yeah." Devin's eyes searched the crowd until his gaze landed on her. His lips curled into a smile and his groin tightened. Liberty was deep in conversation with one of his security escorts. *Come on, baby. Look at me. You know I'm lookin' at you.*

"You sticking around while they load up?"

"No. I'm callin' it an early night. We'll shove off before the rest of you do."

"But you'll be at Patsy's Pancake Plaza tomorrow, right? We always hit Patsy's before the Black Creek Pavilion show."

He'd forgotten about that tradition. "Of course. Save us seats."

As soon as Devin knew he had Liberty's attention, he started toward her.

People gave him a wide berth.

Except Jesse-Belle stepped right in front of him. The silly girl threw her arms around him, pressing her face into his neck and her tits against his chest. "Omigod, what a show! You are totes outstanding onstage!"

Liberty's laser-sharp gaze could've sliced off her limbs.

Devin never looked away from Liberty as he clamped his hands on Jesse-Belle's scrawny arms and set her aside. "Thanks." Then he stepped around her.

But she planted herself in front of him again. "I'd like to talk with you about punching up my stage presence. Did you see my show earlier?"

"No."

"Why not?"

If this girl didn't back the fuck off, he'd show her the meaning of rude. He'd tried polite and disinterested with her and she hadn't gotten the hint. He finally looked down at her, about to let her have it, when Crash intercepted.

"Jesse-Belle, there you are. Boomer and your sound-man have questions before the guys start to tear everything down."

"Oh. Sure. Until next time . . ." She offered Devin a smile—but her attempt at being sexy fell short of the mark.

Way short. He wanted a woman—not a girl pretending to be one.

He mouthed "thank you" to Crash and kicked up his pace until he stood toe-to-toe with his scowling personal assistant. "Something wrong?"

Her eyes were hard, the color of cement. "That girl is trouble. And before you jump to the conclusion that I'm jealous, my issue with her is strictly from a security standpoint. She thinks the rules don't apply to her. All of the problems the venue security guys had tonight were caused by her and her entourage. Since tomorrow night's show is outdoors . . . I'm doubly concerned. Outdoor venues make me nervous."

"Talk to Crash. That was the second time he's run interference between me and her today."

"Crash? Why not me?"

"I don't want some girl-child star who's tryin' to prove herself mucking things up for you professionally by questioning your job if you start makin' security demands. You can set the rules, but let Crash be the one who passes them on, okay?"

Her eyes softened. "Okay. But I can handle myself."

"Baby, I know that." Devin curled his hand around her neck and put his mouth next to her ear. "But I'd much rather you were handling me. So what say we make a run for the bus and hang out the *do not disturb* sign for the next twelve hours?"

Liberty trembled. "Sixteen hours minimum. You don't have to be anywhere until sound check tomorrow."

"Shoot. I forgot to tell you we gotta meet the band at our favorite greasy diner tomorrow afternoon. But I'm yours until then. And I can't wait to strip you outta them bossy pants."

As soon as they stepped apart, he beckoned over his bruiser babysitters.

"Yes, Mr. McClain?"

"I'm done here and ready to head out."

"Your bus is at the back entrance."

They were stopped three times before they reached the exit. When he saw the bus headlights, he forced himself not to throw Liberty over his shoulder and made a break for it so they could finally have some alone time. Naked alone time.

When he saw Reg sitting in the driver's seat, he gave him a thumbs-up.

Liberty had already decoded the alarm and unlocked the door. She raced up the steps and tossed over her shoulder, "Lock up, will you?"

Somehow through the lust clogging his brain, he remembered the code. When he reached the top step, he saw Liberty's discarded shoes on the floor. Then her pants. Then her blouse. "I'm likin' this happy trail." Off went his boots. His socks. He set his hat on the shelf. He unbuttoned his shirt and tossed it aside. Same with his wife-beater. His belt was next. Followed by his jeans and boxer briefs—after he pulled out the lone, hopeful condom he'd stashed in his jeans pocket. Only when he was naked did he track her down.

Liberty was bent at the waist, fully exposing that fine, fine ass of hers.

Oh, hell yeah. That's what I'm talkin' about.

When she straightened up and turned around, her gaze skimmed his chest and went straight to his cock. Then she wrapped her fist around it. "You're packing a surprise yourself." She stroked him a few times and leaned forward, feathering a soft kiss on the side of his throat. "And I like *big* surprises."

Devin lost any ability to take things slow. Palming the condom, he placed his hand in the center of her belly, propelling her against the wall as his mouth crashed down on hers.

The kiss was more explosive than he'd imagined.

Her fiery response and the delicate way she handled his cock drove him insane.

He kissed her without restraint. Twining his tongue with hers, licking and sucking. His brain urged: *more flesh to taste than just her mouth.* Grabbing a handful of her hair, he tipped her head to the side, breaking the seal of their lips. As he dragged openmouthed kisses down the smooth expanse of her neck, he murmured, "Are you wet?"

"Yes. God, yes."

"Show me. Put your fingers in your pussy and then wipe that wetness on my cock."

Liberty's hand that wasn't jacking him slipped between their bodies. He could feel her wrist rubbing against his balls as she jammed her fingers inside herself.

"That's it. I wanna feel you finger fucking yourself." He nipped at the sweep of skin where her neck met her shoulder. "I can hear how wet you are."

She said, "Devin," on a near whimper.

"Show me," he demanded.

She switched her hand and ran two wet fingers up the front of his cock.

He smiled against her collarbone. Appeared Miss Liberty was as good at taking orders as she claimed. Lifting his head, he nuzzled her ear. "I'm gonna fuck you. But first I wanna taste you. Spread some of that sweet cream on your tits."

Once again Liberty's hand dove between her legs. But instead of stroking his shaft, she rubbed the head of his cock over her clit. "Feel that? How plump and hot and ready I am for you to make me fucking scream?"

His cock jerked, and the word *want want want want*

pulsed in his head. Her hips bucked, and he eased back to look into her face.

Lust had turned her eyes stormy gray. She wiped her fingers across the top of her right breast.

Groaning, Devin bent his head and licked. One long swipe of his tongue and then sucking kisses so he didn't miss a single spot. "Can't wait to bury my face in your cunt and gorge myself on this sweetness." He stepped back and pulled his hand away from her belly. The condom package had left a square mark from him pressing it against her skin.

"Glad to see you were prepared."

His gaze never wavered from hers as he ripped open the condom and rolled it on. "I've wanted you so fucking much that I knew we wouldn't make it to the bedroom." His hands followed her sides down to the flare of her hips. "Wrap your leg around me."

For a split second it appeared she might argue, but she raised her leg, pressing her inner thigh into his side.

Devin got a good grip on the back of her standing leg and said, "Jump up." He locked his knees, holding her weight and hoisting her against the wall.

She reached between them and aligned him. But she paused and nestled her face in the curve of his neck.

His body fucking shook, he wanted this so bad, yet somehow he managed to remain calm. "What's wrong?"

"Make me feel it," she whispered.

"Feel what?"

"That first thrust. Don't be sweet. Don't go slow. Slam into me so hard I feel this big cock of yours in the back of my throat. So I always remember this moment."

He angled his pelvis and impaled her in one rough

stroke, bottoming out inside her so fast his balls swung and slapped her ass.

Liberty hissed. "Sweet fuck, that hurt." She panted against his throat. "Do it again." She planted a kiss on his Adam's apple. "And again." Another kiss on his voice box. "And again."

So that's what he did. He fucked her furiously. No break. No stopping to see if she was all right. Her gasps and moans as her nails scored the back of his neck, her heels digging into his ass told him everything he needed to know.

He kept up that driving rhythm until she arched hard against him, her big tits bouncing against his sweat-slicked chest. Her cunt squeezing his shaft in juicy pulses as she climaxed. Then, right on the heels of the first one, she went off again, loudly pleading, "Don't stop."

Devin hadn't been trying to hold off, but he couldn't maintain that brutal pace any longer. His ass, his gut, his balls and his thighs tightened in anticipation. Then he shot his load in a prolonged gush of pleasure that had him gritting his teeth and sent his brain completely offline.

After his body—his entire being—quit shuddering, he dragged a kiss to her ear and gently bit her earlobe. "Not done with you, Liberty. Not by fuckin' half."

"Put me down."

He squeezed her ass cheeks, harder than she expected, and she gasped. "I like havin' you pinned against the wall with my cock still buried deep." He let his mouth follow the slope of her neck to the ball of her shoulder. "Maybe I'll keep you like this until I'm hard again. Which won't be too long because you are hotter than fuckin' fire."

"Devin, you don't have to—"

His head snapped back. "Take the compliment."

"Fine. Then you'll take one from me. You fuck like a dream, cowboy." She scraped her fingertips across his shoulder blades. "Now take me to your bed."

A primitive growl rumbled in his chest. He said, "Hang on," before he pulled her away from the wall and walked them down the hall to his bedroom.

Liberty's breath was a warm caress across his ear. "You weren't bragging. I can already feel you getting hard." She bore down on his cock with her pussy muscles, releasing a borderline evil laugh when he hissed.

He fell onto the bed with her, kissing her mouth like he owned it. She made an unhappy moan when he pulled his cock out of her. "I want to see your hands on the headboard when I get back." In his bathroom, he flushed the condom and washed his hands, checking his face in the mirror. He'd shaved right before his concert so he wouldn't leave beard burn on her—because he planned to have every inch of her chocolate-scented skin beneath his mouth and hands tonight.

When he returned to the bedroom, she wasn't in position like he'd told her. Devin wrapped his hands around her ankles and yanked until she was flat on her back. Then he hung above her, his knees by her hips, his fingers circling her wrists. "Outside this bus you are in charge. I respect that. I respect you. But when we're alone like this? With the world shut out and the bedroom door closed? It's all me." He brushed his mouth across her temptingly full lips.

Those silvery gray eyes of hers didn't waver. "So this isn't a onetime thing between us? We're not scratching the itch, satisfying our curiosity and moving on?"

"Fuck no. I want this for the long haul."

"You mean for the duration of the tour."

Sugar, I'd have you running scared for sure if you figured out how much more I want from you. "That too."

"Then you need to understand that if you're with me, there's no one else for you. No groupies. Not a single one. Yes, fan meet and greets are part of your job, but having those fans blowing you isn't part of it. You want your cock in someone's mouth? It'll be in *mine*. Ditto for this monster dick of yours. Giving you a fast, hard fuck before or after the show to take that edge off? That right belongs to me. *Only* to me."

Sexy as hell, seeing the determination shining in her eyes. "Agreed." Devin kissed her again, letting his lips linger on hers. "I want this one-on-one more than you know." He figured she probably didn't believe him, given his manwhore reputation—something that she'd seen firsthand. So he'd show her. Over and over again until she believed him. He released her wrists. "Press your hands against the headboard."

As soon as she wiggled up, he leaned forward, running his hands down her muscled arms, stopping to feather his thumb over the sensitive crease in her elbow. "I've wanted to get my hands on you since that day you strutted across the parking lot."

Uncertainness darkened her eyes.

"What?"

"You only wanted me after my makeover."

Devin tugged her pouty bottom lip between his teeth and lightly bit down before releasing it. "Wrong. You only enhanced what was already there. I'm the one who's the fool for not seein' it was there in the first place."

Her wary look softened. Her "You're smooth" response wasn't uttered with malice but amusement.

"Mmm-hmm. But, darlin', I'm rough too." He kissed

straight down her chin, over the vulnerable spot in her neck where her pulse pounded. He buried his face between her drool-worthy tits, then slid his mouth up the generous swell, nipping at the skin surrounding the pale pink tip but purposely avoiding putting his mouth directly on the tempting morsel.

"You trying to drive me crazy?"

Devin dragged his mouth back down the slope, stopping to nestle his face into her abundant flesh, kissing up the other side. Treating her with the exact same nip-and-nuzzle combination. But then he detoured to the tender outside of her full breast before his tongue followed the crease back to the center of her torso.

He glanced up at her, mesmerized by the flush on her cheeks, the tousled condition of her hair, the lust in her eyes and the rise and fall of her magnificent chest. "I'll come back to these. But first I need to fuck you with my mouth. Spread your legs."

"Very smooth," she murmured and inched her heels out.

Devin inserted himself between her legs, putting his hands on her inner thighs to push them even farther apart. The dim lighting left those delectable feminine bits in shadow. He stroked the inside of the cleft with his thumbs. So slick and hot. The tip of his tongue flicked over her clit.

Liberty immediately jerked up.

"Stay still." He followed the contours of her sex down to her opening. Once his tongue dipped into that sweet, sticky goodness, his plan to tease her until she begged flew right out the back of the fucking bus. Keeping his tongue stiff, he pushed it into her pussy and licked those silky, pulsing walls.

"Oh, damn. You are very, very good at that."

He rammed his tongue into her again and again. Fluttering

his tongue up her slit to swirl across her clit, then licking back down. All the way down to lap at the juices coating her tight asshole. He wouldn't deny himself any part of her body. The sooner she understood he liked raunchy sex of all flavors, the better.

Liberty clenched her thighs as he pushed her closer to the edge. The friction of the cool sheet against his hot length felt damn good. He forced himself not to hump the mattress. But if he secretly rubbed one off, he'd last longer for the next go.

Nah. He'd had enough of his own hand in the last month.

She urged him, "Devin, please. I'm close."

He suctioned his mouth to her clit and slipped two fingers into her cunt to stroke her G-spot.

That sent her into orbit. She gasped and then seemed to stop breathing entirely as her body writhed and bucked, vibrating like a tuning fork.

It'd been so long since he'd allowed himself this intimacy that he'd forgotten how much he loved going down on a woman. He glanced up, pleased that her arms were still above her head. Really pleased to see the glow of sexual satisfaction on her face.

Liberty sank into the mattress with a sigh.

Devin pushed up onto all fours. He brushed his lips over her right hip bone, stringing kisses over the sensitive skin until he reached her left hip bone. Every long, sweeping upward pass of his hungry mouth brought him closer to the mouthwatering tits he hadn't fully explored.

"Can I touch you now?" she asked, a bit breathlessly.

"Nope. I'm still touching you." He tongued her nipple. "How sensitive are your tits?"

"What do you mean?"

Devin kissed the tip. "You admitted you've kept them bound for years. Has it affected sensitivity?"

"Not that I've noticed."

He enclosed the nipple in his teeth and bit down until she gasped, then drew the tip into his mouth and gently suckled away the sting. The section of skin along her side seemed particularly sensitive, so he caressed and stroked that area while he focused on the other breast.

"You weren't kidding when you said you'd worship my chest," she murmured huskily.

"Hard to tear myself away from perfection." He flattened his palm and inched his hand down the center of her body until he reached her mound. His middle and index finger followed the split in her sex to her wet opening. Then he shoved the fingers in and rotated his hand to manipulate her clit with his thumb. "I want to get you off before I fuck you again."

"And if I said I'd rather you just fucked me now?"

Devin lifted his mouth from her nipple long enough to answer. "I'd say it don't matter what *you'd rather* and you'd better come fast." He blew a stream of air over the wet tip just to hear that throaty moan.

"I can't come again. God. You made me come three times already."

He grinned at her. "And isn't that a helluva nice surprise for me? Because knowing you *can* come like that?" He planted kisses down her belly. "Sweet"—*kiss*—"hot"—*kiss*—"sexy"—*kiss*—"woman of mine. I'm on a fuckin' *mission* to make you come like that every time."

"Devin. Seriously. I can't."

"You know I'm gonna make you eat them words . . ." He dropped between her thighs. "Right after I eat you."

Maybe it surprised Liberty that she came against his mouth in a pulsing wet rush about two minutes after he spread her wide open and feasted on her sweet pussy. But it didn't surprise him.

While she collected her brain cells, Devin rose to his knees and dug into the side dresser drawer, fishing out a new box of condoms.

As soon as he tore off a single plastic packet, Liberty sat up and plucked it from his fingertips. "I'll do that this time." She opened the package with her teeth. Keeping her fist around his shaft as she rolled the condom on, she leaned forward and kissed him.

Devin groaned—from her sure and steady touch on his cock and the kiss that turned him inside out.

She cupped her left hand around the nape of his neck, holding his head in place as her tongue explored his mouth. Then she whispered, "Betcha can't get me to come again."

He laughed against her smirking lips. "Challenge accepted."

∞

Afterward, they were lying side by side in his bed and he still had his hands—and alternately his mouth—all over her. He couldn't *not* touch her. And he'd turned on the lights to see her better while he touched her.

"Go ahead and ask," she said softly.

He traced the thick pinkish scar on the outside of her thigh above her knee. "This is where you were shot?"

"The shooter got me here"—she touched another scar on the upper right side of her chest below her collarbone—"and here"—her fingers slid over to another scar on the same side, two inches lower—"and by some weird trajectory, when he fired the third and fourth bullets, he hit my leg in almost exactly the same spot, so I have one big scar instead of two."

"On a scale of one to ten, how much did it hurt?"

"About a five when it happened. Then, when I was in the hospital, it jumped to a thousand. The first shot went clean through me and came out my back." Liberty rolled. "See that huge scar next to my shoulder blade? That's what an exit wound looks like."

Devin swept his thumb across the mark; his stomach cartwheeled thinking about what she'd been through.

"Open wounds like that take longer to heal. The second shot lodged in bone, so they had to operate to remove it. The medical staff over there is quick and efficient, but they patched me up after surgery and put me on a transport to Walter Reed."

He kept caressing her, wanting to hear about her ordeal and challenges while at the same time he wanted to distract her from the pain of her past.

"The weirdest part? That morning I left the barracks and reported for duty. After the incident, I was aware I was shot, aware I was headed for surgery. But then I didn't wake up again until I was in the hospital in the United States. It freaked me the fuck out."

"I can't imagine."

"By that time they'd called Harper. She and Bran and the boys showed up within two days of my arrival."

Devin wondered if his sister would show up that quickly if something happened to him.

Probably not. When have you been there for her?

"I hated that I was injured and I'd serve out the remainder of my enlistment on disability. Harper is a fixer. It about killed her that she couldn't just slap a Tweety Bird bandage on me and make it all better. Poor Bran had to deal with surly me, his distraught wife, a two-year-old and a baby. But he handled it all in that way he has about him. After a month of bed rest, I started physical therapy with a vengeance. By the time they discharged me, I was in the best shape of my life."

"I'll say," he murmured and bent down to kiss her scar. "Then what did you do?"

"Looked for work. But jobs were hard to come by. My years of specialized training meant I was qualified to be a security guard in an office building or a mall cop." She sighed. "I'm not belittling what they do; I just knew *I* couldn't do it. I hated school, so the idea of enrolling in higher education made me think that janitorial work wouldn't be so bad."

He laughed.

"Then I . . . meandered until I interviewed with GSC. The rest is history." Liberty faced him. "You were so quiet I thought maybe I'd put you to sleep."

"Not even close." He touched the scars on her chest again. "The reason you don't wear cleavage-baring shirts isn't because you wanna hide your impressive cleavage. It's because you wanna hide your scars."

Liberty blushed. "Well, yeah. I have scars everywhere. Not just those. But they are the newest, so they're the most prominent." She brought up her leg. "See this one?"

Devin reached down, curling his hand around her ankle. His thumb swept over the scar above her ankle bone. "What happened?"

"I broke my ankle when I was ten. We never had insurance, so my mom didn't take me to the doctor. By the time the school nurse saw it, I'd done some serious damage to the bones and ended up having several surgeries."

"I hope your mom felt like shit for not getting you in sooner."

"I doubt she even remembers it."

"You never talk about your mom."

"You never talk about yours either," she shot back.

Devin went motionless. Even when Liberty had told him that she planned to call him on his shit, he hadn't believed it. And he really didn't like it.

Except she was the first woman in a long time—maybe ever—who cared enough to even try to get past those monumental walls he'd erected.

"I'm sorry for snapping. There's not much to say—my mother needs a man in her life like she needs air. When men recognized she was the type of woman who'd suffocate them and bleed them dry, they left her. She never understood why. Besides, I haven't seen her in years, and if I never cross paths with her again . . ." She shrugged. "No great loss. I still have Harper and Bailey. I don't need her." She pulled the sheet up, covering her nakedness. "Now, are you done playing doctor with my scars?"

Devin was surprised she hadn't retreated into defensive mode sooner. So he kept it light. "I'm done. But I'm pretty sure at some point in the next two months I'm gonna play connect the dots on your body." He ran his hand down the side of her face. "I'm debating on whether whipped cream or chocolate syrup would be better to draw the lines between your freckles."

"How about . . . both?"

He chuckled. "Definitely gonna be fun goin' to the store with you."

Chapter Fifteen

❧

*L*iberty wasn't used to waking up naked.

Not that she was cold. Devin was practically lying on top of her as she was sprawled on her belly in his big bed.

She shifted slightly and he rolled to his back, freeing her.

Should she sneak out? Wake him up? Hop in the shower and hope he joined her? The bus was still moving, which meant they'd stopped for gas while she and Devin had been conked out. Or they hadn't noticed the bus stopping as they'd banged each other's brains out.

Three times.

Three incredible times.

The man had certainly made her body sing last night. Holy shit, the things he could do with that golden mouth . . .

"What time is it?" he asked, his voice sandpaper rough.

"I was just about to go check."

Then he rolled her to face him. He gave her a soft smile and reached out to run his knuckles down her cheek. "Stay in bed with me a little longer."

"Once I wake up, I'm up. I can't go back to sleep."

"Who said anything about sleepin'?"

"Well, I thought . . ."

"That this was just a one-night thing with me? Wrong. And, sugar, you knew that goin' into it last night."

She blinked at him, unsure what she should say or do.

Turned out she didn't need to do anything, because Devin just took over.

He knocked the pillows aside and traced the length of her arm from her shoulder to her wrist with such erotic intent, she shivered. "I want you. My way. Arms above your head, palms facing the ceiling."

Here was the test between them.

Part of her had attributed his aggressiveness last night to the fact they were finally acting on the sexual tension between them. But the heated look in Devin's eye wasn't playful or teasing.

Liberty had spent her life taking orders from men. But she'd always drawn the line in the bedroom. In her experience, most men needed direction when it came to sex, and she was more than happy to provide it.

But Devin had hit all her hot spots last night without any input from her besides moans and gasps of pleasure.

That's because he's been with so many women he's got a big playbook and he knows all the right moves.

While she waffled and argued with herself, he kept up that sweeping caress, just on her arm. His eyes were a deep midnight blue, his breathing was slow and steady, but his cock was completely hard.

"I don't know how to do this," she admitted.

"That's the thing; you don't need to know anything. You just follow my instructions and I'll take care of the rest. I'll take care of you."

Sounded simple. So why was she making it so damn complicated?

"Liberty, do you trust me?"

She nodded.

"Yes or no. Say the words."

"Yes."

"Good." He wrapped his fingers around her forearm. "And did we do anything last night that you didn't like?"

Liberty started to shake her head, but remembered he wanted a verbal response. "No."

He smiled. "Then, darlin', what's the holdup?"

"What do you mean?"

"Put your arms above your head, palms facing up, like I told you to."

Keeping her eyes on his, she did as he asked.

Devin's gaze moved across her face and down, stopping above her breasts. "Now turn your head to the right and give me that sexy neck."

She closed her eyes as her forehead connected with her biceps.

Then his body crowded hers. His warm lips brushed her ear and he placed his hand on her belly. "You have no idea what it does to me to have this trust from you." His hot breath teased the hollow below her earlobe and she trembled. "So I'll show you. Relax, baby, and let me have you."

That deep, lazy, sex-soaked voice rumbling against her skin set every nerve receptor in her body on high alert.

Devin's mouth followed the cords straining in her neck, treating her skin to nibbles, kisses, licks. The scrape of his teeth caused her to arch and moan.

"Like that, do you?"

"Yes." Liberty suppressed a whimper when he hit the sweet spot below her ear.

Of course Devin noticed. His lips skated over the swell of her upper breast. He latched onto her nipple and sucked, causing her to arch up.

After backing off on the suction, he kept his lips soft around her areola as his teeth sank into the distended tip. At first she loved that nip of pain, but then it was too much. "Ouch. Stop."

He laved the stinging skin and blew a stream of air over the wetness. "Tell me if I go too far. But I wonder if you just need a little distraction while I'm doin' that." He slipped his hand down her belly until his middle finger connected with her clit. His tongue and his finger rubbed each area in perfect synchronicity.

She was already embarrassingly wet and he'd barely touched her. When he teased the nub until it swelled beneath his finger, she fought against her normal response—to tell him exactly how to set her off. It was as much a test of her ability to hand her pleasure over to him as it was to see if he could make her crazy without any help.

About a minute later, Devin proved last night wasn't a fluke and he didn't need any instruction whatsoever. She couldn't stay quiet; she couldn't stay still when that first pulse throbbed against his finger. She gasped when his teeth sank into her nipple, harder than before, but somehow, it turned the pain into pleasure as she was coming.

Then he switched. He enclosed his mouth over her clit. His soft, wet tongue flicked over the swollen flesh, coaxing another orgasm from her as he pinched her other nipple hard. The second climax was short but intense, and she attempted to muffle her cry.

Her body quaked in the aftermath of back-to-back orgasms, and she focused on finding balance since Devin had knocked hers off-kilter.

Devin scattered soft kisses across her lower belly. "Look at me."

Liberty peeled her eyes open and turned her head. He was right there, nose to nose with her. "I expect to hear you come every time unless I tell you to keep quiet. Don't ever hide that from me."

"Okay."

"Now brace your hands against the headboard. And I do mean brace yourself, 'cause I need it fast and hard."

She watched as Devin snagged a condom off the dresser and rolled it on. But even as he did that, his gaze roamed over her with such hunger she shivered again. There was no sign of the charming, laid-back Devin as he scooted closer on his knees. He grabbed her ass cheeks and slowly slid them onto his thighs, the crisp hairs on his legs scraping over the soft globes of her ass in an erotic glide.

Pressing the backs of her legs against his chest, he held her right ankle by his left ear as he positioned his cock and drove into her.

He angled forward, curling his right hand over the top of the headboard and clamping his left arm over her legs as he pumped his hips. "Fuck, you feel good first thing in the morning."

"So do you." He looked good too. That mishmash of golden and dark curls was a tangled mess from her fingers. Stubble darkened his rugged face. There was a determined set to his jaw but a soft set to his mouth. And the way he fucked her—hard, deep, without pause. Damn. First he'd made it all about her; now it was all about him.

He drove into her faster. Sweat dampened his brow. She felt the slickness of his chest and his increased rate of breathing. She couldn't look away from him, hungering to see that moment he lost control. And when it finally happened, she bore down on his pistoning cock, her focus solely on the way his head fell back and how tightly his arm squeezed her thighs.

Devin came in silence, his expression fierce as he rode out his orgasm. But he didn't remain lost in bliss too long. He slid her legs to the mattress and stretched out on top of her, burying his face in her throat. "Christ, woman."

She reached around and ran her fingers through his silky hair just because she could. She'd wanted to get her hands in this sexy riot of soft curls since the first time she'd seen him without a hat on.

He nuzzled her neck. Then he lifted his head, peppering kisses across her lips, on her chin and then the tops of her breasts. "You wanna shower first?" He looked up when she didn't answer right away. "I'd like nothin' better than to shower with you, but we'd end up fucking again, and I don't want you to be too sore for what I've got in mind for tonight."

"Should I be worried?"

"Yep." He pushed up. "But I promise you'll like it."

Liberty crawled to the end of the bed. "I'll shower quickly since you probably want to get to work."

Devin's arm snaked around her just as she reached the bathroom door, and he spun her to face him. "You're okay with—"

"You fucking me raw and then kicking me out of your bed?" She laughed at his shocked look. "Kidding. I've been with you for a month, Devin. I won't infringe on your writing time just because we'll be banging the headboard in here. This change has to be positive for both of us or we should go back to the way things were."

He crowded her against the wall. "No way in hell are we goin' back. I just find it surprising"—he traced the frown line between her eyes—"or maybe I should say *refreshing* that you don't wanna—"

"Monopolize your free time? I'm not a . . ." Shit. *Wrong thing to say.*

"Groupie. Say it."

She lifted her chin. "I'm not a groupie, but after being naked with you, I know firsthand why groupies want to climb on and ride you like a fucking pony."

Devin grinned.

"I can separate my job as your protector from the woman who's your lover." Her eyes searched his. "Can you?"

"In the past, any woman who's been in my bed and on my bus wants me to act like a boyfriend all the time. That's why it's almost too easy for me to switch gears from it bein' about sex to it bein' about work. I didn't want you to feel like after last night and this morning I was bein' dismissive. Of you. Of this."

Dammit. This was recreational sex. Nothing more. She needed to remind him of that. "I need my personal space too. And I'll expect you to leave your aggressive lover side on the bus."

"That I can do." He kissed her forehead. "So many different roles we're playing. Is there any doubt one of us is gonna fuck something up?"

"As long as you let me do my job in public, I'll gladly let you put me in any role you want when the bus door closes."

"Remember you said that."

She stepped back and stared at him.

"What?"

"Handing you control was easier and more freeing than I thought it'd be. I've never done that before."

Devin growled. "Get in the damn shower before I change my mind and join you."

∞

They were thirty minutes late to the pancake house.

They took a rash of crap for it—undeserved because Devin had been working on a song, not working her over between the sheets. As soon as they grabbed seats, Devin scooted their chairs together so Liberty couldn't move any part of her body without bumping into his. While wanting her by his side was a bigger declaration of their together-ness than she'd expected, his closeness impeded her ability to get to her gun.

She murmured, "I'm on duty, so give me some space."

Devin stiffened. Then he placed his lips on her ear. "I'm pretty sure no one is gunning for me in Batesville."

"If they were, you're blocking me in. You know the deal. Our personal parameters changed last night, but the professional ones, especially in public, remain the same. Especially since three people recognized you the second you walked in."

He frowned at her. "Really? Already?"

"I never understand why that surprises you." She placed her hand on his cheek. "This is a memorable face. Too damn handsome for your own good."

"I like this flattering side of you." He angled his head and lightly bit the base of her thumb before he backed off.

She paid little attention to the band's conversation at the table. Or the stack of pancakes Devin ordered for her. Before she'd taken more than a few bites, the group of teenage girls in the corner got up and approached Devin.

"Ah, Mr. McClain?"

He whipped his head around. "That's me. What's up, ladies?"

"Omigod! You're, like, my favorite singer ever! I can't believe you're in my town!"

The other girls behind her squealed their excitement.

"Crash, would you take some pictures?"

Good to head them off before they could ask; it put him in control. Liberty stepped to the side, keeping an eye on the fans and the front door. As soon as the cell phone snapshots were done and he signed autographs, the girls practically floated out of the restaurant.

Then an angry woman stomped close enough to get right in his face. "I've heard your songs. You sing about sex, sex and more sex. And even homosexual sex. It's wrong to put them kind of nasty ideas in young girls' heads. I'm praying for you to find God's guidance in your life and use the talent he gave you to spread the Good Word."

"I appreciate the prayers, ma'am. You have a fine day."

She really had no comeback for that.

Devin returned to his seat. His food had gone cold. But he scooted up to the table and shoveled in what was left. Then he snatched the bacon off Liberty's plate and grinned at her while he crunched it.

"Hurry up," Crash said. "We've got an hour before we reach the venue, and we have to do a quick run-through as soon as we hit the parking lot."

"Why? We've played there before," Gage said.

"They upgraded the sound system since last time. I've been on the phone with Boomer. He's having a shit fit. Nothin' is going right. Half the speakers don't work, and amateurs are trying to tell him how to do his fucking job."

"Amateurs?" Devin repeated.

"Jesse-Belle's crew."

"We're done here." Devin stood and addressed everyone at the table. "Be ready to hit the stage as soon as the bus door opens. Got it?"

Mumbled *yeah*s echoed.

Liberty hadn't seen Devin so infuriated since he'd had front-of-house security haul out a guy in the front row after he'd punched his girlfriend in the face.

Devin had his phone out and was barking orders at someone as he exited the restaurant. She remained a few steps behind him, glancing around to see if the woman with the Bible intended to chase him down and thump him with it.

Reg reached the bus first and unlocked it. He and Liberty exchanged a look when Devin scaled the bus steps without pause.

"Thanks, Reg. Time to put the pedal to the metal, huh?"

"Sounds like, Miss Liberty."

Inside, Devin paced. "I don't give a damn. She can use our equipment, or I'll scratch her from the rest of the dates. Yeah? Go ahead and call Carl at Big Sky. I guarantee if it gets out that I dropped her from the tour, it'll be a long damn time before she gets another offer from anyone. No, sir, that is not a threat; it's a fact. I'm not letting some wet-behind-the-ears twenty-year-old diva fuck up one of my best venues." He paused. "You do that. We'll be there in less than an hour." He hung up. "Motherfucking hell."

"What's going on?"

"In a nutshell, Jesse-Belle's road crew can't get her equipment to work, which has delayed getting my stage show set up. We're sold out for tonight. The damn show starts late anyway, and I'm not sucking up *her* delays. I'll cut her. Double Trouble can do their set damn near acoustically, so I'm not worried about them." He tossed his phone on the bench. "Only ten shows with her, they said. How bad can it be? It's the second night and I want to send her packing."

Here's where the change in their relationship caused her hesitation and some confusion. Was she supposed to try to soothe him like a lover would? Or keep their interaction focused on business?

When Devin plopped down and rested his head against the back cushion with a sigh, she reacted instinctively. She straddled his lap, curled her hands around his face and kissed him. She didn't offer him comfort, but distraction.

He eased back and murmured, "You taste so damn sweet. Like maple syrup."

"And you taste like stolen bacon."

He laughed softly and returned to the kiss. Keeping it just as sweet and soothing as she had. No rush, just focusing on sliding lips, twining tongues and gentle touches.

Something shifted inside her.

No. It was just the bus swaying; that's all.

Devin's lips slid free from hers, and he followed the curve of her neck down to the top button of her blouse. "Thank you."

"Truly my pleasure. Is there anything else I can do?"

"Not now. But it's an understatement to say I don't trust her or that bunch of clowns she calls a management team. So just keep a closer eye on it tonight."

Liberty tipped his head back to look into his eyes. "Should I be worried to the point I'll need to add extra security?" Not that she could at this late in the day.

"Maybe around me so I'm not tempted to throttle her."

"I'm keeping my stun gun away from your twitchy fingers."

Devin sighed again—an agitated sound. "This venue is great for everything except there aren't any backstage accommodations other than sponsor tents."

"Want me to duck into my bunk so you can get into the right headspace?"

"Where would I warm up? In the shower? Wait. That's your special singing spot." His eyes narrowed. "That reminds me. We never talked about why you didn't mention you've got a killer voice."

She tried to squirm away. "Stop teasing me."

Then he wrapped his hand around the back of her neck and held her in place. "I'm serious. When I heard you singing in my shower I thought you were Tay."

"Maybe the manufacturer added excellent acoustics in the shower since this is a rockstar bus."

He made an annoyed noise. "If the acoustics were that damn good, I'd record my next album in there. So try again. Where'd you learn to sing so well that I confused you with a professional vocalist? Have you had training?"

"Are you kidding me? Half the time we didn't have enough money for food. I've always liked to sing. I still do. That's it."

"That's it, she says." He brushed his lips across hers. "So if you like to sing, sing with me."

"What? No way."

"Please." Another brush of his velvety lips.

"Devin. Don't."

"Sing with me one time and then I'll leave you alone."

She snorted. Right.

Then he started to hum. She recognized the song and the next line popped into her head. But her lips remained firmly closed.

"Come on, you know you want to. Sing a little something with me and I promise I'll play a song—any song you want—onstage tonight just for you."

Devin hummed louder. Then he switched to the actual lyrics. And she couldn't help herself when he hit the catchy chorus; she chimed in. So softly at first she doubted he heard her.

But he immediately matched her softer tone, so their voices were the same strength. On the next line, Devin sang harmony as she kept up the melody.

When they reached the end of the tune, Devin grinned and kissed her. "Screw bein' my bodyguard. I'm makin' you my new backup singer."

Liberty blushed. "High praise. Thank you."

"Would it be over-the-top if I said, *Baby, we're gonna make beautiful music together*?"

"Yes, and it makes you a total dork."

"You wound me, darlin'." He slapped her ass. "I gotta get ready."

"I need to make a phone call anyway."

Devin was so distracted he didn't ask who she was calling.

Which was a good thing because the call she needed to make might end everything.

∞

"Garrett."

"Liberty. I'm surprised to hear from you in person. You usually e-mail me your reports. What's goin' on?"

"Something came up, and I don't know what to do."

"What happened?"

No reason to make polite chitchat. She blurted out, "I slept with Devin."

A pause, then, "I assume it was by mutual consent?"

"Of course."

"Is he demanding replacement security?"

"No. In fact, just the opposite. Devin seems to think we're in some sort of personal relationship."

"Of course he does," Garrett drawled. "Think that'll put him in danger? He expects you to act like his girlfriend and not as his bodyguard?"

Liberty leaned her head against the plush padding in her bunk wall. "To be honest, I'm not sure. This is a job, but yet it feels different somehow." Until now she'd avoided drawing parallels between this situation and the one with her commanding officer. They were similar in that she and Sean had to keep what they were doing a secret; they both could've faced disciplinary actions. Devin wasn't asking her to keep their intimate relationship under wraps, but her purpose for being with him, who she really was, was a secret from the rest of the band. Part of her thought that was a harder pill to swallow.

When Garrett didn't respond, her brain chimed in with the serious repercussions she was trying to ignore.

Was fucking him worth losing your job? Worth losing one hundred thousand dollars? Worth losing your self-respect, to think that you're just another woman who fell into Devin McClain's bed?

She couldn't stand the silence any longer. "Garrett? Are you so quiet because you're booking plane tickets?"

"Excuse me?"

"I worried that when I told you about Devin and me becoming lovers, you'd have my ass on the next plane back to Denver."

"Is that what you want?"

"No! It's just . . . the fact that you're not freaking out about this is freaking me out a little."

Garrett said, "Gimme a minute, okay?"

"Fine." He put her on hold and canned Muzak tortured her ear. Who thought an instrumental version of "Smells like Teen Spirit" was a good idea?

Maybe Garrett wouldn't shitcan her. Maybe he'd just pull her off the assignment.

Why did the thought of leaving Devin make her sad and not like she'd dodged a personal and professional bullet?

"I'm back. This might be the understatement of the year, but besides your bedroom antics, you and Devin are getting along well?"

"Yes. He takes the security issues seriously. He listens to me and trusts me."

"Look. If it were anyone else, I'd pull them off assignment, but I suspected something like this would happen. And before your outrage burns through the telephone lines and zaps my brain stem, lemme explain something. It is not that uncommon when people are in close quarters like you two have been that an intimate relationship will develop."

Relief swept through her, followed quickly by a niggling suspicion. "You didn't plan for this to happen, did you?"

"No, but I'm not naive either. So be warned: There's truth in that movie *The Bodyguard*—how it played out and how it ended."

It ended badly, if she recalled correctly.

"When the period of danger is over for the client, the guard and the client go their separate ways." He paused. "Is that what worries you? Have you fallen for him?"

No. Not yet. Okay, maybe a little. "No. I just . . . I wasn't sure if sleeping with the client was a firing offense. The situation wasn't addressed in the employee handbook."

Garrett chuckled. "As long as you can be honest about your ability to still do your job at the same commitment level as when you started the assignment, then I don't have a problem with it. But if there's a change in dynamic on either side, you'll need to inform me ASAP."

"Understood."

"I never doubted your ability to handle this job, Liberty. But I avoid assigning opposite-sex bodyguards to clients for any length of time for this very reason."

"Great. I'm a cliché now too."

"Not yet. So do you want me to tell the promotion company that your relationship with Devin has become intimate and see how they weigh in?"

She chewed on her lip. "I'll leave that decision up to you."

"Then as far as I'm concerned, everything is goin' according to the contract we signed. I'll leave it as is for now. They were the ones who insisted on hiring you. They were the ones who suggested you pose as his girlfriend before we settled on the personal assistant title. They really can't be shocked that you two became sexually involved."

"True."

"Can I give you some advice?"

Unsolicited advice from Garrett Barker? This oughta be good.

"Make sure to take it at face value. The minute you start thinkin' that you've found something real and start makin' plans with him . . . it'll fall apart."

"Are you speaking from personal experience, Garrett?"

A pause followed. "Yeah. Didn't end pretty. I did my job and kept her safe. She walked away intact, which I was paid to ensure. I limped away, half-goddamn-broken, and that fucked me up big-time."

"If you had it to do all over again, would you take the job?"

"Yes. But I'd remember it was just a job. It's not real."

Liberty tipped her head back, knowing in her gut he was exactly right. "Thanks for talking to me."

"Anytime. Stay safe. Keep in touch."

"I will." She ended the call and tossed her phone on the bed, relieved and yet also worried if she and Devin kept up the level of not only sexual intensity, but intimacy, she'd be nursing a broken heart.

Chapter Sixteen

❦

$\mathcal{A}$ week of having Liberty in his bed and Devin still couldn't get enough of her.

And after the high-energy performance he'd just given—he loved rowdy, loud crowds, especially during a rare afternoon concert—he was damn near desperate to prolong that adrenaline rush.

They were in the media room, acting civilized.

He felt anything but civilized.

Devin angled his head and murmured, "I want to fuck you. Now."

No one else saw it, but he felt Liberty tremble against him.

"Devin McClain." A booming voice echoed behind him.

As he turned to face the man, he let his fingers sweep across the bottom of Liberty's ass.

She hissed, "Stop it."

"You don't want me to stop."

He forced a smile for Jarvis Barnes, the program director for the biggest country music station in three states, and held out his hand when the man finally waddled toward him. "Jarvis. Good to see you again."

"You too. Can't believe it's been a year. The new album is doin' great. Congrats on 'Broken Beams' hitting number two."

"Thanks. The fact it's become a fan favorite has taken the sting outta missing that number-one spot."

"Your next single will get there. And, son, I'd really like an exclusive on which song that's gonna be. Especially since we didn't get you booked for an interview at the station this time."

"Tell you what. My assistant and I were just headed back to my ready room to make a few calls and go over some last-minute schedule changes. I'll see what Don at the label says and he'll get back to you."

"Great." He clapped Devin on the back. "Spectacular show today."

"Thanks." Devin stepped back and looked at Liberty. "Let's get this handled."

As soon as they were out of view, he put his hand on the small of her back and said, "I didn't introduce you to Jarvis because he's the type of DJ who's always lookin' to scoop his competition. I don't want him takin' notice of you, let alone mentioning you on air."

"Because you're afraid he'll find out I'm not really your PA, but your bodyguard?"

"No. I don't wanna share what's goin' on between us with anyone in this industry. I deserve to have a private life."

"So I'm just your dirty little secret, Mr. McClain?"

"Yes. And I make no apologies for keepin' all the dirty things we do to each other a secret and enjoying the hell out of every single one."

After a quick nod of acknowledgment to the security guard, Liberty punched in the code that unlocked the door. As soon as they were inside, Devin slid the dead bolt home and pressed the front of her body against the metal door, grinding his erection into her ass.

"I need to be inside you," he said as he trailed his nose down the arch of her neck, filling his lungs with her chocolate and vanilla scent.

"Then stop distracting me at least until I'm unarmed."

"Hurry up."

She pushed him aside, pulling her piece from her waist holster as she walked to the middle of the room to set it on the sofa table.

Devin followed her and snagged a condom out of his duffel bag. As he watched her strip to skin, an animalistic hunger arose. He unbuckled his belt, dropping his jeans and boxer briefs to the tops of his boots. Then he rolled the condom on.

He moved in behind her, and his mouth connected with her ear. "Sexy fuckin' woman. You're a damn drug." He grabbed a handful of her hair, urging her to turn her head. Their mouths met, and the kiss was electric. Passionate. Ramping his need higher.

She made that soft whimper against his mouth when his right hand cupped her mound. He traced her slit with his middle finger, spreading her juices up to her clit. She broke the kiss on a gasp. "We've been in here like three minutes. The second you touch me I'm ready to explode."

"Hands on the back of the couch." Devin slipped two fingers inside her. The tight, slick heat tempted the animal inside him to ignore everything but slamming his cock into her. She'd be good with that—Liberty turned her pleasure over to him completely.

"Devin, I need—"

"Don't push me to get you there faster or I'll make you wait longer."

"You get off on that."

"Yeah, baby, I do. And so do you." But he didn't plan to make her wait this time. With her being tall, he could reach all her hot spots without bending down too far, keeping his mouth attached to her skin as she unraveled.

She started pushing her hips down to try to increase the friction on her clit and shove his fingers deeper inside her. "Don't stop. Please."

"I'll make you come, but you gotta come quietly. Understand?"

She nodded.

He fisted his hand in her hair, pulling hard at the same time he took her earlobe between his teeth and bit down.

A sharp bite of pain, his fingers stroking those wet walls, his teeth on her skin and the rapid rubbing of his thumb over her clit tipped her over the edge.

She bit her lip to stifle the moans as her pussy spasmed around his fingers and pulsed against his thumb.

"Fuck, you're coming hard. This hot cunt is tryin' to pull my whole hand inside you."

She whimpered when he dragged an openmouthed kiss beneath her ear and sucked on the spot that made her wilder yet.

Once the pulses ended, he eased his wet fingers out of her pussy. He growled, "Bend over." As soon as her belly rested on the back of the couch, he aimed his cock at her warm center and plunged inside.

Fuck, fuck, fuck. There was nothing in the world like this.

With both his hands on her hips, his rhythm became

frantic. He should've lasted longer, but the heat that blazed between them was impossible to resist.

She was impossible to resist when she arched her back, allowing him to drive into her deeper yet.

He made a low noise in the back of his throat and slammed into her, completely pulling out on each stroke.

Then *wham*, he was coming, and her cunt muscles clamped down, slowing his thrusts so he felt every spurt almost in slow motion.

When her body squeezed the last throb from his dick, his hands landed beside hers. His chest resting on her back, his mouth at her ear. "You okay?"

"I'm always okay when you're fucking me." Liberty turned her face to his and rubbed their cheeks together. "I've never had a man want me the way you do. So every time you drag me off and press me up against something or bend me over something, I feel . . ."

"What?"

"Like I'm enough."

Devin pulled out and gently spun her around, holding her face in his hands and kissing her. What would it take to get her to believe he didn't want anyone else—just her? Didn't she know how rare and special it was that for the first time in his adult life he'd found a woman who wanted him just for him, not for the outward trappings?

Her arms circled his waist, and she spread her hands over his shoulder blades, digging her nails into his skin.

He slowed the kiss and spoke softly when their lips were a breath apart. "You're beyond enough. You're—this is so much more than anything I thought I'd ever have."

"You trying to turn my knees weak?"

"Yep, because you've got an awfully strong will."

She laughed softly.

Devin placed one last kiss on her sweet lips and he stepped back to right his clothing. He headed to the bathroom to flush the condom. He washed his hands and his face, staring at himself in the mirror. He didn't look different on the outside, but inside was a whole other matter. Being with Liberty changed him. Even if she didn't know it—or believe it—he did and that was all that mattered.

Liberty had already concealed her gun in that funky, slim-fitting pantsuit she wore and waited by the door. "What time are you supposed to be at the children's hospital?"

"In an hour. Traffic is notoriously bad here, so we'd better get goin'."

Those magnetic eyes searched his. "Did you call a car service?"

"No. Crash rented me a car."

"Devin. I don't know how safe—"

"No one will recognize me. Plus, I wanted to take you someplace nice for supper." He tugged on a chunk of her blue hair. "You know how I am after these things. You deserve a decent meal for havin' to deal with my brooding."

∞

Everything started out all right at the children's hospital. The staff had set up a big room for them. In addition to designating a performing area, they'd arranged a table for a craft project. The slightly horrified look on Liberty's face when she realized she'd have to make something out of tongue depressors and cotton balls forced him to turn away to hide his grin.

Devin always spent time with the nurses and aides before the visit. Medical science and the doctors might work miracles, but these people were in the trenches with these kids every day, every night, every step of the way.

These were the true heroes.

As much as he wanted—needed—to do these visits, they weren't easy. No matter how many times he'd done them, he walked into the hospital with a tight knot in his stomach. Usually at the thirty-minute mark he'd realize he'd relaxed and that knot loosened. It felt natural joking around with the kids, singing a few songs. Letting the oldest kid in the room jam on his acoustic guitar.

Normally Liberty remained outside during these visits. But today she sat in the corner—farthest away from the craft table—and closest to him.

He'd just finished playing one of his kid-friendly songs, "That Dog Don't Hunt," when he asked if anyone had a request.

A frail-looking girl in the back shuffled forward, dragging her IV behind her. She stopped right in front of him and wheezed until she caught her breath. "I have a request."

"Sure, sweetheart. What would you like to hear?"

"'You Are My Sunshine.'"

That knot in his belly tightened up again. He never played this song, even though it was great for kids to sing along to. He never played that song because it was the first—and last—song his sister had sung. He managed to ask, "Why that song?"

"My sister sings it to me when I'm sad to cheer me up."

"Are you sad today?"

She nodded.

"Why?"

"Because my sister couldn't come visit me this week. I miss her."

"If I play it, will you sing along with me?"

Her eyes lit up. "Really?"

"Really." He strummed the opening chord. "What's your name?"

"Michelle."

That's when his world fell in. That's when he couldn't breathe; he couldn't move; he couldn't think. He stared at the girl in front of him—the same age, the same coloring as his sister—and for a split second, her image wavered and she *was* his Michelle.

The knot in his stomach crawled into his throat and threatened to choke him.

He must've made some distressed sound, because Liberty was by his side in an instant. She smiled at the girl and said, "Give us a moment, okay?"

Then Liberty's cool hand rested on the back of his neck and her voice broke through the roaring in his ears. "Devin. Breathe. You're all right. Just take a quick break."

He moved his mouth, but no sound came out.

But somehow, tears were streaming down his face. Every anguished second he'd spent missing and mourning his sister rolled over him in an unending wave of sorrow.

Liberty pried his fingers off the neck of his guitar and plucked it out of his hands. She faced the room, blocking him from view.

"You guys ever get a frog in your throat?"

A few kids made a *ribbit ribbit* sound.

She laughed. "Just like that. It even happens to professional singers. So while Devin gets a drink and tries to drown that frog, you're stuck doing a sing-along with me. Problem is . . . I don't play guitar."

While she cajoled the kid from earlier to come up front and play, Devin found the will to move. He coughed a few times as he scooted over to the refreshment table.

A nurse handed him a cup of water. Another nurse

rubbed soothing circles on his back and whispered, "It's okay. It never gets easier for any of us either."

At some point he crawled out of the dark hole of memories and refocused on the present.

Liberty had a rollicking round of "Row, Row, Row Your Boat" started that ended in fits of giggles and laughter.

When he smiled at her, the tense set of her shoulders relaxed. He drained his water and strode toward her.

"How about a round of applause for Miss Liberty Bell?"

She rolled her eyes at him.

He settled on the chair with his guitar. "Before I honor Michelle's request"—he swallowed hard—"how about if I get that frog in my throat to sing like Kermit? Anyone wanna hear 'Rainbow Connection'?"

The kids clapped and a few even whistled.

Still, when he ended the song, he knew what was next.

Devin picked at the strings until he sensed the kids getting restless. Enough stalling. "Michelle requested 'You Are My Sunshine' and I'm thinkin' it must be a Michelle thing, since that was a favorite song of my little sister, Michelle, as well." He strummed the opening chord and started to sing. But when he hit the fourth line, his voice didn't falter; it plain gave out.

Liberty jumped in with her pure alto, and the wave of relief brought tears to his eyes. By the time she started the chorus, he'd chimed back in and harmonized with her to the end.

The nurse in charge took that as her cue. "Everyone say thank you to Devin and Liberty for stopping by to entertain us today."

When the kids mobbed him, Liberty hovered—but not for the same reasons as she usually did. And as they walked out of the hospital, she held her hands out for the keys, knowing he was too distracted to get behind the wheel.

She didn't ask where to. She just drove, leaving him to work through the things he normally tried so hard to forget.

When Devin finally snapped out of his stupor, he realized they were parked in front of a . . . ? He craned his neck to look up at the flashing neon sign with a pin and two bowling balls that resembled a cock and balls. "Where are we?"

"Duh. At a bowling alley."

"Why are we at a bowling alley?"

"Because the name of this joint is Liberty Lanes. Come on, Devin. That's a sign!"

"I think the gigantic dick and balls sign is what first caught your eye," he said dryly, "not your name in neon."

"That too. The big dick and balls reminded me of you, baby," she cooed with total sarcasm.

"Nice. So we just parked here until I got my head out of my ass or what?" Jesus. *Being a dick much?* Liberty had been such a godsend to him today. He hated that he couldn't stop that snappish tone.

But she gave it right back to him. "No, smart-ass. I've let you wallow long enough. You promised me supper of my choosing, and I'm choosing greasy bowling alley food." She tapped on the windshield. "And look. It's karaoke night!"

"You've *got* to be fucking kiddin' me."

"Nope. Usually I'd avoid bringing you into a place like this, but look at the parking lot. Totally empty."

"Don't you think that might be a sign that this place, oh, I don't know . . . *sucks*?"

"Again with the attitude, guitar slinger. Where's your sense of adventure? Besides, being here kills two birds with one stone. You can make good on both promises you made me."

"Food is one. What's the other?"

Liberty grabbed his hand and looked so sincere he automatically went into defensive mode. "Last week when you forced me to sing a little duet with you on the bus? You promised to sing any song I wanted onstage. *Any* song. And you didn't do it that night, so I'm picking this night and this stage for you to fulfill that promise."

"You're joking, right?"

"No, sir, I am not."

He was so fucked. So, so, so fucked.

But he'd show no fear.

Devin grinned. "Bring it."

∞

After thirty minutes passed and no one recognized him, Devin started to relax.

Liberty was in rare form—sarcastic, hilarious and sweet. He realized she needed a place to let her guard down besides the bus. He also realized how much he liked her as a person, beyond her persona as his bodyguard and his uninhibited lover.

The burgers and fries were excellent. As was the enormous piece of lemon meringue pie the waitress insisted was homemade.

They ventured into the lounge. Although smoking had been banned years ago, the place retained that musky odor. It reminded him of the years he'd played in tiny bars and any place that would have him. So he couldn't resist checking out the jukebox to see if any of his songs were offered.

"What're you grinning about?"

Devin pointed to "Broken Beams" on the selection page. "It's corny, but I still love seein' my name and my song on one of these. When I played these places . . . I dreamed I'd see this one day."

Liberty handed him a beer. "We'll each have one." She sipped. "Besides, you'll need it when you see what song I've picked out for you to sing for me."

"Foo Fighters?" he said hopefully.

She laughed. And it had a mean edge.

Shit.

She'd selected a booth right up by the stage. He looked around. There were a total of six patrons in here. Two at the bar, two watching professional bowling on TV, and them.

Devin slid next to her in the booth. "You're really makin' me do this."

"Yep."

"Technically, you can't *make* me do it, but I will do it if you sing a duet with me." He offered her a dazzling smile. "Which I get to pick."

"I'm game." Her eyes flashed a warning. "Just as long as the song isn't 'I Touch Myself' by the Divinyls."

"Deal."

The stage lights came up—a sickly neon green—and the female MC tapped the microphone twice. "All right, ladies and gentlemen, it's that time—time to get up here and shine. Time to strut your stuff. Time to sing your heart out. To get us warmed up for tonight's karaoke, brought to you by Grain Belt beer, I'll get things started."

"Fifty bucks says it's 'The Rose,'" Liberty said.

"You're on. I'm betting it's Patsy Cline's 'Crazy.'"

The MC nodded to the sound guy.

When the repetitive piano chord started, Liberty held out her hand. "Pay up, rockstar."

Devin took out his wallet and slapped cash in her hand. "For the record, 'The Rose' was my first choice for her too."

"Better be quicker on the draw next time. Ooh, and speaking of next time, you'll be up next."

"Take pity on me."

"Not. A. Chance. You could've sung a Maroon 5 song to me the other night, but you blew it."

"You're a Maroon 5 fan?"

"A *huge* Maroon 5 fan," she corrected.

"Why?"

"Have you seen Adam Levine? Dude. He's the hottest man in the universe." She patted his hand. "Present company excepted, of course."

"That's it? You like them because the lead singer is hot?"

"Oh, knock off the indignant act. Your good looks have helped more than they've hindered you." She sipped her beer. "But, honestly, I love their music. From songs that evoke pure sex, to heart-wrenching ballads, to catchy pop tunes, to songs you can dance to. They mix it up on every album."

She'd hit it dead-on why he appreciated their music too.

The loud, totally off-key rendition of "The Rose" ended.

Liberty handed him a folded slip of paper, trying—and failing—to hide a smirk. "You don't get to look at that until right before you hand it to the DJ."

Devin took a big swig of beer before he stood. "I'm gonna sing the hell out of this song."

Why was he so damn nervous as he walked up to the

DJ booth? He sang in front of thousands of people almost every night. When he peeked at the song she'd written down, he had every right to be nervous.

Christ. He needed a shot. Or ten.

His cheeks were flaming when he stepped onstage. He adjusted his ball cap and grabbed the microphone, waiting for the words to appear on the screen behind him.

The distinctive brass sounds of horns started off Shania Twain's "Man! I Feel Like a Woman!" and Devin dove right in.

After he finished the first chorus, he looked over at a laughing Liberty, who gave him two thumbs-up. So he hammered it up, doing his best hip-swiveling, shoulder-shaking Shania impression.

Liberty laughed so hard he swore he saw beer come out her nose.

She leaped to her feet in a standing ovation when he exited the stage. Then she threw her arms around his neck. "That. Was. Fantastic. You rocked my world." She kissed him with such pure happiness that he had to laugh.

The MC returned to the stage. "Thank you. That was, ah . . . interesting. If we don't have any other takers, I've got a favorite or two I'd like to share with you tonight."

"Wanna go double or nothin' on her next selection?" he challenged.

Liberty said, "You got a Benjamin in that wallet you wanna part with? Sure. You pick first."

"I say she sings, 'My Heart Will Go On,'" Devin said smugly.

"Nope. She'll be warbling a different Shania tune. 'You're Still the One.'"

They clinked bottles, sealing the bet.

Devin's jaw dropped when Liberty won the bet again.

He handed her a hundred. "Dammit, woman. Are you psychic?"

She shook her head. "Just spent way too much time around karaoke. Not a lot of other activities to choose from during deployment."

"You ever get up there and sing?"

"Huh-uh. Much easier to make fun of people than to do it myself."

"Well, that's not an option tonight, darlin'. And I know what duet we're singing." His eyes gleamed. "I want a chance to earn my money back. Fifty bucks says you can't guess what song I'm picking."

"Oh, honey, I'm starting to feel guilty about taking all your money, but I'm game. You gotta give me a second to work this out." She tapped her chin as if in deep thought. "A Faith and Tim song is too obvious. You probably want me to think you'll choose a country song, when you'll be thinking of something like 'I Got You Babe' by Sonny and Cher or 'You Don't Bring Me Flowers' by Neil Diamond and Barbra Streisand."

"I ain't got all night. She's about done."

"Hang on. 'You're the One That I Want' is too clichéd. As is 'Don't Go Breaking My Heart.'"

"Ticktock, sweetheart."

She grinned. "Got it." She scrawled on a piece of paper, folded it and handed it over.

"Let's go." He held her hand as they walked to the DJ stand. Then he held her eyes when he said, "Do you have 'Louisiana Woman, Mississippi Man' as a selection?" to the DJ.

Huh. No look of victory on Liberty's face now.

Imagine that.

Devin made a big show of unfolding the paper. "Wow.

Guess you were *wrong*, darlin'. I didn't pick 'Jackson' by Johnny Cash and June Carter."

"You suck."

"Aw, now, is that any way to speak to your duet partner?" He nudged her. "Go on, now. Let's do this thang."

"Jesus."

But he knew she was having a good time when she twirled her microphone cord like Loretta. His pants weren't tight enough for a Conway Twitty impersonation, so he didn't even try. After they finished the song with zero reaction from the bar, she said, "I'm picking the next duet."

Which, of course, was "Jackson."

Back at the table, she scowled at her Coke. "I really want another beer."

"Have one. I'll drive."

"Thanks, but I'm guarding your body after we leave here, remember?"

Devin ran his knuckles down her cheek. "I was havin' so much fun with you that I forgot." He kissed her. Sweetly, but as always, it was laced with heat. "Let's go."

"Wait a sec. Have you ever karaoked one of your songs?"

"Never. Why?"

Liberty brushed her lips over his. "Because this is your perfect chance to do it. Sort of like seeing your name in the jukebox. Won't you feel a little vindicated that you're singing a chart-topping song in a dive bar like you used to play in?"

"No."

"I dare you."

He snorted. "Like that'll work."

"Then I'll make it worth your while." She placed her hand on his groin and started to rub his cock.

"Dammit, Liberty. The last thing I need is a fucking hard-on in here."

"Because you're gonna go up there and sing for me, aren't you?" she cooed. She kept rubbing his cock. His cock kept liking it.

His mind took a hike for a second.

His mind must've taken a longer hike than he realized because when he came to, Liberty said, "See? *That's* the spirit!" and practically shoved him out of the booth.

His cock pouted.

So just for shits and giggles, Devin picked his least favorite song, "Beat-up Truck." At first he planned to totally massacre it, but then he decided to pretend he was just a guy, singing a song to impress his girl. He closed his eyes and tried to remember how he felt the first time he'd ever sung this song.

After he finished the last note, he looked over at Liberty just as someone from the back of the room yelled, "You suck! Get off the stage!"

The MC tried to smooth things over by exclaiming, "Well, I didn't think he was *that* bad. It ain't easy to get up on this stage. Karaoke is a great way to define your vocal limits." She smiled at Devin encouragingly. "If you have the guts to get up here again, I know just the song that's better suited to your abilities. That's why I'm here. To help!"

Finally someone in the back clapped.

"Here's another one of my favorites." The MC practically pushed him off the stage. Then she nodded to the DJ and launched into "Emotions" by Mariah Carey.

The fifty feet to the booth felt like a walk of shame.

"Good thing I don't have aspirations for a musical career," he said dryly.

Liberty was laughing so hard she had to hold her stomach. She slid out of the booth and whapped his biceps. "Stop it. I'm gonna pee my pants."

"Find this amusing, do you?"

"Yes. My God. If they only knew." She hooked her arm through his as they cut out the side door. "Just think what a great sound bite that'll make for an interview."

Devin stopped. He framed her face in his hands. "I'd never do that—use that story. I don't want to share a personal part of my life just for entertainment's sake. That's mine and yours."

She stared at him with such a soft, sweet look that he was momentarily stunned. "Then I'm so glad we had tonight, Devin."

"Me too, sweetheart. And thank you. For what you did at the hospital."

"You're welcome. I'm just glad I got out of making crafts."

He kissed her forehead. "One thing you're not getting out of? You promised to make my humiliation onstage worth my while. And I'm thinking a hand job in the car will take the edge off until we get to the bus."

Chapter Seventeen

❦

*D*evin had her shirt off.
    Again.

He'd talked her into wearing a noncompression bra.
Again.

That wicked, sensual mouth and those skillful hands were turning her mindless as he teased her to the begging point.

Again.

"Devin."

"I'm getting there, sweetheart." He dragged his razor-stubbled cheek over the lacy edge of her bra cup. Then his tongue snaked under the lace and the end almost reached her hard nipple. Almost. He did that twice more.

"Devin!"

The evil man chuckled and then sank his teeth into the top of her breast and sucked hard. Really hard. Hard enough to leave a mark.

"You could do that a few inches down," she murmured huskily. "You can't miss the spot. It's sticking straight out."

"Lord, woman. You've got no patience."

"Says the man who fucked me on the bus stairs last night."

"I don't remember those noises you were makin' sounding much like complaints." His hands squeezed her ass cheeks. "I was insane to have you. In a goddamn fog of lust. Even after five weeks of you bein' in my bed, this need for you hasn't cooled."

"Devin—"

"Let me finish. I saw you waitin' for me at the edge of the stage and I just . . ." He exhaled across the damp love bites he'd placed on her chest. "I thought I was bein' all gentlemanly and shit waitin' until we reached the bus to strip you bare and bend you over."

Liberty groaned. When it came to sex talk, the man didn't mince words.

"Pull down the bra cups so I can get at your nipples," he rasped against her throat. "I want your pussy sopping wet when I fuck you."

She watched the hunger flare his blue eyes to midnight as she lowered her bra straps, when someone started beating on the door.

Devin moved her off his lap and tossed her the baggy T-shirt she'd had on. "Whoever it is better have a damn good reason for interrupting us."

Yanking the shirt over her head, she appreciated that Devin honored the personal and professional line with something as simple as letting her answer the door. At the bottom of the stair bay, she peered through the blind.

Odette said, "Liberty, I need to talk to Devin. It's important. Really important."

She unlocked the door. Odette brushed past her, nearly knocking her over.

"Odette? What's goin' on?" Devin asked.

"Tay is sick. Like, really sick. She's been barfing since last night. Jase and Crash took her to the ER and it's just extreme morning sickness. They prescribed antinausea meds and she's resting, but she can't hardly talk after all that barfing, let alone sing."

"Fuck."

"I hate to say this, but the songs she plays keyboards in won't lose much, but, Dev, she's your main backup singer. A big chunk of your set is devoted to songs with three-and four-part harmony. We can't just say we'll work around it. Some of those songs are the ones fans come to hear. Especially 'Chains and Trains.'"

"Fuck," Devin said again. "What are our options?"

"We could initiate an audience sing-along, and people won't notice the lack of harmony coming from the stage."

"Which will work for a few of the songs, but not half the damn set." Devin stood and paced. "Jesus. I hate to say this, but I wish Jesse-Belle was on this leg of the tour right now. Either she or one of her ten backup singers could fill in for a night."

"I thought of that. Our opening act, Rider Ekman, doesn't have a woman singer in his band."

"Can't you just announce at the start of the show that Tay's on bed rest and ask female audience members to fill in?" Liberty suggested. "The ladies who come to your concerts know all the words. Even if they screwed up, it'd be entertaining."

Devin studied her. "Definitely a last resort." He said, "Hang on," and disappeared down the hall.

Liberty asked, "How is Tay?"

"Miserable. But Jase is being really sweet to her for a change and they're happy about the baby, so that's good."

Devin returned with his guitar and parked his butt next to Odette. He strummed a few chords of "Baby Loves Me like Mama Does" and then pointed to Liberty with the guitar pick. "Jump in when we get to the chorus."

Liberty's mouth fell open, but she couldn't have spoken to protest if her life depended on it.

Good thing Odette demanded, "Devin, what the hell do you think you're doing? She's your girlfriend, not a backup singer."

He faced his songwriting partner. "Liberty sings."

"Devin."

"She sings so damn well that when I first heard her, I thought Tay had broken in to use my shower again."

Odette aimed her skeptical look at Liberty. "Is that right?"

"Yes," Devin answered for her. "And she's been with the tour for months. She knows the set list and all of the songs, don't you?"

"I guess, but—"

"We'll go through the song once so you can get a feel for the harmony sections. Then, the second time through, join in at the chorus. Ready?" he said to Odette.

She nodded.

Liberty's heart jackhammered. Besides her brief kara-oke appearance, the only place she ever sang was in her car or in the shower.

Devin did his thing. Cranked out the tune perfectly, like he'd done hundreds of times; no fancy digital sound engineering, no additional instruments, just a man and his guitar. Odette chimed in with the higher harmony.

Immediately, the missing harmony she'd heard at least once a night flowed into her head. She hummed along. By the second run-through, she closed her eyes and eased into the chorus, making sure her voice blended with the level of sound they created.

Silence stretched after Devin quit playing.

She didn't have the guts to open her eyes. Had she sucked?

"Uh, yeah. Nice little secret you've been keeping, Devin," Odette cooed. "Any other mad skills your personal assistant's got that you want to share?"

"She's also really good with her m—"

"Omigod! Shut up! I was joking! Can't you see you've already embarrassed the poor girl?"

"Liberty. Baby, look at me." Someone nudged her knee.

She peeled open her eyes and focused on Devin's face. His smiling face. His you-rocked-my-fucking-world smiling face.

"You nailed it."

"Really?"

"Really. You up for running through the other songs?"

"Okay." She rubbed her suddenly sweaty palms on her jeans. "What's next?"

"'Show Me,'" Odette said thoughtfully. "That's got a faster tempo."

Devin started playing, and after the first run-through, she joined in. They did this until they had tackled every song on the set list. Twice.

"Looks like we've got our backup singer for tonight."

Panic set in. "But I've never . . ." Been onstage, to say nothing of singing in front of thousands of people.

Then Devin was crouching in front of her, holding her

face in his hands. "We'll get the band together and do a quick rehearsal of these pieces. That'll give you experience onstage and with the earpieces you'll need."

"But—"

He kissed her. Not a sweet shut-up kiss. But one with enough fire that she started to get warm all over.

"Uh, excuse me? I'm still here and not into voyeurism," Odette reminded them.

Liberty tried to break the kiss, but Devin held her in place. "Odette?" he said without looking away from Liberty.

"What?"

"Tell Crash to call a rehearsal. We'll be there in fifteen minutes."

"Yeah, yeah, I know the drill; don't let the door hit me in the ass on the way outta here."

Door. Liberty pushed to her feet. "I'll let you out."

She was so distracted by their impromptu jam session— wait; how much of a dork was she to call it a *jam session*?— that after she scaled the stairs, she smacked into Devin. She glanced up. Damn. That heavy-lidded, impatient-to-get-her-naked vibe rolled over her like an electrical storm. Normally, she'd launch herself at him and fight for who got to be on top.

But right now . . .

"So I take it we're not picking up where we left off before we head into the arena?"

Arena. Why did that word make her gut clench and all the breath leave her lungs?

"Baby. Breathe." Devin plucked her up—something she rarely allowed him to do—and settled them both in the recliner.

As much as she wanted to play it tough and cool, she

buried her face in his neck, letting the clean scent of his skin center her.

After a bit, he said, "You don't have to do this."

"But you need me to."

"Just for this one night. That's it. It'd save a lot of headaches all around if you could embrace your inner rockstar and walk onto that stage. And if you weren't good enough to be on there? Sweetheart, as much as I like you, if you sucked ass, I wouldn't have asked you. I'm a hands-on perfectionist, if you hadn't noticed."

"Gee, really? Somehow that escaped my notice in the past few months we've been together 24/7."

"And she's a comedian."

"I'll admit I'm nervous, okay? But two other things occurred to me that might throw a wrench into these plans anyway."

Devin tilted her head back. "What? Security issues?"

"For one. I won't be thinking about that as I'm trying to remember words to songs, the part I'm singing, and having all those eyes focused on the stage."

"Two guards will walk me to the stage and escort me to the room when I'm done. Will that work?"

"I guess."

"I oughta point out that you cannot be armed onstage."

"Not even a stun gun?"

He shook his head.

"Shoot. Now I'll really feel naked up there."

Devin laughed. "What else?"

"I want to be kept fully in shadow. No one should see my face, either from the crowd or behind a camera lens. No introduction either."

"Makes sense." He traced the edge of her T-shirt collar.

"You'll be on your own up there. You have to pay attention for the song cues because all my energy is focused on what I'm doin' in front of the crowd, not what's goin' on behind me. Understand?"

"Yes." She squirmed out of his hold. "I'd better get dressed in something more appropriate for rehearsal."

Before she reached her bunk, Devin spun her around and stalked her until her spine met the wall. "One other thing I should warn you about. After the first time you're onstage, there's a performance rush, so be prepared for it. I know I am."

"Meaning what?"

His seductive lips moved over her jaw. "You'll see. Now, let's hit rehearsal."

∞

It took three tries for her to get used to the earpiece—it was very different from the military ones she'd used. But the rehearsal went better than she'd expected. Still, she'd be a nervous ball of energy until the final house lights went dim and she was off the stage.

Three hours until showtime, she accompanied Devin to his meet and greet in the banquet hall.

Two hours to showtime, Devin caught her eye and smiled before the two security guards escorted him to his ready room.

Before she could make a break for the bus and figure out what items of black clothing to wear onstage, Odette hooked her arm through Liberty's.

"Alone at last."

Why did something about her tone set off warning bells? "What's up?"

"You and me are having girl time. I've been told to make you presentable for stage."

Her eyes narrowed. "Who said that?"

Odette just slid her a sly smile. "It doesn't matter. What does matter is that you look the part of Devin McClain's backup singer, not Devin McClain's personal assistant. Although, with your funky but professional look, you do have great taste in business attire."

She did? Huh. *Thank you, Harper.* "But it won't matter because I'll be in the shadows."

"It's not about the crowd. You climb on that stage looking hot as fire, girlfriend, you'll *be* on fire. We need you confident to pull this off tonight. Lucky for you, I'm an expert in creating that *wow* factor."

Liberty's gaze moved over Odette, from her shiny black hair casually tossed up in a messy bun to her flawless porcelain skin. Even her lounging clothes were color-coordinated. "No offense, Odette, but you're gorgeous, so your *wow* factor comes naturally."

Odette stood on the tips of her four-inch heels. "You think this is my natural look? Oh, honey. It took me an hour to look like I didn't do a damn thing but roll out of my bunk. I'm as plain Jane as they come."

"I doubt that," Liberty muttered.

"I'll have to prove it, won't I? Let me grab my stage kit and I'll meet you on Devin's bus in ten minutes."

Liberty had just enough time to lock up her guns and bring out her classiest plain clothes before Odette knocked. When she saw the two suitcases of stuff, she felt light-headed. Surely that wasn't all for her?

"Let's treat ourselves to a cocktail while we're putting on the glam. It'll relax you. I promise. And, doll, you need relaxation." She smirked. "I figured Devin would've helped you with that."

"He tried. But someone interrupted us."

Odette laughed and passed her a bottle filled with pink liquid.

"What's this?"

"Cherry pomegranate wine cooler. Drink up while I check out your clothes selection."

Everything Liberty had laid out got the big *no* from Miss Wow Factor. No jeans. No dress pants. She pulled out a lace skirt that Liberty had hidden in the back of the closet.

"We need to see some skin," Odette announced. She tossed two tank tops at her—one silver and one gold. "Try those on. Oh, and show some cleavage."

Cleavage. Right. Not happening. She still had to work with the road crew after her one night onstage. She needed them listening to her, not gawking at her chest. She left the black compression bra on, but it looked good showing beneath the sparkly silver tank top. She stepped from the bathroom and Odette squealed.

"I've got one piece that'll make this perfect." She looked at Liberty's feet. "Provided you have black leather boots? Preferably with spike heels?"

She had a pair of shoes Harper had forced her to buy that she'd never worn. "I have to walk onstage in front of thousands of people. If I wear heels, I'll fall flat on my face."

"Suck it up and show me the goodies you're hiding."

Liberty froze.

Relax. She's not talking about your boobs; she's talking about your shoes.

Odette gasped, "Omigod! These are to die for," when Liberty handed her the spike-heeled booties with black suede strips crisscrossing from the open toe to the zipper at the heel.

Then, from her bag of tricks, Odette whipped out a short black leather jacket.

"That'll never fit me."

"There's no zipper. This is meant to be worn tight." Odette clapped, and Liberty slipped it on.

Hey. It did fit.

"Now the outfit is outstanding." Odette toasted herself and drank. "Makeup time. And I'll warn ya: My motto is more is better."

Awesome.

Odette wouldn't let her look until she finished.

So Liberty was more than a little afraid to see what stared back at her in Devin's big mirror.

"What do you think?"

Her eyes were outlined in black, making them appear enormous. Her irises reflected the shimmery eye shadow, turning her eyes the color of liquid silver. Her lashes were dark and long enough to reach the bottom of her eyebrows. A natural glow highlighted her cheekbones and masked her freckles. Her lips were a frosted purple that should've looked clownish but gave her mouth a sexy pout. Her eyes met Odette's in the mirror. "You weren't kidding. You really are a master at the *wow* factor."

Odette hugged her. "My turn. And, yes, you have to stay while I'm putting on my game face."

Liberty tried to keep the conversation focused on Odette and Steve, but the wily woman directed it back to her.

"What happens when this leg of the tour is over? I mean, you and Dev are together all the time. I assume you'll go to Nashville with him?"

"To be honest, we haven't discussed it."

"I know what you mean. While we were dating, Dev was so great to me when we were on the road. But when the tour ended, we went back to our real lives and it wasn't the same. There are such heightened emotions on tour. Big highs and low lows. That's why Tay and Jase are at odds. In love on the blacktop, but they can't find common ground away from it."

Rather than apply that same logic to her relationship with Devin, she said, "So what's it like for you and Steve?"

"There's some friction when we first start out on tour. Too much togetherness and all that. We settle in and we're fine. But Devin is always restless. He's a great singer, a fantastic songwriter and a generous boss."

"But?" Liberty prompted.

Odette smiled sadly. "But nothing. I chatter too much. A trait Devin didn't like because he needed his alone time. I imagine you can give him that."

Liberty nodded.

"Good. He needs someone like you. You've been good for him. He's been a lot happier lately."

So have I.

Odette fluffed up her hair. "Now that it only took us an hour and a half to become presentable, let's hit it. Show starts in thirty."

Liberty held her hand to her stomach. Thirty minutes.

∞

After the second encore, Devin brought the band up for a final bow. "Thank you, Midland!"

Liberty hung back in the shadows.

It was night-and-day difference, standing beside the stage and being on it when thousands of people were roaring approval. Like the difference between watching porn and having sex.

And speaking of sex . . . The high she experienced during the concert consumed her entire body. She had a desperate need for physical contact, for male heat on her, in her, for rough hands touching her everywhere and a hungry mouth on her skin.

Now Liberty better understood why Devin needed that intense one-on-one connection with her after sharing himself with so many people in the arena.

When she realized the band was exiting the stage, she fell in line behind them. She kept her gaze firmly on Devin's hatted head to the point she stumbled into Gage.

He whirled around. "Whoa. Steady there."

"Sorry. I'm not used to heels."

"You look great. You sounded great too, Liberty. Thanks for saving the day."

"No problem." Then she was vaguely aware of Leon thanking her, as well as Jase before he bailed to check on Tay. Odette hugged her, babbling about a champagne celebration, but Liberty heard little over the throb of need pounding in her lips, her nipples and between her legs. She was annoyed by the two security guards blocking her view of Devin, and she silently willed them to move away.

Somewhere in her head she knew that was wrong, but all she wanted was for the hangers-on to vanish so she and Devin could be alone. Naked.

Then the sea of people parted, providing a path directly to him.

Their eyes met. He didn't flash that million-dollar smile. His sexual heat hit her like a blast furnace and she nearly stumbled again—even though she was standing still. Without breaking his intense eye-fuck, he spoke to the security guys. Then he crooked his finger.

It wasn't her sense of decorum that kept her from running to him, but the reality that she couldn't run in ankle-breakers. By the time she reached him, her entire body trembled.

Devin took her hand and brought her knuckles to his lips for a soft, almost innocent kiss that sent a spike of desire straight to her core. He murmured, "Let's go." He threaded his fingers through hers and towed her through the throng of people, letting one of the security guards clear the way.

When they reached the door to the ready room, the security guard who'd been following her flanked his partner.

Devin said, "No one gets in the room. No one. I don't care if there's a fucking zombie apocalypse. We are not to be disturbed, understand?"

"Yes, Mr. McClain."

He opened the door and hauled her inside, straight to the piano bench. Then he walked back to the door and locked it. He removed his hat and set it on the catchall table. Next he unbuckled his belt and tugged the black leather free from the belt loops. He briefly gave her his back, grabbing something out of his duffel bag and shoving it in his front pocket.

Please let it be a condom.

As he walked toward her, rendering her mindless with that I'm-gonna-fuck-you-hard stare, he shrugged off his shirt, letting it float to the floor behind him.

Liberty's pulse skipped a beat or two hundred when Devin stood in front of her.

He curled his hands around her face, positioning her head where he liked, tracing her lower lip with his thumb. Side to side until her tongue reached out to lick her lip and dampness made the continuous glide easier.

Kiss me; touch me; fuck me.

But he just stared at her. His face, his posture, his eyes didn't encourage her to speak.

Then he bent down and kissed her, tipping her head back to ravish her mouth.

Pleasure, need and lust swirled in her head and zinged through her body. Devin wedged his knee between her legs, keeping the piano bench in place as he arched her back as far as she could go. Liberty slipped her fingers beneath the waistband of his jeans and held on. A moan rumbled from her chest when her knuckles brushed the taut, bare skin of his abdomen.

As the kiss grew hotter and wetter, so did she.

Devin's hands slid down to grip her biceps. He broke the kiss and jerked her to her feet. With his breath teasing her ear, he stripped off the leather jacket and tossed it aside. He kicked the piano bench aside and moved her backward.

Two steps later, her backside connected with the edge of the piano keys.

His mouth attacked her throat. Shivers radiated out from every spot where his lips and teeth landed. His hands followed the curve of her body, over her breasts and belly to her hips. And still Devin said nothing as he yanked her skirt up and her panties down to her shins.

Her thighs clenched when he dropped to his knees in front of her.

Devin pushed her hips down and her ass landed directly on the piano, creating a loud musical crash. He tugged her forward so her pussy was level with his mouth. The tips of her booties barely touched the floor; she was completely off balance. Her palms smacked the keys—the high and low notes jarring the silence at the first touch of his mouth on her molten core.

He removed her panties, spreading her legs wider. His growl reverberated on her sensitive tissues when he jammed his tongue into her wet pussy. Harder and deeper with every plunge.

Liberty gasped. She let her head fall back, squeezing her eyes shut as his greedy mouth consumed her. Licking. Sucking. Nipping her tender flesh.

She didn't stand a chance against Devin's relentless pursuit of her orgasm. Her clit swelled and throbbed as he sucked that little nub until bliss teased the edges of her sanity.

When that first pulsing throb started, she yelled, "Yes, yes, yes!" Her hips pressing up, her ass hit the keys in a dissonant chord as Devin tried to hold her down. They engaged in a war of wills: Liberty arching and bucking for more contact with his mouth, Devin denying her. Giving her the orgasm on his terms.

And holy fuck, what an orgasm it was.

She hadn't caught her breath or her balance before Devin started in again, pushing two fingers into her spasming cunt and driving her higher with every precise lash of his wet tongue.

Almost . . . almost. There.

She arched back, letting the pulsating sensation consume her body and own her soul. Her whole body twitched with aftershocks, her palms pushing into the piano keys, making softer sounds of dissension.

His callused fingertips scraped the tops of her thighs as he dragged an openmouthed kiss down the inside of her right leg. He rolled to his feet and yanked her against him, fisting his left hand in her hair as he plundered her mouth.

She loved kissing him after he'd gone down on her.

Tasting her essence on his lips and tongue mixing with his raw, masculine flavor.

Liberty flattened her palms on his chest and moved them down to the bulge in his jeans. He groaned when she popped the button and undid his zipper. Sliding her hands around his slim hips, she pushed his jeans and boxer briefs until they dropped away.

While she fondled and freed him, he kept kissing her, either on her mouth or on her neck, keeping the passion between them at the same exhilarating level of intensity. She'd gone from having a performance high to being one hundred percent high on him.

He removed a condom from his front pocket and pressed it into her palm, then wrapped his hands around the back of her neck. Breathing hard, his body shaking with need, he rested his forehead to hers.

Liberty tore open the package and curled her fingers around his shaft, jacking him a few times.

He hissed but didn't pull away.

And she was too impatient to tease him. The instant the condom was on, Devin turned her around. He swept her hair to her opposite shoulder, feathering his lips over the cord that stretched from behind her jawbone to her shoulder.

A soft moan escaped her. His sweetness in passionate moments stirred her as much as his dominance.

Then his big hand pressed the middle of her back, urging her to bend forward.

She reached for the only thing within distance—the piano—and the keys made a discordant racket as her fingers fought for purchase.

With a sound akin to a snarl, he placed her left hand on the top of the upright piano, curving her fingers around the edge. He stretched his arm over the top of hers, his fingers circling her wrist. Holding her in place. Proving his power and control.

Keeping his right arm around her hip, he slid his boots between hers and scooted her foot out, widening her stance. Then his hand was on his cock. He dragged it down the crack of her ass, then slipped it between her thighs, letting the tip glide up her wet slit until the head bumped her clit.

Just as she was ready to beg him to fuck her, he poised that thick head at her opening and fed his cock into her inch by inch.

Once he was fully seated inside, he paused.

Devin nuzzled the back of her head. His lips found the top of her ear and he brushed a line of kisses down to the hollow below her earlobe. His rapid breaths flowed across her damp skin, making every hair on her body stand up.

In one breath-stealing moment, he pulled out and rammed his cock back in fully.

Her right hand, still on the piano keys, shifted, playing higher notes as she braced herself against his pounding thrusts.

Devin's body covered hers so intimately that although she was almost fully clothed, she felt the heat of his possession searing her flesh clear down to the bone.

Needing another contact point with him, Liberty turned her head, and his lips grazed her jaw, sending new shivers rippling through her.

The tremors coming from him surprised her.

That's when she recognized he'd reached the edge sooner than he usually did. She also knew he'd hold back, waiting for her to come again, even when she'd already had two explosive orgasms.

His grip tightened on her hip and on her wrist. When he slowed down, she squeezed her inner muscles around his cock. He made a soft grunt and pumped into her with short, shallow jabs.

Against his lips, she whispered, "Let go. I need to hear you roar."

And roar he did.

Musical notes distorted the air as he fucked her without pause. His release was so hot she felt it through the latex.

In the aftermath, Devin's hips kept moving. Swiveling. Driving against her G-spot until she detonated again. As she spiraled down from the place he'd sent her soaring to, she swore he was coming again too.

He nuzzled her ear. "Told you it was a rush."

"Mmm. So does this make you *my* groupie now?"

His teeth nipped her neck. "Since I was on my knees in front of you? Yes." He soothed the love bites with a soft brush of his lips. "You looked fucking hot onstage tonight. But I prefer you like this, half-dressed, my cock in you and a thoroughly fucked smile on your face. Because I know no one else will ever see you like this."

"That was a pretty possessive thing to say."

"I'm a pretty possessive guy." His lips skimmed her temple. "Get used to it."

Chapter Eighteen

❧

*A*lthough Liberty had fun singing backup vocals, she was relieved when Tay bounced back from her pregnancy sickness and returned to her job the following night.

They'd hit the grueling part of the tour. The past fourteen days had been brutally exhausting, travel-wise and performance-wise. Two back-to-back cycles of six nights on, one night off. Hour after hour spent on the bus.

For the past three nights, she and Devin had both been too tired to do anything but crawl into bed, curl up together and fall asleep.

Since the venues were small, mostly county fairs, additional security was limited, and Devin didn't have a separate space to get ready for the show, so he'd resorted to staying on the bus. The problem with that was the zealous fans stood outside the barricade, chanting Devin's name, serenading him with his own tunes. While he admitted he found it more flattering than annoying, he'd had to resort to noise-canceling headphones to drown them out.

Things had gotten tense the first night when she'd stationed the lone security guard in front of the barricade. As soon as Devin stepped off the bus, the crowd knocked down the wooden barrier and charged him. She fought the urge to pull out her gun and fire warning shots in the air to get them to back the fuck off.

Fortunately, Crash had been nearby, and between him and her, they got Devin inside the back entrance without injury.

Devin had been rattled by the incident, but he pretended to take it in stride. He even pointed out his fans hadn't acted with malice.

To which Liberty retorted that if his fans had intended to act with malice, they could have gotten to him way too easily and it would've been too late to do anything about it at that point.

So they'd reconfigured the position of the buses into a V outside the back entrance, which allowed limited privacy and protection as he got on and off the bus.

She had a hard time believing the gigs where Devin played to a crowd of fifteen hundred were worth it. Not just financially, but the back-to-back shows were physically exhausting for everyone involved with the tour. When she'd mentioned her concerns to Crash, he told her that by headlining the smaller venues, Devin was reaching upward of twenty-five thousand people with his music—no different from if he'd played a large arena during that week. Then he'd gone on to point out the only chance some of these people living in rural areas would have to see Devin McClain live is if he came to them—and that decision had been one hundred percent Devin's.

Snapped back to the present when the house lights dimmed, Liberty waited by the edge of the stage after the second encore.

After Devin handed off his guitar to Check, he grabbed a towel. Amid congrats from the crew, they returned to the sponsor's tent, which seemed half a mile away in the middle of a cow pasture. But they were upwind from the Porta-Potties for a change. The rockstar life wasn't all five-star hotels and gourmet food.

The tent was completely empty, so that was a plus.

Devin mopped his face and neck. His black T-shirt was soaked with sweat. Even his jeans clung to his muscular legs.

She sauntered closer. "Great show."

He smiled. "Yeah? Best crowd we've had in the last week."

Pressing her body against his, she draped her arms over his shoulders so she could twine her fingers in those tempting ringlet curls.

"Sweetheart, you don't wanna get that close to me when I'm all sweaty like this."

"I like you sweaty. Especially when we're naked."

He kissed her quickly. "Hold that thought. We'll take a shower together when we're back on the bus. Maybe the reporter won't stick around long if she sees I'm still in stage clothes."

Liberty retreated. She hoped the interview lasted at least until the parking areas were empty and the crowd had gone home.

Devin sighed. "Remind me again what local paper this is for."

She looked at him. "Do you even know where we are?"

He shook his head. "It's all blurred together."

"We're in Berle County. Your contact is Daisy Sue Seftner from the *Tri-City Register*."

"Thanks." He flopped in the folding chair, closed his eyes and tipped his head back. "I'm beat. I don't mean to be a pain in the ass, but it'd be nice to have something better than these hard damn chairs to sit on during the interview."

"Why don't you do these interviews in the bus?"

He peered at her from beneath heavy lids. "Because the bus is my private space. I don't wanna share it with nobody but you."

She loved his sweet, protective side, but it wasn't about her. "Not even if *Celebrity Motor Homes* contacted you to do a segment on your life on the road?"

He shrugged. "This bus is nicer than any I've ever had; it's still not one of them million-dollar motor coaches." Then he offered her a smirk. "And I'm supposed to be keepin' a low profile, remember?"

Crash entered the tent with a young woman who appeared to be fresh out of high school. Then again, the older Liberty got, the worse she was at judging ages.

Devin heaved himself to his feet and crossed the small expanse in three steps. "Daisy Sue? Thanks for postponing this interview until after the show. But I'll warn ya that without a shower I'm a little ripe."

"I don't mind. You earned that sweat. What an outstanding performance."

"Thank you." He gestured to the two chairs in the corner. "How about if we sit over there?"

"I promise I won't keep you too long. I know you've gotta get on the road."

Crash beckoned Liberty outside. "If you've got this handled, the band is gonna take off."

"Are the drivers rested? It seems we're on the road for more than twelve hours every damn night."

"They're all getting the required break. We worked that into the touring schedule, Liberty."

She held up her hands at his brusque tone. "Not an accusation. I just worry about Devin. He's so exhausted, he's not working on music during the day. He just zones out in front of the TV."

"It's the ebb and flow of the tour." Crash frowned. "I'm more worried about you. Is Dev expecting you to entertain him so you're not getting the rest you need? Because it's crucial that you're on your game throughout these next few tour dates."

"My workouts have been about half of what they should be, but besides that, I'm holding steady. And I am armed. That levels the playing field a whole lot."

"Good. And I've been meaning to thank you."

Liberty looked at him quizzically. "For what?"

"For keeping Devin on an even keel. About this time on tour, tempers start to fray. Especially his. Not only does he feel safe with you, but that safety allows him to concentrate on doin' his job every night." Crash grinned. "And he likes havin' you in close quarters. He's never had that before, and he's gotten really protective of it."

Not knowing how to respond, her answer was a little flip. "I'm glad to be of service."

He clapped her on the shoulder. "Have a good night. See you tomorrow at sound check. Be safe."

"Always."

She hovered in the walkway, keeping an eye on the tent where Devin was being interviewed and squinting at the dirt parking lot where the roadies were loading up the last of the equipment. The only good thing about smaller venues is they didn't do a full stage setup, so teardown took less than half of the usual time, but it was tricky to accomplish in the dark with spotlights. Since Devin preferred to stick around until the semis rolled out, she was happy to see they were nearly finished.

An image jogged closer. Between the darkness, clouds of dust and exhaust fumes, she couldn't make the person out. Her hand automatically went to her stun gun. When she realized it was just Reg, she felt like an idiot. Maybe she was more tired than she thought.

"Hey there, Miss Liberty. I'm done with my final check. I'll be waiting on the bus."

She wished Reg could pull the bus around. They were on the opposite side from where it was parked. But the behemoth was difficult to maneuver, so she didn't ask. "Shouldn't be too much longer."

The interview was still in full swing, so she typed her daily report on her phone.

Another twenty minutes passed by. She finally caught Devin's eye and tapped on her wrist.

Devin gave the interviewer his million-dollar grin. "The boss lady is tellin' me we oughta wrap this up."

"I have one last question." Daisy Sue sat a little straighter in her chair. "You've taken some hits over the years as well as had your share of acclaim. Your song 'What Love Isn't' has supporters and detractors. How do you feel when music critics weigh in?"

"Darlin', if I tell you what I really think, you'll get in trouble because you ain't allowed to publish that kinda bad language in your family newspaper."

Daisy Sue laughed.

"In all honesty, critics' opinions don't mean squat. There's no such thing as a 'critical review' because the phrase signifies the reviewer is already a critic lookin' to find something wrong. My fans' response to my music is all I care about. Those supposed professional reviewers, who feel entitled to say whatever nasty stuff they want about my work, are just lookin' for an angle and a way to get *themselves* noticed. In recent years it's come down to who can have the snarkiest sound bite; it's not about my work at all, but how clever they think they can be in dissing it or me."

"Why do you think that is?"

"Some of my peers claim it stems from jealousy because these so-called critics have no obvious talents of their own. I think it's because they have no idea how to create something. Alls they know is how to tear something apart someone else created. So like I said, I'll let the workin' people who plunk down their hard-earned cash for my CDs or to see my shows be my true critics. Life is too short and too precious to focus on negativity or the people who specialize in it."

Liberty wanted to clap. Sometimes she didn't know how he kept doing it, putting so much of himself into his music and into his performances night after night.

"Well, you don't have to worry I'll put you in a negative light. It's been fun interviewing you, Devin."

"The pleasure was mine, Daisy Sue."

They both stood.

"Will you make sure my publicist at the record label gets a copy of the article?"

"Of course." She shook his hand. "Good luck on the rest of the tour."

Devin waited until she'd ducked out before he crossed over to Liberty. "What's the status on the equipment trucks?"

"Gone. As is the band bus. Reg is waiting for us."

"Cool. Let's go."

They exited the tent.

"I probably should've walked Daisy Sue to her car," he said. "Why the hell is it so dark out here? Did they shut off the yard lights to save money?"

"No idea. I can't even see the neon glow from the midway." She listened. She couldn't hear the noise from the carnival games or the music blaring from the rides either. The silence, especially this time of night, set her on edge.

Three more tents were spread out between the back of the grandstand and where the bus was parked. They picked their way through the deserted area; the only sound was the shuffle of their feet in the dirt.

Just as they cleared the last tent, Liberty heard a heavy step and a scrape behind them. She whirled around.

A man wielding some kind of club appeared from the shadows and headed straight for Devin.

Liberty's instincts kicked in as the man charged. Since his focus seemed to be solely on Devin, she held out her foot and tripped him. He went sprawling, but fell only to his knees. She followed through by kicking him in the lower back above his kidney. He let loose a howl of pain before he hit the dirt face-first.

Then she pressed her stun gun into the back of his head as she removed the spiked club from his hand. "Don't fucking move or I will send seventy thousand volts through you."

He puffed out, "Fuck off," and tried to twist his body away from her.

She stomped on his fingers and jammed the stunner more deeply into the fat rolls of his neck. "I said: *Don't. Fucking. Move.*"

The guy slumped to the ground.

She'd fallen for that trick before. "Put your free arm above your head. Palm flat on the ground." When he hesitated, she yelled, "Do it now!"

He slowly reached up.

Liberty didn't ease up on him one bit as she looked over at Devin.

He'd completely frozen.

While she was relieved he hadn't interfered with her doing her job, his state of stock wasn't helping. "Devin," she said sharply.

He snapped out of it and met her gaze.

"Call the cops."

The attacker ran his mouth as he struggled. "Of course you're gonna call the cops. You're a fuckin' pussy just like I thought you were, McClain. Ain't man enough to take me on." He snorted. "You're a pathetic loser if you're gonna let this chick fight your battles."

So tempting to flip the switch and zap this motherfucker. See if that made his lips stop flapping.

Devin pulled out his phone.

"You think the cops will arrest me? I'll be a hero for taking a whack at you. They know what you did when you played here three years ago. How you invited a few girls onto your bus—most of them underage—fucked them and then kicked them to the curb on your way outta town."

"That's why you came after him? Your girlfriend or sister was one of those girls?" Liberty asked.

"She was my fucking *wife*," he spat. "What kind of hard-up piece of shit fucks another man's wife?"

"Evidently, your wife has a thing for hard-up pieces of shit, doesn't she?"

"Shut your mouth, whore."

Do not stun him just for fun. Do not stun him unless he makes a move toward Devin.

"There's a police unit stationed at the carnival tonight," Devin said. "They'll be here shortly."

The small bout of silence was too good to last.

"I could've gotten to you earlier," the man bragged. "Been watching you since your big bus pulled in. You needing a big bus must mean you're trying to make up for your tiny dick."

Devin squatted just out of the man's reach. "Your wife seemed to like my little dick well enough."

Jesus.

The man roared and bucked to get free, spittle and nonsensical words flying from his mouth.

Liberty didn't dare look over and glare at Devin for his taunt because she had her hands full keeping this moose contained. "Calm down."

"I had you in my sights," he wheezed out, ignoring her. "One clean shot from the back row and your brains would've been splattered on the stage."

Her blood turned to ice. "Are you carrying a gun?"

"What do you think, you dumb bitch?"

I think I'm an idiot for not patting you down right away.

Her gaze swept over his body. Nothing in his back pockets. She couldn't maneuver her body to check to see if he wore a holster on the front of his torso.

"I shoulda taken the shot when I had the chance," he snarled.

That did it.

Liberty depressed the button and watched him twitch like a bug on a hot griddle.

As soon as the man quit jerking, she patted down the inside and outside of his calves.

Son of a bitch. There was a hard lump on the outside of his right boot that could be only one thing.

The air rushed from her lungs.

Luckily, the cops showed up before she took a whack at this psycho fucker. They yelled, "Identify yourself and your weapons!"

"Liberty Masterson, Devin McClain's personal security. I am armed with a stun gun. Mr. McClain is unarmed."

The cop—a woman close to her age—hustled into Liberty's space while the other cop moved toward Devin. "I'm Officer Mahoney. What's going on?"

Liberty gave her the basics, ending with "I used the stun gun on him after he admitted he was armed. I believe the gun is in the outside of his right boot."

Officer Mahoney nudged the man's hip until he rolled onto his back. Then she peered in his face. "Emil Chartes."

"You know him?"

"Local loudmouth. Been picked up on drunk and disorderly several times. Domestic disturbance too. His ex-wife took out a restraining order, which means carrying a concealed weapon puts him in a parole violation." She removed the gun and dropped it into a plastic bag.

What a big fucking mess.

Liberty ran her hand across her jaw and glanced over at Devin. The other cop was taking Devin's statement.

Then she watched as Officer Mahoney spun around and pointed her gun at someone. "Hands up and don't take another step!"

She spun around and recognized the interloper. "It's okay. That's Reg, our bus driver. I'm sure he saw you guys pulling in with the red and blues flashing and got concerned."

Officer Mahoney lowered her gun.

Liberty said, "Everything is all right, Reg. We'll give you the rundown when we're done here."

"Okay, Miss Liberty." He backed away very slowly.

"I assume Mr. McClain is pressing assault charges?" Officer Mahoney asked, pulling out her cuffs.

"Absolutely. Will we need to come to the station to file a report?"

"Nah. We can do it here." She rolled the attacker on his belly and yanked his arms behind his back to cuff him. "I'll take your statement once I have him secured in the car."

She jerked him to his feet—none too gently—and hauled him to the back of the cop car. She returned with a clipboard. "All right. Let's hear it from the top."

Liberty relayed the events and waited for Officer Mahoney to ask the same question that'd been kicking around in her head.

"So this attack was based on alleged events that happened three years ago between Mr. McClain and Mr. Chartes's former wife?"

"You'll have to ask Mr. McClain for specific details on that. I wasn't in his employ during the time in question."

"I'm guessing you were in the military," the cop stated.

"Got it on the first try."

Officer Mahoney smiled. "I spent eight years in the marines. Like recognizes like. As far as I'm concerned, you're done here."

"I have a few calls to make, but after the evening's events, you can understand why I will remain very close to Mr. McClain during your interview."

"Understood." Officer Mahoney looked up from her clipboard. "So you're a bodyguard, huh?"

"Officially, yes. To the world at large? I'm his personal assistant."

"Ah. I get it. I say more power to you. You've given me a real boost tonight. I fight to prove every damn day that I'm tough enough to do this job. Maybe when the day comes I'm sick of fighting it, I'll remember there are other options."

"Always."

Liberty kept an eye on Devin and the two cops as she pulled out her phone to call Garrett.

∞

An hour later, Devin broke out his secret stash of whiskey after he shut the door to his bedroom. He knocked back two mouthfuls before he sat on the bed.

He tried to sip, but it was more of a guzzle-until-he-passed-out kind of night.

When the booze hit him, he was able to breathe fully for the first time since that cocksucker had come at him with that spiked club.

And he'd just stood there. Not because he trusted Liberty to do her job, but because he'd frozen in fear.

Fear.

Jesus.

What kind of man did that make him?

A fucking pussy. A pathetic loser.

It wasn't fear for himself that'd turned him into a statue. But fear for her.

Liberty could've died for him tonight.

Died.

That she'd handled the situation—almost too well—scared the crap out of him. Because she'd do it again tomorrow. And the day after that. Put herself in the line of fire for him.

What made his life worth more than hers?

He tipped the bottle and drank, thoughts running around and around in his brain like a damn mouse in a maze.

Obviously, the dude who'd come after him was off his meds because Devin had never played this venue before. But it made him sick to think that the man's ex-wife had somehow convinced her husband that she'd fucked Devin McClain. What kind of crazy person did shit like that?

This isn't the first time this has happened to you. And it probably won't be the last.

Fucking awesome.

It was one thing if people wanted to take shots at him for something he'd done, but Liberty shouldn't be in that line of fire.

Maybe he should call Carl at Big Sky and demand Liberty be pulled off this assignment. It'd be easier to look at some big thug from LaGruder Security as a guy who was paid to protect him. He'd never see Liberty in strictly a professional light. Never. He cared way too fucking much about her.

But he was too goddamn selfish to let her go.

And didn't that just make him the biggest piece of shit on the planet?

Caught between fear and gratitude, between resentment and humiliation, he didn't know what to think. He didn't know what to do.

He stripped and headed to the shower, bringing his bottle for solace.

The hot water pounded onto his tight neck and shoulders, but it didn't ease the tension. Not on the outside. Definitely not on the inside.

The water had gone decidedly cool when he heard the bathroom door slide open.

Devin felt Liberty staring at him, but he didn't have the guts to look at her.

"Are you all right?"

"What do you think?"

"I think I asked you a question and I deserve an honest answer."

"I'm halfway to fucked up." He waggled the bottle at her, held it to his lips and welcomed the burn down his throat as he drank.

As soon as he swallowed, she snatched the bottle away. "Get shitfaced in your room, but not in here where you can drop this on the tile and leave glass all over the damn floor."

"No doubt you'd heroically throw me over your shoulder and save my poor tender feet from big, nasty glass shards."

Liberty pushed his back against the wall. "No, I wouldn't. It's not my fucking job to protect you from your own stupidity." Her eyes searched his. "But that's what this is about, isn't it? My job."

Devin blinked at her. Fire danced in her eyes. She was so incensed, she hadn't even shut off the shower. She'd just stepped in fully clothed and gone toe-to-toe with him.

God, the woman was spectacular. She never held back—her passion or her anger. She wouldn't let him hide.

In that moment, his muddled emotions cleared. He'd always heard Jack Daniel's was truth serum, but he'd never believed it until now.

He reached over and turned the handle, cutting off the water. His hand shook as he attempted to wipe the droplets from the side of her face. "It's stupid, isn't it?"

"What?"

"Me bein' pissed off at you for doin' your job. Me bein' embarrassed—"

"Devin—"

He placed his fingers over her mouth. "Let. Me. Finish."

She just blinked at him.

"I don't like that you risked your life for mine. Not because of some stupid male pride but because your action proved to me that you—your life—is worth more than mine. You're the one who should be protected, Liberty. But instead you're takin' down lowlifes who have a beef with me. It hit me in a way tonight that . . ."

"You're more than just a job to me."

"I know, baby, and that almost makes it worse." He kept his hand curled around the back of her neck as his thumb followed her jawline. "I should send you away."

"Devin. Don't."

"I should send you away," he repeated. "But I can't. If I gotta have someone protecting my ass, I want it to be you *because* I am more than just a job to you. And tonight I saw how good you really are at your job."

Liberty moved in and pressed her body to his, nestling her face in the crook of his neck.

Although he was freezing his balls off, he didn't move. They needed this reconnection. There wasn't anything sexual about the way they held on to each other—but they'd gone beyond physical intimacy to something much deeper. Trust. Acceptance.

Finally, he said the one thing he should've said first. "Thank you for saving my ass tonight."

"You're welcome."

Chapter Nineteen

One week left on this tour and then he could take a break.

Whether it was the heightened security after the incident in Berle County, or Liberty's brilliant protection skills—he firmly believed in the latter—there hadn't been any problems in the past week.

He'd had a few protestors at a performance in Georgia last night. Since they were playing a county fair, he thought they might pelt him with rotten produce. But they'd held signs, urging passersby to boycott the show because of the "unholy" message in his song "What Love Isn't."

Unholy. Wasn't like he'd even played the damn song onstage at that stop.

Plus, Devin had been on his very best behavior. In public at least. In private? A whole 'nother matter.

Spending so much time in close quarters with the sometimes-prickly Liberty . . . Damn, that woman could get him all kinds of riled up. First thing yesterday morning they'd had a stupid fight about a gap in the schedule. He informed her she was wrong; she insisted she was right.

But Liberty was in an ornery mood and wouldn't let it go.

He had shut the bedroom door in her face and concentrated on work. After he finally came out of his marathon songwriting session—at least his anger with her had one positive effect—he'd found her acting overly solicitous. When he questioned her on it, she admitted he'd been right about the schedule.

And she hadn't apologized for her mistake or for her snotty attitude about it.

So Devin had half-jokingly informed her that bratty girls got spanked. When she didn't get all indignant at the idea of him taking her in hand, he knew she was game for whatever he wanted to play.

He'd never been into role-playing. He suspected that was because he hadn't found a woman he trusted not to make him feel stupid for wanting to try it. But he trusted Liberty, and she had no problem putting her pleasure entirely in his hands.

So he'd tested the waters. Toying with her on the bus. A light whack on the butt here. A whisper about naughty girls needing punishment there. Smacking a spatula against his palm during lunch—which made her very, very jumpy and very horny, as evidenced by the shimmer in her eyes and the way she rubbed that smackable ass against his cock at every opportunity. As far as he was concerned, that meant game on.

Before they left the bus, he set a belt on his bed . . . next to the tube of lube.

She hadn't balked when she'd seen it. Or if she had, she hadn't exhibited any sign.

Whenever they had a spare second during the fan meet and greet, Devin had told her exactly what he planned to do to her.

Exactly.

In explicit detail.

The kinky woman had added a couple raunchy suggestions of her own.

So the sexual tension between them hit a new high.

When Devin finally had her alone that night, naked and open to his every whim, Liberty played her role so well they both lost themselves in the moment. He had made her come three times in his version of an erotic orgasm torture. Then he'd spanked her—had spanking always been so fucking hot? After he'd pinkened her butt cheeks, he'd fucked her ass.

Sexy as it'd been watching his cock stretching that tiny hole and feeling the tightness of her back channel surrounding his dick, Devin preferred the hot, wet clasp of her pussy. What made the experience fun, besides that Liberty wasn't an anal sex virgin, was afterward, they'd laughed and cuddled in bed like it was completely ordinary. He loved that they were defining a new normal for their relationship.

"Devin?"

His head snapped up, and he realized he'd completely zoned out while waiting for the sound check to begin. He saw all four members of the Wright Brothers Band leaning on the edge of the stage.

Grinning, he said in his usual corny spiel, "If it ain't the four Wrong Brothers tryin' to make it right." He shook Paxton Wright's hand first. As the oldest brother, Paxton led the band as well as sang lead vocals. "What's with the hair, Pax? You starting a revival of 80s hair metal bands?"

"Gnarly, dude!" Paxton's shoulder-length black hair flew all over in his head banger's impression. Then he flashed devil horns with both hands.

A chorus of his brothers' groans echoed behind him. "Don't encourage him, Devin. Or we'll be covering 'Talk Dirty to Me' in our set," one of the twins warned.

"That's a great idea," Paxton said. "We'll debut it tonight."

All three of his brothers flipped him off.

Flynn, the second oldest brother and the lead guitar player, sauntered up. The physical resemblance between him and Paxton ended with their dark hair color. Their personalities were also total opposites. Paxton was the showman with amazing vocal range. Flynn was the guitar-playing genius who preferred the shadows to the spotlight. He held up his fist to bump Devin's. "Long time no see."

"Yeah. Why didn't you play Gatorfest this year?"

The only time Devin could tell the identical Wright twins, Easton and Weston, apart was when Easton sat behind the drum kit and Weston held his bass. Devin shrugged and said, "Promoters decided to try something new and only have me play events where I headlined."

"How's that going?" Paxton asked.

"Good. Think I've played every casino in the Southwest. The audiences have been great. We've switched opening acts every two weeks or so. Some the record label insisted on, but the rest I got to pick."

"Thanks for choosing us," one of the twins said. "We've been looking forward to opening for you for months."

Devin rolled his eyes. "Thanks for the ego stroke, but we all know I oughta be opening for you guys." The Wright Brothers were one of the few bands who'd successfully sold albums ranging in style from country to pop to blue-grass to light metal. It helped sell records and concert tickets that not only were they incredibly talented, but the brothers had become the bad boys of the music scene. Paxton was notorious for his many messy public affairs with actresses, Flynn for his profanity-laden, equipment-destroying public meltdowns and Easton and Weston for WWE-style barroom brawls and for dating the same woman at the same time.

"See, we're hoping your good ol' boy public persona will rub off on us," Paxton said with a grin.

"Crash mentioned there's more security. Does that mean the leeches from the fucking media are banned from backstage?" Flynn asked with a sneer.

"We've beefed up security. Some weird shit goes along with bein' in the public eye. You guys know that."

Easton and Weston nodded.

"So backstage access is limited. And you'll see more security than normal. Just to be safe."

"Does any of this have to do with backlash from your song 'What Love Isn't'?" Paxton asked. "Because I gotta say, that song is beautiful. Righteous. We even covered it a couple times."

"You have?" If any other act would've said that, he wouldn't have believed it.

"We aren't exactly the poster boys for staying away from controversy," Paxton said dryly.

"You know, I haven't performed that song once on this tour?"

"Your choice?" Paxton asked.

Devin shook his head.

"Man, you can't bow down to the haters," Flynn said. "The song is about the writer's vision, not the listener's."

Simple truths always had the most impact on him.

And sometimes it made him impulsive. "What say we

remedy that tonight? You guys interested in playing it with me?"

Paxton looked at each of his brothers and they nodded. "How about if we go one better? You might've been discouraged from playing that song on this tour, but *we* haven't. We can make it our last song, and you can join us onstage to perform it."

Devin grinned. "Brilliant."

"Devin?"

All five men turned when Liberty skirted the corner of the stage.

And like every other time Devin saw her, his heart beat a little faster and his smile got a little wider. "Come meet the opening band."

Just as he opened his mouth to introduce them, Liberty blurted out, "I can't believe I'm standing here with the Wright Brothers." She stepped forward—way too close to Paxton—and kept blathering. "I have all your CDs. And, wow, all you guys look so much better live in person than in your videos or pictures online. They don't do you justice."

"I'm liking this woman quite a lot already. Is she . . . ?" Paxton's unspoken *yours?* caused his pierced brow to quirk.

Devin snaked his arm around Liberty's middle and hauled her out of mauling distance—not from the Wright Brothers, but because she looked ready to pounce on them. Which was way fucked up because she never gushed or went all fan girl on anyone. Especially not on him. "This is Liberty. She's my personal assistant. This is—"

"Paxton Wright." She wiggled out of Devin's hold and took both of Paxton's hands in hers. "I'd know you anywhere. My roommate in Kabul was obsessed with you. She had posters of you all over her side of the room. I gotta say, you're much hotter without the guyliner. And the earrings." She reached up and touched the end of his hair where it rested against his pectorals. "It looks good longer. Hits that mark between rock-'n'-roll bad-boy hottie and soulful balladeer."

He couldn't believe she fucking touched Paxton's *hair*. His hair! Then she stepped back and giggled. Fucking *giggled*.

"Sorry. Didn't mean to violate your person. I know how Devin gets about that when strange women do it to him."

"No worries." Paxton flaunted his trademark grin and she sighed.

Fucking *sighed*.

But the torture wasn't over yet.

Liberty moved on down the line, chatting and fucking *flirting* with the brothers, who had a revolving door to the bedroom on their bus and were rumored to be major stockholders in a condom company. Jesus. She was acting like she'd never been around anyone famous before, fawning over them like a starstruck groupie.

He froze.

Was this what it felt like to be jealous?

Yes. And just think; this is what Liberty deals with for hours every day.

Devin draped his arm across Liberty's shoulders, trying not to make it look as if he was pulling her away from the Fab Four—aka the Wrong Brothers. "Great havin' you guys here. We won't keep you. We have some things to discuss, so I'll see you at rehearsal in an hour."

Liberty damn near broke her neck craning around to say good-bye to them. As soon as they were out of earshot, she said, "What is wrong with you? You were borderline rude to them."

And you were borderline slutty.

Okay. He had to take this jealousy thing down a notch.

He didn't speak again until they reached his private room.

She flipped on the lights, but as soon as the door shut, he locked it and plunged them into darkness. Then he pressed her against the wall, holding both her wrists in his hands behind her back, immobilizing her.

"Devin, what are—"

"So you want to fuck Paxton Wright." He nuzzled her neck, letting his stubble scrape her tender skin. "Or maybe you want to fuck Flynn Wright." He followed the edge of her jaw up to her ear.

"Fuck you."

"That's the question of the day, ain't it, darlin'? Didn't you say you couldn't tell the difference in the dark?" He spoke in that low, velvety tone that had her trembling from head to toe. "We're completely in the dark. You could live out your fantasy of fucking Paxton . . . with me. I'll even sing one of his songs as I'm doin' you." He started the chorus to their Grammy-winning tune, knowing exactly how much Liberty loved the sound of his voice—*his* voice, not Paxton fucking Wright's voice—in her ear as he fucked her.

She trembled, but she rallied with, "You are an ass. Just because I find him hot doesn't mean I want to bang him. Don't go attributing your practices with groupies to me. I am not a groupie with you or anyone else."

"Former practices," he said with a snarl. "You're the only woman I want. You're the only fucking woman I see whether we're in a room with a thousand people or when we're alone."

Heated silence hung between them.

"God, you slay me when you say stuff like that—you know that, right?"

He placed his lips on the pulse pounding angrily in her neck. "I mean it. Baby, you *know* I mean it."

She found his mouth in the dark and kissed him until they both had to come up for air. "Then show me," she panted against his neck. "Pin me to the ground and fuck me like you own me. Like I never need to doubt that I'm yours."

Devin's grip tightened on her wrists. "Are we role-playing like last night?"

Her softly murmured "No" vibrated through him as loud as a shout in his ear.

It was the first time she'd indicated there was something more between them than just hot sex. He hadn't realized how much he'd needed to hear it from her.

He took her down to the floor. He didn't remember how they got their clothes off or when he'd put on a condom. He only remembered his frantic desire to be inside her, kissing her, marking her, pounding into her, proving that she did belong to him.

∞

The next afternoon Liberty's cell phone buzzed and the ID read: *Private caller.* "This is Liberty."

"Libs! S'up?"

She smiled. "You tell me. Been a while since I've heard from you, Beetle Bailey."

"God, I hate that nickname."

"I know. Why do you think I use it?"

"Fuck you, Liberty Bell."

"Back atcha. So, little sis, how's the army treating you?"

"Like I'm a slave." Bailey sighed. "Some days it's not so bad. Others, I can't freakin' wait to be done."

"I remember those days. You over there? Or over here?"

"Over here. Me'n five other med specialists were selected for a new training program."

"Cool." Liberty propped her feet up on the ottoman. "Spill the details."

After five minutes of Bailey filling her in, she said, "Anyway, enough about me. What's up in your world?"

"Still on assignment."

"How much longer?"

"A week. Then I've got ten days off. And then the final three weeks."

"Any hotties in your bed helping you kill time?"

The images from the past few nights flashed into her head. The erotic spanking he'd administered. Devin's rough hands caressing her before he leveled that stinging slap over and over. And afterward how one stroke of his finger over her clit had made her come so hard she'd screamed. His mouth had seemed cool against her heated flesh as he'd kissed her flaming butt cheeks. Then, after he'd soothed her, he'd lubed them both up and shoved that big cock of his up her ass. She'd loved every minute of it. His hard-driving rhythm. His muscled chest pressing into her back as his body covered hers fully. His deep voice in her ear as he gave her a dirty play-by-play.

Less than twelve hours after that, he'd shown his jealous side, his possessive side, when he'd fucked her in the dark in his ready room. She'd challenged him to prove that he owned her and he had. Twice. Because as soon as he finished his performance that night, he'd dragged her into the shower in his ready room and fucked her again. She'd been completely wrung out afterward. But it didn't escape her notice that upon seeing her wet hair and Devin's, every one of the Wright Brothers fist-bumped Devin as they passed one another on the way to the buses.

"You've been quiet too long, Libs. Spill the deets from between the sticky sheets."

"Nothing to tell," she lied.

"Aha! I get it. The last time you got any was with Spike and Zeke?"

"No." Even those two guys combined couldn't compare to one night with Devin McClain.

"You're such a whore, doing two hot guys at once. And brothers to boot." In her best pouting tone, Bailey continued. "It's not fair! I wanna be a whore! Give me some pointers."

"Mom could give us both pointers." Liberty paused. "Have you heard from her?"

"No. It's been so long, I think she's dead. Is it really horrible that I don't care if she is?"

Liberty's gut clenched. Of the three of them, Bailey had the most issues with their mother, and she refused to tell either of her sisters what had happened in the years Harper had been away at school and she'd been in the army.

"Anyway, I didn't call you to talk about her. I want to make sure you're okay on this long assignment. Especially since I know you can't talk about it."

"It's a different world from any I've ever been in, and to be honest, I'm glad it's only for a few months. I couldn't live this way. That said, I get an equal balance of worktime and downtime." And she did get Devin's undivided sexual attention in that downtime, so that was a bonus. "Thanks for checking up on me."

"Being away from family just reminds me how I didn't appreciate it when I had it. Jesus, I was such a brat to Harper sometimes. I can't believe she didn't wash her hands of me just like Mom did."

"Everyone has a shitty stage in their life where they're dicks to the ones they love. The lucky ones grow out of it and move on. We Masterson girls gotta stick together because we're all we have."

"So true. I talked to Harper last night. She mentioned your upcoming visit to Muddy Gap. I'm jealous."

"I wish you could fly to Denver and drive up with me. Tate and Jake are at that fun stage where everything excites them."

"I told Harper if I'm not mired in training, I'd try to get the week of Thanksgiving off so we can all be together. Of course, she's already planning a family holiday, and we've been drafted to play the part of pilgrims in the Thanksgiving Day reenactment."

Liberty grinned. "I can't wait."

"I can't wait until I live closer. I feel like I'm missing out."

"The time left on your enlistment will go by faster than you know it. And since I'm buying a bigger place in Denver right after I'm done with this assignment, you can stay with me."

"Hang on." Bailey had a short, muffled conversation with someone and then came back on the line. "My study partner is here, so I've gotta go. Love you, sis. I miss you."

"Miss you too, Bails. Love you. Be safe."

The conversation with Bailey increased her melancholy. It was so tempting to pull the covers over her head, stay in her pajamas and sleep until they reached their destination.

Except that you need to be on top of this security nightmare that Devin created.

He hadn't told anyone he planned to perform the controversial song "What Love Isn't." His argument that, technically, it wasn't part of *his* set but the Wright Brothers' set didn't hold water. The crowd's response that night had been overwhelmingly positive. But in this day and age, media response was instantaneous, and word spread rapidly that he'd performed the song.

People in the Bible Belt were serious about lodging protests. So yesterday afternoon, when the bus pulled into the parking lot in Little Rock, a large crowd of protestors had gathered.

That had pissed Devin off. He didn't address the protestors directly—besides playing the song on his set list first thing.

While Liberty understood where Devin was coming from—freedom of speech and not allowing a minority to silence him—it'd created bigger problems.

Trying to get the right media spin on it wasn't her job, but she'd been thrust into dealing with the aftermath as part of *her* job. She'd stayed up late last night worrying about possible security breaches in the next two small venues because she was Devin's lone protector.

Due to her restlessness, and, yes, her annoyance with Devin, she'd slept in her bunk for the first time in weeks. Rather than continuing to obsess over how their professional disagreement also affected their personal relationship, she faced the wall and closed her eyes, trying to shut down her brain.

She had no idea how much time had passed when his warm body pressed against hers and his deep voice in her ear pulled her from dreamland. "Hey."

"Hey, yourself. Are you finished working?"

"Yeah. Had a hard time concentrating today."

Gee, I wonder why. "What time is it?"

"A little after three. We'll be hitting Pine Bluff soon."

"I should shower." She tried to push up, but Devin held her in place, his hand on her stomach.

"Are you still mad at me?"

Liberty sighed. "I don't know if mad is accurate. You know how much I love surprises," she said dryly. "I dread seeing how many zealots greet us today."

"Besides their homemade signs spreading the hate, they've been law-abiding."

"Until they're not. We're lucky that they haven't showed us the throwing things, burning things, Molotov cocktail side of public protests. We've had a good go of it the last few weeks with few incidents."

"Because I played it safe," he said testily.

"No, because I've worked my ass off to keep you safe," she shot back.

"Liberty—"

"Don't, okay? It's your tour. It's your career. It's your song. So it's your choice on how you handle it. When it comes to the artistic side, I'd never presume to tell you what to do."

"But?"

"But nothing. As your bodyguard, you courting controversy makes my job harder. And that comment wasn't meant to say that how it affects me should hold any weight on your decision. Because at the end of the day, no matter what you choose to do, it is my job to adapt and protect you."

Devin nuzzled the back of her head. "I didn't write the song to be controversial. I wrote it because I was pissed off and needed a way to express it."

"What's the real story behind the song?"

"I've watched a friend havin' to hide who he is because the country music industry is highly homophobic. The guy is a brilliant performer and songwriter, but he'll lose everything if he's ever brave enough to step out of the closet to live openly with the man he loves. The whole theme of the song is . . . love is love. No one has the right to judge anyone else and tell them what love is or isn't. When a reporter questioned me whether the song was autobiographical, I said no. But I went off on her, stating that I think gays should be able to marry and that too many people worried what others were doin' behind closed bedroom doors when it ain't nobody's business. That didn't sit well with my demographic—according to the record label.

"I stand behind everything I said and the song because I believe it. But I'd already had enough threat stuff goin' on before I offered such a juicy sound bite. So I agreed to leave the song off the set list for this tour. I thought I'd made the right decision."

"When did that change?"

"I don't know if it did. Now I'm fucked because if I don't play it, the hard-core religious groups targeting me claim they've won. If I do play it, I'm putting myself and you and the entire tour at risk. There's no easy or right answer." He sighed into her hair. "I'm sorry it put us at odds."

"It didn't."

"Then why'd you sleep in here last night?" His lips followed the outline of her ear. "I missed you like crazy."

That delicious curl of heat started between her legs and spread up to where he was dragging his fingers back and forth across her lower belly. "I missed you too."

"Come back to my bed," he murmured against the nape of her neck. "Let me show you."

"Are the servants' quarters below the master's standards?" she teased.

"There's not enough room to spread out this gorgeous body and feast on it like I'm dying to."

"Maybe you should get creative."

Devin rolled her flat on her back. Then he pinned her legs beneath his and shoved her T-shirt up. Instead of taking her shirt off, he did a quick tie that immobilized her arms. A growling noise vibrated against her skin when he discovered she wasn't wearing a bra. His mouth descended, and he pressed hot kisses around the outside of her left nipple.

He kneaded her right breast while he teased the left one with his tongue. Light flicks and his soft breath on the wet tips until she squirmed. Then he suckled sweetly as he stroked the other nipple with a lazy sweep of his thumb. "I need you like this."

"Like what?"

"Sweet and slow."

She melted. "Undo my hands so I can touch you too."

The caresses lingered. The kisses were gentle and teasing. In the small space, their naked bodies were in constant contact. Tangled in the sheets and wrapped up in each other, they turned their passion into comfort. And she was reminded to let their need bring them closer together instead of letting it keep them apart.

Chapter Twenty

❧

*T*hree days until the longest leg of the Heroes and Heartbreakers tour ended. Two more performances and then ten days off. Ten days that he hoped Liberty would spend with him in Nashville.

As soon as the bus parked in the back lot of the event center in the Woodlands, Devin launched the first stage of his plan to convince her. He managed to kill thirty minutes before he left his room.

Liberty sat cross-legged on the chair across from her bunk, playing a video game. She wore baggy tan capris and a baggier T-shirt. He preferred her this way, because no one else got to see her like this. She looked cute.

The woman would knock you on your ass for saying that.

She'd pulled her hair into a ponytail that bounced when she snapped her head up. "Why are you standing there staring at me?"

"I've got a surprise for you. Grab a jacket. And a pair of flip-flops."

"Where are we going?"

"You'll see. And no, you don't need your gun."

Liberty gave him the evil eye. "*I* get to decide where to take my gun."

"It's not necessary where we're goin'. I swear." Up at the front of the bus, he settled his favorite ratty UWYO ball cap on his head. Then he grabbed his backpack and slipped his feet into his sandals.

"What's that for?"

Devin tucked a loose strand of blue hair behind her ear. "Stop bein' so suspicious. We're gonna have some fun."

She muttered something he didn't quite catch as she armed the alarm, but it probably wasn't flattering.

The humid Texas air rolled over him. He wondered how long it took people who lived down here to get used to it, because he doubted he could.

Clasping hands, they skirted the back of the bus. It was the hour before twilight, when the sun had lost its power and most of its heat. He saw the two cars in the middle of the empty parking lot. Right on time.

"Devin, this is making me uncomfortable. You being out in the open like this."

He stopped and faced her, leaning close enough to feel her breath on his lips. "Liberty, relax. There's no one around."

"But—"

He pressed his mouth to hers. "We're leaving. Will that calm you down some?"

"I don't know. This is all so . . . weird. So unlike you."

Which is exactly why he'd set it up. "As of right now, you're officially off duty." He took her hand again and headed toward the two lone cars parked in the lot.

A young guy, probably midtwenties, exited the driver's side and approached them. "Mr. McClain?"

"Yes. Thanks so much for bringing it here on such short notice. Is there anything else you need?"

The guy handed him a clipboard. "Just your signature. Normally we demand a photo ID, but I understand it's an unusual circumstance. Besides, I recognize you. I'm bringing my girlfriend to the show tomorrow night." He grinned.

Devin grinned back. "Excellent. I always look forward to playing here. Good crowd." He scrawled his name and passed the clipboard back. "Soon as you get here tomorrow night, go to the merchandise stand and ask for Sarge. Tell him you met me and use the phrase *Gatlin Brothers* and he'll get you backstage passes for the fan meet and greet."

The guy's jaw dropped. "Seriously? Thank you, man. My girlfriend is gonna be stoked. You are her favorite singer."

"Look forward to meeting her, then. So, are we all set here?"

"Yes, sir." He tossed Devin the keys. "Word of advice when you're in the Gulf region? Put the top up every night."

"Will do."

The guy climbed into the passenger's side of the Enterprise pilot car and they sped off.

Liberty was completely focused on the car. "What is going on?"

He tugged her against his body. "We are practically livin' together. We've been lovers for a little more than two months, and it occurred to me in the past few days that I've never taken you out on a real date. So that's what I'm doin' tonight. Just you and me. On a date."

She looked up at him. "You rented a Mustang? For me?"

"I figured you missed your baby and you'd like to see how fast you can get us to the beach."

"Really?"

"Really. Galveston is an hour or so down the road. We can hit a drive-thru barbecue joint, then sit on the sand in the moonlight and listen to the waves crashing on the beach for as long as you like."

Liberty threw herself into his arms. "This is so perfect! I can't believe you set it up." She slid her hands to his cheeks, holding his face as she kissed him.

He had to pull back because she was bouncing up and down with such excitement he worried one of them might break a tooth.

But she wasn't ready to let him go. She peppered his face with kisses. "Thank you. This means so much to me. Especially since very few people get me." She kissed his chin and stepped back. "Now I know why you said I didn't need to be armed. But I still feel . . . naked."

"You really wanna spend hours cleaning sand out of your gun just for taking it along?" He tucked a hank of hair behind her ear. "We'll be far away from the crowds. I promise."

"Okay." She grinned. "Now, hand over those keys, buddy."

Devin tossed them to her. "Let's go."

Driving down the highway in the early twilight hours softened the breath-stealing humidity. Liberty was in her element, with wind blowing through her hair and a powerful car under her control. Devin was content to watch her, such a rarity in their world because she spent all her time keeping an eagle eye on him. Sometimes after she fell asleep in his arms, he watched her sleep, feeling both guilty and daring, knowing she'd hate that he'd studied her at such a vulnerable time. But her toughness and resilience only made him want to embrace and celebrate the playful side of this complex woman.

"Did you want to listen to music?" she asked.

"No. I like the sound of the wind whistling through the car."

"I thought about buying the convertible model, but it didn't come in the color I wanted." She grinned at him. "I can't believe you rented us a Mustang."

"I can't believe you didn't freak out when I suggested we eat in the car. Aren't car nuts like you vigilant about keeping the interior pristine?"

"Yeah. But this is not *my* car."

"So if we were in your Mustang right now?"

"We definitely wouldn't have chowed down on ribs soaked in barbecue sauce, corn bread muffins and sweet potato fries in here."

He laughed. Seemed he did that a lot around her.

They didn't talk much, but given the people and noise they were usually subjected to, he preferred comfortable silence. Those were his favorite times with her. The two of them tangled in bed, watching TV or playing a video game. Maybe it sounded boring to others, but the normalcy was exciting to him because he'd never really had it.

The scent of the air changed, and she turned to him and grinned. "I can smell the ocean."

"Not far now."

Once they'd crossed onto the island, they hit stop-and-go traffic. Devin expected Liberty would be an aggressive driver, cursing and muttering about idiots, but she remained relaxed. About a block away from the main boardwalk, she said, "Which way? Left or right?"

"Left."

Devin didn't tell her to pull over until they reached a section of the road where there weren't many streetlights and access to the beach was a little more difficult. Since it was summer and tourist season, theirs wasn't the only vehicle, but he knew they'd have more privacy than if they'd come during the day.

"Should we put the top up on the car?" she asked.

"Nah. Nothin' to steal. And it doesn't look like rain." He shouldered his backpack and pointed.

They followed the path to the water single file. Liberty said, "I'm glad you suggested flip-flops."

"I don't like wearing sandals, but I hate havin' sand in my shoes even more."

As soon as they could walk side by side, Liberty reached for his hand.

He loved even the smallest gesture of affection she offered without thinking.

"There it is." She tugged on his hand, urging him to move faster.

Devin laughed. "Baby, slow down. The Gulf ain't goin' nowhere."

"I know. I'm just excited."

He stood beside her about ten feet from the water, watching the waves break on the beach and then flowing back into the water. They remained like that, looking out across the dark expanse. Hearing the steady whoosh and crash that came only from the ocean.

Liberty kicked off her flip-flops and released his hand, shuffling closer to the water's edge.

Devin stayed behind her, watching the slight breeze tousle her hair. She jammed her hands into her pockets and dug her toes deeper into the sand. Tilting her head back, she inhaled an exaggerated breath, letting it out on a long "Aah."

He toed off his sandals and moved in behind her, wrapping his arms around her and setting his chin on her shoulder.

"Devin, this is so awesome. Thank you."

"My pleasure."

Sometimes it was weird to think he had enough money to take her to any beach in the world. He could buy—not just rent—any car she wanted for her. But he knew that wouldn't appeal to her. Because this was more real.

"The first time I saw the ocean was when I went overseas on my first deployment," she said. "I remember being on the troop transport plane, and I snuck over to stare out the window because I'd never seen so much water. I mean, you watch TV shows and stuff and know it's there. But flying over it for hours and hours with no land in sight fucked with my head. Standing on a beach like this seems more manageable."

"Same thing happened to me, that feeling of almost panic when there's nothin' below you but miles and miles of water. I'd never been on a plane before, so it seemed like it took forever to get there. Although the flight wasn't nearly as long as the one you took to Iraq."

"Where did you go?"

Devin felt that same jab in his heart whenever he spoke of it. "Hawaii."

"Sounds fun. I've never been there."

"We did have fun, but at the same time, it seemed forced."

"How old were you?"

"Fifteen."

Liberty spun into his arms and looked at him. "You went with your family?"

"Yeah. It was a vacation of sorts, but it wasn't for us. It was for Michelle. It was her Make-A-Wish trip. The organization is wonderful; everything from our hotel to the sightseeing stuff was top-notch, and they treated Michelle like a rockstar. But for my folks and my sister Renee and me, there was a layer of sadness there the whole time. We all knew it'd be her first and last trip."

She framed his face in her hands. "Devin."

Something about her made him keep talking, allowed him to share a piece of his past he'd never told anyone. He closed his eyes, letting the memory wash over him, almost as sharp and painful as when he'd lived it. "The last night we were there, my mom, dad and sister were packing. Michelle wanted to walk on the beach, so she and I took off. We did all the things kids do when their parents aren't around; we picked up shells, jumped over the waves just as they broke on the beach, splashed each other, kicked sand at each other. She talked nonstop about how much fun she'd had swimming with dolphins earlier that day. As soon as she'd gotten out of the water, before they'd even wrapped her skinny body in a towel, she'd informed everyone that one day she was gonna be a dolphin trainer.

"We'd walked farther down the beach than I realized and she started to get tired. We'd had so much fun just bein' a normal big brother and little sister that for an hour or so I'd forgotten how easily she got tired out and how frail she really was. So I swung her up for a piggyback ride. Since she'd gotten so quiet, I talked for a change and didn't notice that it was a different kind of quiet with her. When we reached the beach house, I turned to let her down and she clung to me. She said, 'No, wait. I wanna look at the water and pretend.' I said, 'Pretend what?' She said, 'Pretend that I really will grow up and be a dolphin trainer.' Then she paused and said softly, 'But I'm not gonna grow up, am I?'

"I wanted to lie, be the protective big brother and assure her that she'd grow up and annoy me for years to come. But I couldn't do it. For a year and a half Michelle had been living with people tellin' her that she'd be fine. Yeah, she was young, but she wasn't stupid. She knew bein' in that kind of pain wasn't normal. Neither was living in the hospital. Or seein' her family cry after a doctor's visit. Or getting a once-in-a-lifetime trip to Hawaii. So I didn't lie. I said, 'Nope, bug. Probably not.' She was quiet for so long, I thought maybe she'd fallen asleep. But she finally whispered, 'Then promise me that you'll think of me every time you go to the ocean.' That's the one promise in my life I've been able to keep."

Liberty's thumbs swept away the tears he hadn't tried to stop. When she buried her wet face in his neck, he knew she'd been crying too. She wrapped herself around him, showing him without words she was a woman strong enough to hold him up.

After a while he felt a little ridiculous. He forced a laugh. "Sorry if that put a morbid spin on what was supposed to be a fun date."

"Don't apologize. We're standing on the beach and it was bound to cross your mind. Although it breaks my heart all around"—her voice caught on a sob—"I'm happy you trusted me enough to tell me."

Tell her she's the only person you've ever told.

But Devin's lips remained sealed. Until Liberty kissed a path up his neck to his mouth and urged him to open up to her kiss. She teased and tormented, licking his teeth, sucking on his tongue. As she used her mouth like a weapon on his, he wanted the same treatment on his cock.

In the time they'd been lovers, whenever she dropped to her knees or slithered down his body to take his dick in her mouth, he'd let her get in a couple of good licks and sucks, but he wouldn't let her finish the job. He wanted more than that with her. Stupid reasoning, but he wanted all the other aspects of sex besides blow jobs that he'd denied himself with the groupies.

When she shivered, he broke the kiss and murmured, "I brought a blanket if you're cold."

She smiled. "I'm not cold. If you haven't noticed, the way you kiss me always makes me shiver. But I wouldn't mind sitting on the blanket."

"Sounds good." Devin kissed her again and then reached for his backpack. He pulled out a sleeping bag, unzipped it, and walked to drier sand before he spread it out.

Liberty left her flip-flops where they were and plopped on the left side of the sleeping bag.

But Devin wasn't having it. He sat in the middle and pulled her up until she sat between his legs, with her back against his chest. "Much better."

"Now there's sand everywhere on the blanket."

"Sweetheart, we're at the beach. There's gonna be sand everywhere no matter how careful we are." He nuzzled the back of her head. "Besides, this is a date. Our bodies are supposed to be in contact as much as possible."

She snorted. "You just wanna cop a feel to see what kind of bra I'm wearing."

"I already know you're wearing a normal bra, not a titty squisher. Because when you hugged me, I loved feelin' all that soft flesh pressed against me."

"So maybe, just maybe, if you are a perfect gentleman the rest of the date, I'll let you get to second base."

Devin bent his head to brush his lips across her ear. "And if I'm not a perfect gentleman?"

She wiggled her ass against his crotch. "Then at the end of the date, I'll let you bend me over the couch on the bus and fuck me until I scream your name."

"Tough choice. But I'll go with option two." He nipped her earlobe. "That okay with you?"

"Mmm-hmm. Gonna be a long drive back to the bus."

They gazed at the moonlit sky and the reflection of the moon on the ocean. The foam on the waves was a fluorescent green, from some kind of algae plankton that was prevalent in the summer months. He remembered Tanna explaining it during one of their beach talks.

After a while, his arms tired of holding them up, and he stretched out on his back with Liberty lying beside him.

"Could you live someplace like this year-round?" she asked.

"I don't know. It'd be cool to have a beach house get-away. But I like the change of seasons. I don't even get as much of that as I'd like living in Nashville. But the last year I've been on the road so much, I walk into my house in Nashville and feel like I'm in a hotel. Not the kind of place I thought I'd come home to."

"Meaning a wife and three point two kids waiting for you in your mansion?"

"It's not a mansion by any stretch," he said dryly. "I'd like to have the wife and kids someday. I'm not in any hurry."

"You don't have to be. You're a guy. You can father kids at any age."

"How about you? Got a burning desire to have munchkins running around?"

"Never thought I'd want that until Harper had Tate and Jake. But unless I meet Mr. Right—not the ones in the Wright Brothers Band, so quit making that growling noise—pretty damn soon, I'll be shit out of luck. My biological clock is ticking furiously."

Devin never thought about this stuff, to say nothing of talking about it, because most women would assume when he discussed having kids, that meant he wanted to have them right now with them.

For some reason he had a flash of a cranky Liberty being pregnant with his child. Then he saw her cradling an infant and him holding the hand of a pigtailed little girl and it didn't scare him senseless. It seemed almost . . . right.

Liberty moved until she hung on all fours above him, pulling his attention away from his strange vision.

"Are you ready to go?"

"No. Close your eyes and keep your hands folded behind your head."

He complied. She kissed him with that blend of fire and control that made him crazy. By the time her hand traveled from his pecs to his belly, his cock had gone hard.

She stroked his shaft through the cotton material until he made a low groan. Then she popped the button, eased the zipper down, and tugged on his camo shorts and boxers until they were past his knees.

Then she scooted backward, planting kisses in a straight line down his torso. The tip of his cock bumped her chin. She didn't look up, didn't speak. Liberty just drew him deep into her mouth on the first pass. Warmth and wetness surrounded his shaft—a feeling of bliss in itself, and then she started to suck.

Goddamn, did that feel fucking amazing.

Her hair drifted across the sensitive skin of his lower abdomen with every vigorous bob of her head.

Her breasts swayed with her body movement, rubbing his thighs until he imagined it was just her hard nipples teasing his skin with no barrier between them.

Fuck. That mouth of hers. She didn't need her hands. She was already turning him inside out.

But Devin needed to stroke her cheek or touch her hair. Look into her eyes. Make it intimate and personal and not like every other blow job, where he just sat there and the woman on her knees went to town.

Not this time.

He sat up and curled his hands over her ears, lifting her face to break the connection between her hot mouth and his dick.

Her eyes glittered in the moonlight. "Don't stop me so you can fuck me, Devin. I want to suck you off."

"I want that too. But I wanna watch this pretty mouth wrapped around the base of my cock. It's fuckin' sexy as hell that you can take me so deep. I want to watch as you drive me out of my mind. I want to watch as you swallow my come. I want you to look at me and see what you do to me."

"Okay, then. But I don't want you to hold back. I wanna feel you spill in my mouth."

He stroked her cheek. "That'll happen sooner than you might think."

"Good. And I want to hear you say my name, Devin. *Mine.* Shout it, groan it or whisper it, but in that moment when you let go, I want you to remember who got you there."

There was a glimpse of her sexual ego he hadn't seen before. "Anything you want."

Devin thought she might tease, drag this out longer,

but she kept her eyes on his as she parted her lips and engulfed his cock in one greedy gulp.

"Fuck."

He kept his hands on her head, not to direct her but to hold her hair back so he could watch her face.

That wet mouth worked him. And worked him. Shallow. Deep. He had one warning shot between his brain and his balls and then *zing*. He started to come. His pulse was thundering through his body louder than the waves crashing on the beach.

She looked up as the first spurt hit the back of her tongue.

He choked out, "Liberty," and she clamped down on his cock, sucking in time to every pulse, until she'd milked him dry.

As he fought to remember how to breathe, she tilted her head, locking their gazes as she slowly released him. She placed a soft kiss on the tip of his cock and grinned when that action caused it to jerk closer to her mouth. She sat back on her haunches. "So that didn't suck?"

Devin shook his head. Maybe his brain wasn't running on all cylinders, but that was an odd response from her. "Not at all. I'm still feeling the aftereffects."

"That's the first time you've let me at your dick for more than thirty seconds. I thought I might've done something you didn't like."

"God, no." He reached for her hand. "I never meant to give you that impression."

Of course Liberty noticed that wasn't really an explanation. He'd tell her why he'd held back on that—just not now. "So how about you hop up here and sit on my face?"

"Tempting, but I'll take a rain check."

Then he hauled her on top of him and rolled them both

down to the ground, his lips sliding over hers until she opened her mouth to accept his kiss. He wanted to taste himself on her tongue. He loved the way she could match his mood, knowing exactly what response he needed from her. The kiss calmed him.

"Are you getting cold with your pants down around your ankles?" she asked.

"Yeah. I think I've got sand in my ass crack too."

She pushed up. "Poor baby. There wasn't any sand on your cock. I licked it completely clean."

"Trust me, I know." Devin stood to pull up his shorts. "You wanna walk on the beach before we leave?"

"Nah. I'm good. This was great." She stepped into his arms and hugged him. "Really great. And just what I needed. Thank you."

"It was what I needed too." He pressed his lips against the top of her head, breathing in the salty air and the vanilla scent of her shampoo. He couldn't remember the last time he'd felt so hopeful. Liberty had to know that the connection between them wouldn't be this strong if it was only temporary. He believed fate had sent her his way for a reason besides protecting his ass.

They shook out the sand and rolled up the sleeping bag. When they reached the car, Devin said, "Don't suppose you'll let me drive?"

"Nope. And be warned; I'm gonna push this bitch to see what she'll do."

With the warm wind blowing and Liberty singing softly to the pop tunes on the radio, Devin dozed off. He came to when they hit the lights of Houston and the always crazy Houston traffic. He squinted at the clock. "Holy hell, woman. How fast did you drive?"

"A little over the speed limit."

"So without coming across as a backseat driver, you remember how to get to the event center?"

"I think so. If you see me taking a wrong turn, let me know."

When they pulled into the back entrance of the parking lot and he saw all the cop cars, he figured they must've taken a wrong turn someplace. But sure enough, the arena was right ahead of them.

"What the hell?" Liberty said.

That's when he realized the activity was centered on his tour bus and his stomach dropped.

She threw the car in park by the police barricade. Then she looked at him, her face a blank mask, her entire body on full alert. There was no sign of the woman he'd spent the last five hours with.

"What do you think happened?"

"That's what I'm going to find out. You stay here. I mean it, Devin. Don't you leave this fucking car."

Devin gave her his back and opened the door to get out. He kept his tone even when she started threatening him. He cut her off with "Do you really think me sitting in a car by myself outside the line of police protection or out of your sight is really the safest place for me to be?"

"Fuck." She inhaled and exhaled slowly. "You stay by me, *right* by me."

"Fine. I get it. Let's go see what happened."

They reached the end of the barricades and were surrounded.

"Who are you? I need to see some ID now!" a cop, pointing a gun at them, barked.

"I'm Devin McClain. This is my personal assistant, Liberty Masterson. Crash Cavanaugh is my tour manager and he can verify who I am."

Thirty seconds later Crash stomped over. "Where the fuck have you been? Jesus Christ. We've been tryin' to get ahold of you for damn near an hour!"

"What happened?"

"Someone shot the hell out of your tour bus. And when we couldn't find you . . . we thought maybe you'd been kidnapped. Especially since there was no sign of Liberty either. And once we got on the bus, it looked like you'd left abruptly. Both your cell phones were on board, as well as Liberty's purse. She'd left her laptop on and your TV was blaring in your bedroom. So where were you?"

"I rented a car and we drove down to Galveston."

"Be nice if you fucking told someone and didn't just go off and do your own damn thing, boss." Crash stomped away.

Devin glanced over to see Liberty in conversation with a cop in plainclothes. He headed toward her.

". . . inside. Different story on the outside."

"Can you tell me what's goin' on?" he asked the guy, not Liberty.

"Someone shot up your bus tonight, Mr. McClain."

"Was anyone hurt?"

"There wasn't anyone on the bus, which was a good thing. Your band had taken their bus to run errands and grab some dinner, was my understanding. Half the road crew went along with them. The rest of the road crew was inside setting up."

"Thank God for that. Did they catch who did it?" *Please say yes. Please say it was some crankhead shooting stuff up on a dare and this wasn't directed at me.*

"No, sir, we don't have any suspects. We don't have any witnesses either."

"So this could've been random." Devin noticed the guy wore a detective badge around his neck.

The detective rubbed the skin between his eyes. "It could've been. Or the shooter knew this was your bus and, for whatever reason, emptied twenty rounds into it, hoping one of those rounds hit you."

Jesus.

Then the detective turned so no one could see what they were discussing. "Your security specialist has informed me because of previous incidents you've been assigned a full-time bodyguard?"

"That is correct."

"Well, you'd better give her a big raise because keeping you away from the arena tonight might've saved your life. You're a lucky man."

Chapter Twenty-one

*L*ucky.

       Yeah, right.

Liberty wanted to throw up. She'd gotten so fucking cocky the last week. Believing that the worst had passed because the protesting had stopped.

But this? Shooting up the tour bus? This was worse than everything else that had happened during the tour combined.

She listened with barely controlled skepticism as the detective in charge and the cops discussed the ballistics pattern, which they were very careful to point out didn't denote intent. The shooter sprayed a wide arc to hit as much surface area as possible. Didn't mean the shooter knew the rear of the bus contained the master bedroom.

She called bullshit on that. If it was random vandalism, why not go for maximum damage and shoot out the windows in the front?

Without any witnesses, chances were good the shooter had left the area undetected. They were waiting for footage from the security cameras scattered throughout the event center's parking lot, but they couldn't access it until tomorrow.

So while she knew the cops were only doing their job, keeping things vague until they had some real answers, it pissed her the fuck off. Especially when the lead detective asked if Crash knew if the venue had sold out for the performance. Like the shooting had been some sort of publicity stunt to sell more tickets. Then he asked if any of the media outlets had been contacted.

That's when Liberty had lost her cool. She pointed out that the dozen cop cars with flashing lights and a police barricade with two dozen cops milling about would clue in the media that something was going on a helluva lot faster than a phone call.

Devin wasn't around for what happened after that, since the detective thought it wise to separate them.

He took her inside the bus and tested her hands for gunpowder residue. He asked to see her weapons. He asked to see her permit to carry concealed. The whole time he was checking to see if her guns had been fired, he gave her a running commentary on how *convenient* it was that no one was around when the shots were fired. And how *convenient* that she and Devin were mysteriously gone and no one could get in touch with them. And since they hadn't bought anything in Galveston, wasn't it *convenient* that they didn't have a receipt to show they'd been ninety miles away on the beach.

That's when she knew that they'd file this as a public nuisance case.

Her fury threatened to consume her. How many more dangerous situations was Devin going to deal with before actual harm came to him? Would something be done about it only when he'd taken a bullet or been beat to shit? Devin's safety had been compromised and no one gave a damn.

The detective's disbelieving look about her being Devin's bodyguard had burned her ass. As had his raised eyebrows and smarmy grin when he was asked to keep her position classified. The sexual innuendo hadn't been spoken, but it had sure as hell had been implied.

She hated that the dismissive attitude of the cops was affecting her confidence. And it didn't help that they were directing all their questions to Crash, not to her. Because he had a dick? Because he wasn't sleeping with Devin McClain?

Liberty snapped out of her fog of anger when her name was called. "Yes, Detective?"

"We've decided to impound the bus until we can access the security tapes."

"Everything we need on tour is on that bus."

"Then I suggest you pack a bag," he said grumpily, turning his head away to expel a phlegmy cough.

She jammed a change of clothes, her laptop, her bathroom kit and her stun gun in her workout bag. Before she left the bus, she made the detective write her a receipt for her remaining firearms and her ammunition.

Crash paced outside the bus when she exited. "What the hell did they do to you in there?"

"Beat me with a rubber hose," she deadpanned.

"Liberty, that ain't funny."

"I know." She sighed. "I don't want to talk about what

they did. What's the status on our accommodations for tonight?"

"We're staying at Benet Tower. It's an exclusive hotel that's not billed as such because the first twelve floors are private residences. Big Sky is providing extra security, and everyone involved with tomorrow night's performance is getting a room. The band and the opening act are on the presidential level, the road crew's one floor down." Crash leaned closer. "Since there wasn't obvious external damage on the other buses, the cops aren't demanding access to them. Which is damn lucky."

Lucky. There was that word again.

But it was good the cops weren't searching the other buses because they'd likely find illegal substances. Devin didn't need to lose his road crew the second to the last night on tour. "The buses will be all right, sitting here unattended?"

"They won't be unattended. They'll be under surveillance by the company that's providing security for the event."

Liberty's eyes narrowed. "Who set that up?"

"I did." Crash moved closer. "Look, I know you're in charge of security, but you weren't here and something had to be done."

That jab stung. A reminder—besides the goddamn bullet holes in the bus—that she hadn't done her job.

"Big Sky is e-mailing all the info to you about the changes, but I don't know if they'll get it to you tonight."

She wondered if Big Sky had contacted GSC. She couldn't fucking wait to have that conversation with Garrett, confessing that she'd been frolicking on the beach with Devin while the bus had been under fire. She glanced over to where Devin was in conversation with Paxton Wright. Two cops stood a few feet behind them, blatantly listening in on their conversation. "I grabbed some personal stuff. Devin should do the same before they take the bus away."

"I already got it for him. He keeps an emergency travel bag packed at all times."

Three long vans pulled up, and she watched band members and crew load their ragtag luggage into the back.

"You and Dev are takin' a car service to the hotel," Crash said. "Looks like it's here."

"Why don't you and Devin go? I'll finish up with the cops and talk with the surveillance crew."

"Liberty, it's been handled. I know you're upset, but the truth is, it's a good thing you and Devin weren't here. I can see you feel . . . guilt or whatever, but you did your job. Devin wasn't in any danger because he was safe with you. Let me repeat it; you did your job."

You did your job.

Right.

"Liberty," Devin said softly. When he set his hand on her shoulder, she flinched and stepped back.

Then she couldn't look in his eyes because she knew he'd either be pissed off or hurt by her reaction. "I know the car is here. Let's go."

"Isn't Crash comin' with us?"

"No. He's staying here." *To do my job.*

Liberty waited until Devin was in the car before she climbed in. Immediately, she opened the notes app on her phone and started typing in what she'd seen while it was still fresh in her mind.

"Sweetheart, are you okay?"

Actually, I'm fucked up by all of this, but telling you

how I feel would further undermine your confidence in my ability to protect you. "I'm fine."

"Then why won't you talk to me?"

"Because I'm dealing with a shitstorm of security changes, most of which I had zero input on, so I'm trying to sort through it all."

"Liberty, look at me."

"Give me a sec."

"Now."

Annoyed by his sharp tone, she looked up from her phone. "What?"

"Stop."

"Stop what?"

"Stop whatever thoughts are in your head makin' you act like this."

"Act like what? Like I need to remember that I'm supposed to be doing my job protecting you and not goddamn rolling around on the beach with you?"

His eyes darkened. "You rolling around on the beach with me did protect me. I wasn't here. I wasn't in the line of fire. Therefore you should get a fuckin' commendation for doin' your job."

She shook her head. "I should've been prepared. I should've known—"

"Known what? That somebody would decide to take potshots at my bus? As far as I know, you can't see into the future, so there's no way you could've been prepared for it. Stop feeling guilty."

"You don't understand."

"No, I don't. But I can see this is another one of them times you won't give an inch or listen to me." He turned away from her and gazed out the window.

They didn't speak at all for the remainder of the ride.

And unlike their drive to the beach, the silence between them wasn't comfortable.

The main floor of Benet Tower looked like an upscale hotel with a restaurant, a bar, a spa and a few retail shops. The elevator system was confusing, with separate elevators for the residences. The concierge led them to an express elevator that served the top five floors in the building and required an additional keycard to access the presidential level.

At least the security was top-notch.

Devin had scored the presidential suite, which contained two bedrooms, a large living room and a small kitchen.

The concierge took their bags into the master bedroom. He told Devin, "There's a fitness facility on this floor and a sauna. Everything else is on the main floor. Don't hesitate to call the front desk if you need anything."

"I appreciate it." He passed the guy a folded bill. After the concierge left, Devin moved in behind Liberty and placed a kiss on her neck. "I need a shower. Wanna join me?"

"You go ahead. I have a few things to wrap up."

An hour later, Devin stormed into the living room. "Enough. It's two o'clock in the fuckin' morning. Whatever you're dealing with can wait a few hours."

Arguing with him would only make him dig his heels in deeper. "You're right."

She'd forgotten to pack pajamas, so she pulled on yoga capris and a sports bra.

Devin was already under the covers when she crawled in. He brought her body against his and nuzzled the back of her head. "You wanna talk?"

"No."

"Me neither." He pressed a kiss below her ear as his hand skimmed the front of her body. "'Cause I know a better way to take your mind off everything."

"Devin, I'm tired."

"That's okay. I'll do all the work." His warm lips trailed down the side of her neck as his hands cupped her breasts. "Sweetheart, we both need this."

"Stop. I'm really not in the mood."

He froze.

Liberty took advantage of his surprise and put some physical distance between them. "We both need to rest."

Devin didn't say a word. But it was like a wall of ice had dropped between them.

∞

As soon as Devin fell asleep, Liberty grabbed her duffel bag and headed out of the room.

She spoke to the guard stationed by the elevators, making sure he'd remain at his post and letting him know where she'd be if he needed to get in touch with her. Then she sprinted to the end of the long hallway, using her keycard to unlock the state-of-the-art fitness center.

Her anxiety had built to the point she had to drop her head between her knees for a couple of minutes to keep from passing out.

Once she'd regained her control, she exited the bathroom and checked out her options.

She could run on the treadmill. She could power climb on the elliptical. She could hop on the bike and spin her wheels. There was even a rowing machine. All those would get her blood pumping, but they seemed too passive for the emotions roiling in her.

Turning, she scrutinized the weight machines, free

weights and kettlebells. Too tempting to throw the kettle-bell like a shot put. In the opposite corner were yoga mats, exercise balls of all sizes, elastic bands for stretching, jump ropes and step boxes.

This was a totally tricked-out space, but it didn't have the one thing that would make it perfect—a heavy bag. She wanted—no, she *needed*—to pound the fuck out of something. Feel her fists connecting with a solid object, imagining it was the shooter's head. Feel her kicks connecting with a solid object, imagining it was the shooter's body. When she noticed the speed bag dangling from the extended arm of the weight machine, she was somewhat mollified. She'd use a cardio workout to get her blood pumping.

During her time on the treadmill, images of Devin's bullet-riddled bus kept up a constant loop in her head. What-if scenarios bogged down her mind, even when she knew it was counterproductive.

How could she live with herself if something happened to him on her watch?

She couldn't. Because she'd fallen in love with him.

Would she have to tell Garrett that? So he could find a replacement for the last three weeks?

She ended her run at the forty-five-minute mark and headed to the mat. Although her lungs labored, she did push-ups and abdominal-strengthening exercises. After slipping on her modified boxing gloves, she dragged her sweat-soaked body to the speed bag.

When her arms finally got tired, she took a break and sucked down several mouthfuls of cold water at the drinking fountain.

The door lock clicked and she whirled around, half expecting to see that Devin had tracked her down.

But Paxton Wright paused just inside the door, looking as startled to see her as she was to see him.

Liberty recovered first. "Hey." She dropped to the bench, next to her duffel bag.

"Hey, yourself. Didn't expect to find anyone here at four in the morning."

"Couldn't sleep."

"Me either." Paxton sat on the bench, keeping the duffel bag between them. "Were you haunted by a melody that kept you up?"

She shook her head.

"Freaky stuff that happened tonight, huh?"

"You were here. Did you see anything? Random people hanging around the buses?"

"No. Flynn and I were arguing about some dumb shit, and we argue loudly, so we didn't hear the gunshots."

"Makes me wonder if the shots were silenced."

"Like a sniper or something?" He frowned. "I thought the cops said it looked like scattershot."

"Or someone wanted it to look random." She felt Paxton's probing gaze and knew she'd said too much. "But what do I know?"

"More than you're letting on, that's for damn sure."

Don't look at him.

"Is Devin freaked out? In addition to all the protestor shit, I heard rumblings that he's dealt with some stalker-type things."

She shrugged. "He's not too freaked out. He's sound asleep in the room."

"And you're not. You're in the fitness room, and judging by the sweat and exhaustion, you've been here at least an hour." He paused. "Interesting."

Liberty faced him. "Why's that interesting?"

Paxton tipped up his water bottle and drank, keeping those assessing eyes on hers. "Because if I ask for the truth, you'll lie. And if I hazard a guess on why there's a stun gun in your duffel bag, you'll hedge. So I won't insult my intelligence or yours by saying anything other than I find it . . . interesting."

"I knew you were smarter than you looked."

He smirked. "I'll sidestep that. Anything I can do?"

She eyed his workout clothes—a long-sleeved T-shirt and baggy cotton pants—martial arts pants if she wasn't mistaken. "I don't suppose you grapple?"

"Mostly I concentrate on tai chi these days and not the combat side of martial arts."

"Pity. I'm in the mood for some ground and pound."

"You any good?"

"Only one way to find out." Then, because she'd obviously lost her mind, she taunted him with "Unless you're scared to fight a girl?"

Paxton set his water bottle aside. "Them's fightin' words. Bring it on. But I've got a couple of rules. Grappling only, no kicks or strikes. And no choke holds. I can't take the chance on fucking up my voice."

"Deal." She rooted around in her bag until she found a long-sleeved shirt and slipped it on.

As they faced each other on the mat, Paxton casually asked, "What discipline do you study?"

"Mostly Muay Thai. You?"

"Formerly aikido."

Liberty rushed him.

Obviously, he wasn't expecting it. He hit the ground hard but bounced back. "Why aren't I surprised you're the strike-first type?" he complained.

"Gotta take my openings when I see them." Then she faked a grab, and when he went to counter the move, she dodged, knocking him to the ground. Her takedown netted her zero gain when he rolled out of it.

She'd missed this physical test of her skills against an opponent's. Chances were slim she'd score a victory; Paxton Wright was lumberjack sized. Six foot five with biceps the size of her head and massive shoulders and thighs. Plus he had a keen eye for detail, so chances were he'd already cataloged her few moves and come up with countermoves.

"You sure we can't kick and strike?"

"No need to." He swept her legs out from under her; then she found herself in guard with no way to escape.

Shit. She tapped.

They went another round, with her managing to get the jump on him just one time. She figured he was just about to flip her on her back again when the door slammed open.

Devin demanded, "What the fuck is goin' on?"

Paxton released her and offered a hand to help her up.

She was flushed and breathing hard when Devin approached her. "We were grappling."

"Why are you even in here?"

"Paxton has experience with a different martial arts discipline, so we wanted to test our skill against each other."

"Awesome. Not only do I wake up at four thirty in the fuckin' morning and find your side of the bed empty—no note, no nothin'—then I find you rolling around on the floor with another guy who's damn near twice your size."

Liberty studied him, matching his icy stance and tone. "What are you insinuating?"

"Nothin'. I'm asking why're you're here."

"And I answered." She looked at Paxton. "Maybe he'll believe you. Tell him this wasn't foreplay."

"Liberty—"

"Tell him."

"She was working out when I got here. We decided to grapple. Probably not the best idea at four in the morning. But I'd never disrespect you by making a move on her."

Devin inhaled. Exhaled. Rubbed the furrow between his brows. "I know that." He looked at Liberty. "Just because we're"—he gestured distractedly—"whatever. Your life is your own. But after what happened tonight, when I woke up alone, I was worried about you. But now that I know where you are, I'll leave you to your grappling." He walked out the door.

Paxton said, "So you just going to stand there, or are you going after him?"

"Shit." Liberty followed Devin and caught him just as he turned the corner to the elevator.

The elevator? What the fuck?

"Where do you think you're going?"

The security guard discreetly walked down the hall, away from the impending explosion.

Devin jammed his hands through his thick, unruly curls. Even sleep deprived and pissed off he looked like a damn rockstar. "Downstairs for a drink."

"There's a minibar in the room."

"Doesn't have what I want."

"Fine. Hang tight for a sec while I get my bag out of the fitness room and I'll come with you."

"No."

"Excuse me?"

"I said no. The reason I'm goin' to the bar is to be alone.

So go back to grappling or to the room, but you're not comin' with me."

Liberty got right in his face. "Wrong. Where you go, I go. Remember?"

"Don't push me on this. I need some time to sort some shit out." His gaze zoomed over her. "Apparently, you needed time alone too. At least I'm givin' you the courtesy of telling you, unlike you just leavin' me in the middle of the goddamn night."

"Totally different situations, Devin."

"Oh yeah? So if you'd awoken to find me gone?"

She would've gone out of her fucking mind. "It's not the same," she said stubbornly.

Devin's eyes searched hers, and whatever he saw—or didn't see—caused him to take another step back. "You're right. But that doesn't change anything. I'm still goin'."

She shook her head.

"Here's how this plays out. I head downstairs for a drink. You leave me be and know I'm safe in the hotel. Or I head downstairs for a drink, you follow me and I'll get in a taxi. I'll be out of touch completely until sound check tomorrow afternoon. Your choice."

He was threatening her? "You're bluffing."

"I don't bluff." His voice dropped. "Ever. So go ahead and push me on this, Liberty. I'll show you how uncooperative I can be when I set my mind to it."

"Why are you doing this?"

The elevator dinged and the door slid open.

Devin stepped inside and immediately slumped against the wall, focusing on the digital panel rather than looking at her. Or answering her.

Then the doors closed in her face.

Immediately, she had a deep sense of loss.

This had gone beyond Devin being upset with her. But what had tipped him over the edge from concern to fury? Her retreat into professional mode once she'd learned of the bus being shot up? Her refusal to take solace for herself or offer it to him by having sex with him? Waking to find her gone? Walking in on her grappling with Paxton Wright?

Paxton. Dammit, she'd just run off and left him with her stun gun.

When she stood in front of the glass door, she wondered how long Devin had watched her and Paxton before he'd barged in. She realized she'd forgotten her room key in her duffel bag, and she'd have to interrupt Paxton's tai chi workout to get back in.

Right after he'd opened the door, she said, "Sorry. I've gotta go . . ." *Where? Chase after Devin and watch him seize the opportunity to elude you?*

"Maybe you oughta take a breather before you race off."

"God. This is so fucked up. I never meant . . ."

"I don't know what's going on, but I do recognize when a guy has been pushed past his limits. I saw that in Devin just now."

"When you've reached that point, what do you do?"

"Tell everyone to fuck off and find a bar."

She sighed. "So that response is a gender thing?"

Paxton's eyes turned shrewd. "Devin went looking for a bar?"

"I don't think he'll go out of the hotel. Unless he sees me, and then all bets are off." She released a frustrated burst of air instead of yelling, *Fuck!* "Even if the bar is closed, he's Devin McClain. They'll open it up for him."

"True. So are you headed down there?"

Liberty shook her head and reached for her duffel bag. "I'll hole up in the room and hope like hell he comes back."

"He will. Might be a few hours. He might be drunker than hell, but he won't be able to stay away from you."

She paused before she opened the door, wanting to ask him how he could be so sure of that, but she said, "Night," instead and fled back to the room.

Chapter Twenty-two

✌

*D*evin bribed the night concierge to let him sit in a booth in the corner of the bar.

Although the bar was closed, the concierge brought Devin five little bottles of Jack Daniel's, two cans of Coke and a large water glass filled with ice.

As soon as he had the booze and the solitude he thought he needed, he didn't want either. He cracked open the Coke and watched the thick brown bubbles forming over the ice before settling into fizzy liquid.

What a totally fucked-up night.

He heard footsteps and looked up. Paxton Wright scooted into the bench seat across from him. Devin sighed. "Hope you didn't pay the dude at the desk more than a hundred bucks, because he's lousy at keeping secrets."

Paxton cocked his head. "Tickets to tonight's sold-out show are worth more and don't cost me a thing."

Devin snorted.

Paxton pointed to the minibar-sized bottles. "Having a pity party?"

"Yep. Hitting the hard stuff." Devin rattled the glass. "Coca-Cola. Straight up. So why'd you track me down? To try to convince me nothin' happened between you and Liberty?"

"You know nothing happened. You trust her. You trust me. Finding her grappling with me wasn't why you were pissed off at her."

He sipped his soda and waited for Paxton to elaborate.

"Liberty isn't just your personal assistant."

"What makes you say that?"

Paxton rested his arms on the table. "Besides the fact I haven't seen her do anything that most PAs do—like fetch food and drinks for you, or coordinate your wardrobe, or deal with media demands—yet she's constantly by your side. I could chalk that up to infatuation on both your parts, but that's not all of it. I couldn't put my finger on it exactly. Knowing you for a few years and that your taste in women runs to the trashy side, I figured maybe you'd hired her because you weren't attracted to her."

Devin's cheeks grew warm. He'd always feel like a tool for what he'd said—and thought—about Liberty the first time they'd met.

"But after watching you with her, the attraction between you two is mutual. It's been mentioned in passing that you work out with her almost every day. So when I showed up at the fitness room because I couldn't sleep and saw her working out, I watched her through the door before I entered the room." He paused. "She doesn't train like a girl. She doesn't fight like a girl. Hell, most women outside of the martial arts community wouldn't know what grappling was. She not only knows her way around submissions and takedowns, she would've forced my submission if I hadn't defined the parameters ahead of time. She carries a stun gun in her duffel bag, and I suspect I never see her in the skimpy clothes most PAs prefer because she's always carrying a gun. I won't put you on the spot and ask you to define her real job title—I can guess well enough."

"So why are you here?"

"I figured you might need to talk to someone that ain't her or Crash. I know how damn isolated this job can make you feel."

He traced the rim of his glass. "Is Crash sitting in the lobby by the doors?"

"Yep. He warned me not to try to sneak you outta the building. Why would he say that?"

"I told Liberty if she followed me down here, I'd leave. But she knows Crash can keep me in line."

"Always good to have one person like that. Sucks when I'm that person for all three of my brothers. You have siblings?"

He thought of how he'd opened up tonight about Michelle. Why had he been able to do that with Liberty and not Renee? "An older sister."

"She whip your ass when you were kids to keep you in line?"

Devin tried to remember. Renee had been more the mother-hen type than the cracking-skulls type. "Not really."

"Huh. That's my favorite part about being the oldest in my family—knocking heads together when my brothers need it, which is more often than you might think." Paxton opened the closest bottle of Jack. "What put you and Liberty at odds tonight?"

Grateful for the subject change, he said, "Her reaction to my bus bein' shot up."

"Come on. Give me more than that."

It wasn't as hard to tell Paxton about the frustrating situation as Devin had imagined.

When he finished, Paxton said, "It'll get harder to keep that line between personal and professional the harder you fall for her."

"Yeah. I know." And it was already too fucking late. If he wasn't so crazy about her, he wouldn't give a shit about her feelings, or her job, or how it affected them.

"So what are you gonna do?"

"I oughta tie her to the goddamn bed until she listens to reason," he muttered.

Paxton raised his hands. "Dude, I don't wanna know about your kinky sex shit."

Devin fought a smile. "If I thought kinky sex shit would work on her, I'd try it. But I'll have to go with the old standby."

"Which is what?"

"Avoiding her."

"Not cool, man."

"Yeah, well, I'm new to this relationship crap. At least if I'm avoiding her, I can buy some time to come up with a way to deal with this."

Paxton stretched his arm across the back of the booth.

Devin's gaze automatically moved to the sleeve of tats. "Every time I see you, Pax, you've got more ink."

"Chicks dig it."

"That's the reason you do it?"

Paxton shook his head. "I don't get off on the pain either. Every one of these images means something. It chronicles my life. Even the shit I wanna forget. Maybe especially that."

Interesting philosophy. But that wasn't a surprise. Paxton was one of the most complex men he'd ever met. Devin doubted anyone ever said that about him. He stood. "Thanks for listening to me bitch and whine. Too bad you don't live in Nashville. We could do this all the time."

"All part of my job as your friend. And thanks, but I'll stick to livin' in Austin, where the real music scene is. But seriously, Dev, you need anything else, call me."

"I will." He pointed to the remaining mini bottles of whiskey. "Keep 'em. See you at sound check."

In the lobby, Devin stopped in front of Crash.

He glanced up from his cell phone. "Better?"

"Some. You got one or two beds in your room?"

"Two. Why?"

"I need to figure some shit out. Can I stay with you?"

"I guess."

They started toward the elevators.

Crash swiped his key and pressed the button for the presidential level.

"Gotta grab my stuff. What room are you in?"

"Fifteen oh five. Don't be too long. I'm dead on my feet, and once I'm out, I won't hear you knock."

Devin nodded to the security guard. He inhaled a deep breath before he unlocked the door to his room and stepped inside.

Liberty stood by the window. Pinkish orange rays of the sunrise teased the edges of the skyline beyond the glass, but her face remained in shadow even as she turned toward him.

He hadn't unpacked much, so it was easy jamming everything into his suitcase.

As he zipped it up, she said, "Where are you going?"

Not an accusatory tone. More sad. That caused him a

pang of sadness too. Only a few hours ago they'd been a normal couple, out on a date, spending a romantic evening on the beach in the moonlight. "It's best if I bunk in Crash's room. I need some sleep so I ain't a damn zombie onstage tonight." He held up his hand. "Before you start in on your security concerns, I won't leave the room on my own, won't order room service, won't do anything but sleep."

"And you can't sleep here?"

By the look on her face, he knew she was thinking of his comment that he slept better when she was next to him. "No, Liberty. I can't."

"Do I get an explanation? Or clarification whether it's me as your bodyguard that you're upset with, or me as your lover?"

"You turned away from me on both fronts. I tried to reason with you about how damn ridiculous you were bein', blaming yourself for something that happened when we weren't even there. But instead of seein' it as a good sign that we were gone, you fixated on how it was some kind of cosmic punishment for you bein' on a date with me. When we got to the room and I needed you to be my lover and not my bodyguard, you shut me out. Then, at your first opportunity, you snuck out." His eyes searched her face, but the room was so dark he couldn't see her eyes. Maybe that wasn't a bad thing because then she couldn't see the fury in his either. "When I tracked you down, did you apologize for worrying me? No. You barked orders and accused me of accusing *you* of fucking around—which never even crossed my mind. You're so . . . blind to the fact that I'm not the one who has the problem separating our professional relationship from our personal one. You are. So, yeah, I'm pissed off. I need a break from all of this. I'll see you after the show tonight." He slipped out the door.

Crash didn't ask any questions after he let Devin into his room.

Devin stripped to his boxer briefs and crawled into bed, putting a pillow over his head to block the coming of daybreak.

∞

The show at the Pavilion went better than Devin had hoped. The Wright Brothers had primed the audience, so when Devin and his band took the stage, the energy from the crowd blew him away.

It sucked he had to deal with mundane business shit after such an outstanding show; it tarnished the glow. His security escorted him to the main room, filled with his crew.

"Now that the star is here, I can share the updates." Crash gave a shrill whistle to get everyone's attention. "Listen up, people, 'cause I'm only doin' this once. Devin's bus is in the repair shop. We have a show in Jacksonville tomorrow night. As soon as teardown is done, the crew will hit the road with the stage equipment since it's a twelve-hour drive. After Jacksonville, we have a ten-day break."

"Thank God," Leon said.

"I think we all feel that way. The promotion company has chartered a plane to take the band from Houston to Jacksonville. Since most of you are goin' home to Nashville, you've been booked on a one-way flight from Jacksonville the day after the gig. Rick will drive the band's bus to Portland. Devin's bus will be repaired here, and as soon as it's done, Reg will drive it to Portland. Then you'll all fly commercial from wherever you are to Portland. So get with our Big Sky Promotions rep as soon as possible on where you'll be in ten days, as I know some of us have vacation plans. Any questions?"

Odette raised her hand. "Did the cops find any suspects in the shooting?"

"I haven't heard anything. We've managed to keep this incident from the media, including fans' social networks, by passing it off as a break-in attempt at the event center. So let's drop it like it didn't happen, people."

"Where are we staying tonight?" Gage asked.

"Same hotel as last night. We've booked the entire presidential floor. Same rules apply tonight. No room service. No one upstairs who's not in the band. You wanna eat or drink, go to the hotel restaurant or bar. We have a car service scheduled to pick us up at ten a.m. Anything *legal* you need off the bus, get it now. The cars will be here in half an hour to take everyone to the hotel."

Devin had tried to ignore Liberty, but his gaze kept shifting to her. She stayed on the opposite side of the room. She looked like the Liberty he'd met three months before—not worried about keeping up pretenses in public. She'd slicked her hair back in a ponytail and hadn't applied makeup, which made the dark circles beneath her eyes more prominent. Even in her severely cut business suit, he had to wonder how he'd ever thought her unattractive. The woman's presence pulled him in like a damn tractor beam.

"All right. That's it," Crash said. "See you all at the hotel."

Liberty leaned in, whispering to Crash, and then she was the first one out the door.

Odette sidled in front of Devin. "Way to kill our post-show buzz, huh?"

"Yeah. And we rocked the motherfucking house tonight."

"I totally agree." She twisted her fingers—a nervous habit that put him on edge.

"Spit out whatever's on your mind, little O."

"Think you and Liberty will be holed up in the back on the private plane tomorrow?"

"Why?"

More finger twisting. "Because I wanna join the mile-high club with Steve. And I wanted to ask before Tay and Jase did."

"Fine. Whatever. Don't blame me if the plane doesn't have a back room. Chartering one this late means we didn't have much to choose from."

"Never hurts to be prepared," she trilled. "What's up with you and Liberty? Are you guys fighting? You two are practically conjoined, and I didn't see you together at all today."

"With all the new changes to the schedule, she's been busy doin' personal assistant stuff," he lied.

"Oh."

He hated that one-syllable word. The only time a woman used that word in a good way was during sex when "Oh" was followed closely by "God." It annoyed him to have to ask her, "Oh, what?"

"Oh, nothing."

His second most hated word from women.

He watched Odette flounce off.

Yeah, he wasn't crazy about that flouncing thing that women did either.

His security guys—he had three tonight—didn't speak as they herded him out the back door into a waiting car.

Devin let his head fall back and relived the low points of the day, not the high points of the concert like he should have been. Waking alone, groggy and cold and Crash hitting him with all the issues before he'd had a cup of coffee. By the time they'd hashed everything out with the promoters, he needed to leave for the arena. When Liberty walked into the banquet room tonight, that was the first time he'd seen her all day. Now that they'd both cooled down, they could talk.

They pulled up to the back entrance of the building and the concierge led them to the service elevator. This stealth stuff was such a pain in the ass.

By the time Devin reached his far-too-quiet suite, he was on edge. He poured himself a glass of water and wandered to the big window in the dining area, staring at the twinkling lights of Houston.

Then he kicked off his boots and cut through the living area—complete with a fireplace—to the closed set of double doors at the end of the hallway. He knocked. "Liberty? Sweetheart, are you up?"

Stupid. Like she'd answer if she was sleeping. He opened the door wide enough to stick his head inside. A lamp burned on the nightstand. The covers had been turned down and a small foil-wrapped piece of chocolate had been centered on the pillow.

He didn't see her suitcase. He searched the room just to make sure.

His edgy feeling escalated. Her stuff wasn't on the counter in the master bathroom. She wasn't soaking in the gigantic Jacuzzi tub with her headphones on. She hadn't barricaded herself in the second bedroom.

Where the hell was she?

He called Crash.

"Yo, Dev. What's up?"

"Where's Liberty?"

"I imagine she's sleepin'. Why?"

"Why? Because she's not sleepin' in my bed. And isn't her job as my damn bodyguard to be close enough to guard my body? Which means she's supposed to *be* in my bed."

Crash sighed.

Not good. "Tell me what the fuck is goin' on."

"After last night's incident and your . . . disagreement with her this morning, she requested her own room."

Devin froze.

"I agree with her. You're secure in this hotel, so you don't need her to stay with you. She had another guard stationed on this floor."

"I don't want another damn guard. I want her."

"Calm down."

The fuck he would.

"You knew this wasn't permanent. Before we left Denver, we discussed the possibility that she wouldn't return for the last three weeks after the ten-day break."

Devin fought his panicked feeling "Has she said she's not comin' back on tour?"

"Not exactly."

"We're not on break yet."

Crash sighed again. "We will be on break tomorrow night. She's traveling to Jacksonville with us. As soon as the show ends, she's on a plane to Denver."

"Not fucking happening. What room is she in?"

"Take it down a notch."

"Tell me what room she's in."

Crash didn't respond.

"Tell me what room she's in or I'll go lookin' for her myself. And I'll do that by banging on every fucking door on this floor, Crash."

"She's in fifteen fifteen."

She'd requested the room farthest away from his?

"Dev, don't do nothin' stupid," Crash warned.

"No promises." Devin swiped his keycard off the table and his spare nylon guitar strap out of his case before he stormed out. He waved guard number one aside, as well as guard number two.

He beat on Liberty's door. "Open up."

No response.

"Open up or I'll get the manager up here to unlock this door."

No response.

"Liberty, I'm not fuckin' around."

The door opened as far as the safety chain allowed. "What do you want?"

"To talk like reasonable adults."

"Says the brattishly behaving man-child who's beating on my door at eleven thirty at night, demanding an audience."

Man-child? "I'm not havin' this conversation through the crack in the door. Let. Me. In."

The door shut. The chain rattled. As soon as she opened the door, he snagged her hand, quickly tying her wrists together with his guitar strap, and towed her out of the room.

"What the hell do you think you're doing?"

"Takin' you back where you belong. In my goddamn room and in my goddamn bed."

"Let me go, you fucking psycho!"

"Not a chance."

Liberty tried to jerk away from him, but he held fast.

When the security guards started toward him, he said, "She's fine. Me'n her are havin' a private chat in my room."

When his bandmates started to open their doors to check out the action, Devin yelled, "Go back in your rooms. This doesn't concern any of you, so butt the fuck out."

"You are such an ass," she hissed.

"Yep. And, sweetheart, I'm just getting started." He unlocked the suite and didn't break his stride until he'd brought her into his bedroom and kicked the door shut. He crowded her against the post on the four-poster bed. "Remember our deal?"

Her eyes said she remembered, but her mouth remained closed.

"Determined to show me that stubborn side, are you? Fine. I'll remind you of our deal. In public, you're in charge. In private, I am. So we'll put aside the professional issues and talk about why you're shutting me out and running away."

"I'm doing neither of those things."

"Requesting a separate room for tonight wasn't shutting me out?"

Her eyes shot daggers at him, and no doubt she'd be thumping him in the chest with her fists if she had use of her hands. "So it's all right for you to sleep elsewhere, but it's not okay for me to do the same? That's utter bullshit, Devin. I spent last night and most of the morning in this suite pacing. Tonight I was fucking exhausted and I just wanted to sleep."

"Meaning you didn't want to sleep with me."

"Meaning it is best if we just let it go."

"No." He framed her face in his hands and repeated, "No. You're not doin' this. I'm not letting you. And I'll stop bein' a man-child and tell you straight up: You hurt me last night. I opened up to you. I told you things about my sister that I've never told anyone—including my family. On the way to the hotel last night after you got done with the cops, you acted like the date with me was the worst thing that had ever happened to you. How the hell was I supposed to take that?"

Understanding dawned in her eyes. "That's not what I meant."

"But that's how it came across. I know last night was a big ordeal for you. I understand why, yet at the same time, I don't. Baby, you did your job keeping me safe."

"Do you know what the cops did after they separated us and took me onto the bus? They tested me for gunpowder residue."

"Why?"

"Because they suspected I'd shot up the bus for publicity purposes. Because, evidently, my job as 'personal assistant cum bodyguard' means I'm your publicity whore."

Goddammit. He remembered how pissed off he'd been when the cops in Kansas City had accused him of the same thing after the attack on JT. "Why didn't you tell me?"

"Because I was more worried about your safety than my feelings. God, Devin. Someone pierced the fucking wall where we sleep with bullets. The only person who recognized the danger to you was Crash. By the time we arrived, he'd already dealt with getting you to a secure place. While the end goal—ensuring your safety—was the same, it still made me feel useless, okay? Useless and weak, and why the fuck am I fucking *crying*?"

Devin undid the strap around her wrists and pulled her into his arms. "You're not useless. And you're not weak, Liberty. You're the strongest woman I know."

"You shut me out too," she said, her words muffled against his chest. "When I tried to talk to you, you went to the bar."

"Didn't I warn you that we'd fuck up at some point? I guess last night was that point."

"I'm sorry."

"Me too, baby." He stroked her back. "Me too."

"I'm glad you opened up to me on the beach. If we ignore the cops and bullets and my crisis of faith in doing my job . . . that was the best date I've ever had."

"I'd argue the karaoke ran a close second."

Liberty didn't try to extricate herself like she normally did.

"Are you okay?"

"Just exhausted. I didn't sleep at all. Well, I dozed off for ten minutes until the bad dream woke me."

Of course she'd internalize everything and end up having a nightmare. "I'm sorry I wasn't there for you." During the months they'd shared a bed, Liberty had had a couple more flashbacks. He'd been there for her with every one, holding her in the aftermath, listening as she shared more of the horrors of war with him. It humbled him, how this strong woman would let him see that vulnerable part of her and that she trusted him to help her through the demons that still dogged her. "Was it Sean again?"

She nodded but didn't elaborate.

"Do you want to talk about it?"

"No," she said hoarsely. "But I will. It was that same nightmare, but this time when I reached the body on the ground, it was you, not him."

He closed his eyes, his stomach in knots, his heart in his throat.

"I couldn't save you either."

Oh, sweet baby, you already have.

Devin pressed his lips to the top of her head. He loved her. Not exactly a revelation, but the first time he'd admitted it to himself. Question was: Should he admit it to her?

No. The woman was dead on her feet.

"Liberty? You still with me?"

"Sorry. I'm fading fast."

"How about if I stand guard for you tonight and chase those bad dreams away?"

"Please."

He swept her into his arms and laid her on the bed between the sheets. Then he shed his clothes and crawled in beside her, wrapping her in his arms.

∞

Early the next morning, Devin paused in the doorway when he realized Liberty was on the hotel phone.

"Hey, it's Liberty. I hate to call you so early, but could you meet me downstairs in the restaurant?" Pause. "In fifteen minutes?" Pause. "Great. See you then." She hung up and turned around.

Those pale eyes cataloged every naked inch of him. The woman about killed him when she licked her lips.

"Who're you meeting?"

"Reg."

He frowned. "Why?"

"Because he's driving the bus to Portland. My guns are on the bus, which the police impounded. I'm going to Jacksonville with you in two hours, which means I can't get the guns before I leave. Crash assured me that the tour company is fine with my firearms being locked up on the bus—as long as the driver knows. I'm hoping Reg is all right with it."

"He will be."

"Don't be so sure of that."

"Sweetheart, you worry too much." He cringed. "Sorry. It's your job to worry. I'll shut up now." His eyes held that unmistakable gleam. "But we do have fifteen minutes to kill."

"Devin. That's not enough time."

"It is if I only make you come once before I fuck you."

He stalked her until her back hit the sliding glass door. "See? This is the fun part of fightin'. The makin'-up part."

"We made up last night."

"With words. Now I want to show you that my nonverbal apologies are so much better."

Smiling, Liberty placed her hand on his chest. "I can't. I have to talk to Reg. If he says no, I have to stay in Houston until the bus is released. Then I'll pick up my guns, pack them in my checked bag and fly to Denver from here."

"But I need you in Jacksonville."

"Why?"

"Because it feels like you're ditching me. That you'll return to Denver and then in ten days you'll decline to finish the tour."

Something—guilt?—flickered in her eyes.

"Tell me I'm wrong."

"Devin."

"Tell. Me."

"You're wrong. I'm seeing this thing through."

His mouth crashed down on hers with more force than he'd intended.

But Liberty twined her arms around his neck without hesitation. She changed the tenor of the kiss, from ferocious to tender. Her kiss soothed him, calming his fear that she intended to sneak out of his life for good.

She broke the lip-lock and murmured, "Better?"

"Some. I'd be a lot better if you were comin' to Nashville with me tomorrow night after the show in Jacksonville."

She looked at him. "You think you need me as your bodyguard in Nashville during the break?"

Tempting to lie and say yes, that he felt safe only when she was around. He stroked her cheek and opted for the truth. "No. I'd want you in Nashville as my girlfriend."

"Devin."

"What? You are my girlfriend and I'll miss you. So is there any chance I can sweet-talk you or sex-hypnotize you into changing your plane ticket?"

"No. Not because it wouldn't be fun, just the two of us getting wild in your hillbilly McMansion in Music City."

He groaned. "You bein' sweet and funny ain't makin' this easier, woman."

"I know. But I've already made plans to visit Harper, Bran and the boys." She kissed him again. "Besides, it's only ten days."

It'd probably feel like ten years.

"I've gotta meet Reg. But when I come back, you'd better be ready to demonstrate your sex-hypnotism on me."

Chapter Twenty-three

∽

*L*iberty hated driving her precious car on gravel, but visiting Harper on the Turners' rural Wyoming ranch didn't leave her much choice.

The sparsely populated roads from Denver had allowed her to rod the piss out of her Mustang and test its performance as well as her driving skills.

She pulled up to the stately ranch house. Bran had had his family home completely renovated right after he'd married Harper. She'd been jealous of her sister when she'd heard that Harper finally had a home of her own—more jealous than when Harper had gotten married.

Soon she'd join the ranks of homeowners. She'd touched base with her realtor in the two whirlwind days she'd spent in Denver. But as busy as she'd been, she missed Devin. They'd spent so much time in close quarters that she'd found herself turning around to tell him something only to remember he wasn't there.

The front door opened and Tate raced down the stairs,

wearing camo shorts, an Iron Man muscle shirt and cowboy boots. The little ball of energy launched himself at her, jumping up so he could squeeze his arms around her neck. "Aunt Liberty!"

She held on and closed her eyes; her love for this kid filled her with joy and chased all the clouds away.

"I thought you'd never get here today!"

If the kid only knew how fast she'd driven. "So whatcha been doing while you were waiting on me?"

"Me'n Jake played outside." He pressed his palms to her cheeks. "Hey, how come you got a piece of blue hair?"

"From eating too many blue snow cones."

His eyes, the same soft brown as Harper's, squinted with disbelief. Liberty kissed his furrowed brow, then brushed a wavy chunk of hair from his forehead. "Don't tell your mama or she might not let us have any."

"I won't." He squeezed her one more time, yammering a mile a minute.

Harper paused on the porch, a sleepy-looking Jake curled into her. She kissed his blond head and hoisted him higher on her hip. "You must've been speeding if you're already here. I wasn't expecting you yet."

Liberty scrutinized her sister. The woman was as beautiful as ever.

Tate wiggled to be let down, and Liberty scaled the porch steps to hug her sister and nephew. "You'd think I'd be used to what a knockout you are, but I swear you look better every time I see you."

"Oh, pooh." Harper gave Liberty a head-to-toe inspection. "You're the one who looks great." She smirked. "I knew that shirt was perfect for you. Love the hair. It's so you."

"Thanks." She held her arms out, hoping Jake would

let her hold him. But the shy, sleepy-eyed two-year-old clung to his mother.

"Come in. It's cooler inside."

Tate took her hand and tugged her into the kitchen. "Me'n Mama made dirt cupcakes," he bragged. "And they have gummy worms on 'em too."

"*Eww.* Gross. Dirt and worms?"

"They're good." Tate scrambled onto the kitchen stool and plucked a gummy worm from a frosted cupcake. He then dangled it in front of her lips.

She slurped the worm into her mouth and chewed. "These are much tastier than your dad's fishing worms."

Tate giggled.

"Coffee with your cupcake?" Harper asked.

"Please. So how's business at Wild West Clothiers?"

"Great. We've become a go-to destination for bargain and Western clothing shoppers. The ads we placed in *Cowboys and Indians* magazine last year helped propel us to the next level. Now Tierney is pushing me to have a bigger online presence. But adding new merchandise and removing sold merchandise from the Web site would be a full-time job. I've been reluctant to hire anyone because I'm happy with how it is now. But Tierney always sees dollar signs first." She smiled. "How weird is it that for the first time in my life that's not something I care about?"

"You're in a good place. I wouldn't want to upset the balance either."

"I'm only working about twenty hours a week."

"Who's working for you the rest of the time?"

"Zinnia was full-time, but after she had her baby, she wanted to work part-time. Did you ever meet Harlow, Tierney's sister? She filled in the summer Jake was born?"

"No."

"She returned to Chicago when I came back from maternity leave. She was visiting here at Christmas and we got to talking . . . Anyway, long story short, she relocated and in the past six months she's really stepped up her game. Now she's indispensable to me." Harper sighed. "While I love the store and it's been a challenge to grow it, I miss my boys when I'm away from them."

By "boys," Liberty knew Harper included Bran.

"Won't be too long before they're in school. So I'm in no hurry to expand." She refocused. "How about you? How's your latest job?"

Liberty wished she could talk to Harper about Devin, but that'd break every professional rule she'd promised to uphold, regardless of whether she wanted personal advice. So she'd have to figure out the *am I really in love with him?* question on her own. And why she continued to torture herself with visions of the future with him, when they didn't have a real future.

"Lib?" Harper prompted.

She managed a smile. "This last assignment has been grueling, as far as the travel."

"I wish you could stay longer than a couple of days, but I'll take what I can get." Harper squeezed her with a one-armed hug. "Now go play with Tate. He's been waiting to show you his new barnyard-themed Legos."

Liberty spent the next hour on the floor, horsing around with her nephews. Literally horsing around, as Tate and Jake turned her into their personal bucking bronc. Then, after riling them up, she snuggled down with them on the couch and watched DVDs of *Bob the Builder*.

When Bran came home, the boys abandoned her.

"Daddy!"

"Hey, guys. You havin' fun with your aunt?"

Tate shouted, "Yes!" first, followed closely by Jake's "Yeth!"

Bran grinned at Liberty. "Glad you could make it. You're lookin' good."

"So are you."

His face lit up when Harper appeared. "Hey, hot mama." He tugged her against his body and kissed her soundly.

"You're back early. I thought you'd check cattle before you came home."

"Thought I'd see if the boys and Liberty wanted to ride along." He ruffled Tate's hair. "Whatcha say, son? Wanna help?"

Tate bounced a couple of times before he announced, "Getting my boots on, Dad."

"Me too," Jake said and chased after him.

"Already got them loving ranch work, Bran?" Liberty said dryly.

"Yep. Trick is to make it look like fun and not work." Bran tucked a hank of hair behind Harper's ear. "You wanna tag along?"

"No. You go." Harper smirked at Liberty. "You do realize the invite is so you'll open gates, right?"

"I figured as much."

After donning the boots and the hats both boys insisted they needed to do "ranch work," they trooped out to Bran's older-model truck.

Liberty didn't see any car seats.

"I know what you're thinkin'; I'm not bein' an irresponsible parent and, yes, Harper lets the boys ride around with me on the ranch without car seats. We don't go more than five miles an hour, since we're just bumping through pastures. We don't go far either. It's just the way it is around here." He pointed to Jake. "He'll hafta sit on your lap." Then he said, "Tate, buddy, hang on."

That's when she noticed the straps hanging from the ceiling. Tate stood in the seat and grabbed the handholds.

Liberty listened to Tate ask ten million questions, and Bran answered every single one with patience. Jake seemed content just to stare out the window and snuggle into her. The trees still had a tinge of green, but the hot, dry, windy months had turned the vegetation brown. Although the area was beautiful, the vastness spooked her. Out here, it was just the ground, the sagebrush, the sky and the sound of the wind. For miles.

It was strange to think Devin had grown up in this landscape. She remembered he'd told her his mom and dad moved from this area when his sister and her family moved to Laramie. She wanted to ask Bran about Devin. What he was like in his younger years. How much he'd changed after Michelle had died. If any of his friends knew how much Michelle's death had affected him and still haunted him.

"So where are you off to next?" Bran asked.

"There are three weeks left of this assignment and we're hopscotching all over the place."

"You really can't tell me where you're goin', can you?"

"No. Sorry."

"But you're happy?"

Seemed an odd thing for Bran to ask. "Working for the company in Denver? Yes. I love it."

"No guys in your life?"

Liberty opened her mouth. Closed it.

Which caused Bran to grin. "I knew it. Harper claims you'd tell her if you were in a relationship, but I said not if it's something you can't talk about." He paused as they bumped over a pothole. "Is it some guy you work with?"

"It's a . . . client. Which is ridiculously stupid, but it's just one of those things. I know it won't last, but I can't seem to stop myself from living in the moment with him. Talking about it doesn't help, which is why I haven't said anything to her."

Bran nodded. "She'll want every detail so she can fix it for you."

"She can't. If I thought she could, I'd gladly tell her."

The boys chattered, and Liberty was happy to let the subject die.

After they pulled up to the barn, the boys bounded out of the truck and raced to the house.

Bran paused in front of her. "I hate to take advantage of you bein' here, but I wondered if you could watch the boys for a few hours tonight?"

"Sure. Why?"

"Because I'd like to take my wife out for a relaxed meal at a nice place where there ain't crayons on the table." He shot her a sheepish look. "That's not a complaint. I love my kids. But I also love their mama, and it's been a while since just me'n her have gone out."

"I'd love to take care of them."

"Thanks, Lib. I mean it."

"It's what favorite aunts do." She smirked at him. "And you don't have to be home early because your teenage babysitter has to go to school in the morning. Stay out late dancing or . . . whatever."

He grinned. "Already a two-step ahead of you."

Harper was taking stock of the refrigerator when they entered the kitchen. "Hope you don't mind leftovers tonight."

Bran wrapped his arms around Harper from behind. "Why don't you let Liberty decide what's for supper? We're goin' out."

She spun in his arms. "That's a great idea. Where are we all going?"

He shook his head. "This is just a you'n me thing, princess. It's already been decided. So go on and get ready while the boys help me finish chores."

Harper hugged him and whispered something in his ear that made Bran smack her ass.

God. These two were ridiculous. But Liberty couldn't help smiling.

Harper took her hand and tugged her toward the stairs. "Come on. Keep me company while I make myself look hot for my man."

Liberty settled in the sitting area across from the big walk-in closet as Harper started tossing outfits on the bed. "I've never worn some of these. That's the downside of owning a clothing store; I'm always tucking away things for myself." She held up a purple dress with what looked like a rhinestone collar. "Too much?"

"Yes. You should wear that one." Liberty pointed to the animal-print dress. "It'll bring out the beast in him."

"The man is already a beast." She held up a sleeveless brown dress with gold accents on the bust line. It looked like it'd hug Harper's every curve.

"That's the one."

Harper smiled and started tossing out pieces of lingerie. Leopard-print crotchless panties slipped off the bed to the floor.

"So since I'm having a romantic dinner with my hubby tonight, I want you to come with me tomorrow night for girls' night out."

Liberty bit back a groan. "Thanks for the invite, but I don't do well with that kinda stuff."

"Oh, pooh. You met most of the ladies at my wedding."

"The . . . older group of ladies who were doing shots?"

"Yep. They're fun, and they'd love to see you again. So would Celia. I don't know if Lainie and Janie can go, but Harlow plans to show up if Tierney doesn't have her babysitting."

Liberty watched Harper's face. For some reason, this was important to her. "What the hell. I'll go. But I'm not the designated driver."

∞

Buckeye Joe's hadn't changed since the last time Liberty had been in. It was her kind of place—cheap beer, lots of laughter, friends and neighbors hanging out.

Still, she felt like a fish out of water, not only because her mother had run off with the married bar owner, but because the table in front of her was filled with all of Harper's friends.

Celia jumped up immediately and hugged her. "Liberty! I'm happy to see you! And wow. You look fantastic."

She said, "Thanks," then whispered, "It's all smoke and mirrors and Harper's doing."

"Wrong. The Masterson girls are all gorgeous."

That was stretching it.

Hooking her arm through Liberty's, Harper said, "You remember my sister. Now she lives in Denver, which is lucky for us." She pointed to a stout woman with carrot-colored hair. "Remember Bernice? I used to work for her at the Beauty Barn." Then she rattled off the names of the rest of the women at the table.

A petite, white-haired woman wearing a tiara and fake gold eyelashes pulled out a chair in the middle of the group. "Now, sweetie, lose the panicked look. We're completely harmless."

Silence lingered.

Someone behind them yelled, "You'll go to hell for lyin'."

All of the women turned and glared at the heckler until the poor man hustled out the door.

Yikes.

Liberty slid into the seat. "I'll apologize in advance. I'm horrible with names."

"I'm Tilda." She pointed to the woman two seats down. "See the one in the floral housedress chomping on a cigar? That's Miz Maybelle." Tilda leaned in and whispered, "She's in her Poker Alice phase. The cigar is her good luck charm. It's won her a whole pile of money at the casino."

A sixtysomething, smartly made-up, impeccably dressed redhead offered her hand. "I'm Vivien. My son was in the army for fifteen years, so I wanted to thank you personally for your service."

"Uh. Thanks."

Then they all started chattering at once.

A whistle rent the air and the lady across the table, wearing purple camo and a lime green beret, shook her finger at everyone. "Girls, you ambushed her. While I'm sure she got used to that in Afghanistan, she doesn't need that here." She smiled and offered her gloved hand. "I'm Pearl, probably the closest thing to platoon leader this group has got."

"Nice to meet you."

"Bet you're good with guns, huh?" Pearl said. "So what's your favorite kind of gun to shoot?"

"Besides an M16?"

The ladies laughed.

"Handgun? H and K P7. Shotgun? Twenty-gauge Ruger over-under. Rifle? AR-15. How about you?"

Each woman rattled off a different firearm and why they liked it; then they proceeded to argue about which one had the most stopping power. Why these ladies had to worry about "stopping power" worried Liberty, but she just went with it.

Pearl whistled again, and everyone held their ears. But the bartender could hear her plain as day. "Sherry! Another round. And don't be stingy on the tequila this time."

Liberty tried to catch Harper's eye, but she was deep in conversation with another blonde she figured must be Harlow.

The drinks arrived, and no one took a sip until Harper stood. "Thank you to my good friends, and to the Mud Lilies, for such a warm welcome for my sister."

"Hear, hear."

The liquid burned like sweet fire as she swallowed. How could that be? Wasn't it a margarita? She lifted it up for a closer look. "What is this?"

"A stargazer, which is a type of lily. It's our signature drink. Like it?" Garnet asked.

"It's . . . unique."

"And it packs a wallop, so we're only allowed to have one."

"By law," Miz Maybelle added.

Liberty glanced over at Pearl, who nodded.

Tilda primly stirred her drink with a straw. "The Muddy Gap council had a meeting and added it to the bylaws after an incident we had last year. For goodness' sake, who knew that it was illegal to ride antelope?"

These women had to be fucking with her. *Had* to be.

But the longer she listened to their exploits, the more she believed they were some kind of ninja badass grannies.

She instantly fell in love with all of them.

"I think it's my turn to buy a round," Liberty said after a bit, feeling pleasantly muzzy from the booze. "Who's up for shots?"

Everyone's hand went up.

"Now, wait a sec. Someone has to be a designated driver besides Harper."

"Oh, honey, we've already lined up a couple of drivers. They just ain't allowed to show up until later and we've had our girl time," Vivien said.

"All right. I get to pick?" She smirked. "I'll go with a man who's near and dear to my heart . . . Johnnie Walker."

Cheers erupted.

The toasts were made. Some of the ladies got up to dance. Or in the case of Garnet, she boogied right in her chair.

"So tell me, Liberty Bell," Miz Maybelle said with a snicker, "you got yourself a fella? Maybe one of them hot special ops types? All muscle and no bull?"

Liberty shook her head. "There's been one guy . . . but it's temporary. I knew starting up with him that it wasn't going anyplace."

"Sweetie, when you look back on your life, you regret the things you didn't do. So I'm glad you decided the short term was good enough."

Harper leaned closer. "You've been holding out on me."

"Not really—there's not much I can tell you." By this point she missed Devin like crazy. She wondered how he was spending his downtime in Nashville. Hopefully, he was keeping a very low profile. She'd lain in bed last night after tucking the boys in, unable to sleep, her phone in her hand, tempted to call him. After she'd heard Harper giggling and Bran's deep-voiced response as they passed down the hallway, she'd felt a serious pang of loneliness.

The ladies all whooped and hollered, and Liberty glanced up to see what the commotion was about.

Several guys were walking toward them. Hot guys. Cowboys.

But the only one Liberty saw was Devin.

Chapter Twenty-four

*E*verything inside Devin settled down when he saw Liberty.

Still, it took every ounce of willpower he possessed not to run over, sweep her into his arms and kiss every inch of the face he loved so much.

And it killed him, fucking killed him not to get to be with her, in front of friends, like he wanted to.

So swallow your pride and stake your claim.

He couldn't. And that made him hate himself even more—that his pride was blocking the path to her.

Liberty looked away, as if she knew what he'd been thinking.

You're an ass. You don't deserve her.

But he sure as fuck couldn't stay away from her.

"Omigod, Devin!" Celia squealed and threw herself at him. "Kyle will be sorry he missed you, but someone's gotta stay home with the princess. What're you doin' here?"

"I had a few days off. I'm crashing with Fletch." He clapped him on the back. "He's batching it this week with Tanna bein' in Tulsa."

Fletch looked around the table. "You ladies getting into trouble?"

"Not yet. Now we can go wild since our rides are here," Miz Maybelle said to Tilda, and they bumped fists.

Harper stood and hugged Devin. "I'm happy to see you. Sorry we missed the concert in Cheyenne. Everyone said it was awesome."

"We were lucky to have such a great crowd." He noticed the chair directly across from Liberty was open. "Mind if I sit here?"

She shrugged.

Liberty still hadn't looked at him. But she was eyeing the other men in the group freely.

"I should probably introduce everyone. This is my sister, Liberty Masterson. She's visiting. Liberty, the guy on the end is Hugh. He's the foreman up at the Split Rock."

Hugh inclined his hat to her.

Harper continued. "Next to him is Tobin; he's Renner's genetics expert and Hugh's right-hand man."

Tobin, that sly bastard, took Liberty's hand, giving her the I'm-just-a-good-old-boy grin that had women sighing as they jotted down their phone numbers. "Beauty must run in the family. Very pleased to meet a real live heroine. Harper's talked a lot about you. Thanks for your service to this country."

Tobin kept holding Liberty's hand, tempting Devin to knock it away and knock him on his ass.

Liberty said, "I never know what to say to that, so . . . you're welcome?"

"And you're just as sweet and charming as Harper too." Tobin winked at her.

Devin wanted to punch him—see if the jerk could still wink with a swollen eye.

"You've met Fletch, our vet extraordinaire."

"Nice to see you again." Liberty didn't mention the connection of working for Tanna's brother. Neither did Fletch. Devin found it hard to believe that could stay a secret.

"And lastly, this is Devin McClain." Harper said it with a flourish, as if he didn't need further introduction.

"A true pleasure to meet you, Liberty."

"Same here." She cocked her head; her eyes were filled with challenge. "You look smaller in person than you do on TV."

Jesus. Really? She was gonna push him? Fine. Two could play at this game. "Ain't nothin' small about me, darlin'."

"Including your ego," she muttered and faced Garnet, blowing him off completely.

Oh, sweetheart. It don't work that way. Dismissing me turns me into a cocklebur you can't shake.

Harper whispered something in Liberty's ear and she shook her head.

"What're you guys drinkin'?" Celia asked.

"I'll have a Coors since Fletch is driving," Devin said.

"Coke is fine for me," Fletch said.

"Me too," Tobin added.

"Make it three," Hugh said.

"So, Devin, my grandson thinks you're 'da bomb' for giving us tickets to the Cheyenne show," Vivien said. "Thank you. I've gone up a notch in his eyes since I know you."

"He seemed like a good kid. It was fun havin' you all there." Devin felt Liberty staring at him. Then Garnet leaned closer, blocking his view.

"My granddaughter, Jade, wasn't impressed when I said you and me were buds," Garnet complained. "Then again, she listens to them fat Italian dudes that sing opera." She adjusted the HOT MAMA bandanna higher on her forehead, pushing back her fluff of cotton candy pink hair. Garnet sported a bizarre biker look tonight, including a leather halter top—a size too big, which exposed way more of her upper body than Devin ever wanted to see. But it was hard not to stare at the two dozen temporary tattoos she'd randomly plastered on her wrinkled skin. Did she even know what the term *backdoor bitch* meant?

"I think that's the first time you've mentioned your granddaughter," Tobin said.

"That's because when she was growing up, my son restricted her visits with her backwoods granny. She's my only grandkid and I gotta go fight the crowds in New York City if I wanna see her. It sucks." Garnet sighed dramatically. "I don't know where me'n his daddy went wrong raising that boy. He lit out for 'civilization' the day after he graduated from high school."

Devin wondered for the first time if people around here said the same thing about him. Because he too had taken off before the ink on his diploma had dried.

Then Miz Maybelle, Pearl and Tilda alternately complained and bragged about their grandkids. Which was one of the first times Devin had seen the Mud Lilies acting their age. He preferred to see them shooting tequila and firearms and mouthing off.

"What's that smile for?" Fletch asked.

"Just happy to be home."

Liberty cocked her head. "Don't you get mobbed when you come in here? Being the big-time celebrity?"

"Rarely."

"Oh, don't play coy," Bernice said. "Tongues will be wagging all over town that you're here. I expect this place to be hopping pretty damn quick and you'll be surrounded."

"So I'm counting on all of you lovelies to protect me."

Liberty glared at him.

Shit. He shouldn't have reminded her that he was here in Wyoming, unprotected. He was supposed to be under guard, even on break.

For the next fifteen minutes, Devin swigged his beer and watched her charming the ladies. And she claimed she was antisocial. She was warm, gregarious and sexy. Every time she laughed, it settled deep in his chest and warmed something inside him.

Fletch leaned closer and said, "Stop starin' at her. It'll just piss her off, and the woman is always armed."

He muttered, "Don't I know it."

"What?" Fletch asked suspiciously.

"I just said that you're probably right."

Harper snagged Devin's attention. "You should stop by and see Bran tomorrow."

Liberty froze midsentence.

"That's a great idea, Harper. Thanks for the invite." He rested his elbows on the table and looked at Liberty. "Will you be there?"

"That's where I'm staying."

He eyed her nearly empty glass. "Can I buy you a drink?"

"No, thanks."

"Since you're not drinking, would you dance with me?"

Liberty's cool gaze met his. "I'm not your type."

Ooh, a punch straight to the groin.

Fletch made a hissing *you got burned* sound.

But Devin wasn't giving up. "Fine. If you're afraid to dance with me, just say so."

"Why would I be afraid to dance with you?"

"Maybe you're afraid I'll sweep you off your feet?"

"Dude," Tobin complained, "give it a rest. She's not interested."

"Gotta give the man points for tryin'," Hugh said.

Liberty held Devin's gaze and he knew he had her. He also realized she was trying hard not to laugh. "So is that a definite no?"

"Will you stop pestering me if I dance with you one time?"

"Worth a shot to find out, doncha think, G.I. Jane?"

Liberty sighed. "For every toe you step on, I'm breaking one of your fingers, guitar slinger."

Devin was on her side of the table before she stood. He offered her his hand.

When she took it, that electric charge between them shot straight up his arm, and she squeezed his hand because she felt it too.

His heart raced as he towed her to the farthest corner of the dance floor. Grateful for the slow song, he wrapped his arms around her and just held on.

"Dammit, Devin, why are you here?"

"Because I couldn't stay away from you." He nuzzled her temple.

"It's not safe for you to be on your own. We agreed—"

"That was before I missed you so fuckin' much I couldn't stand it, okay? I'm always safe when I'm with you. I thought you'd be happy I'm here."

Liberty didn't say anything.

He realized they hadn't moved, so he clasped her hand in his to make it at least looked like they were dancing. "Say you missed me, Liberty. Say you missed me like crazy."

He felt her smile against his cheek. "I missed you, crazy man."

"Thank God." He danced them into a corner. As soon as they were out of view, he pressed his body to hers, kissing her in a full-out onslaught. Pouring all of his heat and need into her. A deep rumble of satisfaction escaped at the familiar taste of her and the familiar sensation of how quickly the passion rose between them.

Liberty ripped her mouth free. "We have to stop." She nestled her cheek against his chest. "Take us back into the crowd before we can't stop."

Devin brushed his lips across her crown before he directed them onto the dance floor.

She held herself stiffly, scanning the room to see if anyone was watching them.

"Are you upset that I didn't let anyone know we're in a relationship?"

"How would you explain it? Besides, this is temporary between us. This is your hometown and these are your longtime friends. I don't want you—or Harper—to have to deal with questions about me and what happened when we go our separate ways."

Why did she always bring that up?

"So in the interest of keeping our cover, you do realize I'll have to dance with Tobin?"

"Only if you want to watch me break his fuckin' arms if he puts his hands on you."

Liberty tipped her head back to gape at him. "What the hell has gotten into you? You never act like this."

You've gotten into me. You're under my skin. You've taken over my brain. Why haven't you grasped the fact that you're mine?

"Devin?"

"You haven't been paying attention if you believe this is the first time I've bared my teeth at another male getting too close to you."

"Seriously?"

"Dead-ass serious." Maybe he shouldn't mention the chat he'd had with his road crew about them acting too friendly with his personal assistant. Or the fact he'd almost come to blows with every single one of the Wright Brothers after he'd caught them eyeballing her ass. And her chest. And her face. He spun her so his back was to the room. "Any chance I can see you alone tomorrow when I come out to Bran's?"

"I don't know. Won't they get suspicious if we sneak off to lock ourselves in my bedroom and then the headboard starts banging against the wall?"

Devin growled. "Don't even fucking tease me with that possibility. It's been days since I've had you."

Liberty rolled her eyes. "It's been four days."

"That's four days too long."

For a moment she must've forgotten where they were because she nestled her face in the crook of his neck. "I almost called you last night."

"What time?"

"Midnight."

"We must've been on the same wavelength because I had my phone in my hand ready to call you. Then I . . ."

Liberty lifted her head. "What?"

"Decided I needed to see you in person, so I called the airline instead."

"You're killing me with this sweetness. You know that, right?"

"You're the only reason I'm here. You know that, right?"

"So you aren't gonna swing by your sister's place? Isn't it on the way?"

Of course she'd bring that up. "Hadn't planned on it."

"Oh."

There was that one-syllable word again. "Oh, what?"

"I just can't imagine being within a few miles of my sister and not at least stopping in to say hello."

"Liberty, I don't have the same kind of relationship with my sister that you do with yours."

"That's a shame. She's all you've got. That'd make me wanna hold on tighter, not let go completely."

He briefly rested his forehead to hers. "But I want to see you tomorrow."

She sighed. "You are relentless."

"Yep. We'll still have five days off after this. I want to spend it with you."

"Where?"

"My cabin in Montana. We could hang out. Get us both a flight out of Missoula for the Portland gig."

"I don't know."

"You weren't planning to spend all ten days with the Turners?"

She blinked those steely eyes at him. "No. But . . ."

"What?"

"We've spent almost every waking minute of the last three months together. Don't you think time apart will do us good? Put everything in perspective?"

"No." Devin slid his fingers across her skin above the waistband of her jeans, needing to touch her. "I still want more of you. Of us."

When Liberty continued to waffle, he pulled out his trump card. "I have fifty acres, no neighbors and a closetful of firearms."

She groaned. "Bringing out the big guns, huh?"

"Darlin', I play to win. You know that."

"All right. You win." Then her eyes narrowed. "Have you told anyone you're spending time at your remote cabin?"

"I hadn't planned on going until just now, so that'd be a no. It's the safest place I could be. Especially if you're there with me."

"God, you're good." She stepped back, breaking their connection as soon as the song ended.

No one seemed to be paying attention to them as they returned to their seats.

Some old guy was grilling Fletch—probably for free veterinary advice. Tobin and Harlow were speaking animatedly as Hugh silently looked on a little too intently. Harper and Celia were talking about their kids. Eli and Summer had stopped over to say hello before they joined another table of friends.

Pearl glommed on to Liberty the second she sat down. Garnet, Tilda, Bernice and Vivien were arguing about the next round of shots. Which left him with Miz Maybelle's undivided attention.

When she smiled at Devin and scooted her chair closer, he knew he was screwed.

"Quite a show you put on," she said, blocking him from the rest of the table.

"I'm glad you were able to make it to Cheyenne. There's nothin' like playing to a hometown crowd."

She snorted. "I'm not talking about the concert—although that was a hoot. I'm talking about the show you and Liberty just put on. Acting like you two don't know each other when it's plain as day that you're in love with the girl."

Devin couldn't hide his shock.

"Relax. I doubt anyone else noticed, since half the table is in the sauce. I assume there's a good reason you're keeping your relationship with her under wraps?"

"It's . . . complicated. That's all I can say. If I could let people know we were together, I would." He imagined sitting next to Liberty in this bar, his arm around her and her head resting on his shoulder like a normal couple. "In a damn heartbeat."

She patted his leg. "She's several steps up from your usual type I see you with in them magazines. And I don't see that look of . . . desperation in your eyes anymore. Which is probably why you're not being hounded by the ladies who showed up here, hoping to get into your Wranglers."

"Seriously?" But as Devin allowed a stealthy look around, he noticed the bar had filled with women of all ages, all focused on him.

Liberty sensed it too. If he hadn't known her like he did, he might've missed the immediate change in her demeanor.

"Let me give you some advice. It'll be damn lonely if all you've got to snuggle up to at the end of the day are bags of money. A good woman who sees you, not just your fame and fortune, is worth more than her weight in gold."

"I know that. I just gotta convince her I feel that way about her—and that I always will." He impulsively leaned in and kissed her cheek. "Thank you, Miz Maybelle."

"Anytime. Now, get Fletch to take you outta here. He's restless and missing Tanna anyway. But at least he's not working to fill his free hours when she's gone."

Devin caught Fletch's eye and gestured to the door.

A look of relief crossed his face and he stood. "I've got an early morning, so I'm headin' out. Come on, Dev. Let's hit the road."

He scooted his chair back. "Great hanging out with y'all, even if it was for a short time." He locked his gaze to Liberty. "Nice meeting you."

"Same here."

Fletch was familiar with the drill. It was easy for him to run interference for Devin because no one wanted to mess with a guy Fletch's size.

Still, even after they escaped outside, the door banged behind them. He automatically turned around to see if he'd been followed, and a pack of four women were approaching.

Then Liberty cut in front of them, shouting, "Ah, Dr. Fletcher, could I ask you a question?"

Fletch stopped. Sighed. "Sure."

"It's about . . . dogs."

Dogs?

"I'm thinking about getting Tate and Jake a puppy. Of course I wouldn't do it without Bran or Harper's say-so, but when is the best time of year to get one? Spring? Or fall?"

Devin noticed the women had stopped. And that Liberty had positioned herself and Fletch so they were blocking him completely from view.

God, he loved this woman, who looked out for him even when she wasn't being paid to do so. That meant something. It had to.

"My usual response is to say spring, but as ranchers, Bran and Harper would have more time to work with the puppy in the fall, not during calving season."

"Dr. Fletcher, did you unlock your vehicle?" Liberty asked in a low tone.

Startled by the abrupt conversational switch, Fletch warily said, "Yeah. I unlocked it when we came out. Why?"

Without looking away from Fletch, Liberty said, "Devin, get in the truck. Now. And try not to be obvious."

He didn't argue and he didn't stick around to hear Liberty explain to Fletch why she was bossing him around.

Chapter Twenty-five

⟨≋⟩

*L*iberty spent the morning outside with the boys, playing cowboys and Indians in their fort. She took them for a walk so they could pick wildflowers—weeds mostly—for their mama.

She cleaned up her dirty charges afterward and then hopped in the shower herself. Since she was heading back to Denver, she dressed in shorts, flip-flops and the AWESOME AUNTIE T-shirt Tate and Jake had given her. No need to slather on makeup or bother fixing her hair. She finger-combed the blue streak she'd re-dyed this morning, figuring it'd be the last time she got to have a teeny bit of personality in her hairstyle. Once she returned to GSC, she'd revert to her normal don't-stand-out hair color.

Her stomach rumbled when she got a whiff of lunch. She slung her duffel over her shoulder and started down the stairs. She nearly missed the bottom tread when Devin walked in the front door, decked out in full rancher gear:

a summer-weight cowboy hat, a long-sleeved white shirt, jeans, boots, spurs and chaps. Chaps. Jesus. The man should always wear fringed leather chaps to showcase his long legs and lean hips. Plus, the cutaway triangle below his belt buckle emphasized what was behind his zipper.

The spurs jingled as he moved toward her.

Somehow she managed to tear her gaze away from his groin and look at his face. "Hey. Uh, wow. I wasn't expecting you. Or to see you in this. Nice, ah . . ." She gestured to his clothing.

"Fletch dropped me off early. Bran was already saddling up, so I tagged along to help out."

"Nice of you. Is that your stuff?"

"All but the chaps and spurs. Why?"

"Because you can wear those for me again sometime. Damn, Devin, you look hot all cowboyed up." Had she really said that out loud? She looked over her shoulder to see if her nosy sister had overheard.

Then Devin's fingers were on her jaw, turning her face back toward his. "You tryin' to get me to haul you up them stairs and bang that headboard?"

Yes. "No. I just . . . wasn't thinking."

"I don't like hiding this, either, Liberty. But not for the original reason I wanted it kept under wraps."

She frowned. "I don't understand."

"I didn't want anyone to know you were my personal security because I wanted to save face about needing a bodyguard, let alone a woman bodyguard." He tenderly stroked her face. "Now I'm protecting us. As far as anyone knows, we met for the first time last night."

"Even Fletch?" she asked skeptically. "After I chased you outside and commanded you to get in his truck?"

Devin smiled. "I told him the Mud Lilies probably sent you to run interference. He's been around enough times that's happened to me that he doesn't question it."

"So why does it matter that everyone thinks we met for the first time last night?"

"Because when this tour is over and we are a couple, we'll have that story as the unofficial version of how we met and we can keep our real story just for us."

But wasn't that still a cop-out? Was he really protecting their privacy? Or just saving face? Why hadn't he asked her if she intended to stay with him? He just assumed.

A noise echoed from the kitchen, reminding her they weren't alone. She stepped back. "Did you need to talk to Harper?"

"No. I came inside to clean up before lunch."

"You can use the guest bath upstairs since I'm done."

Devin inched closer. "It's been five fucking days, Liberty. Do you really think I can be in a room that smells like you and not go fucking crazy because I can't have what's mine?"

She couldn't resist poking him when he got all sexy, possessive male on her. "Maybe we should sneak off to the barn. You could bend me over a hay bale—"

His growl was cut off abruptly when Harper said behind them, "Hey, there you guys are. Lunch is ready."

"Devin was just wondering where he should wash up. It's okay if he uses the guest bathroom?"

"Of course."

"Thanks, Harper."

"No problem. Liberty, I could use your help in the kitchen."

"I'll be right there."

As soon as Harper was out of sight, Devin moved in.

His lips brushed her ear. "I could use your help in the bathroom."

"Doing what?" she said a little breathlessly.

His palm skated up her side and cupped her breast. "Jerking off. It's your fault I'm hard. The next hand that'll be around my cock will be yours." He scaled the stairs without looking back.

Her sister had gone all-out for lunch. French dip sandwiches, homemade sweet potato chips and a veggie tray with dinosaur trees—aka broccoli—that Tate snapped up like candy. She'd have to remember these little tricks when she had kids.

Since when have you thought kids might be in your future?

Against her better judgment, her gaze sought out Devin.

Get that out of your head, Liberty.

Bran and Devin talked about their morning chores. Tate chimed in and Harper coaxed a sleepy Jake to eat two more bites.

When Jake started to fuss, Bran plucked him out of his booster seat and held him against his chest.

Harper sent her husband and son a soft smile.

"Liberty, would you mind givin' Devin a ride into Rawlins when you take off?" Bran asked. "Since it's on your way?"

She took her time chewing the last bite of her sandwich, because her brain conjured up all sorts of naked scenarios that'd happen once she and Devin were alone. "Sure."

"Aw. You're leavin' already?" Tate said with a pout.

"I'll be back."

"Promise?"

"I promise." Liberty looked at Harper. "The road runs

both ways. You guys could take a weekend and come see me in Denver. I hope to have a bigger place soon."

"How much time you got left with the j-e-r-k that demanded you change how you look and dress for this assignment?"

Shit. "Three weeks or so."

"As happy as I was to help you find your style, I'd like to throttle the guy. Who says something like that? Especially to your face? Like you're some kind of robot who doesn't have any feelings? Entitled j-e-r-k-s, that's who."

Don't look at Devin. Don't look at Devin.

"What happened?" he asked, as if he didn't already know.

"Liberty's client said a bunch of mean things about her appearance before he hired her, and he demanded she—"

"It doesn't matter," Liberty interjected. "It's part of my job to be a chameleon. Can we drop it, please?"

"Fine. But I still think it was rude. There's nothing wrong with you. You're a beautiful, strong woman who doesn't need to change for any man." Harper got a little choked up on the last part.

Liberty's eyes started to water. Her little sister had such a tender heart and she was so fierce in protecting those she loved.

"I couldn't agree more," Devin said softly.

She finally looked at him. In his eyes, she saw regret and embarrassment. The part of her that he'd hurt with those words said *Good*. The part of her that had fallen in love with him wanted to soothe him because now she understood where those words had come from—his pride and sense of self-preservation.

Bran handed Harper a napkin.

She dabbed her eyes. "Goodness. I don't know why I'm so teary-eyed today."

"Princess, you know exactly why you're actin' all emotional. Maybe you oughta share our news with your sister?"

"Bran, we agreed to wait. It's so early."

"Tate, buddy, you wanna grab me a book to read for naptime?" Bran said.

Tate hopped down and tore out of the dining room. Jake perked up and followed.

Liberty grinned and let her gaze drop to Harper's flat belly. "Another one?"

"Yes. We weren't trying, but, yeah . . . it happened."

Bran smirked. "We weren't *not* tryin' at every opportunity either, sweet wife."

"See what I mean? I'm surrounded by testosterone. I'm surprised we don't have more kids."

Devin high-fived Bran. "Nice goin'."

Harper rolled her eyes.

"Come on, guitar slinger." Liberty stood. "Let's hit the road."

After they said their good-byes, Devin said, "Where's your car?"

"In the garage."

She backed out and pulled up to the house. She popped the trunk. Before she could get out, Devin loaded their bags and climbed in.

"So I get to ride in your baby?"

"Only if you swear the bottom of your boots are cow shit free."

Devin laughed. "I changed shoes, and I promise they're clean."

Liberty putted down the long driveway.

"Why're you goin' so slow? I wanna see you rip it up."

"On gravel? Are you crazy? Do you *know* what that'll do to the paint job?"

She did open it up when they hit the blacktop. Fuck, she loved this car.

Devin didn't whoop and holler and compliment her race-car driving skills. He was strangely quiet. Then he said, "Take the next left."

"That's not how you get to Rawlins."

"I know. The turn's about a quarter mile ahead."

"Devin—"

"Liberty, it's been five days. I'm not waitin' until we get to Rawlins to touch you. Hell, I thought I was doin' good waitin' five minutes. Take the next left."

She slowed and turned onto a gravel road, glancing at him out of the corner of her eye. He'd balled his hands into fists, like he didn't trust himself not to maul her.

Her stomach cartwheeled. Everything about him was so controlled, yet she knew he'd overwhelm her, own her, when he finally let loose.

"There's a place to pull over just on the other side of those trees."

She focused on driving. Not on the heat of his gaze skating across her body. Not on his rapid breathing. Not on how fast her blood flowed, making her nipples hard and her sex throb. She wanted—no, she needed—him in a way she never had before. It scared her.

The next turn was little more than a glorified goat path. She parked on a grassy area beneath a stand of cottonwood trees and shut the car off.

A cool breeze drifted through the open windows, carrying the scent of water. Bugs buzzed in the grass and the trees.

"Liberty."

"What?"

"Baby, let go of the steering wheel and look at me."

She shook her head.

"Why not?"

"Because it's been five fucking days. Because I'm afraid I'll attack you. Rip your clothes and possibly tear the leather seat to shreds."

His warm, dry hand curled over hers on the steering wheel. "We'll go slow."

"Okay."

He gently pried her fingers free, one at a time. "Breathe, sweetheart."

She nodded.

Then he was brushing her hair from her face, and his rough knuckles stroked her cheek. Steady. Gentle yet insistent.

Liberty turned her head, and before she could say a word, his mouth was on hers in a sweet kiss. A searching kiss. A kiss that soothed. A kiss that inflamed.

Then she was on his lap, one of his hands gripping the hair on the back of her head, the other pressed against her chest. He kissed her like he owned her, like he'd never get enough of her, like just kissing her alone would be enough to sustain him.

But she got a crick in her neck and pulled back. "Ow."

"What?" he panted against her throat.

"I have to move."

A buzzing noise sounded as Devin lowered the seat and slid it back. He shifted her until she was flat against him and his mouth overtook hers again.

The man made her head spin.

He slipped his hands beneath the hem of her shorts and palmed her ass cheeks.

She rolled her pelvis, grinding against his hard cock. Just a little higher. Yes. Right there. She arched back and moaned.

"As much as I love to see you come, you will come either against my mouth or around my cock—your choice, but not from dry humping like horny teens."

Liberty pushed up and looked down at him. With his tousled curls, lazy smile and that big body taking up every inch of available space, he defined male hotness. "I've never had sex in this car."

Devin's eyes heated. "Then let's pop this cherry." He tugged her shirt up. She took the hint and whipped it into the driver's seat. "I'm happy to see you're not wearin' one of them squish-your-tits bras."

"If I were, you could kiss them better."

"Oh, I'm gonna do that anyway. Take it off."

It was difficult, within the confines of the car, to reach around and unhook the clasp.

"Let me," Devin murmured huskily. He had her bra unhooked and his face buried in her cleavage almost before she blinked.

She reached down and popped the snaps on his pearl-button shirt, baring his chest to her greedy hands.

While his mouth latched onto her nipple, his hands moved down her sides, stopping at the waistband of her shorts. He made quick work of the button and zipper, then dragged openmouthed kisses from one nipple to the other. "Need to fuck you."

She shivered from the way his commanding tone reverberated against her skin.

"Since it's your car, I'll let you be on top."

"Do I need to open the door so we can move around and actually get naked?"

"Stretch across me and get into a push-up position." He slipped her shorts and underwear down her legs and she kicked them to the floor. "Stay like that." Devin captured her lips as he hiked his hips up. The stiff denim rubbed against her bare thighs as he ditched his jeans.

Liberty's arms started to shake from holding her body weight at such a weird angle. Then Devin's hands were on her hips, urging her down, and he placed her palms on his chest. He kept their mouths fused as he maneuvered her onto his cock.

Yes. Even when she was revved up, ready to slam all his hardness into her pussy over and over, just being joined with Devin like this, she finally felt complete.

She must've sighed, because he broke the kiss when he smiled at her.

"I know, baby. I feel it too." He lightly slapped her ass. "Now move. Bring those perfect tits to my mouth so I can suck on you while you fuck me."

"I thought *you* needed to fuck *me*."

"You're on top." She hissed when his teeth nipped the top of her breast.

Spreading her knees as wide as the space allowed, Liberty pushed against his chest as she raised her hips. She stopped when only the head of his cock remained inside her; then she dropped down until his cock was buried to the root.

"You feel good."

"So do you." She canted her hips, grinding against him. Given their tight quarters, she couldn't move as fast and hard as they both liked. She struggled not to smack her head into the top of the car or to push his ass into the seat and end up pinching his balls.

But dammit, she wanted that throbbing rush of pleasure that only he gave her. So she ramped up the pace.

"Liberty."

She glanced up, surprised by his sweet tone.

He framed her face in his hands. "Let's slow it down a bit."

"Why? Am I doing something wrong?"

"No." His thumbs made an arc across her cheekbones. "You're doin' everything right. Let's take our time. I wanna enjoy this, enjoy you, lose myself in finally getting what I've wanted for five very long days." He brought his lips to hers. Not only could the man convey such raw emotion with his words, but he poured every bit of what he was feeling into the kiss.

Devin, I love you. I love you so much, and it'll kill me to walk away from you when this tour ends.

But it was inevitable. So she wouldn't dread their parting of ways, but relish every moment they had left together.

Devin's hands stroked and caressed her everywhere. His warm, soft lips teased the spot below her ear. He nibbled on her neck. He traced her collarbone with his tongue. And he whispered such sweet, sexy words in her ear, in her hair and against her skin.

She recognized the change in his body when he reached that tipping point. She increased the pace, tightening her pussy muscles around his shaft when he started to shudder with his release.

His orgasm triggered hers. She gasped softly; her clit pulsed and her inner tissues clamped down, confining his cock to just tiny thrusts as he bathed her walls with his seed.

As soon as they were both spent, his mouth sought hers. Devin's arms trapped her against his body so she couldn't escape even if she wanted to.

Not that she wanted to. She loved the feeling of his hot,

bare skin plastered to hers and the sticky warmth between her thighs.

Wait.

She shouldn't feel that. She wiggled until he released her. "What?"

She stared into his sated eyes. "We forgot a condom."

"Damn." Then, "You're on some form of birth control, right?"

"Yeah, but that's not the issue."

Devin's eyes cooled. "I'm not a walking STD, Liberty."

"Don't deny you had a swinging door for groupies before we became exclusive. And I'm not just talking about the month before we became lovers. I'm worried about all the years before that."

He studied her. "I'm not denying I've earned a reputation as a manwhore over the years. But I will tell you something no one else knows about the groupies invited to my ready room the past year and a half. I didn't fuck a single one of them."

Liberty couldn't help but laugh. "While I appreciate a play on words, Devin, in this case it's not funny. Especially since I know you preferred your women two at a time."

"Like I said, I'll cop to bein' that fuck-any-hot-chick guy in the past, but I'm tellin' the truth. I haven't fucked a groupie in almost two years."

"But . . ."

"What about all the women I've had in my room and on my bus? I let them know up-front that they could blow me. Or give me a hand job." He pushed a damp section of hair behind her ear. "Or if there were two of them, I gave them the option of putting on a girl-on-girl show for me. That's it."

She stared at him, but he wouldn't meet her questioning

gaze. "But I heard some of them talking afterward about your mad sex skills."

"What they said had to be true, right? Because God knows, only fine, upstanding women offer to fuck a guy they don't even fuckin' know just because he's had a few hits and has some money in the bank. No one—especially not women—ever lie about all the sex shit they've done and who they've done it with."

"That's not the point."

"Yeah, it's obvious that the fuckin' point is that no matter what I say, you won't believe me."

Shit. "Devin—"

"Can we talk about this later? I'm getting a cramp in my ass and you need to move."

"Sorry." She scooted back and his dick slipped out of her easily since it'd gone completely soft. She threw her leg over the console and snatched her bra and T-shirt before she dropped into the driver's seat.

Devin already had his jeans on, although his shirt remained unbuttoned. He powered the seat upright and jammed his feet into his shoes. Without looking at her, he said, "I'm walkin' down to the water." He opened the door and he was gone.

After she finished dressing, Liberty let her head fall back against the headrest. Her intent hadn't been to piss him off after such sweet, perfect reunion sex. But dammit, she never did stupid shit like this—getting so caught up in the moment she forgot the most important rule—well, besides the one reminding her not to get attached. She'd forgotten that her health was entirely her responsibility.

While she loved her sisters, she hated that her mother had no fucking clue who her father or who Harper's father was. She hated that her mother's self-worth came only from her sexual conquests.

She let that thought wash over her.

From the beginning, Liberty had attributed that same mind-set to Devin, although she'd conveniently shoved it aside when she'd become one of his conquests.

Turning her head, she let the cool breeze drift across her hot face. Why was she sitting here, feeling guilty? She wasn't the one with the multitude of random partners.

Screw this. She had a right to ask him questions about his past and even question his answers.

After another five minutes of wrestling with her temper and her demons and her stupid need to make sure Devin was all right, she got out of her car.

The breeze coming off the water turned the air chilly, so she grabbed a blanket out of the trunk and wrapped it around her shoulders.

The dry grass was slippery beneath her flip-flops as she started down the slope. A narrow stream zigzagged between the straggly copse of trees on the left and the craggy hill directly in front of her. Given the fairly barren topography, she suspected the stream came from deep underground. Her gaze followed the riverbank to where it disappeared around the bend.

Devin stood on the edge of the bank, in the tall grasses, hands in his pockets. From here she couldn't tell where he was looking, but just by the slumped set of his shoulders, she knew he felt a little lost.

He didn't speak until she was right behind him. "I'm surprised you didn't leave me here after yet another display of my asshole-ness."

"I thought about it," she said truthfully. "But then I

realized running away is how I react when faced with a personal situation that makes me uncomfortable." She rested her cheek on his biceps. "Whereas your reaction is to not let people get close to you in the first place."

"You noticed that."

"You forget I'm a highly trained, keen-eyed observer."

He tugged her into his arms, pressing his chest into her back. "Sorry we forgot to use a condom. It won't happen again." He brushed his lips over the back of her head. "I can assure you that you won't catch anything from me. I got a clean bill of health right before this leg of the tour started. I have to get tested every couple of months or else I can't donate blood. The certificate is in the bus someplace."

"I appreciate that, but you still need to explain those things you said to me."

"I figured that." His resigned breath stirred her hair. "I've never been embarrassed about what I did behind closed doors. Hell, I was proud of it. Women throwin' themselves at me, and I didn't hafta do nothin' except make sure they didn't knock me down."

"Last relationship you were in?"

"Besides psycho China? Odette. I didn't cheat on her, but I struggled with wantin' to cheat on her. She deserved better. How she didn't end up hating me is a miracle. After that, I took what was freely offered. I was livin' the dream. Then all that weird shit started happening. It spooked me. Way more than I ever let on. Around the same time, my buddy Mack LeFabre, lead singer in Southern Cross . . ." He paused. "You know who he is?"

"Yeah. He's another one of those hot, brooding singers, so I'm guessing there are always chicks lined up outside his shows too."

He nodded. "So this woman contacts his manager and says she had Mack's baby. Mack's like, no way. He always uses a condom and he's never with the same woman more than one night. He agrees to the paternity test. It's positive. So he and his lawyers meet up with this skanky Jamie woman and her lawyers. When he sees her, the mother of his kid, he doesn't even remember her.

"He tells me later he was quietly freakin' out the entire time, because something felt off. When she named a ridiculous amount of money she'd need for child support, he lost it, and the lawyers ended the meeting. As they're walking out of the building, another woman approaches him, and he vaguely remembers her. She tells him she and Jamie were both in his tour bus that night, but she—not Jamie—was the one he had sex with. Twice. While they were doin' a little sixty-nine for round three, evidently Jamie pawed through the damn garbage and fished out the used condoms."

"No way," she breathed.

"Sounds like some freaky thing on one of them medical TV shows, but it happened. Not to be crude, but she sucked the come out of the used condoms with a syringe, shot it into herself and made herself pregnant. It's a huge mess because no matter how it happened, Mack Junior is still his kid. He all but offered her every penny he had so the boy could live with him, but she refused. So Mack has limited visitation, huge child support payments and has to live with the knowledge that this psycho bitch is raising his son and there's nothin' he can do about it."

"That's horrible. But, Devin, why are you telling me this?"

"Because it could've happened to me. That's when I decided no more sex with groupies. No more stupid chances.

I had a paternity scare once. And as long as you asked, groupies prefer givin' head to straight-up fucking anyway. Or they get off showing their wild side by providing me with live girl-on-girl action."

"You like girl-on-girl?"

"Darlin', all guys like it. No different jerking off to it whether it's on the computer screen or happening right in front of me."

"God. I can't believe we're talking about this. So you've been hiding these revised 'no sex' groupie parameters from everyone?"

"Yes, because it seemed like . . . by not fucking them, I was makin' a personal choice. Dumb as that sounds. And like I said, the ladies lie about getting fucked by me— regardless if they do or not."

"The last time you had sex—"

"Was about fifteen minutes ago, and, baby, it was amazing," he murmured in her ear in that deep, sexy voice.

"It was amazing. But you know what I mean."

"The last woman was an old girlfriend. She was separated from her husband, and it just sort of happened." Devin spun around until they were face-to-face. "Then came you."

Liberty covered his mouth with hers because she'd heard everything she needed to.

After he had thoroughly scrambled her brain with a ferocious kiss, he backed off, treating her tingling lips to soft nibbles as they continued to share the same air. "Liberty."

"Mm?"

"Come up to my cabin with me. If we leave from here, we can be at Flathead in eleven hours. Less than that if you drive that car as fast as I suspect you do."

She laughed softly.

"You already have extra clothes, but I hope to keep you mostly naked anyway. We'll stop in Casper, get food and any other supplies we'll need."

"So we'll stick with the original travel schedule? Because I'm not leaving my baby in an airport parking lot in Montana for three weeks."

"No, we'll stay at the cabin a couple of days, then drive back to Colorado and fly out of Denver to Portland together." His eyes darkened. "But we're takin' a car service to the airport—you won't need the King Kong twins' services."

"They do draw extra attention."

"So what do you say? You and me in the fresh mountain air?"

"Sounds like fun."

"It will be. Now, to my next question. Ever been fucked on your car?"

Her belly somersaulted. "No, but that'll leave scratches, not to mention a big dent—"

"Not the way I plan on doin' it. And the only place I'm gonna leave scratches? Is the beard burn on the back of your neck when I bend you across the trunk and pound into you from behind."

She shivered. "Uh. Sure. You want to do this now?"

"No. I'll let it be a surprise. I just wanted your permission because I know how much you love this damn car."

Chapter Twenty-six

❧

*L*ate-afternoon sun spilled through the curtains, waking him from his unintentional catnap after a hot, sweaty bout of sex.

Devin rolled over and faced a still-sleeping Liberty. He drank in the soft set of her mouth and the way she angled her chin upward in challenge, even in rest. Propping himself on his elbow, he gently brushed a section of blue hair from her cheek and let his fingers trail down the arch of her neck. His lips curved into a possessive smile when he saw the hickey at the base of her throat. Pity it'd started to fade. He liked seeing his mark on her skin—proof of their passion. A reminder that the woman made him so fucking crazy with heat and need that he'd lost his head entirely.

They'd been out in the woods target shooting. No surprise Liberty kicked his ass on accuracy, no matter which weapon she fired. With the temperate weather, a hint of autumn in the air and his sexy, sassy woman by his side,

Devin couldn't remember the last time he'd laughed so hard, had so much fun, and was so totally relaxed.

When Liberty had finally given in and showed him how fast she could pull her gun, his awe and pride had immediately been supplanted by lust.

He'd taken her right there against the trunk of a tree, their camo shorts kicked into the leaves, her thigh wrapped around his hip, her molten core as wet and ready for him as it always was. He'd fucked her hard, fast and deep, lost in everything that was her—her strength, her heat, her spontaneity. With the ground at their feet littered with spent shells and the air eddied with gun smoke, the moment was perfect. And so perfectly . . . them.

"That's an awful cocky smile you're wearing," she said softly.

His eyes met hers. Then he leaned forward, placing a kiss on the mark on her neck. "It's not cocky, sweetheart. That's how I look when I'm content."

Liberty curled her hand around the side of his face. "I am content too. I'm really glad you invited me to your cabin."

Devin kissed the inside of her wrist. "I could get used to lazing around in bed with you all day."

"Bull. You miss playing, performing and writing music."

"But I like wakin' up late, fucking whenever and wherever we feel like it."

"We have done plenty of that the last couple of days. Plenty."

He grinned. While they'd been in close quarters on the bus for the past three months, being together at his cabin put them on equal footing. Here they weren't protector and protectee. Here they were a couple on a romantic getaway, exploring levels of intimacy. Since she was the first lover he'd ever invited to his cabin, he was determined to christen every room. Twice. And this wasn't the typical small one-bedroom cabin.

She sighed. "It has been the perfect vacation. Not just because of all of your firepower—although you do get serious brownie points for your kick-ass firearm collection. What I like about this place? The freedom to do whatever we want and no one around for miles to tell us what we can't do."

"Exactly. That's why I bought a bigger acreage. I could raise pigs and goats out here, and no one could say shit about it."

A bark of her disbelieving laughter echoed. "Country superstar Devin McClain raising pigs? Never gonna happen, hot stuff. And I know you've heard all about Harper's great goat catastrophe, so that's a double no on livestock."

"I'm wounded, darlin', that you have so little faith in me. But I get what you mean about the freedom. Maybe it's a simple joy, but I like hopping on the four-wheeler and following a random trail to see where it leads."

Shame flitted through her gray eyes and she looked away.

Devin forced her attention back to him. "Hey. It's nothin' to be ashamed of."

"I had a flashback in the middle of the damn day, Devin. On a fucking ATV."

"Something triggered a memory and you dealt with it."

"*You* dealt with it," she murmured. "Thank you for not thinking I'm a total freak."

"Never." Yesterday they'd taken off to explore. One minute they were zipping along through the woods just fine and the next, Liberty screamed for him to stop the vehicle. Then she bailed out and hit the dirt, curling her body into a ball. He'd managed to keep his cool even when he knew she'd literally loaded herself for bear. Then he'd calmly broken through her near-catatonic state and wrapped himself around her until the shaking ended. After they'd returned to the cabin, he'd dealt with her surliness and self-recriminations by mixing them each a stiff drink and forcing her to sit on the porch swing with him as day dimmed into night. It gave him a sense of purpose to offer her his strength when she needed it.

"So admit that you need this break but you are ready to get back to it."

No surprise she changed the subject. "Yeah."

"Why don't you have a guitar at your cabin?"

"I come here only when I really need to get away or during huntin' season. I bought this as a place to have fun, not to work. As much as I love my job, it's still a job."

She poked him in the chest. "Speaking of work, it's your night to cook."

"That's not work, Liberty. I like cooking for you."

"Stop being so sweet, or we'll end up bouncing on the mattress again."

"Like I said"—he brushed his mouth across hers—"I could get used to this kind of life with you." Or any kind of life with her. He rolled away before he saw that guarded look in her eyes. Whenever he'd brought up continuing their relationship at the end of the tour, she turned silent. He'd let it slide for now, but the past three days had just proved to him that they belonged together.

He dressed and eyed his luggage. They had to leave early in the morning for the long drive to Denver and his junk was spread out everywhere. "I need to pack, but I'll get supper goin'."

Right after he entered the kitchen, he heard the shower kick on.

Devin seasoned the steaks, dumped frozen hash browns in the fry pan and took the bag of corn from the freezer. Good thing they were leaving tomorrow since they were almost out of food. He didn't keep staples stocked—no reason to tempt vagrants or bears.

Liberty's cocoa and vanilla scent wafted to him a few seconds before her arms circled his waist. "Steak twice in three days? You spoil me."

"I'm happy you're a meat lover."

"What can I do to help?"

"Get out the plates. The broiler is on, so we'll eat in about ten minutes."

They dined inside rather than fighting the bugs outdoors.

"As usual, the meal is delicious," she said, grabbing the last slice of toasted bread.

"In two days we're back to meals grabbed on the run and bein' at the mercy of the catering company."

"Don't remind me. So what's on the agenda tonight? You've been wearing that secret smirk all day."

He sliced off a chunk of meat and ate it before he answered. "It's a surprise."

Her eyes lit up. "Are you taking me to see a real, live bear?"

"Sweetheart, you don't want to purposely cross paths with a bear. Trust me on this. They're either destructive or grumpy or fiercely protecting their cubs."

"Have you seen one around here?"

"Yep."

"Where?" she demanded. "And when?"

"Last fall, down by that stream we crossed. It was scary

as hell. I was maybe fifty feet from it. I looked at it; it looked at me. I froze, and it lumbered off. Luckily, I've never had a bear come close to the cabin when I've been here, and that's why we'll take every scrap of garbage with us when we leave."

After they finished eating, Liberty said, "I'll clean up the kitchen and get everything ready to go for tomorrow."

"Thanks. I've still gotta pack and lock up all the guns."

"The trapdoor under the bed is a clever idea. Even if someone broke in, they probably wouldn't find them." She frowned. "God, I can't believe I left my guns on the bus. I must've been more sleep deprived than I thought. I should've stuck around Houston—"

"Hey. Stop. We've gone over this. Reg is a responsible guy. He didn't have a problem with guns on board while he's drivin' the bus across the country."

"I should've left him my cell number."

"No service up here, remember? We'll be in Portland the day after tomorrow, and you can check them yourself." Devin dropped a quick kiss on her lips. "I've got an extra jacket you can wear tonight."

Her eyes narrowed. "Last time you sprung a surprise on me, you told me to wear flip-flops. This time you're telling me to wear a coat?"

"Yep." He kissed her again. "I like to keep you guessing."

Fifteen minutes later, they'd climbed into his rag-top Jeep and were tooling down a gravel road.

"Curiosity is killing me. Where are we going?"

"To Flathead Lake. For a romantic boat ride."

Even in the darkness, Devin felt her probing gaze.

After a bit, she said, "You sure that's the best idea? Zipping across a glacial lake, this late at night, with no moon?"

That's exactly why he wanted to do it. "It'll be fine, sweetheart." He plucked up her hand and kissed her knuckles. "I trust you to protect me. Will you believe I'd never put you in harm's way if I wasn't absolutely sure it was safe?"

"When you put it like that . . ."

The parking lot was empty. Only about a dozen boats were moored at this humble dock space. Devin shouldered the duffel he'd brought along and lit the ground in front of them with his big flashlight.

Liberty stuck close to his side. "Is this your boat?"

"Nope. It belongs to Moe, the guy who keeps an eye on my place throughout the year."

"But you have driven this boat before?"

"It can't be that hard to figure out." He stopped at the edge of the dock. "We'll get on board just as soon as I remember which boat it is." He pointed. "Eeny, meeny, miny—"

"Devin!"

He laughed. "Kiddin'. Yes, I've driven this boat quite a few times. Bran would come up here with me and fish—before he got saddled with a wife and kids."

"Funny."

"Follow me." He paused and faced her. "You have been on a floating dock before, right?"

He swore he heard her roll her eyes.

Moe's boat wasn't fancy. Just the basic inboard family-type watercraft, with a platform in the back with seating and a fishing chair up at the bow.

After he untied the front, he said, "Hop in."

Devin fished the keys out of the tackle box and started the motor. Then he unhooked the side clip holding the boat to the dock and stood while he backed the boat out. He looked over at Liberty huddled behind the glass partition on the passenger's side, noticing she'd zipped up her coat to her chin. "Ready?"

She nodded.

He eased into a decent cruising speed. In this section of the lake, they were safe from rock formations rising up out of the water. Because the lake was 197 square miles, they didn't have to go far to reach an open area.

They skimmed along the surface, which was as smooth as black glass. Off in the distance, he saw bobbing lights, but he couldn't tell if they were on the water or the shoreline. Once they'd cleared the cove and were in the main body of the lake, he cut the engine.

The immediate silence was unbroken for several long moments as they both adjusted to the sensory deprivation.

He held out his hand. "Let's get comfy."

She threaded her fingers through his and rose to her feet. "You didn't bring me out here to scare the crap out of me with ghost stories?"

He chuckled. "So suspicious." Scooting the duffel bag within reach, he stretched out in the corner before he settled her between his legs with the top of her head nestled against his neck. "Now we can both look up at the sky."

"I know it sounds stupid, but it's really dark out here tonight."

"The other side of the lake is more developed, so there's some light pollution. The stars don't stand out nearly as much over there."

"Is that what that glow is on the horizon?"

Devin smiled. "No. But keep watching."

The size of the glow increased. A few golden flares zipped across the inky sky. Then columns of rosy pink distorted the darkness.

"Devin? Is this why you brought me out here?"

"Mmm-hmm."

"Is it some kind of fireworks show?"

"Nature's fireworks. That is the aurora borealis."

"Really? But . . . I thought you had to be in Alaska to see it."

"Not this time of year. Tomorrow night is supposed to be the best night for viewing, but I hoped we'd get to see a little bit of it tonight."

They watched in silence as the colors morphed from gold to pink. Every once in a while a whirling flash of purple jetted across the gold, creating a ripple effect. The movement of light was such that it appeared the sky breathed in color.

"That's gorgeous," she said after a particularly vivid flare-up.

"It's something, all right."

"I take it you've seen this spectacle up here before?"

"Nope. I guess March and September are the best months to witness the northern lights this far south, but I'm never around then."

"So you must've always wanted to see them if you've kept track of the best time of year to view them."

"I'd completely forgotten about it until I mentioned to my sister that I'd be up at the cabin for a few days and she told me to be on the lookout for it."

Liberty turned her head and looked at him. "When did you talk to your sister?"

Devin fought the urge to squirm. "The morning I helped Bran, right before I came to the house to get cleaned up for lunch. I called her to let her know I was in the area but I was headed up to the cabin and wouldn't have a chance to stop and see her."

She smiled and kissed his chin. "I'm glad you called her."

He was too. But he didn't tell her that if she hadn't nagged him, he wouldn't have done it. Seeing the love and bond between Liberty and Harper had given him a pang of regret he didn't have that kind of connection with Renee. He wasn't sure if Renee was open to making a change to how they dealt with each other, but for the first time in a long time, he was willing to try.

"You really planned on coming to the cabin by yourself?"

"Probably sounds strange that I vacation alone."

"It sounds lonely."

He kissed the top of her head and whispered, "It used to be. But I almost don't know what lonely feels like anymore."

When she remained quiet, he wondered if she'd heard him. Then she seemed to sink more deeply into him and murmured, "Me neither."

Mother Nature wowed them for the next hour, until even a blanket couldn't keep the cold from seeping into their bones.

After docking the boat, they hustled to the Jeep, their mood somber, as if they'd both realized their time away from the real world would end in a few hours.

Once they were back inside the cabin, Liberty took the lead in the bedroom. Given her public role in his life, she understood and accepted Devin's need to call the shots when her gun came off and they were alone.

So he loved these moments when she surprised him.

Overwhelmed him. She undressed him slowly, taking her time to warm his chilled skin with hot kisses and the sensuous glide of her body against his. Her heated words of praise about how much she loved touching him fired him up as much as the sensation of her wet mouth sucking his cock.

She held him on the ragged edge. Dragging her hair across his sensitized skin. Playing with his nipples. Tracing the checkered pattern of his abs with her tongue. Nipping his neck. Twisting her fingers in his hair as she kissed him with the sweetness he craved and the passion he couldn't live without.

Devin was nearly begging by the time she slipped his aching cock inside her slick center. And he nearly went comatose after she sent him soaring into bliss.

They remained entwined in the aftermath, stealing kisses and extending tender touches, the type of touches that always led to more. But exhaustion set in.

Liberty double-checked the alarm on her phone before she bestowed one last drugging kiss on him. "Morning is gonna come awful early."

"You can sleep in the car." He kissed the sweet spot below her ear. "I'll drive the first leg tomorrow."

"Not a chance you're driving my car."

Chapter Twenty-seven

After taking a private plane to Jacksonville, Liberty could see why celebrities traveled that way. In Denver, they were the last two passengers to board the first-class section of their commercial flight. It helped Devin keep a low profile not to have an entire planeful of people filing past him. But it seemed no matter where they went, that aura of "I'm somebody famous" clung to him, even when he tried to disguise it.

Because face it—Devin McClain is a head-turning man. He'd get attention even if he weren't a singing sensation.

"You okay?"

She looked at him. "Yeah. Why?"

"You seem tense." Devin took her hand and brought it to his lips, placing a soft kiss on her knuckles. "Which is a cryin' shame. I tried my damndest to relax you last night."

"You did." She'd been reluctant to bring Devin to her apartment, especially after staying at his not so rustic

Montana cabin. But he'd just slipped into her space like he'd always belonged there. They'd ordered in from her favorite Thai place. They'd snuggled up on the couch and watched a few episodes of season three of *Sons of Anarchy*—a show she'd gotten him addicted to on the road. Their evening wasn't much different from the nights they spent on his bus. She even did two loads of laundry, so the feeling was very domestic. Which Devin didn't seem to mind.

But when they'd gone to bed, Devin became the sweet, soulful lover. Touching her all over. Kissing her all over and asking for the same type of slow foreplay from her. He didn't show her his aggressive side, or his kinky side, or his playful side. He revealed his loving side and expected nothing less from her. Because even though neither of them had said it, there was love between them. Whether it was long-lasting love, or a bittersweet fling, she didn't know. Apparently, neither did he. So it was easier not to put a name on what had grown between them. During their time at the cabin, they hadn't mentioned what would happen when the tour ended.

"Baby, what's wrong?"

Liberty leaned across the armrest and kissed him. She rarely showed public affection, and she had the urge to prolong the connection they'd cemented in the last week. The kiss turned into a mini make-out session—not the best way to avoid drawing attention to themselves. But there was no maybe about the fact she needed the familiarity of their intimacy as reassurance as they rejoined the real world. His world.

His hand cupped the side of her face and he drew her closer, following her lead until she ended the kiss. Devin pressed his forehead to hers. "Not that I'm complaining, but what was that for?"

"Just because. I don't think I've ever told you how much I like kissing you."

He smiled. "You've told me in other ways how much you like me kissin' certain parts of you." When she didn't respond, he said, "Liberty?"

"Sorry. It's selfish, but I don't want to share you. I like the way it's been between us during this break. It's been . . . normal."

"I liked it too, but that's not my life. It's not your life either." He kissed her temple. "It's remembering those private, normal moments with you that will get me through the next few weeks."

"Fair enough."

"Now, stop them gears from spinning and get a little shut-eye. Gonna be a long-ass day once we hit the ground in Portland, and we didn't get a whole lot of sleep last night."

"No way am I sleeping. I never get to fly first class. I'm loading up on free snacks when the flight attendant brings the snack tray by."

The flight was uneventful except for the woman who'd wandered up from coach and recognized Devin. When Liberty returned from using the bathroom, she found the woman in her seat, practically sitting on Devin's lap. Rather than toss the chick on her ass, Liberty sicced the flight attendant on her.

They made it through the airport without incident. But Devin was nearly mobbed at baggage claim—evidently the overly friendly chick had blabbed to her fellow passengers about Devin McClain being aboard.

Devin dutifully signed autographs while the chauffeur stowed their luggage. Then—she didn't care if it was rude—she separated him from his fans and herded him to the Town Car.

When they were inside and leaving the airport, Liberty asked the driver, "How far to the event center?"

"Half an hour. I'm to drop you off at the buses, correct?"

"Correct." She looked at Devin, but he was already on his phone. She checked her own messages. Made a few notes. Stared out the window when she realized Devin had started a phone interview with a local radio station and wouldn't be finished until they reached their destination.

Crash opened the car door as soon as they pulled up. "Hey, guys. How was your break?"

"Good. Yours?"

"Fantastic. Took the wife on a five-day cruise."

Crash was married? How had she missed that? How could he stand to be away from his wife for so long?

Unless that's what the people in the industry were used to. Maybe it was no different from loved ones gearing up for deployment—except the people on tour weren't worried about getting shot at.

Except Devin is.

"Liberty?"

Her focus snapped back to Crash. "Sorry. What did you say?"

"Just that there's a surprise for Devin." Crash whistled, and a guy using a cane came around the corner of the bus.

Devin said, "I'll be damned."

"Who is that?"

"JT. My bus driver."

"The one who . . . ?" *Was assaulted?*

"That's him."

JT shuffled over and shook Devin's hand. "Bet you thought you got rid of me, huh?"

"Nah. Good to see you, man. How're you feelin'?"

"Better than the last time you saw me."

"That's good to hear. How long have you been here?"

"Flew in yesterday. Relieved that other dude. Told him I was back and we didn't need his services."

"You said that to Reg?" Liberty asked.

JT's eyes slid to Liberty. After his head-to-toe once-over, she felt . . . slimed. "Who's this?"

When Crash opened his mouth, Liberty cut him off. She didn't know this JT guy, and she wasn't sure she wanted him in the security loop. "I'm Liberty. Mr. McClain's personal assistant."

He snorted. "Since when do you need one of those, Devin?"

"Since Mr. McClain's promotion company recommended it and since Crash has other pressing duties as tour manager."

"Outta commission for a little while and everything changes," he grumbled.

"Speaking of . . . Since this isn't the same bus, and we are doing things differently, the promotion company would like me to go over the new safety protocols with you."

JT glared at Crash. "I get fuckin' attacked on Devin's bus, been outta work three months and I come back to this bullshit?"

"JT—"

"I've been driving a bus for you for three tours," JT said to Devin. "I know fuckin' safety protocols. Who does this bi—"

"Choose your words carefully," Devin warned, getting right in his face.

"Why? Are you and her . . . ?" JT laughed. "Now I get it." He winked and nudged Devin. "Of course I'll listen to your personal assistant's suggestions."

He made *personal assistant* sound like *whore*.

Neither Crash nor Devin stood up for her, which wasn't surprising, but it was disappointing. It wasn't the first time she'd been subjected to men like JT. She'd learned to deal with them on the level they understood. JT thought she was a groupie bimbo? Fine. That made her job easier. "When the band is rehearsing, you and I will go over everything. Shouldn't take more than an hour with the paperwork."

"Paperwork?"

She nodded. "New policies. But being as you've been a bus driver for so many tours over the years, you should be used to the paperwork grind, right?"

He harrumphed.

Liberty addressed Crash. "Did the old bus have electronic log reporting?"

"As far as I know. Why?"

"It's imperative that JT knows how to run the new system because the promotion company will accept written logs for no more than a week. I suggest you get Reg back here to train him because this bus isn't going anywhere until we have a qualified driver."

She could sense JT fuming. Good. Once she got Crash and Devin alone, she'd express her displeasure about Reg being pulled from duty. "See you later." She picked up her suitcase before Devin offered to help her. Wouldn't want to look helpless.

Crash walked away with JT as Liberty moved to the bus door to enter the code. But the bus wasn't locked.

"Son of a bitch." She ditched her suitcase, pushed open the door and scaled the stairs. When she reached her bunk, she crouched down and pulled out her padlock key. "If one fucking thing is missing I will have the goddamn cops here so fast . . ." She unlocked the drawer where she'd stowed her guns, her stomach going into free fall at seeing that someone had tried to jimmy the lock.

"Liberty, what the fuck—"

"Ssh. I'm counting." All four guns there. Taser there. No bullets missing from the boxes. She heaved a sigh of relief. Then she grabbed her Kahr Arms PM45 and set it on the bed. She stood and faced off with Devin.

He looked at her and waited.

"Here's where I'm at. And maybe I should preface this by saying that as your personal security, not your . . . whatever we are outside of the hours I'm paid to protect you. After the Houston incident, I agreed to go to Jacksonville only because Big Sky promised me that Reg—and only Reg—would stay with the bus in Houston during the repair stage and he'd be driving the bus across country to Portland. But I get here and discover that JT bulldozed his way into getting his old job back. As head of your security, I should've been consulted on that decision—not informed after the fact.

"To make matters even worse, I also get here to find that the goddamn door to the bus isn't even fucking locked! Who the fuck knows how long it sat here with the contents unprotected!" She closed her eyes and counted to ten before she opened them again. "If the firearms registered to me were to fall into the wrong hands, it's all on me. Not only am I in trouble with the federal government, but I would likely lose my job. Yes, I understand it was my choice to believe the promises Big Sky made me. If I would've had any suspicions at all that Reg would be replaced and your safety would be compromised on the first fucking day back on tour, I would've waited, packed up my guns in Houston and flown with them to Denver."

When Devin opened his mouth, she held up her hand to keep him quiet.

"Now I have to deal with JT, who not only was extremely fucking lax on your previous tours when it came to general safety protocols for someone of your stature, but I had to listen to that smug motherfucker acting like I was just another one of your goddamn bubbleheaded groupies."

"Are you done?" he said coolly.

"No. You should check to see if your guitars are still here. I know your stage clothes are on here too, so grab an outfit for tonight but everything else stays."

Devin's eyes narrowed. "Why?"

"Because you—we—won't be staying on here tonight. And after you get your stuff, I'll have to pass you off to arena security so I can get this handled."

Liberty's heart raced as she dialed Garrett. She explained the situation to the best of her knowledge. He promised to find a Portland company that could perform a full bus security check as soon as possible. Garrett also said he'd deal with Big Sky about why she hadn't been informed of the changes that had caused the security breaches.

When Devin stepped out of the master bedroom, his lips were in a flat line and his eyes were hard. "One of my guitars is missing. I hope like hell that Check came and got it off the bus. And for the record, I just wanted to say I didn't know JT was comin' back. So what happens now?"

"Garrett is tracking down a local security company that will go over every inch of this bus with a fine-tooth comb. I imagine the bus will be taken off site. It'll cost a lot for the expedited service, and it's a good thing you're playing Portland for two nights."

"What do you mean they'll check the bus off site? Check for what?"

She met his gaze head-on. "Bombs. Bugs. Cameras. Poisonous critters. Poison in the food left on board. They'll look for it all. Inside, outside. And no, I'm not being paranoid. The chatter online about all the ways the protestors wanted to 'teach you a lesson' included those types of sabotage. I'm just doing my job. There's a huge security breach here, Devin. Fucking enormous. I'll point out it was caused by the same guy who was involved in the last major security breach."

"In which he almost got beat to fucking death," Devin said sharply. "I'm not questioning you doin' your job, but I also need to point out something my agent mentioned to me. We cannot fire JT for bein' injured while workin' for me. Legally, I have to hold his job for him until he's medically cleared. So him showin' up ain't such a surprise, since he knew he could have his job back whenever he wanted."

"Fuck." She ran her thumb over the edge of her phone. "Big Sky will just have to pony up and pay two drivers, because I trust Reg."

"Fine. Now can I get to rehearsal?"

"Let's go."

The rest of the band was happy to see Devin, as if they'd been apart ten months instead of ten days. They kicked off rehearsal, and Liberty spent half her time on the phone, the other half looking for the hired security to show up.

Devin wasn't happy with the sound and rehearsal went long. When he approached her in the hallway, after conferring with his band, he had that angry glint in his eye.

"What's wrong?"

"Check didn't get my guitar from the bus, so someone stole it."

"What was it worth?"

"Ten grand." He narrowed his eyes at her. "And no, I don't want to call the cops, since it could've disappeared anywhere between Houston and Portland."

Unlikely. Her cell phone rang, and she turned away to answer it. "This is Liberty Masterson. Now? That was fast. Sure. I'll be right there." She hung up and motioned to the event security before she looked at Devin. "The team checking out the bus is here, and I have to sign off on a few things. These guys will get you to your ready room."

"Whatever. See you after the concert at the meet and greet."

"But . . . I thought . . ."

Annoyance pulsed from him. "What? It's two and a half hours until showtime. And since I didn't play a lick of music in the week we were together, I need to get in the right headspace. Especially after all of this shit."

"That's fine." She stayed in place until she saw him enter the ready room. Then she slipped out the side door.

Crash caught up to her. "You wanna tell me what the hell is goin' on?"

"Did you ask JT to rejoin the tour and let Reg go?"

"No. JT was here when I got here."

"Where's Reg?"

"No idea."

"Find him. I wasn't kidding about bringing Reg back. Tell him there was a misunderstanding with JT."

Crash set his hands on her shoulders, stopping her. "I have to ask this, Liberty, and don't take offense, but is all this necessary? Or do you have it in for JT since he insulted you?"

"His insults to me are nothing compared with his dereliction of duty." As Liberty brusquely informed him of what she'd dealt with, Crash's face turned redder and redder.

"That's it. You're done dealing with JT. I will go over safety protocols with him."

"Thank you."

"Devin's always had a soft spot for the guy. Don't know why."

When they reached the buses, JT was squaring off with three guys who could break him like a twig. Crash stepped between them and dragged JT away. When they were out of sight, Liberty said, "You're Marco? I'm Liberty. Let's talk over here." She led them around the side of the bus. "You have the paperwork?"

"Yes." He handed her a piece of paper with the GSC letterhead and Garrett's signature. "There's a warehouse two miles from here. We'll tow it there and check it out. Prelim checks don't show explosives."

She hadn't expected them to find any, but she'd take the same precaution if it were her operation. "Good. You'll keep in touch about what you do find?"

"Of course. You'll have our answer first thing in the morning about problems and any potential delays."

"Thank you, Marco. I appreciate your quick action on this."

"You're welcome."

Back in the event center, JT approached her, Crash hovering behind him. "Look, Liberty, I think we started out on the wrong foot. I had no idea things had gotten so serious with what was goin' on with Devin."

Really? After you were attacked in his bed on his bus, you didn't think it might be serious?

"And I, uh, love this job. This is my family—the band,

the road crew. It about killed me not to be with them when I was recovering." His hand tightened on his cane. "I acted like a jerk to you. I'm sorry. I guess after seein' all this, I know why Devin needs an assistant."

"I appreciate the apology. Crash will keep you updated." She headed down the hall and parked herself outside Devin's ready room because she didn't have anywhere else to go.

∞

The after-party was packed. Liberty lost track of Devin several times, but each time the room security signaled that they had eyes on him.

The concert was, as always, incredible. Time away from the stage seemed to have reenergized him and the band. So they were flying high. There seemed to be a lot of media, which was good and would sell tickets for tomorrow night's show.

But Liberty was too antsy to stand around. She had a shit ton of paperwork to do. At the rate the party was going, she wouldn't get started on it until two in the morning. There were eight security guards posted here tonight. She decided to let them watch over Devin: get him in the car and to the hotel.

She approached Crash.

"Hey, lady, what's up?"

"After all that happened today, I've got reports to finish and file by morning. Devin is well covered tonight, so I'm heading to the hotel."

Crash frowned. "Is everything all right between you two? I haven't seen you together since this afternoon."

"Fine, as far as I know. Been a crazy day, so if you're okay with it, I'll take off."

"You gonna tell Devin?"

"He's busy. I'll see him later."

As she waited back by the band and roadies' buses, she

started getting impatient. Where the hell was the car service? She was about to call them and chew ass when a little voice popped into her head.

Entitled much?

She stopped pacing. Dammit. This wasn't her. She should remember that this life—car services, private jets, multiple residences, first-class hotels and gourmet food—would be a thing of the past in three weeks. All she had to do was complete the job. Then she could move up in GSC.

You'll have the bonus money, but you won't have Devin.

No matter how many times she told herself their constant togetherness was forcing these feelings, she knew that wasn't true.

The car pulled up and she climbed in. At the hotel, she handled her own luggage—better get used to that—and waited her turn for a guest agent.

"May I help you?"

"Checking in for Liberty Masterson. Big Sky Promotions."

"Yes, Ms. Masterson. I see we've had a change in the reservation. Two rooms for one night."

"Two rooms?"

"Yes. Oh, I see we were able to get adjoining rooms at Mr. McClain's request. Is that all right?"

"That's fine." She declined help to her room. She tried really hard not to obsess about why Devin had asked for two rooms without telling her. She unlocked the dead bolt on her side and took a long shower.

Once she'd slipped on her pajamas, she spread everything out on her desk. She opened her laptop and filled out a more personal accounting for GSC and a report for Big Sky. She finished in just under two hours.

And Devin still hadn't shown up.

She stared out the window, unsure where the event center even was from here. She debated on cracking open a bottle of booze from the minibar. Everything was so fucked up. Keeping her fears and feelings locked up inside wasn't healthy. She needed to talk to someone. But who? Too late to call Harper. Bailey had gone off the grid. She scrolled through her contact list, tempted to dial Joe. Even if he'd crashed for the night, he'd be wide-awake if she called.

Between Joe's duties at GSC and her assignment, they'd spoken only a few times in the past three months. In addition to being coworkers, she and Joe were good friends. But this situation put her on a fine line between professional and personal. If she told Joe she'd fallen for Devin, as her friend, he might pull her from duty to save her additional heartache. And as her boss, he might worry she couldn't do her job because of her emotional ties and pull her from duty. So really, a phone call to Joe, lamenting her man woes, would end one way—with her leaving the tour. She'd made it through the hardest part, and she wasn't walking away from that hundred grand now.

Nor was she leaving Devin's security in someone else's hands.

Liberty had almost fallen asleep when she heard the movement in the adjoining room. She watched the clock. Five minutes passed. Then ten. Then fifteen.

At the twenty-minute mark, she knew he wasn't coming into her room.

Maybe this was the beginning of the end.

∞

A strong hand traced her spine, stopping at the bottom curve of her ass.

Warm lips landed on her shoulder. "Mornin'."

She rolled to her back, and immediately Devin's mouth was on hers, gifting her with a lazy kiss.

He murmured, "I missed you last night," against her lips.

"I heard you come into the other room."

"I tried to be quiet." He pulled back to look into her eyes. "Crash said you had a lot of paperwork to do. So I let you be. Wondered if you'd gotten your own room because I'd pissed you off."

She touched his face, sweeping her knuckles down his razor-stubbled jaw. "You didn't ask for two separate rooms for us?"

"Hell no." Those vibrant blue eyes narrowed. "You didn't either?"

"No. But someone changed the reservation."

"Why would someone do that?"

Why indeed? To cause dissension. She and Devin had words yesterday and he'd all but slammed his ready room door in her face. Then they'd stayed on separate sides of the meet and greet room last night. So it wasn't a stretch for those who knew them to assume they'd had a lovers' quarrel. But who had contacted the hotel pretending to be Devin and changed their sleeping arrangements?

"Did Crash mention it was his idea?"

"Not to me."

It left her unsettled.

"Sweetheart, what's goin' on?"

"I don't know. First the bus thing; then you discover another one of your guitars was ripped off. Plus someone had tried to jimmy the lock on my gun drawer. Then someone was screwing with our sleeping arrangements. Anything odd happen at the party last night?"

Devin's gaze turned thoughtful. "Did you see the blonde with gigantic tits lurking around me?"

"Which blonde?" she said dryly.

He bent down and nipped the top of her boob. As soon as she yelped, he kissed the spot. "You deserved that. Anyway, she said she was a gift from one of my roadies."

"Did she say which one?"

"No. She probably made it up. Then she offered to suck my cock like it'd never been sucked."

Liberty slammed a lid on her jealousy. "There's a new line."

"Not really. But it's better than the standard *I suck harder than a Hoover.*"

She growled at him. "How long did big tits stick around?"

"No idea. It happened ten minutes after you left. Why?"

"It bugs me. Not just because I fucking hate women drooling over your dick."

"It's over. Can we forget about it?" Keeping his eyes on hers, Devin teased her lips with fleeting kisses. "So *you* can start drooling over my dick?"

She laughed. "Fine. Bring that bad boy up here and I'll give him a good-morning kiss."

"Damn, woman, I love you."

He'd said it in such an offhand manner and right before she stuffed his cock in her mouth that it didn't count. Right before she kissed the crown, she murmured, "I love you too."

Chapter Twenty-eight

❧

"This is Devin," he answered distractedly.

"Hey, Devin. It's Chelsea Lynn from *Country Music Today*."

He smiled. Although Chelsea was a reporter, she was unlike the others he'd dealt with over the years; she had integrity. They'd clicked on a deeper level at their first formal interview, when she'd broken down and told him how much his song "Won't Be a Tomorrow" had affected her after the death of her older brother. So in a moment of sharing, he'd told her about Michelle. Afterward he kicked himself, suspecting he'd been played and the rookie reporter would pen an angsty article about Devin's personal tragedy to scoop the competition and to prove herself. But she'd never broken his confidence and he trusted her—which said a lot.

"Great to hear from you. Did I forget I had an interview or something?"

"No. But when you get back to Nashville, I'd love to

have lunch and talk about the Heroes and Heartbreakers tour." She paused. "Rumor has it there have been some unsettling incidents. You've got a killer PR team if they're keeping it out of the press."

"I learned my lesson with the China Marquette fiasco on how best to game the system. Don't quote me on that."

She laughed. "I won't. And I'm asking this as your friend, not a nosy reporter looking for a story, but you're all right?"

"I'll admit it's been a trying tour. The logistics of it, not the fans or the venues."

"I definitely want the details on that. But like I said, that's not why I called."

A bad feeling started to take root. "Now you've got me concerned, Chels."

"You should be, so I'll get right to it. I received an anonymous e-mail two days ago that offered me the real inside story on your tour. With pictures."

"Pictures? Of what?"

"Of you and your new girlfriend. And the first picture attached to the e-mail was really provocative."

Jesus. Liberty would blow a fucking gasket. "There's more than one picture?"

"Uh-huh. I played a bit of a cat-and-mouse game with this person. Acting like I didn't believe they had more to offer. I said we didn't pay for innuendo and hearsay."

"And how'd that go over?"

"I received four more pictures. All of them in pretty intimate positions with you and this woman. They're not porn by any stretch, but the shots were taken by someone who has close access to you, Devin."

He closed his eyes against the rage churning inside him. "What'd this person want?"

"A hundred thousand dollars. With more exclusive photos. Not only of you with her, but the inside story about how this woman has ruined the tour. She turned your bandmates against you; she made ridiculous demands at venues; she's keeping you from your fans and is manipulating the media. This person said your bus was shot up and broken into and your bus driver beaten—in three separate incidents. And she's put so much stress on Tay, your keyboard player, that she was rushed to the emergency room for stress-related seizures?"

"Are you fucking kiddin' me?" he shouted. "That's so far from the truth, it's . . ." He inhaled a deep breath. "Shit. Sorry. I didn't mean to yell at you. But this is just insane, mostly because there is a kernel of truth to some of it."

"That's what I suspected. Because we're friends, I have to ask if this new woman you're involved with is some kind of Svengali?"

Wasn't it ironic that he'd kept most the important people in his life in the dark about Liberty's true purpose on this tour and he was about to tell a tabloid reporter? "Chels, I gotta know we're one hundred percent off the record right now."

"We are."

"The woman in those photos is my bodyguard. I've had some fucked-up stuff happen to me over the last two years. The tour promotion company insisted I have protection twenty-four hours a day. She's former military, and our cover story is she's my personal assistant. But if her picture gets out, with all the 'who is this mysterious woman' bullshit, it might ruin her career. I won't let that happen. The woman has saved my ass a couple of times."

Chelsea was quiet for a moment. "So who do you think is doing this? Any jealous ex-girlfriends on tour with you?"

"Jealous ex? No. Odette is my ex, but she's got no beef with me." She did have opportunity, but Devin refused to consider that. Odette was his songwriting partner. He trusted her.

"What about your tour manager? No offense, but he's a little gruff and kinda shifty."

"Only because he doesn't want me talkin' to reporters. So Crash would be last on my list of suspects. Besides, he's the only one on tour with me who knows she's really my bodyguard."

"Oh. From the e-mail, this person isn't aware of that. Doesn't sound like that narrows the list of suspects very much."

"No. But I will figure out who is involved." Devin couldn't come up with a delicate way to word his question, so he just asked it straight out. "I have to ask what you're doin' with all of this?"

"Nothing. I'd never run this story, Devin. And not because it wouldn't sell magazines, because it would. It's just . . . I owe you. You gave me the time of day when no one else would during my cub reporter days. You've proven yourself to be a good guy time and time again. You don't deserve this kind of press. That said . . ."

Devin knew his laugh had a bitter edge. "When this is all said and done, you want a story or an exclusive interview, right?"

"Yes, sir."

"Fine. But I need to ask you a favor. If you haven't offered to pay this person, is there any way you can stall? Make 'em think you're getting approval for funds and editorial and all that? My gut feeling is this person doesn't know how tabloid journalism works."

"No problem. I already laid the groundwork for that so I could contact you."

"Good. What I don't want to have happen is this person takes it to your competitor and then it's out of my control. If you hint that the payday could be even bigger if they get more proof, I'm hopin' I can catch whoever is doin' this in the act."

"I'll pass that along too. I haven't responded after the second batch of photos. I'm assuming you'll make your bodyguard aware of this situation?"

Hell no. Liberty was already on double alert because of all the shit that'd gone down. He'd handle this one on his own. Maybe bring Crash in on it—if his manager promised not to go running straight to Liberty with the information.

"I'm sure it's no surprise the pictures were taken with a cell phone. Where do you want me to e-mail what I've got?"

Devin had one private e-mail account that wasn't associated with any of his social media. Since he rarely used it, he had to look it up on his phone. He rattled it off and then ended the call.

He flopped back onto the bed and closed his eyes. Getting more pissed off wouldn't be productive. There were ten days left on the tour. Maybe this person would be careless since the opportunity to cash in was nearing the end. He tried to look at the situation logically, not emotionally. But Christ. Who worked for him that he'd pissed off to the point they'd look for such extreme payback?

Two knocks sounded on the door and he said, "Come in."

Liberty came in and locked the door. The mattress moved and then she curled into him. "Hey."

"Hey, yourself. What's up?"

"You've been in here an hour longer than you usually are. I came to see if everything was all right."

"Just resting my eyes and wishing I could take you to my favorite Italian joint in this town. Great atmosphere. Best pizza outside of New York City."

"Sounds like fun. The only good part about us not going is no extra calories for us to work off tomorrow morning."

Devin rolled on top of her. "How about we work off some preshow calories now?" He nuzzled her neck. Her scent filled his lungs and blood filled his cock. "Unbutton your blouse, baby. I wanna suck on you."

"You know the drill. If my chest is bare, yours is too."

Pushing to his knees, he ditched his shirt. Then he thought, *What the hell?* and got completely naked.

Liberty's upper half was bare. Bare and beautiful.

He dragged a fingertip between her breasts, over her navel, stopping at the waistband of her pants. "You still have your period?"

"Yeah. Why?"

"Will it bother you if we mess around?"

"No, just as long as you don't shove your hand down my pants." She reached for his cock and smirked. "Why don't you let me take care of that for you. You want my hand or my mouth?"

Devin crawled up her body and kissed her. The second their lips touched, his hunger for her was all consuming.

As she arched into him, her hand worked his cock exactly the way he liked it.

He broke the kiss and followed her jawline to her ear. "I don't want your hands or your mouth." He traced her earlobe with his tongue and tugged with his teeth. "I want to fuck your tits."

"I wondered when you'd get around to that, self-admitted tit-loving man that you are."

God, he loved her. She was always up for anything. Even after almost four months together, he found it a total fucking turn-on to be with a woman who embraced her sexuality without apology.

Devin scooted down, dislodging her hand from his cock. "What about me usin' your vibrator on you? Buzzing that sweet little clit right through your pants?"

"You don't have to—"

"I want to." He nuzzled the top of her left breast. "I love getting you off. So where's your vibrator?"

"In the drawer where I left it last time we used it. Next to the lube."

"That'll come in handy." After he found what he needed, he said, "Touch yourself. Get your nipples nice and hard."

Liberty trailed her fingers up her belly and over her slim torso. She pushed the globes of flesh together. Squeezing and caressing as she worked her fingers ever closer to her nipples.

Devin stroked his cock as he watched her.

She rubbed the tips with the palms of her hands before sweeping her thumbs around the aureolae until her nipples constricted. Then she pinched the rigid points with such force that she cried out.

He was right there, enclosing the abused tip in the wet, suctioning heat of his mouth. He sucked until she writhed. Then he kissed her other breast, teasing it with soft caresses. Scraping his stubbled chin across the wetness he created. Using his hands and his mouth to nip and soothe. Burying his face in her softness like he planned to bury his cock.

"Devin."

"Say my name like that again," he demanded as he palmed the battery-operated wand.

"Devin, baby."

"I love that husky sex-voice of yours." He turned the vibrator on and set it at the top of her pubic bone, while he kept his mouth moving between her nipples.

"Slide it down," she panted.

"Here?"

"No. More to the . . ."

Taking her hand, he curled it around the vibrator. "You do it and I'll watch."

Liberty pushed the flared tip of the vibrator right where she wanted it and held it there.

He fisted his cock, keeping a tight grip as he stroked. Knowing by the soft sounds she made that her orgasm was close.

"Yes." She canted her hips up and arched her neck, beautiful in her abandonment. Half a minute later, she sank into the mattress and opened her eyes. "That never takes long."

"Still fun to watch."

She tossed the vibrator aside and licked her lips. "I want you in my mouth before you fuck these." She pushed her tits together.

Devin straddled her, tucking his knees beside her ribs. Holding on to the headboard, he lowered his hips until they were level with her face. He painted her lips with the fat cockhead, knowing she wouldn't taste him until he gave her the go-ahead. Her rapid exhalations on the wet tip were such sweet torture. He ran his knuckles down the side of her face and murmured, "Lick me."

She swirled her tongue around and around the rim. Stopping to rub the sweet spot beneath the head with the stiffened tip of her tongue.

"Open these pretty lips and relax your jaw." He eased in a little at a time, his breath hissing out as the wet heat of her mouth engulfed almost every inch of his shaft. He pushed in the last two inches until he felt her teeth digging into the base of his cock. Stroking the hollows of her cheeks, he gritted out, "Swallow."

Her throat muscles shifted, giving the head of his cock an intimate kiss.

"Jesus, that's good. One more time." After her throat muscles contracted again, he withdrew slowly, enjoying every second of the extra suction as he pulled out. His grip tightened on the headboard and he rested the rim of his cock on her lower lip. He watched those beautiful pale eyes, glittering with lust, as she opened her mouth for him again. "So tempting just to fuck this greedy mouth and forget those luscious tits." Then he was balls deep in her mouth and he groaned. "Especially when it feels like this. Swallow. Harder. Fuck. Yes. Like that."

Liberty hummed, and the vibration traveled straight up his dick and electrified his balls.

"Jesus, woman. That's like . . ."

Hard for her to smile with her face stuffed full of cock, but she managed. And she hummed again.

Devin groaned. "You're killin' me." He held her jaw as he withdrew. Then he reached for the lube, squirting a thick line between her breasts and another on the top side of his cock. Watching her eyes, he pressed the soft flesh together. "Too much?"

"No. You can go more."

His palms pushed the abundant softness with more force, creating a smaller, tighter space. He canted his pelvis, sliding his cock across her sternum and entering the channel. Not as tight as her cunt or her ass, but warm and soft.

"I need your hands on me," he panted.

Liberty trailed her fingertips up and down the muscles straining in his forearms. "This part of you is so sexy, guitar slinger."

Devin glanced down to watch her tits bounce. To see the reddened tips of her nipples poking up, making him wish he was flexible enough to suck on her while he fucked her like this.

Careful not to crush her, he tried to bear most of his weight on his knees. He thrust faster.

Then Liberty started pinching her nipples, knowing that would drive him crazy. "You're so close. I can feel it. You're so fierce-looking when you come. Let me see it. Come all over me, Devin."

Fuck, that dirty talk did it for him every time. Devin slid back and started beating off. "Hold those tits up."

Come shot out the end of his dick in a long arc, the first spurt landing below her left nipple, the second spurt right on it. He growled through each hard pulse, pushing upright onto his knees, bracing his hand on the headboard so he could mark her. Making sure every hot drop dripped onto her skin. He jerked and twisted on his shaft until nothing remained but the bliss of release; then he let his spent cock slip from his hand.

Fingers clamped onto his ass cheeks. Then Liberty's hot—*sweet baby Jesus, her mouth was so fucking hot*—mouth swallowed his cock to the root. She released his shaft, licking and nuzzling the crown; her fingers gently stroked his balls.

His brain was so fuzzy, his dick so sensitive that he couldn't take it anymore. He croaked, "Please. Baby. Stop. It's too much."

"Just a little more."

That's when he realized the buzzing sound wasn't only in his head, but in Liberty's hand. She used the vibrator to get herself off again as she sucked on his softening dick. Her hot breath teased his damp cockhead in rapid puffs of air that sent chill bumps across every inch of his skin.

Liberty rolled down to the mattress with a very contented sigh. From beneath heavy lids, she gifted him with a sated smile.

Devin dropped to his hands and knees and hung above her. Keeping his gaze on hers, he thoroughly licked a milky trail of his come from her breast. And another. Then he smashed his mouth to hers, sharing the taste and the passion she brought out in him.

Her hands came up to cradle his face. She gentled the kiss, quieting the storm raging inside him. Devin wanted to shout to the ceiling that he loved her. Promise her anything and everything if she'd agree to share her life with him.

"Devin?"

He was afraid to open his eyes, knowing she'd see right into the heart of him. "That was so fuckin' hot. I think you fried my brain cells. Hang on; I'll get something to clean you up." Then, like a chickenshit, he escaped to the bathroom. He soaked a washcloth in warm water and returned to her.

She was in the same position, staring at the ceiling.

Devin gently wiped the stickiness from her chest. He tried not to feel guilt upon seeing the finger-shaped marks on her pale skin. By the time he finished wiping her down, the cloth had gone cold.

Was it his imagination or had the air gone cold too?

"You okay?" he asked.

A beat passed before she answered. She sat up and twined her arms around his neck. "Thank you."

"For what?"

"For never holding back with me."

Baby, if you only knew.

Devin didn't know what else to say to that, so he said nothing. He just breathed her in.

For a man who made his living with words, he sure couldn't come up with the right ones to say to her.

And he was running out of time to figure them out.

Chapter Twenty-nine

∞

They had one week left on this last leg of the tour. Things had settled down since the bus incident, but Liberty was still twitchy.

She trusted her gut enough not to discount the feeling that something wasn't right. Her job was ninety percent awareness and ten percent instinct. And instinct had her holstering her forty-five tonight instead of her stun gun.

The banquet room was packed to capacity. With one exit, she'd stationed Devin at the front of the room. People who wanted to talk to him could come to him.

No matter where they went in the last week, she felt as if they were being watched. Not in the normal, *Omigod, I can't believe I'm in the same room with Devin McClain!* type of gawking they dealt with every day. But even when she and Devin had a spare moment to themselves, it felt like they had an audience.

She scanned the room for the hundredth time and saw the same thing as the other ninety-nine times. The band was there. Sarge, Check, Boomer and the road crew were huddled in the corner. They always came for the food, but they never mingled. Several ladies—heck, most of the ladies—were eyeing Devin like a juicy slab of beef. She couldn't quite keep her smile to herself because he *was* a burning-hot hunk of man flesh. And he was all hers.

For the next seven days, anyway.

"Only two things bring a smile that wide to a woman's face. Sex or chocolate. And if you've had both today, I might actually punch you."

Liberty didn't move; she waited for Odette to stand beside her. "Start punching."

"Damn. I gotta do something to get that spark back with Steve. The bag of M&M's I scarfed down ain't cutting it."

Liberty pointed to the chocolate fountain in the corner. "Maybe have yourself a *man*due instead of fondue. Coat him in chocolate and lick him clean."

Odette blinked at her.

"What?"

"So much for me thinking that you're the shy, retiring type behind closed doors."

She grinned. "Still waters don't run deep; beneath the surface they run very dirty."

"Liberty!" Odette giggled. "You are awesome. I'm so glad you're on tour with us. You're part of the family now."

That caught her off guard. But it was true. She genuinely liked the band and the road crew. They had a lot of respect for Devin and looked out for him. "Thanks."

"Thank you for the *man*due idea."

"You're welcome." Liberty leaned closer. "I need a really huge favor."

"Name it."

"I need to talk to Devin alone. It seems every time he

has a spare minute, we get interrupted or intercepted. So once I get him out of here, could you keep an eye on the room? See if someone follows us?"

"You want me to try to stop them if that happens?"

"No. Just keep watch."

"Of course."

"Thanks." She would've asked Crash to run interference if he'd been around, but she hadn't seen him since the show ended. As she cut through the crowd, several women were downright nasty about letting her pass. One skank even stomped on her foot, then offered a lame "Did I do that? So sorry."

Liberty flashed her teeth, thinking that she'd much rather be flashing her gun. She finally reached Devin. Without breaking the conversation with his fan, he held his hand out and tugged Liberty against his side. She caught the eye of the foot stomper and smirked. A girl had to take tiny victories where she could get them.

Devin said, "What's up?"

She put her lips on his ear. "I need to speak with you alone. It'll take just five minutes."

"What happened?"

"Nothing."

Devin smiled at the people in line. "Duty calls, but I promise I'll be right back."

The only exit in the room was also the entrance. They had to wend through the throng to escape.

Once they were in the hallway, Devin said, "What was so all-fired important—?"

Liberty clamped her hands on Devin's cheeks and kissed him, trying to keep an eye on who'd followed them out of the room.

Devin wasn't on board with a mini make-out session.

He twisted out of her lip-lock. "*This* was why you pulled me away from a fan meet and greet?"

"Sort of. You looked like you could use a break."

They weren't alone in the hallway. Liberty grabbed his hand. "Let's go backstage where we can talk in private." She towed him behind her and didn't stop until they were in the wings.

"Liberty, sweetheart, have you been drinkin'? 'Cause this is unlike you."

"I never drink on the job. Have you seen Crash?"

"Gotta be more specific."

"Have you seen Crash since the show ended?"

"Not that I recall." His gaze turned suspicious. "Why are you so interested in what he's doin'?"

"Because he was supposed to help me," she lied, "and he's been MIA. That's not like him. Usually he hovers around you as much as I do."

Devin kissed her forehead. "He'll turn up. He always does."

Stall. Think of another reason to keep him back here to see if anyone followed you.

"Anything else? I need to get back in there so we can leave at a decent time tonight." He traced the scoop neck of her shirt. "Because I have plans for you."

"What kind of plans?"

"Naked with a can of whipped cream and a Ping-Pong paddle kind of plans."

"Yum. And ouch. My two favorites together."

He whacked her butt. "Take me back before I blow off my responsibilities and fuck you right here."

She took his hand and returned him to the room but didn't go in.

Odette waved at her from down the hallway, and Liberty sauntered over. "I'm afraid I'm not a good Nancy Drew. Only person I saw follow you out was JT. Then he got a phone call and took off like a bat outta hell. All the rest of the people who left just went to the bathroom."

"Thanks for your help. I did get to talk to Devin about what I needed to."

"Cool." She turned to head back to the party room.

"Odette, which direction did JT go?"

She pointed to the only side exit where there wasn't a guard stationed.

Even in Northern California the night air held a chill. Liberty shivered in her jacket and strode over to the bus. No sign of JT in the driver's compartment. Out of habit, she rounded the front end of the bus and checked to see that the alarm was armed.

That's when she heard it. A muffled thump.

What the hell was that?

She followed the sound, stopping when the noise became sporadic and she couldn't tell where it was coming from.

Then she heard it again.

Sounded like someone was smacking a heavy bag with a baseball bat.

She picked her way along the back wall of the event center, lured by grunts and low-pitched male voices. She paused in front of a concrete loading bay and scanned the area. Pale yellow light from the lone lightbulb shone ten feet above the ground by the loading dock's back door.

In the corner were two figures, and one guy was whaling on the other.

Silently creeping along the concrete wall into the loading bay, she kept her hand close to her gun.

"Stop." The guy on the ground wheezed. "I'll get the money. I promise."

"Heard that one before. Carny ain't happy. Been six months that you owed him, JT."

She froze. JT?

"Chumley fucked me up bad in Kansas City. I was outta work for three months! You gotta cut me some slack. I said I was working on it. Alls I got on me is five grand. I swear I got something goin' on that'll pay Carny in full."

Jesus, what the hell was JT into?

Right then she decided not to get involved. But she couldn't take a chance they'd see her, so she pressed her body against the wall where the shadows were the deepest.

"Gimme the fuckin' money. And I'm keeping half of it as personal compensation for havin' to track you fuckin' down *again*."

"But—"

The standing guy smacked JT across the shoulders with some kind of club.

JT yelled in pain.

"Shut the fuck up. Anyone comes running and I bust you in the face, understand?"

All she heard was a whimper.

"Good. Now get your flabby ass off the ground and gimme the money."

JT rolled to all fours and pushed upright with no help from the thug. Then he stood and dug his hand into his jacket pocket and passed over a thick wad of bills. "That's all I got. That don't even leave me money to eat."

"Boo-fuckin'-hoo. I saw you stuffing your face in that room with all the tables of fancy food. You don't look like you're starving anyway, lard ass." The thug swung the club and laughed when JT leaped back. He started to walk backward out of the docking bay. "Stay right there until I'm gone. One week, motherfucker."

Liberty's heart raced when the thug passed by her. But he was too busy watching JT to see if he attacked him to notice her. After the guy cleared the area, she counted. She hit one hundred and twenty when she heard an engine start and tires peel away.

"Fuck! Fuck, fuck, fuck." JT wiped his face on the sleeve of his jacket and took out his phone. He started to pace. "I need to talk to Waverly O'Brien. No, you can't tell him who's calling. Just tell him it's about some pictures he'd be interested in."

Waverly O'Brien. Why was that name familiar?

Then it clicked. The reporter from the religious magazine *Song of Solomon* who wrote the nasty article about Devin turning his back on his core audience by performing "What Love Isn't." So why was JT contacting him? And what pictures was he talking about?

Son of a fucking bitch.

Of course JT would have pictures of Devin and his groupies since he'd been Devin's bus driver for a few years. Given the fact she'd just heard he owed someone money, the bastard planned to sell them to get himself out of debt.

Or maybe, all those feelings of being watched meant that JT had been snapping pictures of Devin and her. But why? She was nobody.

But Devin isn't. His love life had been reported on for years.

"No, I won't hold," JT snapped. "I'll leave a message. You tell him to expect a call from me tomorrow or I'll find another magazine to publish these pictures of Devin McClain and he'll lose out."

JT hung up, muttering to himself.

No way was she letting this piece of shit hand-grenade Devin's career. No. Way.

When he started to shuffle up the ramp, Liberty stepped out of the shadows. "Hey, JT."

The man jumped about a foot. "Oh, uh, hey, Liberty. What're you doin' out here?"

"Getting some fresh air. But it's funny. Something out here smells rotten. Like really rotten. Rotten to the core."

JT froze about fifteen feet from her, his hand in his pocket. "Did you follow me?"

"I figured what goes around comes around. You've been following Devin and me everywhere."

"Lady, you're whacked."

"So you don't plan on selling the pictures you've taken of us to settle a debt?"

"I have no idea what the fuck you're talking about."

"Don't lie. I heard your phone conversation. And I heard you whining to that enforcer. That attack on Devin's tour bus never was about him, was it? It was all about you. You've been fucking him over since the second you started working for him."

The shift from clueless bus driver to slimeball was instantaneous. "You think you're so fuckin' smart. But you ain't the first bitch to suck Devin's cock and you ain't gonna be the last. So why don't you just go and get back on your knees where you belong and keep your mouth shut unless you're blowing him?"

Liberty laughed. "You are such a pig. But you're smart enough to keep Devin and the tour company snowed. You stole his guitars and hocked them, didn't you?"

"Back off."

"All the other weird shit that happened, you did that

too. Changing the hotel reservations. Sending groupies Devin's way."

"Shut your mouth and back off or so help me God I'll—"

"What?"

Then he pulled a gun out of his jacket, pointing it at her with a very shaky hand. "I said back off, bitch."

Her heart raced, but she kept a calm facade. "You gonna shoot me now?"

"If I have to. I'll tell people you were being attacked and I jumped in to save you and some crazy motherfucker shot you dead."

"How much money do you owe?"

"Why? You got a spare two hundred grand? Right. If you did, you wouldn't be trying to fuck your way into Devin McClain's bank account."

Liberty kept walking backward, letting him think he was pushing her forward against her will. "Why didn't you ask Devin for the money? Two hundred large is chump change to him."

"Because I don't wanna lose my job! I told you these people on this tour are my family."

A few more steps and he'd clear the concrete wall protecting him from all sides.

Come on. Keep moving.

"Bullshit. Family doesn't steal from family. Family doesn't lie to family."

JT reached up to wipe his bloody nose with the back of his free hand. "Maybe not your family, but mine sure as fuck did."

Footsteps skidded on the cement behind her.

Please don't let it be Devin.

"Jesus, JT, what the fuck is wrong with you?" Crash boomed.

"This is your fault," JT yelled at her, and his hand holding the gun wavered enough to worry her.

"Put down the fucking gun," Liberty said evenly.

"You're making me do this. Right now I'd be better off in jail. Carny's guys can't reach me there. At least not in this state."

"Liberty," Crash snapped. "Just fucking shoot him."

Events never happened in slow motion for her. For her, they happened in a nanosecond. She saw the shadowed form in her peripheral vision and then a split second later the form tackled JT. She turned to reach for her gun, saw the muzzle blast and heard the pop as JT's gun fired.

Then she felt the bullet rip through her flesh and a warm gush of blood. In shock, she staggered backward before she fell forward onto her knees.

Devin's roar vibrated through the air.

Dozens of footsteps pounded past her. Shouts sounded, and a male voice yelled in pain.

Crash crouched in front of her. "Liberty, are you okay?"

"He shot me."

Then Devin shoved Crash aside. "He fucking *shot* you?"

"Devin—"

"Where did the bullet hit?"

"My left arm. Fuck. I always forget how fucking much it hurts to get shot."

"Ambulance is on its way," Crash said. "Cops too."

"She can't wait for the fucking ambulance," Devin snarled.

Then Check was right there. "Move. I know what to do." He spoke in a low, soothing voice, asking where it hurt, gently poking the outside of her biceps and fashioning a tourniquet out of his bandanna.

Liberty needed to focus on something besides the pain. "Who's dealing with JT?"

"Event security guys. They stun gunned him a couple of times."

"Wish I coulda had a go at him," Crash grumbled.

"Good timing on your part, but how'd you find us?"

"Devin and I suspected JT was up to something, so in the past couple days, I started watching him."

"You suspected JT," she said evenly. "And yet you didn't think to oh, *discuss* it with me? Since I'm—"

"Not thinkin' clearly," Crash interjected, jerking his chin toward Check, who had no idea that Liberty was Devin's bodyguard.

Dammit. Even now, sporting a goddamn gunshot wound, she had to keep her mouth shut.

"Tonight I had to deal with equipment breakage, so I couldn't keep an eye on him after the show. SOB probably vandalized the equipment so I would be occupied," Crash said bitterly. "How'd you find JT?"

"I was by the bus and I heard a strange noise. I tracked the sound and came upon JT and some enforcer type guy beating on him."

"Devin said you were lookin' for me, so I went lookin' for you. When I couldn't find you, I knew something was up."

"Did you bring Devin along as your crime-fighting partner?" Liberty asked, unable to keep the disapproval from her voice.

"Fuck no." Crash glared at Devin. "Odette told him you were worried someone was watching you two and you'd followed JT outside. So Odette distracted security and Devin snuck out."

Liberty aimed a cool stare at him, hoping it masked

the pain in her eyes. "You decided it'd be a good idea to jump in front of a gun?"

Devin's jaw tightened. "I was just supposed to let him shoot you?"

She opened her mouth, snapping it shut when he made a snarling noise.

"I lost a hundred years off my life seein' him with a gun pointed at you. I reacted like any normal man would when the woman he's in love with is threatened."

"He could've shot you."

Devin curled his hand around the side of her face. "Baby, he *did* shoot you."

She blew a raspberry. "Please. He winged me. Barely a flesh wound."

"Jesus."

At that point the cavalry arrived. The EMTs helped her up and led her to the ambulance.

Devin was right there with her, every step of the way.

After she warned the EMTs that she was armed, they very gingerly cut away the ripped and bloody sleeve of her shirt. She hissed when they started poking around in the wound.

Her eyes met Devin's. He reached for her hand and kissed her knuckles. He'd stayed so close to her side that she figured the EMTs would boot his ass any second. They tried; Devin snarled and they let him stay.

The EMTs conferred in low tones. The medical jargon meant nothing to her, but the wound was getting to the excruciatingly painful stage. During a break in their conversation, she said, "So? What's the prognosis?"

"The bullet grazed you. But given the caliber of the bullet, it took a decent-sized chunk of flesh out of your arm. Not sure if there's muscle damage, so we need to get you to the ER."

"Is there a veterans hospital around here?"

"Liberty, you don't have to worry about that. We'll take care of the bill."

She rolled her eyes. "The VA has all my medical records. It'll save time. Plus, if they've got a wound care unit, that's who I want treating me."

"There is a VA close by," the female EMT offered.

"Good. Let's go."

Crash jogged over. "You all set here?"

"They're takin' her to the VA. I'm riding along with her."

"Uh, no, you're not," Liberty said. "I'm not exactly in the best position to protect you."

Devin smiled at the wide-eyed EMTs. "Can you please give us a moment alone?"

As soon as they stepped aside, Devin lit into her. "Not another fuckin' word about you protecting me. The guy who caused the problems is under arrest. And there's no way in hell I'm gonna sit on the bus with my thumb up my ass while you're in the fuckin' hospital from a goddamn bullet wound, Liberty."

Liberty looked at Crash, expecting he'd talk sense into Devin.

But Crash just shrugged. "I'm with Dev on this."

"Why?"

"Because if I know he's with you, I won't have to worry that he'll pull some dangerous dumb stunt trying to *get* to you."

"Fine." She gave Devin a hard look. "But we're going to a military hospital. I'm a former soldier, so there will be no fucking coddling me, got it?"

"Yes, ma'am. Now give him your gun," Devin told her in that bossy tone of his.

She reached around with her right hand—thank God she hadn't been shot in her right arm—and pulled the gun from her Undertech concealment shorts and handed it to Crash. "It's got one in the chamber."

"You are one scary-ass woman." Crash handled it like it was a snake, which amused her to the point she had to bite back hysterical laughter.

Possibly she was coming down from the danger high and was about to crash.

Hey, she could crash *into* Crash. Wasn't that funny? She had to chomp on her tongue to keep from chortling like a hyena at her awesome play on words.

"I won't be able to keep this from the media. So how do you want Big Sky to spin this?" Crash asked Devin.

"The official immediate statement should be: 'Unstable tour bus driver took a member of Devin McClain's road crew hostage. After a brief scuffle, the bus driver is in police custody awaiting charges. The crew member suffered a non-life-threatening wound and is expected to make a full recovery.'"

Liberty cocked her head. "Wow. If I could clap right now, I would. Damn, guitar slinger, you're quick on the uptake."

Devin smiled. "Ain't my first rodeo, G.I. Jane."

Chapter Thirty

❧

*F*our hours later, Devin was stretched out on the bed
on his bus beside Liberty. After she'd given her statement to the cops, the docs had doped her up on pain meds
since she'd refused to spend the night in the hospital. She'd
gone comatose the instant her head had hit the pillow.

He'd wanted to cosset her in a nice hotel with room
service, but they'd hit the road so he could make his next
performance.

A performance he'd be a zombie for since he couldn't
take his eyes off her. Devin had never been so terrified as
in that moment when he realized that JT *would* shoot her.
He'd reacted instinctively and he'd do it again, despite
Miss Professional Bodyguard's ass chewing for his macho
behavior. She'd pointed out—repeatedly—that he could've
hit JT at the wrong angle, sending the bullet ricocheting
into her head or into her heart. To which he'd calmly
replied that her head was so fucking hard the bullet
would've bounced off it like rubber.

She'd not found that amusing.

Eventually his eyelids drooped. Before he succumbed to slumber, he wondered if the drugs would keep Liberty from having combat nightmares. Because guaranteed this event would stir them up.

∞

The next morning Devin had showered and dressed by the time Liberty woke up. "Mornin', bullet catcher."

"Fuck off."

He raised an eyebrow. "Did JT hit part of your funny bone last night when he shot your arm? Because, woman, that was funny."

"Ha. Fucking. Ha. Better?" She struggled to sit up. "God. Did they slip me elephant tranquilizers last night?"

"No. Just enough to keep you down for at least twelve hours."

"What time is it?"

"Almost two."

"In the afternoon? Shit. I have to call Garrett."

"I already did. I told him you'd check in when you were feeling up to it."

"Oh. Thanks."

"How's your arm?"

"Sore. It'll be better once I start moving it. You did remember to grab that sheet with the recommended rehab exercises?"

Devin sat on the edge of the bed. "Before you start doin' physical therapy, are you hungry?"

"Yeah." She wilted against the headboard. "I could use a shower."

"Shower first because I need to change your bandage."

She scowled. "I can do it."

"I'm sure you can, sweetheart, but you ain't gonna do it. I am."

"Fine. How bad is the media?"

"No idea. Been avoiding it. I did call Chelsea Lynn from *Country Music Today* and gave her an exclusive, since she was the one who'd tipped me off to someone trying to sell pictures of us to the tabloids. See, JT had created this whole spin that you were a controlling bitch and causing problems on my tour. Which just goes to show you how stupid he was. Everyone likes you—except for him. And he got a bunch of his 'insider information' wrong, so we narrowed it down to him causin' the problems pretty easily."

"I heard him on the phone trying to get in touch with Waverly O'Brien."

"Fuckin' douche bag. JT was desperate. According to the statement the cops got, JT owes more than two hundred grand to some Vegas bookies."

"He didn't look like a junkie, so I figured he must be into gambling."

Devin pushed her damp hair off her cheek. "So observant. That's why you get paid the big bucks."

A worried look entered her eyes. "Why would you want me here if I can't do my job?"

"Stop. You're with me for the duration of this tour. Don't you think I'm safe now that the threat has been eliminated?"

Liberty shook her head. "You had incidents in the three months JT was recovering."

"But the worst of it, the attack on JT on my bus, the lax security, my guitars bein' ripped off, all a thing of the past."

"But what about your bus getting shot at? And—"

Devin put his fingers over her lips. "We knew the bus incident might've been random. And the protestors I brought on myself. I'm not bein' reckless. I'll continue to have security at all the events."

"But it won't be me."

"No."

"Then what good am I to you?"

"You really just asked me that?" He tamped down on his temper. "And by the way, when I told you I was in love with you last night, you didn't even respond. You just continued ripping into me for tackling JT." Devin kept a firm grip on her chin, not allowing her to look away. "Are you surprised that I have feelings for you?"

"No."

"Am I alone in those feelings?"

It took her a second to answer. "No."

"Good. I'm takin' care of you. That'll give us plenty of time to sort out what happens between us when the tour ends in a week." He kissed her. "Now, would you like scrambled eggs and toast? Or oatmeal?"

"Both." Then she purred, "And that's not all I'm hungry for," with a glance at his crotch.

"One thing at a time, sweetheart."

∞

On day five of Devin's mission to keep Liberty under his watch, he would've happily shipped her—and his entire crew—to Disneyland to see if being at "the happiest place on earth" would change their shit attitudes.

They'd had a lousy rehearsal. Everyone was ready to be done with the tour and get home. He chewed collective ass until the band and the crew understood he'd keep the rehearsal going until he was satisfied they weren't just phoning it in.

After the marathon session, his security escorted him to the bus. The second he emerged from the stair bay, he saw that Liberty's bad mood exceeded his and she was loaded for bear.

She sat on a folding chair in the middle of the living area, working on her physical therapy—bouncing and squeezing a tennis ball. Except she'd modified the exercise. She whipped the ball at the wall above the driver's cab. If he hadn't ducked, she would've nailed him in the head.

His eyes narrowed. Had she done that on purpose?

"Glad you could grace me with your presence," she said snottily.

He snagged the ball midair when she threw it again, this time at his groin. "Attitudes during rehearsal sucked, so I kept everyone until the attitudes improved. Why're you in a bad mood?"

"Because I've been a fucking prisoner in this goddamn bus for the last five days."

Devin flashed her a smile. "Welcome to my world, sweetheart."

"Oh, go to hell."

"Just spent two hours there, so no, thanks. How's the arm?"

"Perfectly fine. One hundred percent healed. It's a fucking miracle."

"Great. Get your shit packed. I'll have Crash book you a flight outta here tonight."

Liberty stared at him, and he saw the edge of fear in her eyes.

Such a little liar you are, tough girl. You don't want to go any more than I want you to.

She stood. "I'm not looking to leave. I'm looking to get back to work."

"No. The doctors said one full week of no strenuous activity."

"So is that why you haven't fucked me? Because it's always so fucking strenuous?"

"That's what you're so pissy about?"

She pushed the chair aside—using her injured arm, fully aware that he'd notice her little act of defiance. "Yes. Why haven't we had sex in six days?"

"Because you have a bullet wound."

She cocked her head. Devin braced himself for the barrage of bullshit she was about to spew. "Last I checked, I didn't get shot in the pussy; I got shot in the arm. And since you're not into armpit fucking, there shouldn't be a problem." Her gaze dropped to his crotch. "Or is there?"

He laughed. Goddamn, she was a piece of work. "No problem on my end." His eyes made a very slow, very hungry pass up and down her body. "You lookin' to get fucked?"

"Yes!"

"Then strip."

"Right here?"

"No, out in the damn courtyard. *Yes*, right here." He raised an eyebrow. "Unless that's a problem?"

Keeping her eyes locked on his, she dropped her sweatpants. No underwear. Then she unbuttoned her shirt and tossed it aside. No bra.

Yes, his hot, sexy woman did want to get fucked.

Too bad he wasn't going to oblige her.

"Very nice. Now walk down the hall nice and slow so I can see every jiggle of that fantastic ass of yours."

Liberty turned. She spread her legs and bent forward, dangling her head between her feet, exposing her pussy and that sweet little asshole. "Remember when you fucked me like this? And I braced one hand on the floor so I could play with your balls as you rammed into me? You fucked me so hard I nearly passed out. Let's do that one again."

He growled, "Get your ass into the bedroom. Now."

She sashayed off. *Sashayed.* G.I. Jane never sashayed.

When Devin reached the bedroom, Liberty was spread out on the bed, her vibrator in her right hand. "You priming the pump?"

Her husky laugh zinged straight to his cock. "No. I've been making do with Slim, here, oh, a couple . . . three times a day since I've been left to my own devices."

Own devices. She cracked him up. But he kept the smile from his face. "That right?" Devin kicked off his boots. Yanked off his T-shirt. Watched those silvery eyes focus on his fingers as he unhooked his belt, lowered the zipper and shed his jeans and boxers. "You and Slim wanna give me a show?"

"No. I want the real thing."

He reached in the drawer and pulled out a neckerchief.

Liberty's eyes zoomed to the silky black fabric. "What's that for?"

"For fun and games. Right arm up by the headboard."

"But I don't need fun and games, Devin. I need you to fuck me."

He crawled across the bed and stopped to kiss her with brutal possession. "I'll give you what you need. Now, arm up."

She sighed dramatically, but she obeyed.

After he tied her, he started to touch her. First with his hands. Featherlight caresses all along her supple body. Taking time to marvel at the softness of her skin and the strength beneath it. Her graceful neck, her strong shoulders, her luscious chest, her compact rib cage. Then he moved on to her taut belly, her rounded hips, her muscular thighs, defined calves and the delicate tops of her feet.

Then he let his mouth have a turn. Kissing. Licking. Sucking. Paying particular attention to the spots he sometimes overlooked in order to focus on the obvious body parts that made her scream and cream for him. The ripped musculature of her forearms, biceps and triceps. The bend in her elbow. The valley between each one of her fingers. The stubborn jut of her chin. The outer curves of her breasts.

He rolled her over to properly worship her backside. From the sexy sweep of the nape of her neck to her shoulder blades and the curve of her spine. The tempting dimples above her ass. The soft arc of flesh where her hips flared into her thighs.

As he teased and explored, her breathing grew shallow.

He looked up, expecting she'd have her eyes closed. But they were open and focused on him.

"Don't treat me like I'm fragile."

"I'm not." He kissed the swell of her breast that covered her heart. "I'm treating you like you're precious." He kissed her again. "Because you are so very, very precious to me, Liberty."

"Devin."

He looked up at her again, seeing a combination of fear and hope on her face. "I love you. Been wantin' to say it to you again. But this is better."

"What?"

"Showin' you that I love you. Every inch of you. Because I know every inch of this beautiful body. I know where to touch you to make you sigh. To make you moan. To make you cry out. This body knows me. It knows my intent every time I'm naked with you. But today I want your heart to know my intent. Because, baby, I want to prove to you that if you give it over to me as easily as you do your body, I'll cherish it."

"You . . ." She swallowed hard. "Have a way with words."

"They come easier when they're spoken from a place of truth."

"So how long will you continue this erotic torture? Until I beg?"

He traced the sharp edge of her jaw. "This isn't about power."

"Then what is it about?"

"Makin' love. Showin' love. Bein' in love."

Liberty's lips trembled. "I don't know how to do that."

"Sweetheart, we've been learning how to do *exactly* that for the last four months we've been together." When their mouths met, the kiss was scorching hot. But Devin wouldn't be rushed. When he kissed her, that's all he focused on. Her taste. The feel of her tongue tangling with his. Their synchronized breathing. How perfectly their mouths fit together.

How perfectly they fit together.

When the time was right, Devin levered himself over her, wedging his hips against hers, and slowly slipped inside her. He forced himself to stay still. To not give in to that powerful need to thrust. He looked down at her.

She lifted her free hand and touched his face. "I love you."

He'd never been happier than in that moment. "I love you too."

Her hand moved down his side to his ass. She slapped it hard. "Now fuck me."

Devin laughed. "Whatever you want."

Chapter Thirty-one

∽

The final performance of Devin McClain's four-month-long Heroes and Heartbreakers tour had arrived.

Liberty would be intimately familiar with the term *heartbreaker* at the end of the night.

The late-afternoon sun shone through the skylight above Devin's bed, sending sunbeams across his skin.

They'd spent the last hour in bed. The first time had been so fast—clothes off, hit the mattress and *boom* he was thrusting inside her—that she wondered if they were playing *Beat the Clock*.

The second time had been slower. Climbing that peak together until they both tumbled down in a dizzying, blissful rush.

Devin's rough-tipped finger circled the white bandage on her biceps. "I know it's been a week, but sometimes . . . I can't believe you got shot."

"I'm happy there wasn't muscle damage."

"Me too. Still . . . you'll have a scar."

"It'll match the others."

"Liberty—"

"I'm not being flip." She looked at his fingers gently stroking the inside of her arm. "Now I'm officially two for two."

"Meaning what?"

"The ambassador I saved? First and last security assignment."

"But I thought . . ."

"My security specialist skills Garrett brags about were securing transport trucks, not people."

"That tears it. I'm gonna demand my money back for false advertising," Devin drawled.

Liberty smiled. "Too late. And now, with my very first private security job, I end up with another damn bullet hole. It's enough to put a girl off bodyguard jobs for good." The instant she said it, she wished she hadn't.

"So ditch your job workin' for GSC and come to work for me full-time. You can handle security for my tours." He smoothed his hand over her shoulder then curled it around her cheek. "Although you never want to talk about this, you know I don't want this to be an ending. Let's make it a beginning."

"Devin—"

"Hear me out. I need a security coordinator. You're the very best I've ever had. You could run your own business, set your own hours. We'd be together on the bus during tours and the rest of the time we can live at my place in Nashville. We could be out as a couple everywhere."

The way he phrased it sounded perfectly logical.

But not for her.

Didn't he see that? How could he not realize that she'd suffocate in that no-purpose role? She'd never fit in his lifestyle. She needed something for herself beyond seeing to his needs.

But doesn't he see to yours? In ways you never imagined any man would?

Yes. But still, Liberty had known their relationship would end when the tour did, despite all of Devin's hints that he wanted it to continue. She could tell herself that she hadn't meant to fall in love with him, but from the moment he'd hauled her out of bed and comforted her after she'd had a nightmare, she realized falling for him was inevitable.

So her options were to end this with a big fight, or nod her head, play along with his delusions of their togetherness and then leave him like she'd planned.

Shame on you. Act like a soldier, not a coward running away again, and face this thing head-on.

At least a fight would allow her to tell him exactly why they wouldn't work. It'd hurt him—something she didn't relish doing. She wanted a clean break, not a cruel break. Which is why she'd never tell him about the hundred-thousand-dollar bonus she'd earned for staying with him on tour.

Walking away from him would be hard, but she'd survive. She always did.

So why was she crying just thinking about it?

"Darlin', what's wrong?"

She rolled to the side of the bed and started putting on her clothes.

"Liberty? Say something."

Inhaling a deep breath, she turned around and said, "No."

"No what? No, you don't want to say something?"

"While I appreciate the offer, no, I won't be handling your security on a permanent basis."

Devin shifted to his side of the bed and pulled on his clothing.

Then they faced each other in the middle of the room, ready for battle.

"What don't you understand? I love you. I want a life with you."

"Stop. Your declarations are just making this harder. This will never work."

"Why not?"

"Because we don't want the same things."

"You don't want a man who loves you more than he ever thought he was capable? You don't want to make a home with me and maybe a couple of children?"

She wiped her eyes, but the tears kept coming. "Don't be stupid. Of course I want that. The problem is I can't have that with you."

"Why not?"

"Because I love my job and that job is in Denver. I'm finally in a good place where I can have a home of my own—something I've never had. I lived the nomadic lifestyle my entire life, Devin. First growing up and then in the military. I'm thirty-five years old, and for the first time I'm putting down roots.

"Can you really see me in your life, Devin? At some fancy record label party? I'll never be the polished type of woman you need on your arm. And can you imagine the looks of horror if you told them I ran your tour security? It brings us right back to the issue you've had since day one on this tour."

"Don't go there," he warned.

"I have to! You don't want anyone thinking that you've got a woman protecting you. I won't let you be the butt of jokes in an industry where you work so fucking hard to earn respect. I've worked hard to earn respect too, and I'm not walking away from something that is more than just a job; it's my career."

There was only about ten feet between them in the room, but it might as well have been ten miles.

A lifetime of silence hung between them.

"You never saw this ending any other way, did you?" he said softly.

She shook her head. "And I fell in love with you anyway."

"That is exactly why we can make this work. We have to at least try."

"Fine. Let's compare schedules. I'm training in the field for a month after I return to Denver. It's not a Monday to Friday, with weekends off kind of job. It's whenever and wherever Garrett needs me to train. So I have no idea when I'll be around. You plan to sit in my apartment and wait for me to get home?"

He scowled.

"Oh, does that conflict with *your* schedule?"

"Yes. You know damn well I've booked studio time and I'm playing at the Ryman."

"So you couldn't kill time waiting in Denver anyway. We're back where we started. Living our lives, but not together."

Devin shook his head. "I can't accept that. Maybe next month won't work as far as seein' each other, but the month after that might. And the month after that. We can take it month by month. Who knows what'll happen next year? My career might tank and no one will schedule me to play anywhere. And you could get—"

She held up her hand. "Please don't say I could get injured in the line of duty."

"But it happened to you twice, and it can happen again." He shoved his hand through his hair. "I lived my worst nightmare when JT had a gun pointed at you."

Here was the moment of truth. "Do you wish that I didn't have such a dangerous job?"

"Honestly? Yes."

"Then we're even," she said softly. "Because I see those hordes of women clamoring for you, and I wish you wouldn't step foot on that stage. But that's who you are, Devin. That's a big part of the man I fell in love with. I'd never ask you to change who you are to be with me."

He stared at her for so long she wondered what the hell was going through his head. "And I'd rather have a few sleepless nights worrying about you than demand you change what I love and respect most about you."

When Devin wrapped himself around her, she knew he finally understood. They clung to each other, neither one willing to be the first to break away.

"I love you," he whispered. "That ain't ever gonna change."

"I know. I love you too."

Then, in almost perfect synchronicity, they both stepped back.

"Will you be at the show tonight?"

"Wouldn't miss it for the world. Since it's the first time I'll see it as a fan and not your bodyguard."

"It's the same show. I'll see you at the after-party?"

"All the bigwig sponsors will be there. Your time will be at a premium."

"That's not an answer."

Liberty was hedging because she'd already booked her

ticket on the red-eye flight from LAX to Denver. She'd stay for the performance, but not the after-party. It'd be easier if she didn't tell him. If she just . . . wasn't there. "Are you doing any new material tonight?"

"Haven't decided. Crash is bugging me to do a couple of cover tunes to make the set just a little longer, so we'll see." He reached for her hand. "I've gotta get to rehearsal."

"Go."

Devin kissed her. It was a sweet melding of mouths that left her feeling breathless and even more brokenhearted.

"See you in a few hours."

But as soon as he was out of the bus, she packed up.

∞

The band and the crowd were rowdy. More wound up than any other night she'd seen them play. She chalked it up to it being the end of the tour.

After playing all his big songs and a new one that he and Odette had written, the house lights went down.

Devin situated himself on a stool, stage center, and strummed his guitar. Then he adjusted the microphone and looked at the audience. "I'm doin' something a little different tonight, so bear with me." He plucked a few more strings.

Why did he look nervous? That made her nervous in turn.

"I've got a . . . friend who's not a big fan of country music."

Boos rang out.

He laughed. "Now, hold on. Everyone's entitled to their opinion, even if it's wrong."

It seemed like everyone in the arena laughed at that.

"It's tempting to take a pop song and countrify it to prove that if the song is good, it can be played country style."

Leon did a traditional steel guitar riff; then Odette joined in on fiddle and Steve on drums.

"But some songs don't need extra flash. Some songs don't need to be countrified. Some songs are best as is. Stripped down to basics. Like this one." He bent his head so his hat cut the glare of the stage lights. "This one's for you, Liberty."

As soon as Devin hit the first chord progression, everything inside her tightened. And when he started the chorus of "She Will Be Loved" by Maroon 5, her tears fell without shame. She wrapped her arms around herself, keeping her eyes glued to the stage, letting Devin's beautiful, soulful voice fill her—even when it was breaking her into a million tiny pieces.

There was a moment of stillness throughout the stadium when Devin finished. Then thunderous applause created a roar that moved through the building in a deafening wave. Even the people behind the scenes were abuzz.

Which made it easier for Liberty to avoid everyone on Devin's crew and disappear into the night.

Chapter Thirty-two

❧

Liberty was gone.

Gone without saying good-bye.

Isn't that what you were doing in the hotel room earlier today? Saying good-bye?

He signaled for the cocktail waitress to bring him another beer as he tuned out the hipster blowhard from some LA indie label.

"Here you go, Mr. McClain," the cocktail waitress with gigantic fake tits, a fake tan and fake white teeth cooed at him as she handed him the bottle of Coors.

"Thanks, darlin'. And don't go far because I'll need a lot more of these tonight."

"I'd be more than happy to provide anything you need," she said in a husky tone.

As she sauntered away, Devin decided his cocktail waitress really had a cock—no woman he'd ever met had shoulders and arms that size. No way.

"Gah. Why are you drinking that?" indie label guy said

with disdain. "I know there's a decent selection of craft beers."

"Nothin' wrong with Coors."

Indie guy opened his mouth to challenge that statement, but Devin cut him off. "Coors sponsored my tour. Which I'm sure offends your sensibilities, assuming I sold out. I didn't. I don't accept sponsorship money from companies I don't believe it. I've been drinking Coors since I was old enough to buy my first six-pack."

The challenging look Devin leveled on him sent the guy scurrying away.

Carl moved in beside him and sighed. "You're usually a lot more charming than that, McClain."

"After four months on the road, I'm all out of charm."

"Can't say as I blame ya." Carl tipped back his own bottle of Coors. "If that small-potatoes label didn't have an artist that your label was trying to poach, that guy wouldn't even be here."

"Gotta love end-of-tour parties. Not."

"I know you're glad this tour is over, and I have to tell ya, we couldn't be happier with the preliminary numbers. Even with the added expenses after the Houston incident and the Portland incident, we're still ahead. That makes the investors and the sponsors happy, so kudos to you. Anytime you're ready to talk about setting up another headlining tour, I'm game."

Carl was game as long as Devin had songs in the top twenty and a new album to promote. Once that dried up, so would the offers. "I'll keep that in mind. But for now, I need a break."

"I imagine so. Especially after all that happened with JT."

It burned his ass that a man he'd befriended had lied to him, stolen from him and used him—from the very start. Not to mention he'd shot Liberty. "I still feel like an idiot over that."

"The guy passed all the security checks. Who knew he had a gambling problem? Don't beat yourself up about it. I'm just really glad Miz Masterson was so fast on her feet or things might've turned out differently."

While Liberty had been undergoing treatment in the ER, Devin had told the cops what'd happened. Mostly. He stretched the truth a bit and said Liberty had wrestled with JT—that's how she'd ended up getting shot. Devin had changed the details because he didn't want anyone reading the police report and thinking he was some kind of hero when he wasn't. Liberty was. He'd told Garrett the truth and let him decide what to tell the promotion company. Liberty didn't know any of this and never would.

Carl drained his beer and seemed to sway more than usual. Awesome. The man was drunk. "She was worth every damn penny, including the bonus."

"What bonus?"

"Performance bonus. Extra cash if she lasted the entire tour."

Right. It was a fucking bribe for her not to sue them for getting fucking shot. "She oughta be surprised."

"Not a surprise to her. She knew about the money when she signed on. In fact, she insisted the bonus be paid within three days of the end of the tour."

The truth sent his stomach churning even worse than the idea of a bribe to stay with him. "How much was I worth?"

"A hundred thousand dollars. I was willing to double that, but GSC didn't counter for more for her and I wasn't gonna offer."

That was a lot of money. Now he knew why she'd been looking at property in Denver. A hundred K was a hefty down payment on any house.

Had she only pretended to be in love with him?

Fuck that. She loved him. She loved him so much she was running scared.

Or had she run away, laughing, with dollar signs in her eyes?

You're just a commodity to most people. Money, sex, publicity—if you don't provide it, they don't want you.

"Hi, Devin. You're looking good."

Devin was tempted to sprint toward the door at the simpering voice of his ex, China. Of course he'd see her when he was all pent up, wondering if Liberty loved him, or if she'd merely played him.

"Hey, China. Surprised to see you."

She stuck out her lower, heavily Botoxed lip in a fake pout. "I remember when you used to call me China doll." She put her hand on his chest and leaned close. "Can we let bygones be bygones?"

"Really?" he said in a hoarse tone, trying not to breathe in the artificial smell of her. And did she really think he'd just forget about all the crap she'd put him through? Not fucking likely.

"Seeing you onstage tonight got me all hot for you again."

"How about if I do something to put out that heat?"

She dug her nails into his chest and purred, "Now we're talking, lover."

Devin stepped back. "I'll get you a drink." He headed for the bar, snagged another bottle of Coors and walked right out the door.

∞

Ten minutes later, he'd tracked down his tour manager, who was glugging down a bottle of Jack.

They sat side by side on the cement ledge of the docking bay watching the roadies load equipment. "I'm starting to feel the booze."

"Getting shitfaced is unlike you, Crash."

"This has been a tour unlike any other." He swigged from the bottle. "I'm getting too old for this shit."

Devin sent Crash a hard look. "Jesus. Don't tell me you plan to quit. I've already had one person leave me today."

"Liberty didn't leave you. She finished her job and returned home."

"That ain't helping."

"Come on. How else did you expect it to play out?"

"I didn't expect her to take off without a fucking word." He drained his beer and was tempted to throw the bottle just to hear the angry sound of crashing glass. "But I imagine she's gotta be in Denver, at her bank Monday morning, to cash that big fucking check."

Crash frowned. "What check?"

"The big fat bonus check from Big Sky for makin' it through the whole tour." He looked at him. "You didn't know?"

"No. But it's not like that's something new."

Startled, he said, "What do you mean?"

"You've never been interested in the nuts and bolts of the tour side beyond the venues, but almost everyone associated with the tour, even the roadies, get a performance bonus if they finish the tour."

"Even you?"

"Even me. So see, it's nothin' personal. From what I've

seen of Liberty, as much as she earned that money, I imagine she feels guilty for keeping it."

"Because she had to pretend to be in love with me for four fucking months?"

Crash laughed. "You are an idiot. The woman is in love with you for real. Goddammit, Devin. How many other women would've taken a bullet for you? How many other women really, truly don't give a good goddamn about your celebrity? Or your money? She doesn't. You were more open with her than I've ever seen you with anyone, including people who've worked for you for years, including your own family."

Really tempting to throw that bottle now—except right at Crash's drunken head.

But he's not telling you anything you don't already know.

"I know you don't like me nagging, but did you see your family when you followed Liberty to Wyoming during the break?"

He shook his head.

"Why not? And don't tell me it's too hard."

"It's not that."

"Then what is it?" Crash demanded.

Devin snagged the bottle and knocked back a slug of whiskey. "It's like we're not even family—just strangers who survived a tragedy with nothin' else in common now that the crisis is over."

"Your family never talks about Michelle? Or you never talk about her with them?"

"I talked about Michelle with Liberty."

"Did it help?"

He sighed. "Yes. And no. It stirred up all that shit I've been avoiding."

Crash snatched the bottle back. "Tried to tell ya at the Cheyenne show that your folks and your sister and her family were disappointed you didn't hang out with them. They saw you with your hometown friends, so it wasn't like you didn't have the time. You just didn't choose to spend time with them. I imagine that's a little hard to swallow."

"I suck. I know that, all right?" he said hotly. "Maybe I'm stayin' away from them for their own good. What broke between us . . . Maybe it just can't be fixed."

"Whatever, man. You sure can't fix it if you don't ever bother to try."

The same exact thing Liberty had said to him.

Which made him suspicious. "Were you and Liberty talkin' about my private family stuff behind my back?"

"A few times. Mostly after you visited a kids' hospital. It wrecks you. In the past I'd been the one to pick up the wreckage, and she gladly took on that burden."

He had been a big damn burden to her. But she'd never been anything but supportive after those visits. Sweet. Caring. Or she let him wallow. Or she encouraged him to talk. She had the uncanny ability to know exactly what he needed.

"Despite the family situation that's still weighing on you, in the last four months you've been happier than I've ever seen you. It's like she gave you back a piece of your-self that's been missing."

"What piece?"

"Your heart."

Crash wasn't wrong, but he'd sound like a fucking pussy if he said the reason he didn't give out his heart was because the son of a bitch always got broken. "What am I supposed to do?"

"You'd be a damn fool to let her get away now that you finally found her. Gotta say, man, that'd drive me fuckin' nuts, knowing where she is and not goin' after her. Me'n my missus have been married thirty-five years. It sucks balls bein' away from her. But we made a deal that I'd do only one tour a year. The other eight months I'm underfoot, driving her ass insane. We found a solution that works for us."

"That's what I told her! We could figure out a way to make it work if she just trusted me."

"Talk is cheap. Put your cards on the table so she can't miss what you're offering her."

Devin let that sink in. He swiped the bottle from Crash and drank. "Did you see her leave tonight?"

"Yeah. She was crying so damn hard that she couldn't even talk. I helped put her bags in the cab. Christ. She had four pieces of luggage. How the hell she'll manage that with her injured arm is beyond me. Probably not beyond her though. That woman is a beast."

"Where was she goin'?" *Please say a hotel.*

"Airport. Imagine she's in the air by now."

His throat burned, imagining Liberty alone, struggling with her baggage and her emotions. He returned the bottle without taking a drink. "Thanks for the advice." He hopped down. "It's easy to let the family stuff slide, because I have you and the rest of the crew as my family these days."

"And you, more than anyone, know how to fix things when they start to go bad with all of us. Maybe it's time you put that into practice with your own family."

"Maybe." He clapped Crash on the shoulder. "Later."

"Where are you goin'?"

"To make a couple of calls."

∞

Liberty understood why they called it a red-eye flight. With few passengers on board, she just let her damn tears fall. There wasn't anyone around to see them.

You did the right thing.

It's painful now, but in time you'll see it never could've worked.

You're an idiot.

You'll never ever find another man like him. He gets you. He loves you.

With the warring thoughts pinging in her brain, there was no way she could sleep.

"Ma'am? Would you like another drink?"

Liberty eyed the empty beer can. Might as well. It wasn't like she was driving home from the airport.

And nobody will be anxiously awaiting your arrival home. Get used to being alone again.

She bit back a sob.

Oh, stop feeling sorry for yourself—you did this to yourself.

"Ma'am?" the flight attendant prompted.

"Sure." She wiped her eyes. "I'll have another beer. No. Make it two."

"I'm sorry. I can only sell you one at a time."

"Shame."

The beer wasn't as cold as she liked and it was plenty foamy. She set it aside.

She stared out the window into the inky blackness. Would she have a text message from him when she landed? Would he have tried to call her?

No. She'd left him. She'd made it clear they were done. He'd offered her the best of himself, trying to find common ground. What had she offered him besides the word no? She hadn't even considered compromising.

Fuck.

She slammed the beer, grabbed her iPod and shoved in her earbuds. She'd drown out the unhelpful voices. She deliberately chose songs that wouldn't remind her of Devin. No country. No Maroon 5. No Foo Fighters. No Wright Brothers. Incubus, Staind, Nickelback or Evanescence oughta do the trick.

Liberty jumped when a hand landed on her shoulder. She looked around, momentarily forgetting where she was. Somehow she had dozed off.

The flight attendant smiled. "Sorry. We're about to land."

"Thanks."

After she'd cleared the security exit point, she tried to ignore the passengers being met by loved ones—even in the middle of the night. She saw their smiles, their tears, their hugs and kisses. Their joy should have no bearing on hers.

But it did. She'd never felt so alone.

Jesus. Don't fucking cry.

She dragged her weary body past the luggage carousels, looking for her flight number. That's when she saw him.

"Garrett? What are you doing here?"

"Makin' sure you get home safely. Lots of crazies out there this time of night." He closed the distance between them. "Liberty, you look like hell."

You should see how shredded I am on the inside.

"Did I accidentally send you a copy of my itinerary?"

He shook his head.

"Then how did you know I'd be here?"

Garrett gave her a very level look. "He called me."

Her heart nearly stopped. "When?"

"Tonight. After you left LA. He didn't want you to come home with no one to meet you."

That's when she lost it and started bawling right there in baggage claim.

Garrett—strong, tough, take-no-shit Garrett—pulled her into his arms and held her while she cried.

By the time she'd calmed herself, the carousel had stopped spinning and her four bags were the only ones remaining.

Garrett leaned back to look at her intently, keeping his hands on her shoulders. "I never should've let you take this assignment."

Not having the life-changing experience with Devin was more awful to contemplate than walking away from him. "It's fine."

"No, it's not. You're not. We need to talk. But you need to get your head straightened out first, okay?"

"Okay."

"In the meantime, you're officially off duty next week. And, yes, that's SOP after a long assignment, not special treatment because you're a girl." Garrett strode to the carousel and hefted two of the duffel bags. "Jesus, woman. What do you have in here?"

"Clothes. Shoes."

"I don't even want to know what's in those." He pointed to the other duffel bags she'd hefted. "You have a lot of baggage."

You have no idea.

"Come on. The car is double-parked."

Liberty settled in Garrett's plush Lincoln Navigator. She lived a solid thirty minutes from DIA—without traffic. Her boss wasn't the type to make idle chatter, but the silence just caused the voices in her head to get louder and louder.

"Liberty? You okay?"

No. "Why?"

"You sort of growled."

Jesus. Would this emotional basket case shit never end?

"Look. I know you said I needed my head on straight before we talk, but the deal is, I need to talk to someone now. Since this . . . entanglement with Devin grew out of an assignment, and because of nondisclosure agreements, I can't call either of my sisters and cry on their shoulders. So it looks like you're my only choice as confidant—whether or not you like it."

After a few moments, he nodded. "Keep the sex stories to a minimum, okay?"

"Deal." Liberty inhaled a deep breath and started to talk.

Chapter Thirty-three

⚜

*D*evin was more than a little jet-lagged when he pulled up to his sister Renee's place in Laramie two days after he'd left LA. But guilt quickly replaced exhaustion when he remembered he hadn't been here in three years.

He might've hidden in his rental car all damn day if Renee hadn't come out and pointedly waited on the deck for him.

Grabbing the bouquet of fall flowers off the passenger's seat, he climbed out and followed the brick path up to the deck, noticing the new landscaping and all new siding.

He stood in front of her, not knowing where to start or what to say.

Renee smiled at him. "Flowers? The only time Chuck gets me flowers is when he's done something to piss me off."

Devin took the first step and hugged her. "I haven't

done nothin' wrong. Besides bein' the world's shittiest brother." Maybe he shouldn't have started with that. "I saw them and thought you had some like these in your wedding?"

She put her nose in the bouquet. "I'm surprised you remembered that."

"Like I could forget you got married earlier than you planned just so you could fulfill Michelle's dream of bein' a flower girl before . . ." He cleared his throat and looked away. "She had so damn much fun tossing them petals in the air. I don't remember much else, besides Michelle wearing that big floppy hat because she didn't have hair."

Renee's breath caught.

Devin's gaze snapped back to her.

"That's the first time I've heard you mention her name in . . . years."

"It's not because I don't think of her," he said brusquely.

She hugged him. "I know. I'm glad you called. I'm really glad you're here. Let's go inside."

Renee's house was a standard three-bedroom ranch, a family place filled with everything that made it a home. Comfy furniture, pictures, and the clutter from a husband and two kids. She pointed to the dining room. "Have a seat. I'll bring coffee out." He heard her humming while she put the flowers in water. She returned with two cups of coffee and a plate of homemade banana bread.

"Mom's recipe?" he said, stealing a slice.

"Nope. Mine. And it's better."

He took a bite and nodded. "It is."

They sipped and nibbled in silence, and Devin wondered if he had the guts to start this conversation.

Renee fiddled with the quilted place mat. "So, Devin,

what brings you by? Because even when you're in the neighborhood, we don't always see you."

"Yeah. Well. I'm a piece of work, aren't I?"

"Let me start over. Do you have bad news you want to deliver in person?"

He met Renee's eyes then. Eyes identical to his. Eyes identical to Michelle's. "No. I've just come to some realizations. You probably think I don't come around here or don't call much because I think I'm too good for—"

"Stop." She put her hand on his arm. "I know why you don't come around here. Why you talk to Mom and Dad just enough times throughout the year that they don't think you've forgotten about them. It's not because of you being famous. It's because of Michelle."

Devin looked at the banana bread crumbs on his plate.

"You started pulling away well before you became Devin McClain country superstar. I also know that's why you can visit your friends in Muddy Gap and Rawlins and drive right past here."

"Like I said, Renee, I ain't been up for brother of the year for a lot of years."

She was quiet for a moment. "During those two years Michelle was so sick, you never let your friends know how bad it was, did you?"

He shook his head.

"So they didn't know why you dropped out of all your activities?"

"No." He'd come home every day after school to be with her. His biggest fear was the day he'd get home and Michelle wouldn't be there. After that happened . . . he stayed away from home as much as possible.

"Then, after she died—at least with them—you bounced

back to being charming, fun-loving Devin Hollister. I bet even now if I asked Kyle Gilchrist or Hank Lawson or Eli Whirling Cloud or Bran Turner or Reese Davidson about that time, they never saw the broken part of your soul."

"Mostly because they were goin' through rough times of their own. Kyle almost died in a motorcycle accident. Hank, Abe and Celia lost both their parents at once. Eli's dad went to jail. Bran watched his grandparents' health failing. Reese enlisted to avenge his brother's death. It's harder for people to know what to say or what to do when it's a kid who dies, so no one brought it up with me. I think the fact we could put all that sorrow, avoidance, hurt and anger aside, at least when we were together, it's what's kept us friends throughout the years."

"I don't disagree. But . . . you wouldn't speak of Michelle even to us. Mom and Dad were so lost in grief for two years after Michelle passed that by the time they came out of it, you were gone."

Sometimes when Devin was really feeling sorry for himself, he felt he'd lost both his sisters and his parents that year. Renee had her own life with Chuck. Mom and Dad had each other. Devin had no one. But that's when he found music. "I don't have any resentment toward them for that." He paused. "Do they know that?"

"I think so. But I'm sure they'd like to hear it from you."

"I . . ." He inhaled and blew out a puff of air. "I'll keep that in mind. I plan to swing by and see them today."

"That's progress." She paused. "Do you resent me?"

He frowned at her. "Why would I resent you?"

"Because I was so wrapped up in my new husband and trying to be there for Mom and Dad, even when they shut me out, that I didn't have enough energy left for you. I shoved aside how awful it must've been for you, having them shut you out too—but you had to live with them."

"It was like livin' with ghosts," he said softly. "They were shells of who they'd been. The house was so . . . quiet."

"That breaks my heart. You were just a kid yourself. I had my own place and didn't have that loss constantly in my face."

"Didn't mean it wasn't there."

"You were closer in age to her than I was. Your rooms were right next door to each other. I can't imagine having to walk past her room, knowing Mom and Dad had left it exactly as it was before she . . ."

Devin hadn't ever gone back in her room. And when his parents decided to sell the house and asked him if he wanted anything of Michelle's, he still couldn't face stepping foot in the place that was her safe haven.

"She was so lucky to have you." Renee attempted a watery smile. "She thought you hung the moon and stars."

"I did. Literally. Remember that damn solar system she had to have hanging above her bed?" He pointed at her. "You bought it for her. She worshipped you, Renee."

"It was mutual," she murmured. "I remember being so annoyed when Mom and Dad told us they were having another baby. I was thirteen and totally icked out by the idea they'd had sex. Then they brought that screaming, pink bundle home from the hospital and I fell in love."

"You carried her around everywhere like a princess. And I mostly ignored her until she started to do tricks."

Renee laughed. "She would do anything to get your attention."

"She was such a pain in the ass sometimes." And then she was gone. For the first two months after she'd died, he'd beaten himself up, remembering all the times he'd been impatient and mean to her before she'd gotten sick.

"It's good, us talking like this."

"Yeah. It's been . . . hard for me to remember the good times before everything changed." He spun his coffee cup. "How did you deal with it?"

"Poorly. Very poorly. Poor Chuck. Eventually it got better—but never easier. Especially not when Chuck was ready to have kids. I put him off for nine years."

"Why?"

"I was so terrified that I'd have a child and it would . . ." *Die.*

He stared at her in shock. He knew they were married a decade before starting a family, but he'd never asked why. "What changed your mind?"

"Mom did." Tears freely spilled down her cheeks. "She said she'd never regret having Michelle even when losing her nearly broke her. Then we talked about the joy Michelle had brought to all of us, even though it was only for a short time." She sniffed. "Lord, I think I was pregnant the next month." Renee wiped her cheeks. "Christopher and Becca are such blessings to me now. I can't imagine my life without them."

"They seem like good kids." Not that he'd spent much time with them. He remembered watching Liberty with her nephews and being jealous of her easy, loving relationship with them. He had no idea how he'd ever get that with Chris and Becca since he'd missed a good chunk of their growing-up years.

"What happened in your life that you're ready to deal with all of this?" Renee asked cautiously.

Thinking of Liberty, he managed a smile. "I met a woman. An amazing woman."

"And she's encouraging you to . . . ?"

"Open up about family stuff. I told her about Michelle right after we met."

Renee raised an eyebrow.

"It caught me off guard, her bein' so easy to talk to. It's rare in my life, not knowin' who I can trust. I have good friends who don't know that I had a younger sister, let alone lost her. As far as dealin' with it back then? I just plain cut and run. How I'm dealin' with it now probably ain't much better, but in my defense, I'll say I handle it in my own way."

"By entertaining kids at children's hospitals, by donating blood, by being in the bone marrow donation database, by creating and funding the Hollister Foundation that pays for siblings to have outings and sleepovers near the hospital when one sibling is in treatment."

It was strange to hear his sister speak of those things with such admiration, because they never talked about it. "How'd you hear about that stuff?"

"Mom and Dad. They're proud of what you do in Michelle's memory, but they're afraid if they tell you, you'll pull away even more."

Devin snorted. "Is that even possible?"

"Honey, give yourself a break. I know you don't do any of it for the publicity, and you blush and stammer like you're doing now if anyone brings it up. But it will get out one of these days, and you'll have to address the questions about why you do it and why you hid it."

"I know. I'm ready for that. In the past four months I've talked about Michelle more than I ever remember. It's been . . . good. And Liberty—"

"Wait. Your girlfriend's name is Liberty? Geez, Devin. Please tell me she's not a stripper."

He grinned. He could hardly wait to tease Liberty with that one. "Actually, she's been my bodyguard." It felt good to tell Renee everything about how they'd met—including his demand that the former soldier make herself over, which earned him a whap on the arm. Just like old times.

After he finished, Renee said, "She does sound amazing. I can't wait to meet her."

"You will." Devin had a plan to put in place as soon as he returned to Denver. "She's close to her sisters. They didn't have it easy growin' up, but they're determined to be part of one another's lives as adults. It's a good example for me to see what they've got and what we've been missin'. I wanna change that, Renee. I really do. With you and your family and with Mom and Dad."

Renee squeezed his hand. "I'm glad."

"Liberty's sister Harper lives in Muddy Gap, which is why she took a job in Denver, to be closer to her."

His sister looked at him with surprise. "Is there a chance you'll be close by too? Like . . . permanently?"

"If I have my way? Yes."

"You always get your way."

Devin grinned. "Yep."

"God, you've been that cocky little shit since you were a kid." She smiled. "I've missed seeing it."

He smiled back. "You'd better get used to seein' it again."

∞

Four days had passed since Liberty had left LA.

Four days that seemed like four thousand years.

She forced herself to keep the appointment she'd made with her realtor, back when she believed looking at houses would keep her mind off Devin.

Ha. Fat fucking chance of that.

Looking at real estate only reminded her of how foolish she'd been in thinking she could focus on the big bonus at the end of the job and not the emotional devastation from leaving the man she loved, who'd been way more than just a job to her from the start.

After her talk with Garrett, where she'd laid it all out, her boss insisted she take the week off to think things through. *Quit being a dumb-ass; call Devin; decide what level of commitment you can give him and GSC before you even think about walking into my office.*

Yeah. No pressure.

So here she was, trying to act enthusiastic about housing choices, when she wanted to be holed up in her shitty apartment, deciding if she should be buying property in Denver at all, or buying a pair of cowgirl boots to wear on her way to Nashville.

A pair of shiny red shitkickers was currently winning.

She usually met Jada, her realtor, at her office, but today Jada insisted they meet at the first property.

After scanning the general literature on the building, Liberty dropped her head back and stared up at the funky metal and concrete high-rise. "I don't remember asking to see this one."

"I know. When you told me your base price had increased, I figured you should see what's available in the next price bracket. Sometimes it helps you decide if you're settling for something that fulfills a basic need rather than going after what you really want."

Liberty gave her a sharp look. That seemed to sum up everything going on in her life.

Jada smiled. "How about we head inside?"

461 ∞ HILLBILLY ROCKSTAR

The "lobby" of the high-rise reminded her of the hotel/condo place they'd stayed at in Houston. An armed guard parked at the desk immediately requested IDs. He took Jada's driver's license and checked it against a master list before he handed her a keycard.

According to the spec sheet, this building had twenty-seven floors. Besides the penthouse, which took the entire top floor, the main floor lobby, and the second floor, which held the business offices and the building's janitorial services, the remaining twenty-four floors were all privately owned condominiums. Some floors had six units, some had three or four units, and the floor right below the penthouse had two units.

"What do you think so far?" Jada asked brightly.

"I think it looks expensive."

"Let's go up to the unit I wanted to show you. The square footage and pricing information is detailed on the seller's sheet."

In the elevator, Jada ran a keycard through the digital reader and hit the button for the twenty-sixth floor. "The cool thing about this building is not only is it just under three years new, close to downtown and public transportation, but most of the units have mountain views. The security system is state-of-the-art. The elevators are coded by keycard and only the owners have access to their specific floor."

"That is pretty cool."

"Very safe for a single woman," Jada added.

Talk about a hard sell.

"The underground parking garage is under security twenty-four hours a day, and each unit is able to rent two spots per month."

The elevator didn't stop until it deposited them on the twenty-sixth floor. They stepped into an elegant hallway with doors at either end. The doors were crafted with architectural details that resembled the entrances to upscale houses in the suburbs.

"Which one is for sale?"

"They both were, but that one recently sold." Jada sashayed to the archway on the left, using an old-fashioned key to open the door. She held the door open and said, "Go on and look around. I need to make a call."

The instant Liberty walked in, she fell in love. Like hard-core in love. The view? Amazing. The connected living room and dining room provided an unobstructed view of the Rockies. She opened the sliding glass door and stepped out onto the balcony.

Cool wind stirred her hair, and she could see herself out here, stretched out on comfy patio furniture, drinking coffee and lazing in the sun.

Devin would love this outdoor space. She saw him with his feet propped up, dinking around on his guitar, the breeze wreaking havoc on the sexy curls in his hair she loved so much.

Not helping.

She returned inside.

The kitchen was strategically placed, keeping separation of spaces but with doorways to the dining and living areas. Since she wasn't much of a cook, the bells and whistles of the granite and stainless steel space were lost on her.

A gas fireplace was centered on the far wall in the living room. She envisioned cozy seating areas scattered throughout the space. No place for a TV, but with that view she'd spend her time staring out the window.

Just past the dining room was a funky octagonal-shaped hallway with eight arched doorways going in every direction. Behind the first door was a half bath. The next door led to a decent-sized bedroom with a big closet and windows facing the mountains. The next bedroom was bigger. It had an attached bathroom with a tub/shower combo. She opened the door to the master bedroom and stopped.

Holy shit. This room was enormous. She could put two king-sized beds in here. And check it out. Another freakin' fireplace and another balcony that boasted a view of downtown Denver. The master bathroom had a gigantic black marble shower with half a dozen showerheads in the walls and two hanging from the ceiling. At the back of the bathroom was a set of pocket doors that revealed a tiled corner garden tub with whirlpool jets. The main part of the bathroom had cabinets galore, big mirrors and a double vanity.

Devin would love this suite. He'd want to christen every feature in these rooms, making love to her in front of the fireplace, banging her against the wall in the shower, bending her over the balcony railing.

Not helping.

She returned to the bedroom and peered into the closet. Not a single closet—his-and-hers walk-in closets. Half the bedrooms she'd slept in growing up weren't this big.

Back in the hallway, Liberty opened the three remaining doors. Behind door number one—a laundry room. Behind door number two—a storage room with another built-in pantry. The last door revealed a media/family room, complete with a small wet bar.

Devin would love this room. She saw them cuddled up, watching movies, playing video games, installing a card table so they could outdo each other in a game of strip poker.

Liberty rested against the wall. Dammit, she loved everything about this place. The feel was casual and contemporary without being weird.

Anything else she looked at would pale in comparison.

She decided to bite the bullet and get the sticker shock over with.

Jada stood in the empty living room, holding a clipboard, waiting for her reaction. "Well?"

"It's gorgeous. It's perfect. *Perfect.* It's got everything I was looking for and more. I know it's out of my price range. And it's far too much room for a single woman—"

"But not for a couple," a male voice said.

The deep, sexy male voice she'd feared she'd never hear again unless she flipped on the radio.

Liberty watched in utter shock as Devin strolled out of the kitchen. "Devin? What are you . . . ?"

Jada patted Liberty on the shoulder. "Let yourself out when you're done and I'll talk to you tomorrow."

Neither she nor Devin moved until the door shut.

She probably should've played it cool, but she couldn't. She launched herself at him, nearly knocking him down. "I can't believe you're here."

Devin's arms came around her, pulling her body even more completely against his.

She buried her face in his neck, filling her lungs with his scent, letting his heat and his solid presence fill the empty parts inside her.

His hands slid up to cradle her face. Without saying a word, he slanted his mouth over hers, blowing her mind with a kiss that might've been the single most perfect kiss in the history of the world.

Devin only released her mouth to wipe the tears from her face. "Baby, please stop."

Liberty turned her head and kissed his palm. "I can't. I've hardly been able to stop crying since I left you in LA."

"Chickenshit move on your part, G.I. Jane."

"I know." She kissed his palm again. "Thank you for the song you dedicated to me that night."

"Maybe I oughta change the title to 'She *Is* Loved.'"

"Or maybe you should change it to 'She Is an Idiot for Running Away from the Man She Loves and Can't Live Without.'"

"That's a little long for a song title," he said dryly, "but I get the gist of what you're sayin'."

"Good." She curled her hand around the back of his neck and brought his mouth down for another kiss. "Tell me what you're doing here."

"After you left, I returned to Nashville. I lasted less than twenty-four hours there before I flew to Denver. I'd been thinkin' nonstop about some of what you'd said, some of what Crash said, so I nutted up, rented a car and drove to my sister's place in Laramie. Then I spent the night with my folks."

As much as she hated that he'd faced that alone, she was glad he'd done it. "How did that go?"

"Better than I expected. I took the first step and they were more than willing to meet me halfway. So I thought, what the hell?' I'd try the same approach with you." He gave a soft, embarrassed laugh.

"What?"

"Last night I sat outside your apartment for an hour, workin' up the courage to knock on the door, rehearsing what I needed to say to you. Then an alert sounded on my phone and I saw the picture someone had taken of me and China at the after-party in LA."

"I saw the picture online."

"Nothin' happened between us. You believe me, right?"

Liberty nodded. "I was pissed. But mostly pissed at myself because I had no right to be so insanely jealous since *I* left you and I had to resort to cyberstalking you. So I have to ask again. Why are you here?"

"I called Garrett to see if I could surprise you at work, and he said you had the week off to house hunt. He gave me the realtor's name and I contacted her." He stepped back and spread his arms out. "This place is great, isn't it?"

"Yes, but it's out of my price range."

"That hundred K bonus you got for lasting the whole tour with me doesn't knock it down to a reasonable mortgage for you?"

Her jaw dropped and heat flushed her cheeks. "You knew about that?"

"Not until Carl got drunk at the after-party and told me." He looked at her. "You thought I'd be upset when I found out, didn't you?"

"I know you feel like a commodity and people don't see beyond that. I didn't want you to think all I ever saw in you were dollar signs."

Devin moved closer and twisted a section of her hair around his finger. "But it was an incentive for you to take the job, wasn't it?"

"Yes." She locked her gaze to his. "In one of those sappy romantic movies, not only would I have not walked away from you, but I would've refused the money. Is that what you wanted from me?"

"God no. You earned the money. You more than earned it." Devin reached into his front pocket and retrieved a piece of paper.

"What's that?"

"Your money."

"But Big Sky already sent the money to GSC."

"This is in addition to that. Carl indicated GSC hadn't negotiated for a higher bonus and he was willing to pay you double what you agreed to. So I forced his hand. Actually, I forced a checkbook into his hand." He grinned. "The man shouldn't drink and start running his mouth because cash falls out of it. Anyway, this is yours. Garrett already approved it."

Liberty squinted at the check and then her eyes got wide. "Another hundred K?"

"Yep. That oughta help you get the home of your dreams. But the reason I'm here is because I was hoping we'd look for a home of *our* dreams in Denver."

"You're moving here?"

"Yes. Let me make this perfectly clear. I love you. I want us to make a life together—I don't care where. I want to make a home with you that's not on a damn tour bus or fifteen hundred miles away from our families." He touched her cheek. "On the road we started bein' an everyday part of each other's lives. I want that for longer than four months, Liberty. I want that forever."

Dammit. She started to cry again.

"Lord, woman, I don't know what to do with your tears. You didn't cry this much after you were shot." He hauled her against him and kissed the top of her head.

"But what about your life in Nashville?"

"I don't have a life in Nashville; I have a house. No one ever said I have to live there. Sure, I'll have to be there once in a while, but I don't need a big house that I'm never in. I put my house on the market the day after I left LA."

"So do you really see us living together? Here?"

"I know it's important for you to buy this place yourself, so I won't offer to buy it outright as a gift for you."

This was really happening. She could have Devin and this awesome condo. "Hang on a second. Let me do a quick calculation."

Devin snatched the sales sheet out of her hand. "I'm not bein' flip when I say makin' this decision about our life together can't be about money. I'll match the amount of your bonus as a down payment, even if my name ain't on the mortgage. I'll pay half the utilities. Hell, I'll even take out the garbage."

She laughed.

"There's something else you oughta know."

"What?"

A sheepish look crossed his face. "I already bought the other unit on this floor that was for sale."

Another jaw-dropping moment in a day filled with them. "Why would you do that?"

"Because I knew you'd love this place. As your new neighbor, I planned to wear you down, one way or another. Come over and borrow a cup of sugar. Fuck you until you agreed to be my woman forever. That sort of annoying neighbor thing."

She laughed again. "So you'll live there and I'll live here?"

He brought her against his body. Hard. "No fuckin' way will we *ever* have separate houses. We'll live here. Because of my celebrity, I have certain security requirements, and this building more than meets my safety standards—and yours, I would imagine. I figured it'd be safer if we owned the whole floor."

"Really? You're playing the safety card *now*?"

He turned serious. "I need somewhere private to work on my music, so part of the space can be a studio. Plus, we'll have a place for our families and friends, and my bandmates to stay when they visit us." Devin rested his forehead on hers. "I want our lives entwined together on every level. So you know this isn't a temporary thing for me."

"I know. I thought it was all too good to be true, so I didn't believe in it—in us. For that, I'm sorry. I love you, and we will make this work or we'll die trying."

He smiled.

"I have something to tell you too." She tried to step back, but Devin wasn't having any of it. He kept them face-to-face.

"What?"

"I had a talk with Garrett. I told him I didn't want to permanently upgrade to full-time fieldwork."

"Which means what?"

"No more being assigned as a bodyguard. For anyone."

"Seriously?"

"Seriously. Getting shot is not my idea of fun, and that's happened twice now. So I'll be in a supervisory and training role for GSC. Garrett is actually thrilled because he wanted to get back into the field and away from his desk."

Devin frowned. "You're takin' desk duty? Baby, are you sure you want that?"

"I'll still get to kick asses in the training room on a daily basis. You're making big changes to be with me; it's only fair I meet you halfway. When I have my evaluation, I also planned on telling him that as long as you're still touring, I'll spend a month on the road with you." Liberty looked into his eyes. "Not as your bodyguard. But as the woman who loves you and wants to take care of you."

"You'll be my permanent—my only—groupie, otherwise

known as my wife." He kissed her before her mouth could fall open.

"That's a big step for a man who claimed he wasn't attracted to me."

"You're never gonna let me forget that, are you?"

Liberty twined her arms around him. "Nope. But I'm sure we'll still be talking about it when we're old and gray."

"Baby, I can't wait."

Epilogue

∽

Two months later

Devin sorted through the stack of mail as he rode the elevator to their apartment. After a long day of setting up temporary studio space until his studio was finished, all he wanted was a quiet night. But as he shuffled through bills, one magazine in particular caught his eye and he flipped to the back page. His grin widened as he read the text.

Country Music Today news—
Chelsea Lynn, contributor

December 10th—Pass the tissues, ladies, because country music heartthrob Devin McClain is officially off the singles' market.

The singer/songwriter, named Sexiest Male Artist by this very magazine, married Miss Liberty Masterson, his former bodyguard, in Devin's hometown of Muddy Gap, Wyoming, over the Thanksgiving holiday.

Vows were exchanged in a private ceremony in front of family and friends.

While the details of the wedding haven't been publicly disclosed, someone close to the happy couple confirmed the after-party included skeet shooting, karaoke and a wedding dance with music provided by none other than the Wright Brothers Band. The newlyweds planned to honeymoon in Hawaii.

Our sincerest congratulations go out to the couple!

That article wasn't too bad. Liberty would be happy, and Chelsea had gotten the scoop he'd promised her.

Good thing he'd bribed Miss Maybelle to keep from writing her usual gossipy column for the *Muddy Gap Gazette* with the down-and-dirty details of their wedding. An invitation-only concert for her seventy-fifth birthday was a small price to pay to keep the most important day of their lives as private as possible.

After unlocking the door, he tossed everything on the table in the hallway. It drove his wife crazy—and how much did he love calling Liberty his wife?—but he pointed out it was called a *catchall* table for a reason.

He yelled, "Honey, I'm home!"

It was her first day back on the job after their honeymoon. After spending all their time together the past two weeks, he missed her when they were apart for even nine hours. Within a week of moving in together and after he'd spent five long days alone in Nashville, he'd popped the question. It hadn't been the most romantic proposal in the world, but the end result was the same; now she was his and he was hers.

Liberty sauntered into view and his heart stopped. She wore her favorite ratty ARMY STRONG sweatpants and a Devin McClain concert tour T-shirt. But he barely paid attention to her attire; he was enthralled by the best thing she wore these days: the look of love.

"Hey, guitar slinger. I wasn't expecting you yet." She met him halfway and twined her arms around his neck, tilting her head back so he could kiss her.

"I wanted to see how your day went."

"Good. Except for the smart-ass men I work with spray painted my gym locker pink and wrote Mrs. Hollister in big black letters down the front."

"I hope you made them pay for that."

"Damn straight. Just because I'm married doesn't mean I'm soft."

Devin tugged her more firmly against his body. "You're soft in all the right places."

"And it's all for you." Liberty played with his hair. "So now that we're an old married couple, do you want to watch the news and have a beer in the den until supper is done? Or is that too clichéd?"

"Damn right it's clichéd. Which is why I'm takin' you to bed first." Devin picked her up and raced down the hallway to their bedroom, amid her shrieks of laughter.

Yeah, this married, normal life with her would work out just fine.

Don't miss Lorelei James's

What You Need

Available now.

BRADY

*S*aturday night I waited outside the restaurant to meet Siobhan.

I'd worked all day. One of the perks of being CFO was my executive office that had a private bathroom as well as a dressing room where I kept several changes of clothes. I'd never voluntarily admit how many nights I've spent sleeping there after working until close to dawn the next day. Most people didn't know I'd been there all night; they just assumed I'd gotten in early.

I forced myself not to pace as I waited. I'd worn a blazer, not in an effort to impress but because October in Minnesota meant the weather could change from balmy to frigid in as little as an hour. What I had on wasn't club wear by any stretch, but I'd never grasped the need for a different look when hitting the bars.

My cousin Nolan constantly harassed me about dressing like a stuffy old man. The pushy jackass had even brought his personal shopper into my office to stage an intervention.

The guy seemed nice enough, if more enthusiastic about men's fashion and grooming than I was accustomed to. Plus, his personal clothing choices set off my warning bells. No fucking way was I ever wearing skinny jeans. Or a neon yellow shirt that would stop traffic on Hennepin Avenue. Or a fedora.

Nolan had given up on me. He'd sworn I'd have to beg him for help when I finally came to my senses.

As if that'd happen.

The black Lincoln Town Car pulled up to the curb and I pasted a smile on my face. The driver came around the back to open the door and a redhead stepped out.

A young redhead. Christ, the girl—and yes, I mean girl—looked barely legal. Then it occurred to me I'd never clarified why Maggie's niece was here. A horrid thought crossed my mind. What if this girl was a high school foreign exchange student?

Upon closer examination, I decided Siobhan was college aged. But it made no sense why Maggie had chosen me to be her niece's companion. I was easily a dozen years older than this girl. I had two younger brothers who were better suited.

You agreed to do this because you just had to know what opportunity your dad was springing on you. Maybe if you weren't such a control freak, you'd just go with the flow once in a while. Then you wouldn't be in the situation of having to card your fucking date.

I offered my hand. "Siobhan? I'm Brady Lund."

She sized me up. "Well, Mags din't tell me to expect an older gent."

Great.

"But I'm happy to meet you, Brady Lund, if for no other reason than to get out of me aunt's flat."

"Shall we go in?"

Siobhan glanced up at the marquee. "Fancy place, eh?"

"No, just a good steakhouse."

"Mags didn't tell you I'm vegetarian?"

I froze. "No, she didn't."

"No offense, but you'd better be comin' up with another place to chow down. Meat is murder and all that."

"Of course."

"I'll get the car back here." She let loose a piercing whistle that rivaled an air horn for loudness. When that didn't work, she stepped into the street and started waving her arms. She'd dressed like a street urchin in a skirt over leggings, heeled boots, a ruffled blouse and a long cardigan. I felt as if I'd stepped into a Dickens novel.

Right then, I should've gone with my gut instinct and called off the evening. Instead, I pulled her out of the street and said, "I have the car service number, so there's no need for that."

She rolled her eyes. "Whatever."

I took out my phone and typed "vegetarian restaurants Uptown Minneapolis" into the search engine. "There are five places around here. Would you like to choose?"

"Are any of them within walkin' distance to Steel Balls, the club I wanna hit after?"

Steel Balls? "I have no idea. And what makes you think that going to that club is on the agenda tonight?"

"*Agenda?* Dude. You are uptight. This club is right hard to get into, but I thought a guy with your connections—"

"My connections?"

"Business bigwig, flush with a lot o' the green."

"Well, you thought wrong." I scrolled through the restaurant list. "There's sushi or Indian a block either way."

"Sushi."

I hit the walk option on the map and spent our short stroll staring at the cursor blinking on the map image, half hoping I'd trip off the curb. Surely an ambulance call was a valid reason for ending a date.

I held the door open for her.

"Now this is more like it."

The restaurant had a small sushi bar in the middle of the room and tables scattered throughout.

The hostess appeared. "Two for dinner?"

"Yeah, and put us close to the bar, will ya?" Siobhan said.

She stated that as if it would be a drunken free-for-all. Like hell.

After we were seated, I said, "No bullshit, Siobhan. How old are you?"

"Twenty-one. Why?"

She was lying; I was sure of it. "Because if you order a drink, they *will* card you. America isn't like Ireland."

"Hey. What's that supposed to mean?"

"Like you don't know Irish bars don't really give a damn if you're only fifteen. As long as you have money and don't act like a pain in the arse, they'll serve you."

"Been to Ireland, have ya?"

"Twice."

That surprised her.

The waitress came by to take our drink orders. I opted for a Leinenkugel Red Lager.

"That's sounds good. I'll have the same—but bring me two. Bein' from Ireland, one gets tired of drinkin' Guinness. Although you Yanks serve it way too cold." She winked at the waitress.

The Asian waitress smiled. "Yes, these Yanks try and improve on everything, don't they?"

Then the two of them launched into a discussion about all the foreign things Americans had gotten wrong.

When I took out my phone, the waitress got the hint to skedaddle and fill our drink order.

"That was rude," Siobhan said.

I tucked my phone in my pocket. "Not as rude as your comment about Americans and their misuse of the word football."

She smirked. "Got your back up, eh?"

"Since my brother plays for the Vikings? Yes."

"One of the more hapless teams in American football, I've heard."

Enough. "How about you don't malign a true sport that you don't understand and I won't have a hard go at your beloved footie, eh?"

Her eyes flared with anger. "You're more than a bit of a puss face."

"I don't know what that means. But I can't imagine it was a compliment."

"'Twasn't. Least you aren't completely daft. Ah, perfect timing," she said to the waitress as she dropped off the beers.

Siobhan gulped her first beer and leaned back in her chair, daring me to say anything.

I clamped my teeth together. The little brat wasn't getting the best of me.

I hoped the service was fast, because I couldn't wait for this to be over.

She probably feels the same. Story of your dating life, isn't it?

LENNOX

Of all the sushi joints in town . . . Brady Lund had wandered into mine.

Well, not mine as in I owned it, but mine as in my roommate Kiley and I splurged every other week and had a girls' night out at the Sake Palace. Since we'd been coming here so long we were considered regulars—and I didn't like that he was on my turf.

With a date.

I checked out the redhead sitting across from him at his cozy table for two. Not at all the type of woman I imagined Brady Lund would go for.

Woman? She's like twelve. Maybe he's babysitting.

I snorted. That'd be the day.

Kiley glanced up. "What's so funny?"

"Nothing."

"Then why the self-amused snort?"

I hated that she knew my tells. I leaned in. "Don't look—" I put my hand on her shoulder to keep her from whipping her head around. "Seriously, *don't* look, but the CFO of Lund Industries is here with a date."

"Where?"

"Back and to your right."

Kiley shrugged her shoulder to dislodge my hand. "I hate it when you do that. I can be discreet."

I bit back another snort.

"This is the clueless dude who didn't know about the temp department?"

"Yes."

"The one who is so freakin' gorgeous that you could orgasm just from looking at him?"

"Kiley! Shut up! I never said that."

She poked her chopsticks at me. "But you've thought about it and it's all over your face whenever you talk about him."

I snatched up a piece of pickled ginger and popped it into my mouth.

"So, since I can't look, give me a play-by-play on what's going on."

"They just got their drinks. I can't believe Jailbait is old enough to drink."

Kiley choked on her sake. "Jailbait?"

"She looks really young."

"Maybe it's his niece."

I shook my head. "Neither of his brothers nor his sister is married."

"Scary that you know how many siblings he has, Lennox."

"I work for Lund Industries, so I know about the entire family because that's part of my job," I retorted. "His sister, Annika, is in the PR division of Lund, his brother Walker does something in construction, and his other brother, Jensen, plays for the Vikings."

Kiley's eyes widened. "No shit? Jens 'The Rocket' Lund is his brother?"

"I didn't know you were a football fan."

"I wasn't until he started playing. Man. Have you *seen* The Rocket's ass in his football pants? It really emphasizes his *tight end* position. He shoulda got the Heisman for that alone."

I barely resisted smacking myself in the forehead. But then I saw Jailbait lean back in her chair, with her arms crossed over her chest. Mr. CFO ran his hand through his hair. Neither of them looked like they were having a good time.

Why that made me happy made no sense.

Jailbait stood, grabbed her beer and headed to the sushi station.

"Hello?" Kiley snapped her finger in front of my face.

"Sorry." I refocused on my friend. "Before I got distracted by the orgasm generator"—I grinned at her—"you were telling me about your newest project."

"I was telling you about it because I need your help." Kiley set down her chopsticks, serious face in place. "One of the centers my kids attend got closed down because of drug activity. While I'm glad the cops are following through with their promise to get rid of the troublemakers, it feels like these kids are being punished. So if they've got nowhere to go on Saturday, and nothing productive to do, what do you think will happen to them?"

My roommate was passionate about "her" kids and the work she does with them. That was part of the reason I adored her, since it took a special person to see the potential in kids who couldn't count on family to raise them. "They become even more at risk."

"Exactly. A couple of them have already been in juvenile more than once."

"How can I help?"

"Once we nail down a place to have an activity outside of their neighborhood, I'd love it if you'd hang out with them. If they give you shit, you can share your success story."

Success story. Oh, it was a helluva story, all right. I was still working on the success part. "You let me know when and where."

Kiley squeezed my hand. "You're such an awesome person, Lennox. I'm so glad you answered my Craigslist ad."

"Me too." My last year of school my roommate had flaked out on me and decided spontaneously to move to

Iowa with her boyfriend. Since the apartment was in her name and the lease was up, I'd been pretty much screwed. Even though the place had been a total dive, it'd still cost more money each month than I could swing alone. And I would've had to go through an entire approval process to take over the lease, in addition to forking over first and last month's rent. So I'd had no choice but to look for a new living arrangement.

I'd always gotten a kick out of reading the *City Pages* ads for roommates, but those "Must love craft beer and quinoa" roommate ads were less funny when I needed a place to stay. On a whim I checked Craigslist and saw Kiley's ad for a roommate to share a house. The private bathroom and second-floor sitting area trumped the requirement for snow shoveling and summer yard maintenance. I'd shown up in the area known as Dinkytown and fallen in love with the older house.

The first month Kiley and I were respectful of each other's spaces. She'd bought the house after her sister assured her that she'd pay half the mortgage—then she'd left her high and dry. Making the mortgage payment on her own had proven difficult since she was just starting out as a social worker. But our polite distance around each other changed the night she'd come home from work a complete mess after one of the kids in her program had been killed in a drug deal gone bad. Problem was, the kid wasn't buying or selling drugs; he'd been walking his little sister home from the playground because they lived in a dangerous area, and he ended up with a bullet to the chest when a gun accidentally went off.

That night she and I downed a bottle of wine, swapped life stories and then started hanging out regularly. What I loved most about Kiley was that she didn't need a man to validate her. So many women my age felt like failures if they didn't have a boyfriend, whereas Kiley and I were open to a relationship if the right guy came along, but we were both focused on our careers. I loved that we were beyond the pressure of heading out to the meat market bars every weekend in hopes of a hookup.

"What's the hottie CFO up to now?" Kiley prompted, pulling me out of my ruminations.

I glanced over at the sushi bar. Lund and his date were chowing down on sushi as if they had somewhere else to be. They weren't talking—at all. "Looks like they're ignoring each other."

"I think you should go over and say hello."

My pulse jumped. "What? Why would I do that?"

"Because it'd be fun to see if he's embarrassed about the age of his date."

"You're evil."

She shrugged. "Maybe he'll try and explain her."

"Maybe I don't care."

"Uh-huh. You don't care and that's why your gaze keeps darting over there every five seconds."

When she phrased it that way, I felt a little pathetic.

"Think of it this way: You're approaching him first, so the control of the situation is yours. If he admits he saw you in here but didn't acknowledge you in any way, then you know he's a tool. If he genuinely seems surprised—"

"Then he'll think I want something from him, when I don't."

Kiley sighed. "You are using skewed logic. But whatever. You're too chicken to do it anyway."

I watched as Jailbait got up and headed to the ladies' room. She'd just given me a chance to casually swing by and say hello. I pushed my chair back and stood.

"Thatta girl!" Kiley said. "Go get 'im, tiger."

Lund was the tiger. He'd probably eat me alive.

So in a total chickenshit move, when I was within four feet of him, I cut around the side of the sushi bar and headed for the bathroom.

I swore I heard Kiley clucking behind me.

I used the facilities, and when I stepped out of the stall, I froze.

Jailbait stood in front of the mirror, affixing piercings to her face. She now sported a nose piercing, two nose rings, as well as snakebite piercings in her lip. I continued to watch as she shed her skirt, revealing skintight leggings. Beneath the blouse was a Sex Pistols Tshirt, strategically ripped and then held together with a row of safety pins.

At that point, I was helpless to look away. I washed my hands, trying to discreetly watch her apply thick black eyeliner to her eyelids and then outline her lips.

"What're you lookin' at, eh?"

She had an accent I couldn't place. British? Irish? Scottish? And because the "What're you lookin' at?" question annoyed me, I didn't temper my answer. "Your outfit. Wondering if you're going to an eighties costume party? Or if I somehow missed the update that punk fashion from that era was back in style."

For a moment anger sparked in her eyes. Then she grinned. "Ballsy one, ain't ya?"

I shrugged.

"Punk never went out of style where I'm from."

"Where's that?"

"Great Britain—specifically I was born in Ireland and went to uni in London."

"Ah."

She pulled a long studded belt out of her bag and wrapped

it around her hips and waist. Then she attached studded bracelets to each wrist. "Look, you seem like an okay lass, so could I get you to do me a wee favor?"

"What?" I said cautiously.

"There's a man sitting out there. Can't miss him, right stodgy as hell. If you look closely enough, you might see a stick up his arse."

"What about him?"

"Tell him I left, yeah?"

"Wait. Is he your date?"

"Hard to believe, ain't it? Him 'n me on a bloody date."

Hard to believe indeed. "Why are you ditching him?"

She snorted. "Because I don't like old dudes."

My eyes narrowed at her. "How old are you?"

"Twenty-one. Can you believe the arsehole asked to see me ID? After the bloody waitress didn't card me? What kind of bastard does that?"

A smart one. "Why'd you agree to go out with him if you think he's too old for you?"

"My auntie set up the date—though now I know why she was very careful not to call it a date, eh? But I can see why he agreed to go out with me. I bet the poor bugger never gets his pole waxed. I might've given him a ride because he is right nice to look at, but he's such a cold wanker."

Wow. Harsh assessment of Brady Lund. But how could she have come to such a fast judgment about him when they'd spent less than an hour together?

"Anyway. Tell him I bailed, yeah? And I'll find me own way back to Auntie's." With that, she sailed out of the bathroom.

I followed her and watched her yell at the kitchen workers before she bolted out the back door.

Freakin' awesome.

But there was no way I could tell the CFO of a multibillion-dollar company that his blind date had dumped him.

I carefully kept out of his line of sight as I returned to the table. When I told Kiley what'd happened in the bathroom, she had no problem switching seats with me. So I didn't see when he'd left. I only know he was gone when I turned around.

Connect with Berkley Publishing Online!

For sneak peeks into the newest releases, news on all your favorite authors, book giveaways, and a central place to connect with fellow fans—

"Like" and follow Berkley Publishing!

facebook.com/BerkleyPub
twitter.com/BerkleyPub
instagram.com/BerkleyPub